Acclaim for Tim Downs's novels

Head Game is an exciting page-turner that will keep the reader guessing.

—*Christian Retailing*

[In *PlagueMaker*] Downs evenhandedly dispenses humor, interesting technical details, and the trademark "ick" factor that characterizes his previous books. He throws in enough surprises and unusual events to keep the story fresh . . . Downs's best book to date.

—*Publishers Weekly*

PlagueMaker is a novel that can proudly be shelved beside any [book] featuring Crichton or Clancy and hold its own.

—Infuzemag.com

Top-drawer thriller about moral grudges—and fatal fleas . . . Downs (*Chop Shop*, 2004, etc.) knows his bugs and his techno stuff, but what makes this work so well is the appeal of the characters . . .

—*Kirkus Reviews* of *PlagueMaker*

Reading *PlagueMaker* may cause rapid page turning and accelerated heart-beats. Breathing may come in gasps and sleeplessness could occur. However, the treatment is simple. Keep reading to the last page to experience an outrageously great book . . . The author has seamlessly woven a thread of love and hope in this tale of impending disaster.

—inthelibraryreviews.com

A page-turning, exciting book, Downs has used research and skill like few other authors to provide a real life thriller. His twists and turns will keep you up at night . . . *PlagueMaker* is an excellent suspense read.

—Dancingword.net

D0109635

With its fast-paced, action-packed storyline, *PlagueMaker* by Tim Downs is an all too realistic glimpse into the modern world of terrorism . . . a heart-stopping albeit terrifying look at modern day biological warfare.

—romancejunkies.com

[*PlagueMaker* is] an intense, riveting, deeply emotional and yet gently instructional read that is well worth the investment of your time and money.

—*ASSIST News Service*

Tim Downs has written an exciting thriller that will engross the reader. This book [*PlagueMaker*] is highly recommended.

—Bestsellersworld.com

Few [virus novels] have the tightly wound plot going for them as Downs does [in *PlagueMaker*]. The scientific details of the crime, from fleas to flammables, [were] well-researched and spelled out in an entertaining, Crichton-esque manner . . . The speed is close to break-neck, and the tension—particularly in the final 100 pages—is palpable as its story is plausible.

—Bookgasm.com

OTHER BOOKS BY TIM DOWNS

PlagueMaker

Chop Shop

Shoofly Pie

TIM DOWNS

THOMAS NELSON
Since 1798

NASHVILLE   DALLAS   MEXICO CITY   RIO DE JANEIRO   BEIJING

Published in Nashville, Tennessee, by Thomas Nelson. Thomas Nelson is a trademark of Thomas Nelson, Inc.

Thomas Nelson, Inc., titles may be purchased in bulk for educational, business, fund-raising, or sales promotional use. For information, please e-mail SpecialMarkets@thomasnelson.com.

Library of Congress Cataloging-in-Publication Data

Downs, Tim.
    Head game / Tim Downs.
        p. cm.
    ISBN 978-1-59554-023-2 (hc)
    ISBN 978-1-59554-323-3 (tp)
    1. Persian Gulf War, 1991—Fiction. 2. Psychological warfare—Fiction. 3. Information warfare—Fiction. I. Title.
    PS3604.O954H43 2007
    813'.6—dc22

                                                                                2006023178

Printed in the United States of America

07 08 09 10 RRD 6 5 4 3 2 1

For my beautiful Joy,
whose voice always calls me back.

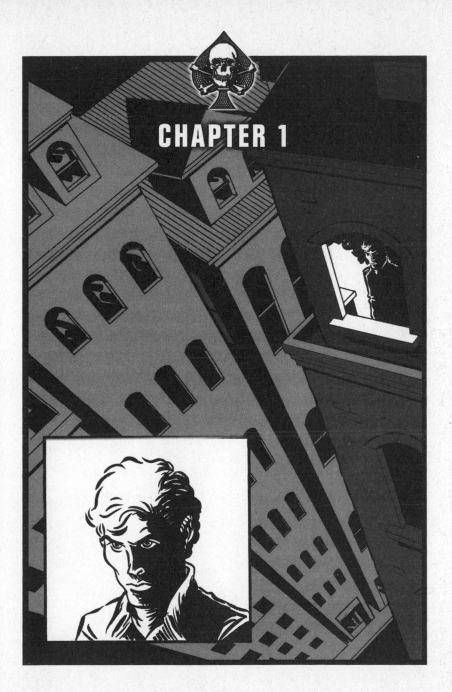

CHAPTER 1

He held the two-ply bristol board up to the light and carefully studied the final page of his drawings. A few pencil lines still showed through the ink; he took an art gum eraser and began to lighten them, carefully rubbing outward

6

toward the edges of the paper—but he stopped. *What difference does it make?* he thought. The pages weren't for reproduction anyway—only the originals mattered, and only a couple of people would ever see them. But he was an artist to the end, and the pursuit of perfection was so deeply ingrained in him that it was almost an obsession—so he returned to his work, gently blowing off the eraser shavings with a can of compressed air.

Spreading the pages across his drawing board, he studied the work as a whole. He reviewed the layout, the frame design, and the narrative flow—that was the most important part. He looked at the work with a fresh eye, trying to pretend that he had never seen it before. Was it clear that the opening scene took place in his own apartment? Were the various settings in the city recognizable? Was the flow of action clear and unmistakable? And most important of all: Was the central character recognizable? Had he made the likeness strong enough? Would the viewer know at a glance that the man in the story was him?

Nodding with satisfaction, he gathered the drawings into a stack. It was a nice piece of work all in all, one of his best—and it only seemed fitting. His editors would have been proud of the drawings; too bad he'd never have a chance to show them. He found himself wishing that the NYPD detective who found them might turn out to be a comics buff, someone who could appreciate them. But then, that wasn't really important either. There was only one thing that really mattered; there was only one person on earth who really had to see the drawings, and even he didn't have to appreciate them—he only had to understand them, because his life depended on it.

The only thing left to do was to find a place in the apartment to leave the drawings where they were sure to be discovered. Then everything would be ready; then it would be finished.

He looked around the room for the last time.

CHAPTER 2

Kuwaiti Airspace, February 1991

Cale Caldwell sat strapped to a web seat in the forward cargo hold of the massive MC-130. The aircraft flexed and groaned with every pocket of turbulence—and there were plenty of them in the rising plumes of heat above the Arabian Peninsula.

Cale's eyes wandered over the cavernous interior. It was like being in the belly of a whale. *Just like Jonah,* he thought, *swallowed by a monster and dangling from a strand of seaweed.* The floor was like the monster's belly, with alternating rows of gleaming silver rollers and nonskid patches of sandy gray. The walls were a rib cage of arching aluminum struts joined together by pale green strips of vinyl-covered flesh. Cale stared into the shadows at the rear of the plane; that was the monster's maw, and he wondered when it might gape open again to swallow up another victim—or maybe to vomit him out along with the wooden crates and tarpaulin-draped equipment that lined the monster's gut.

An hour ago Cale was standing on the tarmac at King Fahd Airport, and now here he was riding in the belly of a beast through an ocean of air. Less than twelve months ago he was still a student at the University of North Carolina at Chapel Hill—just a Tar Heel from the Piedmont town of High Point, the "furniture capital of the world," paying his way through college with an Army ROTC scholarship. Tuition, books, and a monthly stipend that just about covered room and board—it sure made sense at the time. Vietnam was a distant memory, the cold war was ending, and there were no military conflicts anywhere on the horizon. "Iraq" was just a thing that held your .30/.30 in the back window of your pickup, and ROTC was just a free ride through Chapel Hill followed by an easy six-year payback in the Army Reserves.

Who could have known?

Last spring Cale was still an advertising student at the Kenan-Flagler Business School at UNC; by summer he had landed a to-die-for position as a creative director at Leo Burnett, a top ten ad agency in Chicago; but by autumn the buildup in the Persian Gulf had begun, and Second Lieutenant Cale Caldwell found himself summarily summoned to active duty and attached to the Fourth Psychological Operations Group, commonly referred to as 4POG. The group was stationed at Fort Bragg in Fayetteville, just a stone's throw from High Point—but a world away from that nice little office in Chicago. And now he was another world away, thousands of feet above the rocky plateaus of Saudi Arabia's eastern province, preparing to rain down propaganda leaflets on frontline Iraqis defending the stolen oil fields of Kuwait.

Cale shook his head. *Does life get any stranger than this?*

Across the aisle from Cale sat a second passenger, clutching the vertical supports with blanching knuckles like a child on his first swing set. The man was almost exactly the same age as Cale; he also wore "butter bars" on his lapels; and he, too, hailed from the Piedmont Triad of North Carolina. All this was more than coincidence—the man was Cale's onetime college roommate and his oldest friend in the world.

"Hey, Kirby, you having fun yet?" Cale asked with a grin. "You're supposed to be enjoying this."

"Says who?"

"It's a chance to get out of the office. You know: join the Army, see the world."

"I joined the Army, not the Air Force."

"Who are you kidding? You didn't join anything."

"You got that right," Kirby grumbled.

One short year ago Kirby was also a student at UNC, courtesy of a scholarship from the Reserve Officer Training Corps—but he was not in the business school like his roommate. Kirby had no interest in business, or psychology, or any other field of study at UNC. Kirby was an artist, and ever since he was a boy in High Point, he'd been interested in only one thing: comic books. Kirby's life goal was to one day move to Manhattan and work for Marvel or DC Comics, spending his days penciling massively muscled superheroes and curvaceous superheroines in spandex suits. That was Kirby's dream—and it was his reality, too, until he was also called up to active duty and assigned to 4POG at Fort Bragg.

Kirby was born Alderson Dumfries, a name that for many years hung around his neck like an albatross. And so, upon entering college, he simply announced to Cale one day that he was changing his name—to King Kirby, after the legendary Marvel artist Jack "King" Kirby, in hopes that he would soon become known across campus as "King." But royalty eluded Kirby; it took only one glance to recognize that Kirby was a Kirby and not a King. But even "Kirby" was preferable to "Dumfries," and so the man who would be King was forced to settle for a parallel move instead of the promotion he had hoped for.

Cale found the floor surprisingly stable. The enormous aircraft seemed to give with the turbulence, softening the motion. "Let's get the leaflets ready," he said. He looked over at Kirby, who was staring at the metal rollers that lined the floor. "What's wrong?"

"Those rollers go right up to the door. It's like a big slide."

"Just step over them."

"Didn't you ever see *Jaws?* Remember that scene where the old guy went sliding down the deck, right into the mouth of the shark?"

"Not many sharks around here."

"That's what the old guy said."

Cale nodded at Kirby's shirt. "This looks like a job for Superman."

Kirby fingered the buttons on his desert BDU.

Ever since childhood Kirby had worn a red, yellow, and blue Superman tee under every button-down shirt or jacket. He wore it to school, and to church, and under his pajamas at night—he even wore it under his high school prom tuxedo. Kirby would no more forget his Superman undershirt than Clark Kent would, because it served the same purpose. It was his secret identity, his means of leaving Alderson Dumfries on the floor of the phone booth and emerging as someone else—someone bigger, someone braver, someone stronger.

Cale remembered playing dodgeball with Kirby in their grade school gym class back in High Point. Whenever their team was being mercilessly pounded, mild-mannered Alderson Dumfries would strip down to his Superman T-shirt and save the day—or at least think he did. Once, delivering a speech in front of his high school English class, Kirby was overcome by stage fright. He grabbed his oxford button-down with both hands and ripped it open, revealing a scarlet *S* emblazoned across his bony chest. Buttons ricocheted in every direction and the class erupted in laughter, but Kirby felt no fear or shame. How could he? Superman is invulnerable. Whenever a little more courage was needed, whenever a little more strength was required, all Kirby had to do was unzip his jacket and reveal the man beneath—the man he really was.

Kirby opened just the top two buttons of his BDU. At the first glimpse of that royal blue field, he felt the power flowing through him.

"Let's get those leaflets," he said.

Cale and Kirby were not alone in the cargo hold; a flight engineer and two loadmasters made notations on clipboards and tested the restraining tethers that held crates and equipment in check. Cale turned just in time to see another figure enter the cargo hold through a narrow door in the forward bulkhead. The man was a captain in rank, two decades older than Cale or Kirby. He appeared to be much shorter, though mathematically it was only a difference of two or three inches. The difference was one not of height but of proportion; squeezing through the narrow doorway, the man looked as wide as he was tall. He had a neck like a water buffalo and the trunk of a century oak. His arms were like pipes, thick but without definition, and his catcher's-mitt hands ended in five blunt stubs. *Like the udder of a cow,* Cale thought.

The most interesting thing about the man was his face—interesting, Kirby once said, the way a camel's face is interesting. His nose was broad and flat and his eyes were set wide but not deep, giving him a look of constant alert-ness or surprise. His forehead seemed flat, too, like all of his facial features. Kirby said that most faces are like mountain ranges, but his was more like a plateau: just a few boring landmarks and not much change in elevation.

Overall, the man looked like a boxer whose features had been perma-nently fixed by one massive blow to the center of his face, which probably accounted for his nickname: Pug. The name tape on his right shirt pocket said MOSELEY in large block letters, and "Captain Moseley" was the required form of address by all subordinates—but to everyone else he was simply Pug. Nobody knew his Christian name; nobody cared. Pug was a career PsyOps officer whose tour of duty extended back to Vietnam. In the Army, Pug said, you call it like you see it: an infantryman is a "grunt," an Iraqi civil-ian is a "Haji," and a Muslim woman in traditional garb is a "BMO"—a Black Moving Object. In 1965, somewhere outside Da Nang, some wise guy in a moment of boredom or divine inspiration referred to young Private What's-His-Face as "Pug," and the moniker stuck—for good.

Pug spotted Cale and Kirby and headed toward them. As he approached, Cale noticed that Pug seemed completely unaffected by the rolling and lurch-ing of the plane; his stride was just as solid and deliberate as always. Cale once quipped that in the event of an earthquake, Pug would be the only stationary object around; you could duck and cover or you could just grab on to Pug.

"How you two doin'?" Pug called out.

"Just getting our sea legs," Cale said.

Pug glanced down at Kirby's open battle dress uniform and the non-regulation undershirt beneath. "Excuse me, *Lieutenant,* but your underwear is showing." Pug enjoyed addressing Kirby by his inferior rank, and he had a knack for making the word "lieutenant" sound like a derogatory term.

"That's my uniform," Kirby replied.

"*That* is your uniform," Pug countered, jabbing Kirby's BDU with one of those cigar-shaped fingers. "*That* thing is your underwear—and according to regulations it's supposed to be brown."

Kirby reluctantly refastened the top two buttons.

"Look, Superboy, if this Combat Talon takes a nosedive, stripping down to your skivvies won't save your hide."

"Super*man*," Kirby corrected.

"Coulda fooled me."

"Pug's got a point," Cale said to Kirby. "Suppose the plane does go down, and suppose the Iraqi army finds your body in the wreckage. Think of what the headlines would say in Baghdad: 'Superman Dies in Plane Crash'. What would people think back home?"

"Yeah, but what if I survived?" Kirby said. "Suppose the Iraqi army approaches the wreckage and the only thing left intact is me, standing like this." He widened his stance and placed his fists on both hips. "Man, this war would be *over*."

Pug shook his head in disgust. Kirby's nonregulation undershirt was a point of contention between them, but it was just one of many. Virtually everything about Kirby was nonregulation. Pug found it difficult to imagine anyone less suited to military life than this skinny, hyperactive artist with delusional fantasies. As a Vietnam volunteer with no education beyond a GED, Pug had a general disdain for what he called "ROTC pretty boys"—but Kirby was almost more than he could bear.

Yet at the beginning of the conflict in the Gulf, the Army in its infinite wisdom assigned Pug, Cale, and Kirby to the same three-man PsyOps team at 4POG's Propaganda Development Center in Riyadh. Their mission: to create propaganda leaflets designed to strip the enemy of his capacity and will to resist—or as Pug so eloquently expressed it, "to put an idea in his head instead of a bullet."

Cale served as the PsyOps officer of the team, the one responsible for developing the original propaganda "theme." Cale was highly qualified for this role, though his Army training consisted of nothing more than a four-week Basic PsyOps course at Fort Bragg. In fact, Cale was simply doing for the Army what he did back at Leo Burnett: He was selling a product—a different kind of product, granted, but the Army was betting that a man who could talk a welfare kid into shelling out a hundred bucks for a pair of Nikes could also talk an Iraqi soldier into laying down his rifle and raising his hands in the air.

It was a good bet, because Cale possessed an exceptional natural ability: a horse trader's uncanny insight into human motivation and behavior. Cale listened to the human heart the way a concert musician listens to his instrument, and he knew how to tighten one string and loosen another until the instrument produced precisely the sound he wanted to hear. Cale's study of advertising didn't produce this ability—just the opposite: It was his inborn talent that made advertising such a hand-in-glove fit. Cale's natural gift was what allowed him to land a coveted internship with Leo Burnett before his senior year of college, and the same gift helped him create a campaign for Nintendo that brought home a Clio in his very first year at the agency. And now Cale found himself working for a different kind of agency—the Hell, Fire & Brimstone Agency, Kirby liked to call it. Their motto: "Repent—or the end is near." The product was different this time; Cale was no longer selling shoes, or light beer, or popping-fresh dough. The client was different too: Now it was the U.S. Army instead of McDonald's or GM or Hallmark cards. But the process was still the same—only this time the Arab culture was the market segment, and the Iraqi soldier was the consumer.

The product the Army was selling was simply *life:* survival; continued existence; the chance to see your loved ones again; the chance to get your first decent meal in weeks; the chance to abandon your outdated Soviet equipment and walk away before the Second Marine Division ground you into desert dust. But at first the product wasn't selling—not the way the Army hoped it would anyway, and Cale knew why: the Army was selling down to them. The product wasn't tailored to fit the consumer's needs. To a devout Muslim—to a man guaranteed a place in Paradise simply for dying in battle—

the offer of life was just not enough. The offer needed to be life with honor; survival with dignity; and continued existence with the respect of family and friends.

Cale understood this intuitively. He told Pug, and Pug knew he was right.

"Just like the end of World War II," Pug said. "On islands in the South Pacific, they were trying to round up all the Japs still holed up in the hills. The PsyOps boys tried dropping a leaflet on 'em. The title said 'I Surrender'—but nobody did."

"How come?"

"'Cause in the Japanese culture 'surrender' is a dirty word—better to die than to surrender. So we changed the title to read, 'I Cease Resistance,' and the Japs came down in droves. Go figure."

To Cale, it did figure. The Army had subtly but shrewdly changed its sales pitch—from simple *surrender* to *surrender with honor*. The distinction might be lost on some, but to an ad man it was no different than a fast-food restaurant changing its pitch from "Great-tasting food" to "You deserve a break today."

So that's what Cale began to do—change the pitch. The propaganda themes that he began to create were specifically designed to capture that missing sense of honor. He began to address the enemy with dignity, as a powerful and worthy opponent instead of a second-rate force doomed to annihilation. His themes appealed to Arab brotherhood; they made surrender sound like an investment in the future of the Arab world instead of capitulation to an arrogant foreign power. With Cale's savvy and cultural insight, a different kind of PsyOps theme began to emerge.

But someone had to take Cale's concepts and visualize them—that was Kirby's job. Words can be ambiguous, and translations from English to Arabic are notoriously problematic. One leaflet produced by another PsyOps team bore the message, "Brother Iraqi soldiers, our great tragedy is we do not want you to come back to Iraq dead or crippled." But because of a subtle error in translation, the message actually read, "Brother Iraqi soldiers, our great tragedy is to want you to come back to Iraq dead or crippled."

That's why images were so important, and that's why reservists like Kirby with artistic abilities were so eagerly snatched up by 4POG. Images are a universal form of communication—though images are not without difficulties of their own. One leaflet portrayed the face of an Iraqi soldier; in a "thought bubble" above his head was the image of his wife and children back home. Unfortunately, the Arab culture has no equivalent for the "thought bubble." An Iraqi POW, asked for his opinion of the leaflet, asked, "Why are those people floating in the sky?"

But images say things that words alone cannot: images of exploding bombs, dismembered bodies, and grieving loved ones—and no one captured those images better than Kirby. When Kirby first arrived in Riyadh, he reviewed all of the current propaganda leaflets, summarizing the level of artwork as "Crap, crap, and more crap." And he was right—though his candor didn't win him many friends.

"In the Army you call it like you see it," Kirby said, reminding Pug of his own words.

"That's right," Pug replied, "but after you call it, remember to duck."

Kirby brought a whole new level of artistry to 4POG. His images were simple, clear, and powerful; his representations of Iraqi soldiers were respectful and dignified—even heroic at times. Kirby's leaflets had become collector's items among the Coalition forces, gathered and traded with the same enthusiasm as any past issue of the X-Men or Fantastic Four. Kirby drew constantly; there was almost always a pencil in his hand, as though it were an extension of his arm. He doodled on every flat surface—every notebook, every desktop, every restaurant napkin. His knowledge of anatomy was flawless, and his caricatures were unerring. At the headquarters of 4POG in Riyadh, Kirby was almost a legend. Lonely GIs brought him tiny, faded snapshots of sorely missed wives and girlfriends, and Kirby returned to them enlarged and generously enhanced caricatures that were featured on many a wall and locker.

Pug served as the Intelligence Officer on this three-man team. His assignment—one he had done without peer since Vietnam—was to gather intelligence on specific enemy units, to identify targets of opportunity, and to evaluate the results of previous propaganda efforts. Pug was the old warhorse of this team; his was the voice of practical knowledge and experience. Cale understood human motivation, and Kirby knew art—but Pug knew PsyOps inside and out, and the mere offer of a beer was enough to get Pug started on some bizarre story from the history of psychological warfare.

In the Hell, Fire & Brimstone Agency, Pug served as market researcher, identifying new markets and suggesting products to fit. One of his favorite duties was interviewing prisoners of war, employing them like focus groups to fine-tune upcoming campaigns. One leaflet in development had displayed a bowl of apples and oranges, suggesting a bounty of food for hungry soldiers who surrendered.

"Add some bananas," one prisoner suggested. "To the Arabs, bananas are a delicacy." Pug made a note, and bananas were added to the menu.

Another leaflet portrayed a friendly, clean-shaven American soldier extending his hand in friendship to an Arab soldier—but to the Arabs a beard is a sign of maturity, brotherhood, and trust. Under Kirby's hand, images began to show American soldiers sporting Arab-style chin beards.

Just as General Motors spent millions every year to remind the buying public of basic themes like safety, reliability, and trade-in value, so the Army worked to keep four basic messages in front of its "consumers": "Your Defeat Is Inevitable," "Abandon Your Weapons and Flee," "It's All Saddam's Fault," and "Surrender or Die." That last message was the Army's particular favorite, and that's why MC-130s like this one were currently dumping more than eleven million leaflets bearing that simple and powerful message—with Cale's special spin.

"Your drop zone is coming up," one of the loadmasters called out over the drone of the engines. "Get your boxes on deck."

Cale, Kirby, and Pug began to carry a series of simple corrugated boxes to the rear of the plane, arranging them side by side on the rollers of the cargo ramp. Each box was about eighteen inches on a side, and packed with thousands of five-by-eight-inch leaflets. The top of each box bore a fifteen-foot tether secured to a tie-down on the floor of the plane. The bottom of each box had been crisscrossed with a razor knife to weaken the cardboard. When they reached the drop zone—a specific location calculated by their altitude, prevailing wind speed, and distance from the target—the cargo ramp would lower and the boxes would roll out. When the tethers jerked tight, the bottoms of the boxes would rip apart, scattering their contents to the wind—and hopefully into the hands of impressionable Iraqi soldiers.

Kirby didn't loiter on the cargo ramp; the instant each box touched the floor, he released it and leaped aside in a kind of grand jeté that Superman was rarely known to make.

Pug rolled his eyes. "Whatsamatter, your underwear give out on you? Superman's not afraid to fly."

Kirby muttered something that the engines drowned out.

"Aren't you boys enjoying our little field trip?" Pug asked. "That's gratitude for you. I went to a lot of trouble to set this up."

It was true. Ordinarily, PsyOps teams are deskbound and rarely ride along on leaflet drops. But a sergeant in the Dissemination Battalion at King Fahd Airport owed Pug a favor, so today they had a rare opportunity to witness the fruit of their labor firsthand.

"Thirty seconds," the loadmaster announced. "Clear the ramp."

Kirby didn't have to be asked twice.

A few seconds later the ramp actuators activated. The cargo ramp began to lower as a hatch above it began to rise, and the two sections of the fuselage slowly separated like the jaws of opening pliers. Pug and Cale stood in the center of the deck, watching, but Kirby kept one hand on the cargo behind him, fearing a sudden vacuum might suck him out—but there was none. In fact, it was surprisingly still; the opening ramp flooded the cargo hold with sound and light but remarkably little wind.

Now the boxes began to move, and one by one they slowly rolled forward and disappeared over the edge of the ramp. The tethers snapped taut, and then—nothing. The three men stood staring at empty sky and a dozen nylon tethers dangling into space.

"What a rush," Kirby called out. "Let's do it again."

Cale looked over the ramp at the ground below. He had expected to see nothing but a vague, khaki-colored landscape, but found to his surprise that he was able to make out specific details.

"We're a lot lower than I thought we'd be," he shouted to Pug.

"You can thank the flyboys for that," Pug shouted back. "They've knocked out all the ground-to-air defenses—all it took is a couple thousand air sorties. It's a big help for us; better to fly low when you're dropping leaflets. More accuracy—less wind drift."

Now tiny bits of paper began to appear behind the plane, spinning in the air like a blanket of confetti. The leaflets were designed to spin—to "autorotate," that was the word 4POG used—so they would be dispersed as they slowly descended toward the ground.

"Don't they have any antiaircraft?" Cale asked.

"They don't have much of anything. That's one of the reasons our leaflets work. They've got nothing and they know it—we're just reminding 'em. Hey, there's a leaflet idea for you—an Arab guy singing, 'I Got Plenty of Nothing.'"

Pug turned and grinned at Kirby. "Hey, doughhead, whaddya think about—"

Suddenly, there was a sound like a hammer rapping on the side of the plane. A series of small holes appeared in the padding on the starboard fuselage, as though someone had plunged an invisible ice pick through from the other side.

Kirby let out a cry and collapsed.

Pug grabbed Cale by the shoulder and dragged him to the floor. "Stay down!" he shouted. "The floor's got plenty of metal—those shots came through the wall." He twisted toward Kirby and started crawling. Cale was right behind him.

At the same instant the loadmaster lunged to the port side of the plane. He slammed his fist against a large switch, and the jaws of the monster began to hiss and slowly grind shut again. Through a wall-mounted intercom he shouted instructions to the pilots. A moment later the cargo plane rolled left and began to climb rapidly, baring its armored underbelly to the direction of fire.

Kirby was in agony. He pressed his hands against wounds on both sides of his left thigh, and blood trickled freely between his fingers. Pug grabbed Kirby's right hand and pried it away.

"What are you doing?" Kirby shouted.

"Gotta see if they hit an artery," Pug said. "They didn't—lucky you."

"I thought they didn't have antiaircraft," Cale said.

"That was just small arms fire. If it had been an AA round, he might not have a leg left. I'll take a bullet over shrapnel any day."

By now the loadmaster was at Kirby's side with a portable medical kit. He quickly jabbed an antibiotic syringe into the muscle and began to unwrap sterile gauze pads and a compression bandage.

"Bullet went clean through," the loadmaster said, noting the exit wound. "Must have missed the bone completely. Lucky guy."

"Everybody says I'm lucky," Kirby moaned. "I don't feel so lucky."

"Relax, doughhead. You'll need a couple units of blood, that's all. Might be awhile before you can leap tall buildings with a single bound, but you'll be fine."

Within minutes the bleeding was under control and Kirby was lifted to a stretcher rigged in place of the web seats, his left leg so thickly bandaged that it resembled a Thanksgiving drumstick. Cale did his best to remain by his friend's side, but the plane's steep angle made standing difficult. When the loadmaster had first shouted his warning to the pilot, the plane's engines roared so loudly that Cale thought they were going to explode. Then the plane began to climb, and he felt as if his body weight had suddenly doubled; he wondered if he would have collapsed to the flight deck if he hadn't been there already. He felt glued in place until their angle of ascent grew so steep that he gripped the floor for fear of rolling back onto the cargo ramp.

Cale pulled himself to his feet next to Pug, half-standing and half-hanging beside his wounded friend.

"How you doing, buddy?" he asked, patting Kirby on the shoulder.

"I'll feel better when I get off this plane."

"Guess the Superman long johns didn't work," Pug said. "I'd take 'em back if I were you."

Kirby looked up at him. "You think this is my ticket home?"

"Forget it. You sit on your butt all day. So what if you got a hole in your leg?"

Kirby groaned.

"Hey, I just thought of something," Cale said. "You get a medal for this."

"A medal?"

"Yeah—the Purple Heart. And guess who gets to pin it on you? Your *commanding officer.*" He grinned at Pug.

Now it was Pug's turn to groan. "There is no way I'm pinning a medal on this two-digit midget."

"It's regulations, Pug."

"Then I'll pin it on with a nail gun. That'll be your ticket home."

Kirby winced. Humor was a distraction, but it wasn't an anesthetic.

Cale turned to the loadmaster. "How much longer back to Riyadh?"

"Sorry, Lieutenant, we've got another drop to make first."

"We've got a wounded man here."

"The lieutenant's in stable condition. We can't scrub a mission unless it's a critical injury. Besides, we can't land the plane with this thing still on board." As he spoke, he dragged a canvas tarpaulin off an object the size of a Volkswagen in the center of the cargo bay.

Cale looked. The object was metallic, cylindrical in shape, tapering to a point at the fore end and slightly rounded at the tail. It looked like the stub of a pencil magnified a thousand times. It was at least four feet in diameter and ten feet long—maybe fifteen end to end. At the tapered end a slender rod protruded forward another three feet. The entire object was fastened with thick straps to some kind of movable sled.

"What is that thing?" Cale said. "It looks like a grain silo turned on its side."

Pug stepped forward and ran his hand along its side. "It's a BLU-82—used to be called a Daisy Cutter."

"Largest conventional bomb in the world," the loadmaster said. "Fifteen thousand pounds of GSX slurry—ammonium nitrate, aluminum powder, and polystyrene."

"You're going to drop it?"

"That's the general idea, Lieutenant."

"We started using 'em in Vietnam," Pug said. "It was tough to find clearings in the jungle big enough to land a Huey, so we started using these babies. It's got a blast radius of six hundred yards. You drop one of these, you got a landing site." He walked around to the tapered front and pointed to the protruding rod. "See this thing? That's called a fuse extender. The bomb drops nose-first, lowered by a parachute. The minute that rod touches down, the bomb goes off. That keeps the blast aboveground—keeps it from cratering."

The loadmaster nodded. "At ground zero a BLU-82 causes an overpressure of a thousand pounds per square inch—that's about the same pressure you'd find two thousand feet underwater. Turns everything around it into mush."

"Is that why we're still climbing?" Cale asked.

"You'd better believe it—you don't want to be anywhere around when this thing goes off. Coupla weeks back we dropped one of these; there was a British commando unit a few miles away. They thought it was a nuke."

"But this is a cargo plane," Cale said. "Why isn't it on a bomber?"

"Won't fit," Pug said. "There isn't a bomber in the world that can carry it."

"I thought we were just dropping leaflets."

"We have to consolidate missions, Lieutenant," the loadmaster said. "It's not exactly cost effective to take this big boy up just to drop off a few cardboard boxes."

"So what's the target? There are already plenty of places to land a helicopter around here."

"This isn't Vietnam," Pug said. "The BLU-82 has a different operational objective here."

On his stretcher, Kirby rolled his head to the side and looked. "I've seen that thing somewhere before. Where was it?"

"Probably on a leaflet," Pug said.

"That's right. I drew that thing for a leaflet—it was a series of three."

"Yeah, that's the one. The first leaflet says, 'Tomorrow we're going to bomb you at noon.' So the next day we bomb them at noon, just like we promised. Then we drop the second leaflet. That one says, 'We told you so—and tomorrow we're coming back to do it again.' Next day, we bomb them again. Now they know we mean business, so we drop the final leaflet. That one says, 'Tomorrow we're dropping the Mother of All Bombs. Flee and preserve your life, or stay here and meet your death.' And right there on the front of the leaflet is a picture of this."

"The Mother of All Bombs."

"That's her. By the time we drop the BLU-82, there's nobody left down there. Nobody sticks around to see if we'll do it. They know we will—we proved it twice before."

"But if there's nobody down there, why drop it?"

"To keep our word. That's the first principle of PsyOps: Always tell the truth. If you make a threat, you better deliver on it—or they'll never believe you again."

Cale shook his head. "We drop the world's largest bomb on nobody?"

"There's always a few who stick around, I suppose. But I guarantee you one thing: After we drop this baby, there's *nobody* around."

"Seems like a waste of an awful big bomb. Why not drop it on some troops?"

"You drop it on some troops, you kill a few troops. But if you drop it here—exactly when and where you said you would—the psychological impact is enormous. This isn't an antipersonnel bomb, kid—this is a PsyOps bomb. When this thing goes off, they can feel the shock wave for miles around, and they can hear it a lot farther than that. Pretty soon everybody's talking about it; everybody knows we can do it to them too. After that, all we need to do is yell, 'Boo,' and they all go running for home."

"Drop zone approaching," the loadmaster said. "Clear the flight deck."

Pug and Cale stepped back while the two loadmasters readied the BLU-82. The restraining straps that anchored the sled to the floor were released, and a drogue chute was attached to the aft end by a long nylon rope. Once again the ramp slowly opened, flooding the cargo bay with glaring sunlight. One of the loadmasters edged precariously close to the yawning door with the drogue chute bundled in his arms like a load of laundered sheets. The second loadmaster listened on a headset, awaiting the drop command.

"We have release in five, four, three, two, one—bomb away!"

The loadmaster made a long, sweeping arc with both arms and tossed the bundled parachute as far as he could. It slid quickly down the cargo ramp and dropped over the edge, and the nylon rope chased after it like a snake after a mouse. Seconds later the rope stretched taut and the chute snapped open behind the plane, shaking and dancing in the wind.

"Clear!" the loadmaster shouted, and in response they all pressed back tighter against the fuselage. The loadmaster leaned down and pulled a lever mounted on the floor; an instant later the sled shot backward, rolled down the ramp, and silently disappeared. The Combat Talon, relieved of its fifteen-thousand-pound burden, heaved a sigh of relief and rose higher into the air.

The ramp door closed again. Cale just stood there, his eyes readjusting to the near-darkness, blinking at the empty space where the BLU-82 had rested just a moment before. It seemed impossible that an object so seemingly immovable could be whisked away so quickly and with so little effort.

"How long?" he shouted to the loadmaster.

"About thirty seconds. The bomb tips nose-down; twenty seconds later the sled falls away. Don't worry, you'll know when it hits."

They waited.

Less than a minute later they felt the shock wave slam through the plane. It felt like a hard landing; everything in the aircraft seemed to shake at once, but it lasted for only an instant. Cale turned and looked at Kirby.

"You okay?"

"Man," Kirby said, "I'm glad I'm up here and not down there."

Cale turned and crossed the cargo bay to the port-side crew hatch. He stared out the porthole-shaped window at the Kuwaiti desert far below. By now there was no sign of the blast. He wondered if anyone really was down there when the BLU-82 went off—if anyone was stubborn and stupid enough to stick around. He wanted to believe they were all long gone, but like Pug said—there were always a few.

Pug stepped up beside him. "How you doin'? You look like you swallowed something."

Cale looked at him. "I always thought of PsyOps as a way of saving lives."

Pug nodded. "Y'know, kid, you write some pretty clever stuff, but no matter how you say it, it all boils down to one message: 'Surrender or else.' The fact is, there has to be an 'or else' or none of it works."

Cale looked out the window again. Somewhere, several miles back, his leaflets had reached the ground. By now the lonely, hungry, frightened front-line troops had picked them up and read the carefully crafted message. He wondered if they felt the shock wave from the BLU-82; he wondered if they heard the blast. And he wondered if they would believe the leaflets that told them their cause was hopeless, they were facing overwhelming odds, and they had no other option but to lay down their weapons, abandon their positions, and surrender.

Or else.

CHAPTER 3

New York City, Present Day

Cale placed the stack of comic books in the box along with the others. The pile was too tall to allow the lid to close flat, so he took off two Captain Americas and a book-length Spider-Man and tossed them aside. He pressed the flaps down again and stretched out a strip of clear packing tape with a rubbery, ripping sound.

It was the twelfth box of comic books Cale had packed, and it was beginning to look as if Kirby had owned nothing else. Cale hadn't even started on Kirby's personal effects yet, and that was his whole reason for being there— that was why Kirby's mom had asked him to come. The old woman might have been strong enough to face the secondhand furniture and anonymous household items that once belonged to her son, but the personal mementos were more than she could face—things that carried the imprint of a dead son's fingers; things that reminded a mother of a life she once carried.

Cale took the box into the living room and stacked it beside the others. The furniture was already gone—what there was of it. Kirby wasn't exactly into decorating—but then, Cale supposed, neither was Clark Kent. After all, when the fate of the whole universe rests in your hands, you probably don't spend a lot of time at Bed Bath & Beyond.

Cale tried to work quickly and stay focused on the task at hand, but he felt like a dinosaur hurrying through a tar pit. He knew that if he stopped for even a moment, the objects would trigger memories, and the memories were sure to mire him down in a pit of grief and pain. And pain was something Cale was tired of feeling; he had felt enough pain in the last six months to last a lifetime.

But Cale did stop, because he knew somewhere in his heart that grief was something he owed his friend. Cale tried to envision his own death someday, and he could imagine an army of cheerful, efficient volunteers arranging his final affairs in record time, scurrying over his half-cold body like ants on a roadside raccoon. It felt cheap and it felt cowardly, and Cale knew that Kirby deserved better than that.

So he stopped in the center of the room and let his feelings catch up to him like the wake of a slowing boat. And when they did, he discovered that he felt two things in almost equal measure: grief over the loss of his oldest friend; and anger—because Kirby had killed himself.

Cale wondered: If he could see his old friend one more time, would he throw his arms around his neck or punch him in the nose?

There was a knock on the open door. Cale looked up to see a familiar face.

"Heard you might be here," Pug said. "Long time no see."

Cale shook his head. Pug hadn't changed in thirteen years. The man had to be in his late fifties now—maybe sixty—but you wouldn't know it from the neck down. Pug was the same brick outhouse he was back at 4POG a life-time ago. Only his face had changed: he was even more weather-worn, if that was possible, and his coarse black hair was definitely steelier at the temples. But he looked good, Cale thought, and he was a welcome sight—especially here and now.

The two men embraced like rams butting heads. After a hearty slapping of backs, Cale pulled away and looked at his old friend and mentor.

"Man, you got old," Cale said.

"Not you," Pug said. "You still look young and stupid."

"Who you calling young?"

Pug looked around at the half-empty apartment and the stack of corrugated boxes that lined one wall. "Looks like you're making some headway here."

Cale nodded. "When did you hear?"

"Few days ago—got a call from his mother. Didn't know she had my number."

"I gave it to her."

"Didn't know *you* had my number. Guess it's been awhile."

Cale gestured to the room around him. "Pug—does this whole thing make any sense to you?"

"What—you mean Kirby offing himself?"

Cale winced. *He still calls it like he sees it,* he thought. "They say he jumped off the Verrazano Bridge. You know the one? It connects Brooklyn and Staten Island, right where the bay narrows down."

"I know the one," Pug said. "I talked to the Port Authority. Two hundred and twenty-eight feet from the lower deck to the water. He musta hit like a bug on a windshield."

"There's no walkway on the Verrazano—I asked. How do you get out to the middle of a bridge if there's no walkway?"

"I guess you use the road. How many people jump off the Verrazano every year? Did you ask about that? Port Authority won't give out numbers, but I hear they get maybe twenty a year."

"But they never found his body—I asked about that too. Doesn't that seem a little odd?"

"Do they ever find the body? You asked the wrong questions, kiddo. They call it the Verrazano-*Narrows,* where the upper bay dumps out into the sea. They say the current's pretty wicked there when the tide rolls out. Did they tell you they found his car on the Brooklyn side near the bridge?"

Cale nodded reluctantly. "But he jumped off a bridge in the middle of the night—without any indication or warning to anyone—and then his body washed out to sea without a trace? C'mon, Pug, it's almost like—"

"Like he wanted to disappear? That's sorta the point, isn't it? Maybe he didn't want a body left behind, ever think about that? Maybe he didn't want to do that to his friends and family."

"It doesn't make sense," Cale said.

"It never does."

Cale eyed his old friend cautiously. "I never saw you take anything at face value, Pug—but you don't seem to have any problem buying all this."

Pug reached into his jacket pocket, took out an envelope, and handed it to Cale. Cale opened the envelope and removed several sheets of paper that looked as if they had been torn from the pages of a comic book—only in black and white.

"Recognize the drawings?" Pug asked.

There was no doubt about it—they were Kirby's. Cale studied the drawings frame by frame. It was a story laid out in comic book form, but without any text—the images alone were left to convey the meaning, and the central character was unmistakably Kirby himself.

In the opening frame Kirby stood at the window of his own apartment, staring out at the darkened city. His face had a look of anguish, or anger, or—what was it? Even Kirby's hand couldn't make it certain.

The second panel showed Kirby sitting at his drawing board, apparently producing the very drawings Cale now held in his hands. It gave him an odd sense of prescience, and it made him feel as if Kirby were looking over his shoulder right now.

The third page opened with an ominous silhouette of a bridge, and Cale felt an icy finger run down his spine. Kirby sat on the bank beside the water, his head hung low, brooding, maybe hesitating—then his eyes rose with a look of determination. He turned and climbed the long escarpment toward the bridge; he worked his way down the roadside, keeping to the shadows along the edge, ducking the headlights of a passing car.

On the next page Kirby stopped, turned his back to the viewer, and stared over the railing and down into the darkness below. By the second panel he had climbed over the railing and steadied himself; in the last frame he stepped off and hurtled silently down toward the water—not in a flailing panic, but in perfect balance, like an Olympic diver stepping off a ten-meter platform.

Cale looked up at Pug. "This is unbelievable—he drew his own suicide."

"You got to admit, the guy had style. Guess you can't expect somebody with his talent to leave an ordinary suicide note."

Cale turned to the final page, where the point of view shifted dramatically from the bridge to a bird's-eye view above the water. It showed Kirby with his face turned heavenward, his eyes squeezed tight, plummeting downward. On his face he wore an indistinguishable expression: maybe fear, maybe regret, maybe an astonished comprehension of the irreversible step he had just taken. In one final act, Kirby grabbed his shirt and ripped it open, revealing nothing but bare skin underneath.

"He wasn't wearing his Superman shirt," Cale said. "Why not? What does that mean?"

"Beats me," Pug said. "Maybe it means he ran out of guts—that there was no way out this time. Your guess is as good as mine."

Cale held the pages up to the light and studied them more closely. He could detect the hairlike remnants of half-erased pencil lines and the faint gloss of India ink. The drawings were clearly originals.

"Where did you get this?" he asked.

"From his mother—she got it from NYPD. They found it right here in his apartment."

"What else did they find?"

"Nada."

Cale shook his head. "This tells us what happened, but it doesn't tell us why."

"No," Pug said, "but it tells us what we need to know right now—that Kirby is gone, and that he did it to himself."

"I can't accept that."

"Believing is one thing; accepting is another. Right now you need to believe it; you can accept it whenever you want to. Or don't—whatever gets you by."

Cale carefully folded the pages and handed them back to Pug. "How come she gave this to you and not me?"

"Jealous?"

"Yeah, a little."

"She gave it to me because I asked for it, that's why—I asked if her son left a note. If it makes you feel any better, I didn't believe it either—not at first."

"But you do now."

Pug shrugged. "Seeing is believing."

Cale took a deep breath and slowly let it out. He glanced around the apartment again, then turned back to Pug. "So—are you here to pitch in or just stand around and give orders like you used to?"

"Not much point giving orders," Pug said. "You never could follow 'em."

The two men began in separate rooms, which was the most efficient way to complete the project—but neither of them was in the mood for efficiency, and thirty minutes later they were both in Kirby's bedroom.

"What happens to all this stuff?" Pug asked.

"Most of it I'll ship to his mom back in High Point. The personal stuff I'll take to her myself. I want to be there when she gets it."

Pug opened a desk drawer and began to transfer Kirby's drawing supplies to a waiting box. There were bottles of Pelikan drawing ink, a small jar of Graphic White, a half dozen crumpled tubes of Winsor & Newton gouache, and a stack of slender sable and nylon brushes with black lacquered handles. Pug transferred the objects one by one, as though their personal significance gave each one weight. Cale watched as Pug stretched his clublike fingers toward a box of delicate pen nibs.

"So," Cale said, "where you been keeping yourself for the last thirteen years?"

"Fayetteville," Pug said. "I finished out at Fort Bragg."

"Still a captain?"

"You kidding me? You don't retire on a captain's pay. I left a full colonel."

"Colonel Moseley—I'm impressed."

"Took a job across town at Fayetteville State. I'm on the faculty there."

"Now I'm really impressed—a full colonel and a college professor to boot. When did you get so smart?"

"I was always smart—you were just too dumb to recognize it. I teach a couple of courses in behavioral psychology, but it's really just PsyOps. A bunch of the officers from 4POG take courses at Fayetteville State as part of their master's."

"So you're really still in PsyOps. I can't think of a better place for you."

"Hey," Pug said with a shrug, "you do what you can do."

Several minutes of silence passed before Pug asked, "How's Gracie?"

Cale felt a sudden twinge of something he couldn't quite identify—worry or fear, maybe even guilt. It was the feeling he used to get as a boy when he awoke to remember a school assignment that was due that day—an assignment he hadn't finished yet. He was angry that he felt that way at the mention of his own daughter's name.

"Grace is getting by," he said and offered nothing more.

"Is that your full report, Lieutenant?"

Cale didn't answer.

Pug sat down on the edge of the bed. "Look—I heard about Hannah. I should have come to the funeral. I should have at least called, but I didn't. No excuses. I'm sorry, kid. I truly am sorry. I only met her twice—once at the wedding and once at Gracie's baptism—but I could tell she was something special. To lose her like that—to have her taken away, and you with a teenage daughter. That's got to be tough. How's Gracie handling it—losing her mom like that?"

"It's only been six months," Cale said. "How do you think?"

"How're you handling it?"

Cale paused. "She blames me, Pug. Grace blames me for Hannah's death."

"Hannah was killed by a drunk driver. That makes no sense."

"She's thirteen, Pug—it doesn't have to make sense. Grace grew up in Chicago, remember? I'm the one who got sick of the city; I'm the one who wanted to go back to North Carolina. Not Hannah, not Grace—me. So I finally talked them into it and we all moved down to Charlotte, just one big happy family—and a month later her mom gets broadsided by a drunk with two prior DUIs. She blames me, Pug. Everything was fine until we moved to Charlotte. Grace blames me."

"She needs to get her head on straight. I should talk to that girl."

"Great idea. You could say, 'Hi, I'm your uncle Pug. You don't recognize me because I never call and I never drop by, even though I only live two hours away—even though I'm your godfather, for crying out loud.'"

Cale stopped. Pug was right: it didn't make sense for Grace to blame him, but it didn't make sense for Cale to blame Pug either—and that's what he was doing. True, Pug didn't call and Pug didn't stop by—but Cale didn't call or stop by either. There was blame enough for everyone; no sense trying to pawn his off on someone else.

"Sorry," Cale said. "I was out of line."

"No—what you said is true. I was wrong, and when I'm wrong I say so."

Cale smiled. "When did you start that policy?"

"Always had it," Pug replied. "I've just never been wrong before."

Cale turned back to Kirby's dresser and began to unload rolls of socks and piles of folded T-shirts into an open box. "What the girl needs is a mom," he said. "What do I know about daughters, Pug? Hannah's the one who raised her—Hannah's the one who brushed her hair and took her shopping for clothes. Now she's thirteen and she's about to become a young woman. What do I do now?"

Pug shook his head. "Don't know much about women."

"Well, I need to learn—and fast."

Pug drew in a deep breath and then stopped, as if considering his next words. Cale turned to him and waited.

"I got something to get off my chest," he said. "You were right—what you said about not calling and all. I haven't been a very good friend. Maybe if I were a better one, we wouldn't be here packing up Kirby's stuff."

"Pug, you don't have to—"

"No, let me finish. I don't believe in beating yourself up over the past—it just doesn't do a whole lot of good. I haven't been the friend I oughta be;

okay, that's the past, and what's done is done. The point is: I want to be a better one in the future. I want to stay in touch; I want to drop by and see my goddaughter."

"I'm not sure she could handle it," Cale said with a grin. "We told her there were no wild animals in North Carolina."

"Tell her my bark is worse than my bite. But tell her I'm coming—I mean that, okay? I want to be a better friend than the one I've been in the past."

Now Pug looked down at his watch. "I hate to leave the rest of this to you, but I've got to catch a red-eye out of JFK. I got a class in the morning."

The two men embraced again, and Pug started for the door.

"Hey," Cale called after him.

Pug turned.

"You, and me, and Kirby—we were good, weren't we? As a team, I mean."

Pug winked. "Buddy, we were the best—don't let anybody tell you otherwise. Eighty-seven thousand Iraqi soldiers surrendered during Desert Storm, and 75 percent of them were carrying one of our leaflets when they did. That's eighty-seven thousand men who didn't have to die. You think about that: eighty-seven thousand men owe their lives to that doughhead and his drawings. I think that's something to be proud of."

"You'd think that'd be reason enough to live," Cale said.

Pug shook his head. "You can't live for the past; you need a future for that. Who knows—maybe Kirby didn't think he had one."

CHAPTER 4

By now the stack of boxes was head-high and two deep. Cale stepped back to take a final count, and as he did so he noticed through the open doorway a young woman step into the apartment directly across the hall and close the door behind her.

Cale crossed the hallway and knocked. After a few moments the door began to open, then stopped with a *chink* at the end of a security chain. The young woman stood behind the door, peering around the edge with one eye.

"Hi," Cale said. "I was across the hall and I saw you come in here."

That didn't seem to do much for her confidence. She remained safely behind the door, waiting for him to continue.

"My name is Cale," he said. "I was a friend of Kirby's. A very old friend, in fact—we grew up together in North Carolina."

"You knew Kirby?"

Past tense—she must know. "Kirby was my best friend."

"Then how come I've never seen you around?"

"I live in Charlotte. Look, I was wondering if I could ask you a few questions." He gestured past her at her apartment.

She glanced quickly over her shoulder. "You expect me to let you into my apartment? Welcome to New York."

"You could come over to mine," he said with a smile, "but all I've got is a pile of boxes. No sofa . . . no throw pillows . . . no coffee, black with just a little bit of sugar . . ."

She smiled but still hesitated.

Now Cale leaned closer to the door, lowered his voice, and added a touch more Southern drawl. Cale's accent was something he controlled like a rheostat, and he could adjust it at will from High Point hayseed to Chapel Hill academic, depending on the need of the moment—and what the moment needed now was a touch of Southern comfort.

"I'm going to have to trust you with something," he whispered. "Under Kirby's shirt, he always wore something very special—*always*." Cale slowly drew a large *S* across his chest.

The woman let out a laugh.

"Then you know about his secret identity," Cale said. "That makes us practically family. Please? I promise I'll only take a moment of your time."

Cale heard the rattle of the chain; then the door swung wide and she turned away, waving for him to follow.

"Sofa's over there," she said, pointing as she disappeared into the kitchen. "Pillows too. Coffee black with just a little bit of sugar—right?"

"Right."

"I'm Rachel," she called from the kitchen.

"Nice to meet you, Rachel. How long did you know Kirby?"

"Not long. I only moved in about a year ago."

"You must have known him pretty well."

"You mean the Superman thing? It wasn't exactly a secret, you know. Kirby kind of liked to show it off."

Cale paused. "When did you hear about him?"

"Just after it happened, I suppose. The cops were in his apartment, and they make a lot of racket."

"Did they question you?"

"Sure—I'm the girl across the hall. They just asked basic stuff—pretty much the same things you have: Did you know him? How well did you know him? Did you have any reason to believe he was suicidal?"

"That was my next question."

She poked her head around the doorway. "You sound like a cop yourself."

"I'm not, I promise. I just lost someone very close to me and I'm trying to make sense of it, that's all."

She returned from the kitchen with two steaming cups.

"Thanks," Cale said.

"Are you single?"

The question stung. As a boy, Cale had never expected to be married one day. It wasn't that he didn't want to be; there were just so many things to do that he never thought he'd get around to it. And there were so many women—how would he ever choose? Cale didn't trust men who longed to get married; how would they ever know if they were in love with a woman or just in love with love? But then he met Hannah, and he had a sudden and complete change of mind. The desire to marry came with the woman, and that's how he knew she was the one. For Cale, their marriage was more than a relationship—it was a sort of metamorphosis, a complete change of identities, and asking him now if he was single was like asking a butterfly if it was back to being a catepillar.

"Yes," Cale said reluctantly, "I'm single."

"Funny. Could have sworn you were married."

Cale paused to let the subject pass. "How well did you know Kirby?" he asked again.

"Like I said, I'm the girl across the hall—that's all. We knew each other in passing: Good morning, Good evening, Let me help you with that—that's about all."

"Did you know him well enough to get a baseline? You know—to have some idea what he was like on a regular basis?"

"Kirby was friendly and outgoing. He had his ups and downs like most creative types, I suppose, but on the whole he seemed like a fairly level-headed guy."

"Did you notice any significant change of attitude toward the end? Any signs of deep discouragement or depression?"

"That's pretty hard to tell from 'Good evening' and 'Let me help you with that.' I didn't see any difference. That doesn't mean there wasn't any—I just didn't see it."

"Did Kirby get a lot of visitors here?"

"People were in and out all the time—mostly artist types, you know? From his work, I suppose."

"Was there anything different about those last few days? Anything unusual —anything different at all?"

Rachel stopped and considered. "There was one thing," she said. "There was this guy."

"What guy?"

"That's just it—I never saw him before or since. He stopped by one evening, just a few days before . . . you know. I remember I heard a knock and I thought someone was at my door, so I looked through the peephole—but it was somebody at Kirby's door instead. He was dressed in a suit and he carried a briefcase—very professional-looking. Not like the guys that Kirby worked with. I guess that's why I remember him: he stood out because he didn't stand out, you know? He was dressed like normal people."

"Did you see his face? What did he look like?"

"He was facing Kirby's door. He had black hair and dark skin—that's all I could see."

"Dark skin—you mean black?"

"No, like Hispanic—or Indian—or Middle Eastern, I don't know. Hey, this is New York. There are people from everywhere around here."

"So what did the guy do?"

"Well, I only saw him for a few seconds. I heard the knock, I went to the door, I looked; I saw the man standing and waiting, and then I saw Kirby's door open. Kirby greeted the man and invited him in—then the door closed and I went back to what I was doing."

"Greeted the man how? Did Kirby look surprised to see him?"

"No, now that you mention it. He looked like he expected him."

"And how did Kirby seem? Happy? Friendly? Did he look glad to see him?"

She tipped her head and studied him. "You sure you're not a cop?"

"Cross my heart."

"No, Kirby looked serious—like this was some kind of business deal."

"Did you tell the police about this guy?"

"I didn't remember him until just now. Should I have?"

Cale considered for a moment. "No. It probably doesn't matter."

He set his cup down on the coffee table and rose from the sofa. "Thank you, Rachel. I don't want to take up any more of your time."

"You're welcome to stay longer," she said with a smile. "You're sure you're not married?"

"Pretty sure. Thanks for the offer—maybe another time. I would like to ask one favor, though." He took out his wallet, pulled out a business card, and handed it to her. "If you think of anything else—anything out of the ordinary—would you give me call? Call me collect, day or night. And if you ever see that guy again—the guy in the business suit—be sure and let me know, okay?"

As she walked him to the door, she said, "Can I ask you something?"

"Sure."

"Kirby did commit suicide, didn't he?"

"That's the way it looks."

"You're asking a lot of questions. Are you trying to prove otherwise?"

"Not really," Cale said. "I'm just trying to understand why an old friend would leave without telling me good-bye."

CHAPTER 5

Bushwick, Brooklyn

The dark-skinned man stood on an empty street corner in a run-down section of abandoned German breweries and crumbling brick town houses. The crossing light slowly changed from WALK to WAIT again and again, but the man made no motion toward the street. He simply waited, staring straight ahead and occasionally glancing down to check his watch.

The man smoothed the front of his business suit and straightened the knot of his tie. He seemed strangely out of place, a kind of anachronism in these dilapidated surroundings. His dress was contemporary, professional, yet he stood in a section of Brooklyn frozen in time, where three decades ago a gluttonous spree of looting and arson during a summer blackout reduced this neighborhood to a smoldering ruin. Businesses withdrew, residents fled, and the only inhabitants left were precisely the people he was hoping to find.

He looked across the street at an abandoned brownstone. The first-floor windows and doors had all been bricked in to prevent the interior from becoming a crack house. The second- and third-floor windows were empty black rectangles with jagged shards of glass projecting from the edges like the teeth of a shark. *This is America too,* the man thought. *Not the one they show us in the sewage they pump into our homes from Cairo and Beirut—not the one they want us to see. But this is America too.*

Twenty minutes passed before another figure appeared. The man heard the woman before he saw her. The click of her brittle heels was audible a block away. He watched her approach from the corner of his eye; he did not turn to look at her. In his peripheral vision he saw a long-legged creature in a black leather skirt that barely covered half her thighs. She walked directly to him and stopped less than an arm's length away.

There was an awkward moment of silence. He waited for her to speak first, as he was told he must. He had heard about such encounters, and he could not afford any mistaken intentions or misunderstandings.

"Don't you look yummy," the woman purred.

"Good evening."

"Waiting for a friend?"

"No."

"Lucky me. Would you like to make a new one?"

He turned and looked at her for the first time, and it was all he could do to keep from taking a step back. Her thick plume of hair was unevenly colored an odd reddish-brown. Her skin was plastered smooth with a heavy foundation that left a distinct edge along her jawline, and her rather ordinary features were enhanced by bold streaks of red and blue and black.

Why are such women allowed to walk the streets in America? he wondered. *At home she would be in prison where her kind belongs.*

"One never has enough friends," he replied.

"Interested in a little companionship this evening?"

The woman spoke in riddles, in vague suggestions. It was just as he had expected—just as he had been told. The woman must be certain that he was not an undercover police officer, and he must do the same. In America, he knew, the authorities sometimes hire women like this to ensnare the morally corrupt. The initiative must be hers. He must not answer her directly, and he must not be the first to mention money.

"I'm sure you would make a fine companion."

"I can be any kind you like. Interested?"

"I am always interested in companionship."

She smiled and hooked her arm through his. "How does a hundred dollars sound?"

He let out an audible sigh. "You are a prostitute, then."

She pulled her arm away and frowned. "Honey, you're a big disappointment, you know that?"

"I assure you, I am not with the authorities."

"No kidding."

"I had to be certain that you were not either."

She gestured to her outfit; it fit like a second skin. "Do I look like I got a badge under here? Now are you interested or not?"

The man took a step away and began to study her more closely.

"You are too tall," he said.

"Well, I'm in heels. Here," she said, kicking them off.

He shook his head—even in her bare feet she almost looked into his eyes. He looked down at her legs. Even in the fading light he could see a lacework of blue and purple veins. She was much too old. *She may even have a child,* he thought.

"How much do you weigh?"

"Forget this," she grumbled, wriggling her feet back into her shoes. "I don't need this kind of—"

"I am interested," he said again, "but not in you. I am looking for someone much younger, slighter in build, with much more delicate features."

"This isn't eharmony.com," she said. "You want somebody else, you find her yourself."

He removed a wallet from his lapel pocket and opened it. "You mentioned one hundred dollars. I will pay you two hundred dollars if you will help me find the one I am looking for." He handed her a crisp hundred-dollar bill. "The rest you will receive later."

She eyed him suspiciously. "And just what is it you're looking for?"

From the same coat pocket the man produced a small photograph and handed it to the woman. "I am looking for someone like this—someone *exactly* like this."

The woman studied the photo. "How old is this girl?"

"The one I am looking for need not be the same age—but she must be able to pass for this age, with suitable alterations to her hair and dress."

"You've got very specific tastes."

"I have very specific needs. Do you know such a woman?"

She examined the photo again. "You're in luck," she said. "I happen to know someone who could be this girl's sister."

"Where can I find her?"

"I can take you to her—but not for two hundred bucks."

The man forced a look of impatience and frustration, though her maneuver was expected. That's why his original offer was only half what he was willing to pay.

"I do not wish to haggle," he said. "Please name your price."

"Make it three hundred and I'll take you there right now."

"Agreed," he said, sealing the arrangement with a second hundred-dollar bill.

She turned and started down the sidewalk, and the man fell in behind her. He watched her legs as she walked—her stride was long, and she walked briskly. *Time is money for this creature,* the man thought. At the end of a long, desolate stretch of pavement, they came to a bronze statue of a winged Victory streaked with black patina. Then they passed through the shadow of an elevated train, crossed a narrow street, and turned left. A few blocks later they came to an old brick building, the onetime residence of some wealthy brewmeister recently converted into a hotel of dubious distinction.

They entered the building without a word and headed up a narrow stairway to the second floor. They passed open doorways on both sides, but the man looked neither to the left nor to the right. He kept his arms pinned tightly to his sides as he walked, hoping to escape as much defilement as possible.

The woman stopped in an open doorway. "I'm looking for Jada," she said.

"You know the one I'm talking about? Sweet young thing from the Lower East Side. About so tall, skinny, looks half her age. Have you seen her?"

A female voice gave an inaudible reply and the woman laughed in response. She moved from doorway to doorway with the man following behind, watching her collect bits of information like a bird assembling a nest. Half an hour later they had worked their way to the fourth and final floor. The woman knocked on a door, waited for a muffled reply, then opened the door and stepped inside.

"Jada, honey, I brought you something."

The girl was lying on her back on a queen-size mattress between two windows on the opposite wall. She lay propped up against half a dozen pillows, flipping through a copy of *Entertainment Weekly*. She dropped the magazine in her lap and glanced up with a look of total boredom.

The man stepped into the room and looked at her. The girl's hair was dark, shoulder length and straight. Her build was very slight: Her collarbone and shoulders showed beneath her blouse like coat hangers, and her crossed legs looked like a pair of entwined serpents. The woman was right, she did not exaggerate—although she must be in her twenties, the girl could easily pass for someone half her age.

At the sight of the man, the girl sat up on her bed and flashed a mechanical smile.

"Stand up," the man demanded.

"Hey, good looking. How about—"

"Stand up," he said again. "Let me look at you."

The girl glanced up at the woman, who responded with a shrug. The girl returned the gesture, rose from the bed, and held out her arms like a scarecrow.

"See anything you like?"

The man took a step closer and removed the photograph from his coat pocket again. The girl was shorter and more slender than necessary, but that could be compensated for. Her hair was the wrong color, of course, and the wrong length—no matter. He looked at her face. On this point the woman had exaggerated—she bore only the slightest resemblance.

"Turn," he said.

She rolled her eyes but obeyed. "Choosy, aren't we?"

"How old are you?"

"Old enough."

He considered the width of her shoulders and the heft of her arms. He observed the basic proportions of her torso: the taper of her back, the thickness of her waist, the curvature of her narrow hips. Most of all, he studied the shape of her head—and he was satisfied.

"Yes," the man announced, "you will do."

"Lucky me."

"I have a business arrangement I wish to discuss with you."

"What a surprise."

The man turned to the woman in the doorway and handed her the balance of her finder's fee. "This concludes our business," he said to her. "The rest does not concern you. Please leave us."

The woman raised her eyebrows at the girl.

"It's okay," the girl said. "Thanks for the referral—I owe you one."

The man waited until the door closed behind her, then turned back to the girl. "What is your monthly income?" he asked.

"Who are you, the IRS? None of your business."

"I wish to offer you a business proposition."

She sat down on the edge of the bed.

"This is a different kind of employment than what you are used to."

"I'm listening."

"I would like to hire you for a period of one month. This will require your full time, day and night, and you must be willing to travel. In exchange for this service, I will pay you fifty thousand dollars—in cash."

The girl paused but never changed expression. "Whoa," she said. "Let's back up for a minute. What would I be doing—*exactly*—for this fifty thousand dollars?"

"There is too much to explain at this time. Your instructions will change each day."

"Forget it."

"Perhaps you should consider what you would *not* be doing. For a period of one month you would not have to live in this filthy hovel; you would not be surrounded by the constant threat of violence and substance abuse; and you would not have to sell yourself to disgusting vermin for the insulting fee of one hundred dollars—perhaps less."

She paused again.

"You would live with me in a respectable apartment. You would have your own room. I would not touch you, and I would insist that you never touch me. As I said, it is a business arrangement."

She narrowed her eyes. "And when do I see this fifty thousand dollars?"

"I will pay you five thousand dollars now, if you accept. You will receive the balance upon completion of your services."

"How do I know that?"

"You don't."

"And I'm supposed to just trust you?"

"No, you are supposed to enter a business arrangement with me. Like all business partners, you must keep one eye on me—and I on you. Please consider that you are not the only one taking a risk here. I am offering you five thousand dollars just for the promise of your services. That is a significant amount of money. I have no way to prevent you from simply taking the money and disappearing."

"Suppose I do?"

"Then I will lose five thousand dollars—and you will lose forty-five. I am in need of your services; you are in need of my money. That is the basis of a good partnership."

The man reached into his pocket then and removed a white envelope. He took out a stack of hundred-dollar bills, fanned them like a blackjack dealer, and laid them on the bed. Five thousand, he knew, was just a number; the eye is more easily persuaded than the ear.

"I want to count it," she said.

"You would be a fool not to."

"This 'service' you want from me—is it illegal?"

"It is undetectable."

"That's not what I asked."

"No, it's not."

"So there's risk involved."

He glanced about the room. "Every occupation has its risks, as I'm sure you know."

She took the money from the bed and slowly counted it.

"Is the amount correct?" he asked.

"Yeah."

"No, it isn't," he said. "There is an extra hundred-dollar bill, as I'm quite sure you noticed."

She frowned. "What is this, a test?"

"I simply wanted to make a point: I am not the only one who requires trust."

She took a single bill from the stack and tore it in half. She handed him one of the pieces. "You keep an eye on me, and I'll keep an eye on you—fair enough?"

"Fair enough."

"When do we get started?"

"My business in New York has recently concluded. I will call for you tomorrow before noon."

"What should I bring?"

"Nothing you currently wear would be suitable. Your clothing will be provided. Pack only your personal things. Please do not bring alcohol, tobacco, or any controlled substance."

"What a fun party this is gonna be."

He turned to the door, opened it, then looked back at her. "Will I find you here tomorrow?"

"Trust me," she said. "By the way—they call me Jada."

"Jada," he repeated. "I suppose that will do."

"Nice doing business with you, Abdul."

"My name is not Abdul. It is Hashim."

Hashim's own Brooklyn hotel room was no larger than Jada's and no better furnished. The few pieces of flimsy furniture were made of particleboard covered with a thin veneer of wood-grain vinyl that curled back from every corner like the peel of a banana. His metal-frame bed had no headboard or footboard, and the only desk in the room was a folding card table set up at the foot of the bed. There wasn't a single poster or mirror or cheap art rip-off on the walls; in fact, it was almost impossible to determine the color of the walls because every square inch of available space was covered with paper.

There were newspaper clippings of all shapes and sizes, and magazine articles with portions highlighted and underlined in red. There were Post-Its, "While You Were Out" notes, and even scraps of grease-stained fast-food bags bearing handwritten notes in Arabic. There were maps of every portion of the city, but especially Midtown Manhattan just below the park. There were bits of paper everywhere—and in the center of it all was a glossy 8x10 photograph of Kirby.

One by one Hashim pulled or peeled or unpinned each item from the wall and carried it to a shredder by the foot of the bed. Each one disappeared into the slot with a high-pitched whir. There were transcripts of telephone interviews with Kirby's past employers, neighbors, and childhood friends in High Point. There were photocopied pages from the ROTC section of the *Yackety Yack*, the UNC–Chapel Hill yearbook; there were dozens of printouts from the website of POVA, the Psychological Operations Veterans Association.

And there was Kirby's Army service record, with detailed notations about his awards and citations: the Army Service Ribbon, the Overseas Service Ribbon, and the Kuwait Liberation Medal presented by the grateful Saudis. Hashim had paid special attention to one particular award: the Purple Heart, awarded to Kirby for a wound received in the line of duty.

An hour later the walls were barren again, and the final facts and details of the life of King Kirby vanished into a sea of confetti.

Now Hashim reached into his coat pocket and removed the small photograph of the young girl. He studied it for a moment, then opened a thick file folder and placed it atop another photo: a glossy 8x10 of her father—Cale Caldwell.

CHAPTER 6

Charlotte, North Carolina

Cale stood in the yawning doorway of his great room, the traditional Southern name for a living room and family room joined together to form a single living space. In this house, that space was the size of a small airplane hangar. Cale and Hannah clearly traded up when they moved from their tiny two-bedroom condo in Chicago to this sprawling two-story-with-a-basement in the newest suburb of Charlotte. The condo had been fine for a young married couple, but a dozen years later they had outgrown the space—and the city too. It wasn't a matter of size, but a matter of *feel*. Cale was from rural North Carolina, where houses were tiny but lots were immense, and homes were never built closer than a cornfield or a truck garden apart. In High Point you could walk in a straight line for five miles without interruption; in Chicago a man could barely reach his stride before he came to a wall or a fence.

Cale had been a bright and shining star at Leo Burnett. His print ads had taken top honors at the One Show and NYAD; his commercials for Dean Witter, Allstate, and Disney had been featured at Chicago's Film Fest and had even been short-listed at Cannes. In just twelve years he had rounded up every award the industry had to offer, and he found himself about to become the youngest executive creative director in the history of the agency—and that's when he decided to quit.

It wasn't Burnett, and it wasn't the advertising field. It was the relentless pace, and the endless commuting, and the at-the-drop-of-a-hat red-eyes from O'Hare to New York or Los Angeles. It wasn't the work—it was the *time*. Cale had a twelve-year-old daughter, and he made a little mental calculation one day: Two-thirds of Grace's childhood was already past, and he knew that the remainder would fly by in a flash. He decided he might like to be there to see it.

So he began to talk to Hannah about returning to North Carolina—to a smaller ad agency and a slower pace of life. He mounted an ambitious sales campaign; he brought up the topic at every opportune moment. He shamelessly oversold the virtues of the area—he made the Carolina Piedmont sound like the Elysian fields. Hannah finally agreed to a compromise: North Carolina was acceptable, she said, but she had no intention of moving into a double-wide trailer in the middle of a High Point soybean patch. Hannah still wanted a city—something with malls and parks and a respectable football team. So they settled on Charlotte, the largest and grandest city in all of North Carolina—though less than a fifth the size of Chicago.

They sold their little condo, cashing in on a dozen years of inflation and soaring property values, and went shopping for a single-family dwelling in Charlotte—not in the city proper, but on the outskirts of town: somewhere unincorporated; somewhere without all the rules and ordinances; somewhere the dog could run without a leash. They found such a place, surrounded by tobacco fields on one side and a forest of lodgepole pines on the other—and they were astounded when they realized what Chicago money would buy in Charlotte.

In Chicago they had two bedrooms, a breakfast nook, and a nice little kitchen with a butcher-block island. In Charlotte they now had a four-thousand-square-foot French country manor complete with screened-in porches, a gourmet kitchen with granite countertops, and a master bedroom with its own stone fireplace and cathedral ceiling—that's the room Cale liked best.

What Cale didn't know—what he never expected in a thousand years—was that Hannah would not be there to help fill this house. Even in their little condo, Hannah's absence would have been palpable; but here, the vast emptiness of these cavernous rooms reflected the loss of her like an echo in a canyon.

Cale looked into the great room; it was dark except for the flickering glow of a plasma-screen TV. Across from it he saw Grace sprawled sideways on an overstuffed Thomasville chair.

Cale watched her for a moment, as he often did when Grace was unaware of his presence, and he felt a familiar longing. It was a wonderful, terrible thing that Grace looked so much like her mother. The brightness of her eyes, the delicacy of her hands, even the way she tossed her hair when she was angry—she was like a miniature replica, growing every day in size and detail until one day she would look like a virtual duplicate of the original. It didn't seem fair for his daughter to be swallowed up by her mother's memory. Cale hoped that it would never happen—but a part of him hoped that it would.

He entered the room and crossed between Grace and the television. Her eyes never shifted; she showed no recognition of his presence. He reached down and clicked on a table lamp beside the chair. Grace frowned in annoyance and cupped her hand over her eyes.

"Bad for your eyes, sweetheart."

"That's an urban legend."

"It's in the Parenting Manual—section 27, paragraph 4: 'All parents must warn their children about the dangers of eyestrain, junk food, and running with pointed objects.'"

Grace said nothing.

Their golden retriever, Molly, stretched out in front of Grace on the floor. Grace's right arm swung back and forth like a pendulum, stroking the dog's long back as she stared at the TV. The dog was Hannah's; she bought her on a whim at a garage sale one Saturday morning in the suburbs of Chicago. Cale told her she was crazy—a retriever is a hunting dog and a hunting dog needs room to run. It's not the kind you keep in a little two-bedroom condo in the city. It'll chew the place apart, he told her, but it was too late; Hannah already loved the dog. She was like that—she loved things quickly—and in the long run, whatever Hannah loved was good enough for Cale.

When Grace came along, they had their doubts about the dog. When Grace was just a toddler, barely able to stand, Molly would lumber through the living room like a brontosaurus and send Grace sprawling—then lick her face in apology until she burst into tears. But soon Grace learned to manage; she learned to wrap her arms around Molly's neck and shriek with delight while the dog dragged her around the apartment like a rodeo queen.

Strangely, it was Molly who first caused Cale to think about leaving Chicago. One evening, walking down a city sidewalk with Molly straining at the end of her six-foot tether, Cale suddenly felt trapped—confined—boxed in. He returned to the condo and told Hannah that he felt sorry for the dog—that a dog needs room to stretch her legs. Hannah smiled and listened, and somehow sensed what Cale wouldn't understand for months yet—that the dog had never once complained about the constraints of city life. It wasn't Molly who needed more room to run—it was Cale.

Cale loved the dog, but even more he marveled at her. What a strange creature a dog is, to give so much pleasure with so little effort. Molly was like the hub of a wheel, and everyone in the Caldwell family seemed to somehow connect through her. When Molly was full grown, she could lie across all three of their laps at once, and each of them would take a section and stroke, groom, or scratch to their heart's content—and Molly, for her part, was more than happy to oblige. "The Love Sponge"—that's what Hannah called her. Cale wondered if somewhere in that dull canine mind Molly knew that Hannah was gone forever—and in her own way, grieved.

Cale sat down on the carpet beside Molly and began to scratch her neck. When he did, Grace took her hand away.

Cale got up from the floor and walked to the kitchen door. "C'mon, Molly," he called back. "Time to go out—time to get some exercise."

The dog rose, stretched, and reluctantly obeyed. Cale opened the door and waited for her to trot out—then he looked at Grace again.

"Guess where I was today," he said.

She shrugged but said nothing.

"I was at your school."

Still nothing.

"Want to know why?"

"Not really."

Cale picked up the remote and switched off the TV. "Grace—look at me."

She turned her head just enough to see her father from the corner of her eye.

"I was asked to come to your school today by your counselor. You know why?"

Grace rolled her eyes and made a heavy sigh. "Because I made the National Honor Society and they wanted to tell you in person."

"Not much chance of that," Cale said. "Your counselor says your grades are dropping like a rock in a pond. How come?"

"Because I hate my teachers," she said. "They're stupid, and boring, and they don't know how to explain things."

"But your grades were great at the beginning of the year."

She threw him a quick and pointed glance. "Things were different then."

He paused to let her know he got the message. "Your counselor says you're not turning in your homework."

"Homework bores me."

"You can't stop doing homework just because it bores you. You—"

Cale caught himself. He knew he needed to tread lightly because so many of these conversations had gone so badly. He tried to evaluate each line before he said it, like an editor checking copy before it goes to press. Parents often revert to annoying clichés, and if he wasn't careful, "You can't stop doing homework just because it bores you" would be followed by, "What would happen if everybody stopped doing everything that bored them?" capped off by the inspirational, "If I stopped doing my work every time it bored me, you wouldn't have anything to eat." And by that time, Grace would have long ago checked out.

"Do you need help with your schoolwork?"

"No," she said indignantly.

"I see two options here," Cale said. "Either you can't do the work, or you won't do the work. If you can't, let's get you some help; if you won't, well—I'd like to know why."

"Because I hate this school, and I hate the kids, and I want to go home!"

"Grace, this is your home."

"No, this is *your* home. My home is in Chicago—that's where my school is, and that's where my friends are—my *real* friends."

Packing up and returning to the city of Chicago was something Cale had seriously considered after Hannah's death. But Cale knew that it wouldn't solve the problem—the real problem. Cale hoped that Charlotte would be a step up for them, a chance for an even better life, but instead it had become a place of death—at least for Grace. Unfortunately, the Chicago that Grace was longing for no longer existed—because in that city Hannah Caldwell was alive and well, and that city was no longer on this earth.

Cale said nothing for the next few minutes, and Grace sat as quietly as a fly in a web, waiting for the ugly spider to decide its next move. This was how every conversation between them seemed to end—at the point where Cale knew exactly what he needed to say next, but couldn't say it. He needed to talk about Hannah. He needed to tell Grace how sorry he was that she died but that it wasn't the city's fault—it wasn't *his* fault. That was what he wanted to say most—and he could say it with a lot more conviction if he really believed it himself.

At least he could tell her how much he missed her too—that there were ways a husband missed a wife that a little girl couldn't even understand. And he wanted to invoke the power of Hannah's presence; he wanted to tell Grace that somewhere, somehow, her mother was still alive and watching—that she was counting on them; that she wanted them to love each other and to do well—for her sake if not their own.

He wanted to say all these things, but he knew that it was infinitely more than Grace could bear. The mere mention of Hannah's name—the simple use of the word "Mom"—was like setting off an incendiary bomb.

And so, after several minutes of silence, Cale simply said, "Okay, here's what we need to do: I want to see your homework every night before you go to bed. Got it?"

She answered with a dramatic groan.

"By the way, your uncle Pug says hi."

"Who?"

Cale smiled. "The last time you saw him you were about the size of a football. Pug's not really your uncle—he's your godfather."

Grace rolled off the armchair and started for her bedroom.

"Too many fathers," she grumbled.

Across the street, a solitary figure sat in a parked car, watching the front of the house. It was evening now, and porch lanterns and landscape lights washed the house in a warm yellow-orange. The man in the car saw a side door open, casting a shaft of light across the lawn. A moment later a golden retriever bounded out and trotted toward the woods.

The man checked his watch and jotted a note in Arabic.

CHAPTER 7

"More lemonade, Cale?"

"No ma'am. Thank you just the same."

"I'll fetch those lemon bars, then."

Cale sat in the tiny living room of Kirby's High Point home, while Kirby's seventy-year-old mother darted about like a mosquito. He wished she would stop moving; he wished she would sit down and face him and talk. But it's no easy thing to talk about a dead son—an only son—and Cale supposed that some things are easier to face when you don't look at them head-on.

He felt a dull ache growing in the muscles of his groin, and he realized that he had been squeezing his thighs tightly together to keep from touching anything on either side. It was something he had always done at Kirby's house, ever since he was a boy, because the rooms possessed a brittle, museum-like quality. There were lacework doilies on every flat surface that looked as fragile as gaslight mantles. There were delicate glass candy dishes, eggshell-thin porcelain vases, and china display plates perched precariously on little wooden easels. *It's like living in a house of cards,* Cale thought.

Cale could never relax at Kirby's house, and that's why the boys always ran out to play as soon as they could—because even when he was a small boy, the house made Cale feel big and clumsy, as though at any moment his body might lose control and crash into some priceless and irreplaceable object. He realized now that none of the fragile objects had any monetary value—but since none of them had been moved more than an inch in the last thirty years, he imagined that each had great personal significance. Maybe they were handed down; maybe they were family heirlooms. He could imagine how devastated the old woman might be if a single item were chipped or cracked, and he wondered how she was holding up—because the only thing she ever owned of any real value was now broken beyond repair.

The woman disappeared into the kitchen again, and Cale decided to follow.

"Miss D.," he called after her. "Miss D." is what Cale had called her ever since he could remember. "Dumfries" just didn't seem like a nice thing to call anyone, so Kirby's mom quickly became known to all the neighborhood kids as "Miss D."

"Miss D., sit down with me for a minute, will you?" He pulled out one of the kitchen chairs.

"Let me get those lemon bars."

"No, sit down first. C'mon—over here."

She approached the chair without a word and slowly sank down.

Cale looked at her eyes, but she didn't quite look back. He considered what to say next—he wondered what she could bear to hear. He knew he had to avoid the things he wanted to say most, but he was used to that—that's what he had to do with Grace every single day. He wanted to say, "I loved your son," and "Did you see this coming?" But that would be like asking the old woman to stare into the sun—so he decided to take a back road instead.

"I wonder if I could ask your advice," he began.

"Of course, Cale."

"You raised a child by yourself—out here, in the country. That had to be hard to do."

"It had its moments," she said.

"But you raised a *boy*. You—a woman. How did you manage that?"

"You're asking about your own daughter."

"Yes ma'am, I am."

She smiled. "You know, Romulus and Remus were raised by wolves. It wasn't any harder than that."

"Thanks, Miss D.—you're a big encouragement."

"I was raised by wolves myself," she said, "the only girl among four brothers. You might could think I grew up just like them—but I didn't."

"Why not?"

"Those boys beat the tar out of one another—it's a wonder any of them survived. But if they ever laid a hand on me, my father would raise the stars and bars on their backsides. He rarely had to; the boys knew I was different. They didn't know what to do with me, but they knew what not to do. I think that's a pretty good start."

"Well, I know what not to do," Cale said.

"Do you? That's not as easy as it sounds."

"What do you mean?"

"Some people think that only a man can raise a boy, but that's not quite true. If a father looks at his son and thinks, *He's a boy, so he's just like me,* that man is in for a truckload of trouble. You can't raise anyone to be what you are—you have to raise them to be what they are. In a way, you're lucky—you won't make that mistake with your daughter."

"But there's so much I don't know about raising a girl."

"Do you love her to death? Do you treat her with respect? Do you listen to her?"

"I try."

She nodded. "The rest is details, and details take care of themselves. I raised my boy to be good and kind, because I believe that's how everyone should be. But in the ways he was a boy, I just let the boy come out."

"How did you put up with it?"

"The same way that wolf did—I howled at the moon sometimes."

"I've done some of that too."

"Of course you have. On a quiet night you can hear parents for miles around."

Cale grinned.

The old woman reached across and patted Cale's hand. "Your daughter is what God made her to be," she said. "You can shape her, but you can't change her. 'You can plant a tater in a melon patch, but that don't make it a melon'— that's what my daddy used to say. He raised a tater; so did I; so can you. You just keep loving her and she'll turn out just fine."

Cale paused here, because the thought that came to mind was something he could never say: *Not necessarily—she might jump off a bridge someday.*

The old woman seemed to read his silence.

"You know," she said, "I used to give piano lessons. Do you remember?"

"You bet I do. You were the terror of the neighborhood."

"Now, that's not true."

"I heard the stories."

"What stories?"

"About sitting on that hard bench in your parlor, with nothing but the sound of that metronome—*tick, tick, tick*. And you, standing behind the bench, staring down but never saying a word . . . That's why I took up football."

"I tried to make Kirby take lessons—you talk about howling at the moon."

"He didn't take to it, huh?"

"Mercy—the boy couldn't sit still for five minutes. Kirby had what they now call an 'attention deficit.' They didn't have a name for it back then—we just called it the 'fidgets.' The shame of it is, he had real talent."

Cale looked directly into her eyes. "Sometimes talent's not enough."

She smiled slightly. "You know, the piano is a complicated instrument. It has about two hundred and seventy strings—did you know that?"

"No ma'am, I didn't."

"Strings break sometimes, especially when the piano's being tuned—when a little too much tension is applied. You know, it's the treble strings that break most often—the high notes. I believe that's what Kirby was: a treble string."

Cale reached out and took her hand. "I set the boxes in Kirby's room, Miss D."

"Yes. Thank you, Cale; that will be fine."

"The rest will come by UPS in a few days. I wanted to bring these myself. They're his personal things: letters, photographs, things like that."

"It was very kind of you."

"I left some mail on top. Just a few bills and advertisements—things that arrived while I was at his apartment. If you like, I'll go through them for you."

"Would you? I don't expect I'll open those boxes just yet."

"It'll just take a minute," Cale said, sliding back his chair. "In the meantime, why don't you fetch those lemon bars? I'm not leaving here without one."

In Kirby's room, Cale flipped through the stack of envelopes and circulars, quickly sending most of it into the wastebasket. There was a final water bill and a prorated rent notice. He tucked those away to pay himself; he wasn't going to leave the old woman with bills.

He came to a plain white business envelope with no return address, and he cocked his wrist to send it sailing into the trash—but then he took a closer look at the address window and thought better of it. He opened the envelope and removed a thin sheet of paper with a series of holes punched across the top. He studied it carefully.

It was a lab report from the Community Healthcare Network on Madison Avenue in New York, announcing the results of Kirby's recent test. According to the lab report, Kirby did not, in fact, have HIV.

"Is there anything I should know about?" Miss D. asked from the doorway.

Cale folded the letter, stuffed it into his shirt pocket, then turned and smiled. "Not a thing," he said. "Now, how about our dessert?"

Cale was on I-85 just outside Kannapolis when his cell phone rang. He hooked the earpiece of his hands-free headset over his right ear, opened the phone, and pushed Talk.

"This is Cale."

"Hey, I got your message. What's up?"

"Pug—thanks for calling back. Where are you?"

"On the other end of this phone. How 'bout you?"

"I'm on my way back from High Point to Charlotte. I was visiting Kirby's mom—I dropped off some of his things."

"Good for you."

"Pug, I found something in Kirby's things I want to ask you about."

"I'm listening."

"It's a letter that was mailed to Kirby—it arrived the day I left New York. It's a medical report from a lab in Manhattan—one of those confidential testing places."

"Testing for what?"

"HIV."

There was a pause on the other end of the line. "Kirby had HIV?"

"No. According to the report, he was tested for HIV—but the results were negative."

"Okay. So what's your question?"

"Pug, don't you find it a little strange that Kirby had an HIV test just before he committed suicide?"

"Can't say as I do."

"Why not?"

"When did you say this letter arrived?"

"The day I left New York."

"*After* he did himself in."

"Right."

"Dunno about you, but I think I'd wait until *after* I got my test results before I jumped off a bridge."

Cale said nothing.

"Look, I know what you're trying to do. You got a dead buddy and you want to know why. But suppose you do find out why—then whaddya got?"

"Peace of mind," Cale said.

"Don't you believe it—you still got a dead buddy. Don't rack your brain, kid. If Kirby wanted us to know why he did it, he would have told us. Who knows—he might have drawn us a whole comic book."

Cale heaved a sigh of resignation. "You're right," he said. "Sorry—hope I didn't interrupt anything important."

"As a matter of fact, I'm at the day spa—you interrupted my treatment."

"You could use treatment," Cale said.

"You know, I been meaning to call you anyway. How're things going?"

"Which things?"

"You know, things—things in general."

"What am I supposed to say? Things in general are okay."

"Okay, lousy question. Look—if things weren't okay—if something happened, if something was really wrong—you'd tell me, wouldn't you?"

Cale paused; it was an odd question. "Sure, I guess so."

"Good. So how's Gracie?"

"In general? Okay."

"Did you tell her Uncle Pug says hi?"

"Yeah. She said, 'Yippee! Who the heck is Uncle Pug?'"

"Well, tell that girl I'll pay her a visit sometime soon."

"Right. We'll see you when we see you, Pug."

"Hey, kid."

"Yeah?"

"Stop worrying about Kirby. You got enough on your hands."

CHAPTER 8

Cale slumped back in his canvas-backed director's chair with his arms folded lazily across his chest. He sat in near-darkness, but thirty feet away from him, the film set glistened like a stadium at night in the center of the soundstage. Overhead, banks of glowing lekos and Fresnels looked like satellites orbiting in space, their barn doors angling out around them like solar arrays, flooding the planet below in blinding light.

For some of Burnett's creative directors, a commercial shoot was the be-all and end-all of the advertising field. The chance to do LA; the chance to hang out in the bar at the Four Seasons; the chance to hit on some gorgeous and potentially grateful actress—it was the American dream. But Cale hated commercial shoots: the monotonous meetings and endless consultations, the temperamental directors who thought of themselves as the next James Cameron, the constant breaks for lighting corrections and technical details. Cale estimated that a thirty-second commercial could probably be shot in about six hours, but all the crap that went with it filled up an entire week—an entire week in Los Angeles.

To Cale, LA seemed just like the soundstage: a vast, open space dominated by one enormous movie set. Like all sets, it was definitely glamorous and impressive—until you took a look backstage. That's the problem with a set: it only looks good from the front. From behind it's just canvas and plywood with a few braces and sandbags to prop the whole thing up.

Maybe it wasn't all LA's fault, Cale thought; maybe it was just the way it felt to a boy from North Carolina—a real and solid place located midway between Disneyland and Disney World. Or maybe the problem was really Cale himself: Maybe it was his gift—his natural ability to look inside human hearts and understand their workings. Maybe he was just tired of looking inside people and finding nothing much going on. Whatever it was, every time Cale returned from the West Coast, he felt a little emptier and a little more cynical—and he found himself thinking more and more about his Carolina roots.

Cale's chair had been arranged beside the director's, but he dragged it back about ten more feet and took up position there. Part of the reason was to get the big picture of everything going on in front of him, but part of it was just to distance himself from the chaos of production. The set was designed to look like a typical kitchen—a typical TV kitchen, that is, with twice the space and half the clutter of any real-world counterpart. They were shooting a spot for Procter & Gamble, introducing the latest in a long line of whizbang household cleaners from the longtime client of Leo Burnett. The cast included a husband, a wife, and a pair of freckle-faced, cute-as-a-button tykes just like the ones you find next door—except that these two happened to be represented by the William Morris Agency.

It wasn't going well. On the set, the actor playing the husband waved his arms and stopped the taping for the fifth time.

The director turned in his chair and glared at Cale. "I'm going to kill him," he said. "I'm never working with this casting director again."

"Let me talk to him," Cale said with a reassuring nod.

When he stepped onto the set, he had to squint against the dazzling light. He approached the husband and asked, "Is there a problem?"

"This is all wrong," the actor said. "You've got me coming around the island like this and stopping here." He demonstrated, rounding the island and taking his mark at the right of the sink.

"So?"

"So my back is to the camera the whole time."

"That's the way I planned it. When you hit your mark, you look across at your wife. The viewer follows your eyes to her, and she holds up the product."

"But then the focus will be entirely on the product."

Cale blinked. "It's a commercial."

The actor put his hand on Cale's shoulder. "Look, can I share my heart with you here?"

Cale almost laughed. It was another way of saying, "If I say something really stupid, will you promise not to think I'm a *total* moron?"

"Go ahead," Cale said.

"You've got a product, and I've got a product. Yours is soap, or dishwasher detergent, or whatever. *This* is mine." He held up both hands, framing his face. "You see what I'm saying? My face is my product. My face is what got me this part, and my face is what will get me the next one. Now if your client doesn't see his product in this commercial, he's not going to be very happy, right? Well, it's the same with me—I need to get my product in front of the camera. So how about this: I round the island, but instead of stopping here, I cross the aisle, turn, and lean back against the counter. That way I'd be facing the camera, see? And I can still turn and smile at the little woman and all."

Cale stood silently, listening, but thoughts went buzzing through his mind like mud daubers from a nest. *It's a commercial, you moron, not your movie debut. Yes, the focus is on the product—that's what commercials are for. That's what a client pays ten thousand bucks a second to produce, and if you want your own commercial, you can pay for one. I don't care about your product—I hired you to show off mine, and if you draw attention away from my product for even a second, you're out of here.*

But Cale said none of those things. He knew that if he did, it would probably cause a major meltdown in the actor's ego, and that would be just one more headache he'd have to deal with. Instead, he said, "You're looking at this the wrong way. Did you ever see *Silence of the Lambs?*"

"Of course," the actor said.

A split-second hesitation told Cale he was lying. "Anthony Hopkins, remember? That's who everybody remembers—he stole the show. The film was a hundred and eighteen minutes long, but Hopkins was only onscreen for sixteen minutes—and he still took home the Oscar. You know why? *Presence*."

"Presence?"

"The way he carried himself, the way he stood. A good actor doesn't have to grin at the camera—he just has that presence. Now let me tell you something, just between you and me." Cale leaned in a little closer. "I cast you for this part. Not the director, not the casting agency—me."

It was true. As producer, Cale was responsible for final casting decisions. He didn't take part in the original "cattle calls," when the casting agency sifted through hundreds of résumés and headshots and sat through dozens of readings to narrow the contenders down to a final few. But it was Cale's job to make the final decisions, and he did so based on a simple criterion: he looked for people who looked good on camera. He never wanted to meet the actors in person; he never wanted to see them except on a TV monitor. It didn't matter if they looked good in person; it didn't matter if they were pleasant or nice—and they frequently weren't. This actor was no different; in person he was arrogant and fragile and difficult to work with, but it made no difference. For some mysterious, unexplainable reason, he just looked good on camera—particularly from behind, according to one focus group.

So it was not really a lie when Cale said to him, "I think *you* have that presence—that's why I cast you in this role. Look, I can get anybody to stare at the camera; I need something deeper from you. Can you give me that? Can you do that for me?"

The man began to nod solemnly, searching deep in his soul for that mysterious quality that would somehow give his backside Oscar-winning appeal. Cale patted him on the shoulder and turned away.

On the opposite side of the set, the "wife" waited patiently for shooting to resume.

"You're doing a great job," Cale called over.

She smiled. "I haven't done anything yet."

Cale stopped and looked at her. "Do you have everything you need?"

"If I did, I'd be doing feature films."

Cale walked over. "What I mean is: Do you know what I need from you?"

"Boy, how many men have asked me that?"

Cale grinned. "Let me put it another way: Do you understand the part?"

"It's pretty straightforward," she said. "I read the script."

"So did he," Cale whispered, nodding to the other actor.

"Maybe you could give me that 'presence' speech," she said. "That was very inspirational."

"You think so? Which part did you like best?"

"The part about, 'I need something *deeper* from you.' I got tingles."

"That was good, wasn't it? That belongs in a movie."

"Where I come from, we put that on rosebushes."

"You're not from LA?"

"Nobody's from LA. LA is like a bus stop. At a bus stop you don't ask people where they're from; you ask them where they're headed."

"So where are you headed?"

She shrugged. "That depends on which bus comes along first."

Cale cocked his head and looked at her more closely. He had cast her, too, but somehow he felt as though he were seeing her for the first time. The camera loved her, there was no doubt about that. On a nineteen-inch screen she was drop-dead gorgeous, but she was even better looking in person. Her long brown hair had a distinct auburn highlight that seemed to glow under the powerful lights. Her face was almond-shaped, and like those of most beautiful women, her features were perfectly symmetrical. Her nose was thin, turned up and chiseled at the tip—a detail that the camera particularly liked. Her eyes were a penetrating shade of green that no camera could capture, and even under her heavy stage makeup, it was obvious that her complexion was flawless. She was a model, Cale recalled from her résumé, and like a lot of LA models, she was apparently trying to make the jump from print to film. Like most models, she would probably fail—though in her case Cale wasn't so sure. She had something special—something that came through on camera—but Cale had never expected that quality to come through in person. In person, most of the models he had worked with had no more dimension than their photographs. But there seemed to be more to this woman—a whole lot more, and Cale found himself wanting to know exactly how much.

"Something wrong?" she asked. "You're staring."

"Sorry. I bet you get that a lot."

"Yeah, I do. I was hoping for more from you."

Cale blinked.

"So where are you from?" she asked.

"North Carolina."

"You like it there, I can tell. I can hear it in your voice."

"I don't live there now. I live in Chicago."

"If you like North Carolina so much, why don't you go back?"

"I've been asking myself that question. What about you? Are you happy in LA?"

"It's hard to feel at home in a bus station."

"I don't think you'll be here long," Cale said. "I bet all kinds of buses would be glad to pick you up."

She paused. "That was either very sweet or very rude."

"Would you have dinner with me?" he blurted out, then abruptly stopped. He didn't plan to say those words—they just came out. His timing couldn't have been worse, but there was no way to take them back now.

"You need to understand something," she said. "I'm waiting for a bus, not hitchhiking. I'm not desperate."

Cale felt his face flush. "I'm sorry," he fumbled. "I'm saying all the wrong things."

"Not really," she said. "I think you're improving. You know, when you quit schmoozing, you're a pretty nice guy."

"You didn't answer my question," he said.

"I know. I want to be sure what you're asking."

"I'm asking you to have dinner with me."

"And that's all?"

"Cross my heart and hope to die, stick a million pins in my eye."

"Is that what they say in North Carolina?"

"We do if it gets us a date."

"Well, it worked," she said, "but I'm bringing some pins just in case."

"I'm Cale Caldwell." He extended his hand and she took it. Her hand was warm and soft, and she didn't let go until he did.

"Hi, Cale. I'm Hannah Grace."

"Hannah Grace," he said aloud, and then to himself: *Hannah Grace Caldwell.*

Cale rose from the bench and stepped over to the granite headstone. He slowly ran his hand across the curved top and wiped it on his jeans, leaving a smudge of yellow pine pollen behind. The speckled gray-and-black monument consisted of two massive slabs: a horizontal stone that lay upon the ground, rough-hewn around the edges, and a vertical stone resting upon it whose surfaces were as smooth as glass. On one face of the vertical stone, carved in relief and gilded in gold, was the name *Hannah Grace Caldwell.*

CHAPTER 9

Cale could remember the day he bought the headstone. The salesman from the monument and memorial company kept emphasizing the sheer mass of the black granite. *A hundred and seventy pounds per cubic foot, two-point-six times the weight of an equal volume of water*—as though there might be a problem keeping Hannah down. It seemed ridiculous at the time, but now he understood. The salesman wasn't talking about weight, he was talking about permanence—immovability—some small testimony to Hannah's existence that couldn't be washed, worn, or weathered away—at least not for a few hundred years.

Now Cale understood how important it all was, because the world is in such a hurry to forget. Life belongs to the living, and the dead have no place in it. Bodies are consumed by bacteria, grave sites are covered by grass, and headstones are dusted with pine pollen—tiny, living spores that can force down roots into stone itself. And Cale didn't want that to happen. He wasn't ready to forget Hannah; he was trying, with all his power, to remember.

"It's a beautiful day," Cale said aloud, "the kind you always loved. The azaleas are mostly gone now. I think spring's about over—you can already feel the humidity starting to move in." He rested his hand on top of the stone; it felt warm in the afternoon sun.

"I drove over to High Point today. I visited Kirby's mom—dropped off some of his things. I asked Grace if she wanted to come. She didn't—big surprise. I could've made her come along, I suppose, but that wouldn't solve the problem, would it?" He glanced down at the stone and for an instant expected an answer, but there was none. It made him feel a little angry—not because Hannah failed to reply, but because God did. Sending a message from beyond the grave was beyond Hannah's power, but not God's—not from what he'd always been told. He could really use a voice from above right about now, but God seemed strangely silent—and he didn't understand why.

He walked back to the small stone bench across from Hannah's grave and sat down again.

He found himself drifting back to his days at 4POG. The first thing they taught you in basic PsyOps training was to *know the mind of your enemy*—if you failed to do that, there was no telling what could go wrong. The Iraqis were famous for their ignorance of the American culture; during Desert Storm they once put a woman on the radio we called Baghdad Betty—the Arab equivalent of Tokyo Rose. One day she announced to our troops, "While you men are fighting overseas, your wives and girlfriends back home are being seduced by Tom Cruise, Tom Selleck, and Bart Simpson." It was a ridiculous blunder—but it was just the kind of mistake you can make when you don't know the other guy's world.

That's the way he felt about Grace right now: She was from another world, and he had no idea what she was thinking or what she really felt. At times he found himself wishing that he could drop some leaflet on her that would cause her to turn around and come back to him. But he hated himself for thinking that way. Grace was not some frontline soldier who needed to be analyzed and exploited. She was his daughter; how was he ever supposed to win her back with an attitude like that?

"What am I going to do with Grace?" he asked the headstone. "Grace was always your department. Miss D. says all I need to do is love her and the rest will take care of itself—but I do love her, Hannah, and it's not enough. Her grades are falling; she's dropped out of all her activities; she's pulled away from all her friends. It's like she's got her bags all packed but there's nowhere to go—and I can't help her because she won't talk to me. She's so angry. She blames me for—for everything."

Cale looked up into the sky. "Did I screw up, Hannah? Is all this my fault? Were things good enough in Chicago, and I just got greedy? Did I—"

Cale stopped. He suddenly became aware of a presence behind him; he turned and looked. Less than twenty feet away, an old man was standing on the asphalt footpath that passed behind the bench. Beside the man was a gray rolling trash can with the handles of a rake, a shovel, and a broom protruding like antennae. His khaki work shirt was clean and pressed and buttoned all the way up to the neck. The cuffs of his sleeves were buttoned, too, disappearing into gray leather work gloves. His shirt was tucked neatly into crisp khaki trousers, giving him an almost military demeanor.

Though he was dressed as a common laborer, his clothing showed no signs of physical exertion: There were no dark blotches of sweat under the arms, no green and yellow stains tattooed across the knees. He looked like a retired general, still wearing his combat uniform but only for parade. But there was little doubt that the man had seen his share of active duty; his broad back and rounded shoulders revealed years of backbreaking labor. He reminded Cale of an old hickory tree, with its branches hanging a little lower than in years gone by, but with more than enough root to still hold its ground.

"Beg your pardon," the old man said. "I hate to interrupt a man's prayers."

"Can I help you with something?"

"Just stopped by to place these flowers."

In his two gloved hands the old man cupped a crude papier-mâché cone containing a beautiful bouquet of perfect white roses; the niveous petals stood out against his khaki shirt like seagulls on a beach. Cale counted at least a dozen roses—maybe a dozen and a half. It was a rarity to see such beautiful and expensive flowers in a graveyard; these days it was uncommon to find real flowers at all. Artificial arrangements were now the order of the

day, because of financial realities and the practical considerations of wind
and rain and bleaching sun. The delicate roses would last only a day or two
on the exposed hillside. It was a beautiful and extravagant gesture on someone's part—but not Cale's. He hadn't sent them.

"Is there a card?" Cale asked.

The old man poked a thick, gloved finger into the center of the bouquet.
"'Roseland Floral Company,'" the old man read. "That's all it says. Roseland's
over on Central, not far from here."

"I think there might be a mistake," Cale said. "I didn't send those."

"Family then, maybe."

"Not likely. My wife didn't have family around here."

"Just you and Grace, then?"

Cale blinked.

The old man smiled. "Heard you mention her name. I seen you here before,
many a Lord's day."

Cale felt a little embarrassed. "I don't remember seeing you."

"I been here. I'm always here. I know how to walk real quiet so's I don't
interrupt."

Cale didn't reply; he hoped the old man would get the point. Instead, he
carried the bouquet of flowers around to Hannah's grave. In the ground in
front of the headstone was a rectangular slab of concrete; in the middle of the
slab was a circular bronze disk with a handle across the center. The old man
slowly knelt down and laid the roses on the grass beside him. He turned the
bronze handle and the disk released; he pulled up, revealing an inverted bronze
flower vase. He turned the vase right-side up, placed the base back into the
hole, and twisted it to the right; it locked into place with a click.

"Never did like these things," he said as he worked. "In the old days folks
put real flowers graveside—planted whole gardens if they wanted to. Weren't
no rules then; folks used to dig up the area all around, planted tulips and daf-
fodils this time of year—gladiolas and chrysanthemums too. Me, I always
liked tulips best. But it took too much time to trim around all those gardens,
and time is money for the folks what run this place. So nowadays they got

rules. Nowadays you can't plant no flowers; you got to have one of these things put in. You just turn it upside down and stick it back in the ground; then the people they hire to cut the lawn can run the mower flat over it."

He picked up the roses again and placed them neatly in the vase, taking a moment to spread the stems apart.

"I hate to waste your time," Cale said, "but I think somebody made a mistake—those flowers are for somebody else."

"Could be," the old man said. "Might as well put 'em to use while I'm here, though." He leaned back on his heels with a look of satisfaction. "Now don't that look nice?"

Cale looked at the brilliant white flowers standing in stark relief against the charcoal stone. The old man was right—they were perfect. The phony silk arrangements that decorated most of the grave sites were gaudy barrages of pink and yellow and blue. By contrast, the simple white roses had a magnificent elegance. Cale found himself wishing he had sent them himself.

His task completed, the old man collected himself to rise again—and the process was much slower than on the way down. He made no sound as he rose, but he took his time. He planted each foot deliberately, and he tested it carefully before trusting it with his full weight. He stretched out each leg gingerly, then slowly straightened from the waist like a great crane rising erect. Once standing, he placed one hand on his lower back and arched.

Cale felt his own joints ache as he watched. "Would you like to sit down for a minute?"

"Don't mind if I do," the old man said. "Take a load off these old dogs."

He pulled off one of his work gloves and extended his hand. Cale took it; the skin felt as thick and as leathery as the glove itself. His fingers were long and the knuckles were knobbed and gnarled from arthritis, but his grip was strong and steady.

"Name's Walter," he said.

"I'm Cale."

"Cale Caldwell, no doubt." He nodded to Hannah's grave. "*Hannah Grace Caldwell.*"

"My wife."

"Figured as much. And Grace?"

"My little girl. Well—she's not exactly little anymore. She's almost fourteen."

"Hard time for a girl to lose her mother."

"Is there a good time?"

Walter turned and looked across the manicured cemetery lawns. "Mm-mm," he said. "Mr. Caldwell, I got to say, you picked about the prettiest spot in this whole cemetery."

Cale looked around the sprawling grounds. Walter was right; it was a perfect location—if there was such a thing in a graveyard. Hannah's grave rested near the crest of a hill, just out from under the canopy of an ancient oak tree. The cemetery itself covered hundreds of acres, and most sections were packed tightly with headstones and monuments. But Hannah's was the first grave in the newest section, and so far the hill belonged only to her. It was as if she had a graveyard all to herself, and that's the way Cale wished that it could stay.

"You must know this place pretty well," Cale said.

"I know every grave in it," Walter replied. "Buried half of 'em myself."

"You're kidding."

"Dug most of 'em by hand—got the bad back to prove it. 'Course, these days we use a backhoe. See that part down there what backs up to the scrub pines? Those are Civil War boys down there—that's how old this place is."

"Did you bury any of them?"

Walter smiled. "Only the Union boys."

"So you're a grave digger."

"*Caretaker* is what they call me. But that's mostly what I do: I open graves, I close 'em up again, I set markers. Not as many as I used to—they got some younger boys now." He turned and looked at Cale. "I opened your Hannah's grave, though. Near about six months ago."

"Thanks," Cale said, though the word seemed strangely inappropriate.

Both men sat silently for a minute, staring at the perfect white roses nodding lightly on their slender green stems.

"Seems like a waste," Cale said.

"How's that?"

"Seems like a waste to put such nice flowers on a grave."

"I don't follow you."

"You should send flowers like that to somebody in a hospital. Maybe it would cheer them up; maybe it would help them get better." He glanced around. "Nobody's getting better around here."

"You're wrong about that," Walter said. "People get better here all the time— it just takes awhile, that's all."

Cale didn't reply.

"Is there something I can do for you, Mr. Caldwell?"

"What do you mean?"

"I'm the caretaker round here—I'll be taking care of your Hannah for you. I'll clip around her headstone, I'll keep the bird mess off it—we get the pine warblers with the woods nearby. If there's anything else I can do for you, anything extra, you just let me know."

"Thanks, Walter. I appreciate that."

Walter slowly rose from the bench.

"You'd better take the roses with you," Cale said. "Somebody else will be looking for them."

"Tell you what I'll do," Walter said. "I'll check down at the office to see where they belong. Meantime, I'll leave 'em right here. Can't imagine a nicer spot for 'em."

The two men shook hands again.

"It was a pleasure, Mr. Caldwell, a real pleasure. I seen you here many a Lord's day, and I expect I'll see you again."

Cale nodded. "I expect you will."

CHAPTER 10

Grace sat by herself in the corner of the school cafeteria and picked at the tray of inedible food. She knew she wouldn't eat it, but she'd bought it anyway. It gave her something to do with her hands—and more important, it gave her an excuse to pass the lunch hour staring at the table in front of her instead of at a roomful of prying eyes.

She didn't need to look up—she knew where everyone was sitting anyway. By the second week of school, everyone had staked out their place in the cafeteria, and things rarely changed after that. The jocks sat closest to the food line, of course, and nobody in their right mind sat near them. The cheerleaders always huddled in the center of the room as if they might get the sudden urge to jump up and form a pyramid. The band geeks and nerds were spread evenly around the room like little clusters of molecules. There were ethnic groups, and skater groups, and "I get a Mercedes when I turn sixteen" groups. There were club members, and student council members, and members of silly middle school gangs. And then there was Grace, sitting by herself in the corner of the room, just as she had done every day for the past six months.

And near the door, three tables over and a dozen seats to the left, sat Grace's friends—her ex-friends, that is. Theirs were the eyes she felt the most; they were the ones she especially despised.

The first weeks were the hardest. She detested the feeling of being singled out, of being the subject of rumors and whispers. She wished her teachers would just stand up in front of each of her classes and announce, "Grace's mom died, okay? Does everybody know now? Grace feels just terrible, but she doesn't want to be reminded about it every day—so go ahead and say you're sorry, then treat her like you used to." But everyone was afraid of saying the wrong thing, so no one said anything at all. Everybody talked about her, but no one talked to her.

Her friends should have been different; they should have understood, but they didn't. They didn't understand why she got so angry, so they began to get angry back. And then their whispers began to change. They said that Grace deserved what she got, that God was punishing her for something she had done. They said things so dark and so cruel that Grace couldn't bear to hear them, because they were things she had thought herself. And she was allowed to think them herself, but a friend would never think them—not a real friend. That's when Grace knew they were never friends at all; they were phonies, and she hated them—every last one.

"Gonna eat your tots?"

Grace looked up. She didn't recognize the girl who stood across from her, grinning from ear to ear. No, wait—now she remembered. It was the new girl, the one who was introduced in her math class just this morning.

"You know, *Napoleon Dynamite*—Gonna eat your tots?"

Grace didn't know what to say. She thought about just looking down again, but it seemed too cruel a rejection for a girl on her first day at a new school. Grace noticed the girl when she was introduced this morning, and there was something different about her. She didn't seem as self-conscious as most of the girls her age; she didn't seem to keep one eye on the rest of the room, wondering about how she looked or what everybody else might think—she didn't seem to care. Her parents let her wear lipstick and eye shadow—even fake nails. *I'd never get to go to school like that,* Grace thought.

Her outfit and earrings looked a little different, too, like maybe she'd borrowed them from an older sister.

Before Grace could decide on an appropriate response, the girl dropped her books on the cafeteria table and sat down across from her.

"My name's Jada," she said brightly.

Now Grace did look down again. The girl's enthusiasm was blinding, and Grace was in no mood to connect on that level—especially with a stranger. "Grace," she said to the table.

"Saw you in my math class," Jada said. "My history class too. What have you got after lunch?"

Grace said nothing. She hoped the girl would take the hint and just go away, but she made no move to leave. Instead, she opened a three-ring binder and studied the top sheet.

"I've got English with somebody named Kennedy," Jada said.

Grace glanced up for only an instant. "Me too."

"No kidding? Hey, we're three for three. Let's see—I got biology last period."

Grace looked at her. "With Mr. Joerling?"

Jada searched her schedule. "Yeah, that's the one. I hate biology—how 'bout you?"

"It's okay," Grace said.

"I hate math too—I really stink at math. I stink at biology and I stink at math." She let out a laugh. "Come to think of it, I stink at everything!"

Grace wasn't sure what to say in reply, so she said nothing.

"I know," Jada said, "you're probably thinking, *What's she doing in all these advanced classes if she stinks at everything?* It's my dad—he makes me take 'em. He says the other classes are all for morons, and he doesn't want his kid to hang out with morons. I keep telling him, 'But I'm a moron—that's where I belong!' But he says, 'I'm not living with a moron!' And I say, 'Why not? I do!'" She laughed again. "No, I don't really say that—if I did, he'd crack me a good one."

She leaned forward now and spoke in a lower tone. "Do you like this school?"

"No, I don't."

"Neither do I. It's like going to school in Mayberry—everybody talks like Gomer Pyle. Shazzam!"

Grace cracked her first smile.

"You don't talk like that," Jada said.

"Neither do you—I could tell right away."

"Well, I'm from New York."

"I'm from Chicago."

"Hey! I knew you were different—I could tell just by looking at you. You're from a city like me—a *real* city. See, I think city people are different."

"So do I."

"I mean, it's not like we're better than they are—we've just been around more, that's all. We've seen things."

"Have you seen the Statue of Liberty?" Grace asked.

"That's nothing—I lived in the city; I've seen all kinds of things. I've seen all the shows, I've been to some really great clubs—"

"Really? How did you get in?"

Jada paused. "Well—I had to sneak in. See, I know this older boy—he has a fake ID." She seemed to slow down now, and several seconds passed before she spoke again.

"Thanks for talking to me," she said quietly. "First days are the worst. This is my third school this year."

"How come?"

"My dad—he switches jobs a lot." She paused. "I hate him."

Grace listened intently but didn't respond.

"You know he made me ride the cheese wagon this morning? My first day and he wouldn't even give me a ride—even though he drives right by here on his way to work."

"Why not?"

"He says I'm new here and I need to learn where things are—like riding the bus is going to show me the town or something. I mean, hey, I'd see the same things riding in his car, wouldn't I? He just doesn't want me around, that's all. I hate his guts."

"Couldn't your mom give you a ride?"

"I don't have a mom," Jada said. "I mean, I did—then my mom and dad got divorced, and I went with my mom 'cause my dad didn't want me. Then my mom married this guy, a total loser, and now I have to live with him."

"Why?"

"'Cause she died, that's why. Now I have to live with a guy I'm not even related to. He doesn't even like me—he just takes care of me, like I'm his dog or something."

Now Jada leaned across the table and pointed a finger at Grace. "Don't you dare tell anybody my mom died."

"Why?"

"'Cause then everybody feels sorry for you, and I hate that."

Grace looked as if she had been slapped in the face. "I know."

Jada squinted at her. "How do *you* know?"

"Because my mom died too."

Jada's mouth dropped open, but she said nothing. The two girls sat in silence, staring at each other across the table.

Grace waited for Jada to say something in reply. She had just handed a stranger her most precious gift, and she waited to see what she would do with it. Would she ignore it and turn the conversation to a different subject? Would she try to one-up her by telling a story of her greater suffering? Or would she put on an act of phony sympathy, just like her other two-faced friends? But Jada did none of those things; she responded exactly the way Grace hoped she would.

"It sucks not having a mom."

"Yeah," Grace said. "It really sucks."

Now Jada took on a look of genuine sorrow. "I'm so glad I met you," she said. "I can't talk about these things with anybody else—nobody understands."

"I understand," Grace said.

"I know you do. I can tell just by looking at you."

The bell rang, and both girls began to gather their books.

"Maybe we can talk again," Grace said. "Maybe at lunch tomorrow."

"I doubt it," Jada replied.

"Why?"

"'Cause I'm a moron, remember? It's my first day of school and already I'm behind in math. I have to get help during lunch. Looks like I'm gonna be pretty busy."

"I could help you," Grace offered, "after school."

"Really? You understand this stuff?"

"I used to get A's in math."

"No kidding? How about biology?"

"Biology too."

"A freakin' genius!" Jada shouted. "My new girlfriend is a freakin' genius!"

The two girls left the cafeteria arm in arm, and Grace felt better than she had felt in the last six months.

CHAPTER 11

Hashim parked the car just out of view of the Charlotte Pet Rescue Shelter and turned to the passenger seat.

"Do you understand your instructions?" he asked.

Jada rolled her eyes. "Gee, let's go over it again: I wait ten minutes, then I walk in. Is that it? Did I remember everything? I'm not a real moron, you know. I just pretend to be one—for the money, remember?"

Hashim exited the car without responding.

The front door of the Pet Rescue Shelter opened with a pleasant jingling of bells that was quickly drowned out by a cacophony of barking and yapping from the back room. Hashim curled his nose at the pine-scented disinfectant that barely disguised the stench of urine and feces. *Americans*, he thought. *They treat animals like gods and human beings like refuse.*

"Can I help you?" A pleasant-looking man in a well-stained smock stepped out from the back room.

"Yes," Hashim said. "I am looking for a dog. I understand it is possible to obtain one here."

"You've come to the right place," the man said. "All our dogs are current on their vaccinations and they've been screened by a vet—spayed or neutered too. The adoption fee is fifty-nine dollars, the best bargain in town. All you've got to do is pick one out. We've got all shapes and sizes—all voices too. What are you looking for, a soprano or a bass?"

Hashim didn't understand the question.

The man grinned apologetically. "What kind of dog are you looking for?"

"I am interested in a dog for security purposes."

"Well, a lot of these dogs would do—very loyal, very faithful. All they need, really, is a lot of love and—"

"Yes. I require a large dog, one with an aggressive nature. What breed do you recommend?"

The man grinned again. "We've got all kinds of breeds, but most of them are in the same dog, if you know what I mean."

Hashim did not.

"Look, this is an animal shelter—we take dogs that have been abused or abandoned. These are all mixed breeds here. You want a purebred, you go to the American Kennel Club—here you get a pure *dog*. We've got plenty of those, and any one of them would make a good pet for the right owner."

"I understand," Hashim replied. "A 'mixed breed' will suffice—but it must be a large and powerful animal."

"To scare away all the bad guys, right? Well, come on back and let's see what we can find."

Hashim followed the man into the back room. It was a large and sterile-looking space with cinderblock walls and a bare concrete floor that sloped slightly toward a drain in the center of the room. A green garden hose wound across the floor like a python, and a small terrier on the left barked at it incessantly. The walls were lined with row after row of chromed wire cages with metal tray bottoms covered in layers of last week's *Charlotte Observer*.

Hashim started at the left and slowly passed by the cages, examining the occupant of each. The term "mixed breed" was too generous. Some of the dogs were the product of so much crossbreeding that it would take an expert to isolate all the contributing genes. Only bits and pieces were recognizable: a spaniel's head, or a beagle's coloration, but most of them were identifiable only as dogs—and some were barely that. There were absurd and laughable combinations: heads that didn't fit their bodies, and bodies that didn't match their legs. There were tails and ears of various length and coats of all possible colors and textures, some pocked by patches of mange.

Most cages contained a single animal, though a few held one or more puppies snoozing in furry piles. Some animals poked pleading snouts through the bars as Hashim approached; others, holding a lower opinion of *Homo sapiens*, turned and cowered in the corners of their pens. Hashim passed close to the cages, searching for a specific response: a dog that sought no affection but did not retreat or cower; a dog that stood its ground, laid its ears back flat against its head, and glared back at him with challenging eyes. Hashim knew little about dogs, but he knew that look—he knew it from his own mirror, and he would recognize it when he saw it.

"This one's a sporting dog mix," the man said. "We get a lot of these—part retriever, part Lab, part setter, that sort of thing. Great outdoor dogs—might be what you're looking for. And I wouldn't ignore the smaller breeds if I were you. Some of them are very territorial—they make good watchdogs."

Hashim ignored him and continued his search.

Along the back wall, in a cage at eye level, he found what he was looking for. The dog fixed its eyes on Hashim as he approached and coolly tracked him as he passed by. It was a large, muscular animal with a thick chest and shoulders and a neck that looked like a bound bundle of cords. Its head was triangular, tapering from its sinewy jaw to an almost pointed snout—*like the jackals of western Iraq,* Hashim thought. Its eyes were small and still and cold, and they did not blink. Hashim took a step closer. So did the dog, as if to say, "These bars are here for your protection, not mine."

Hashim studied the front of the cage. It was not locked; it opened with a simple sliding mechanism.

"Now here's a good-sized dog," the man said, continuing his tour. "He's got a little boxer in him—I'm not sure what else. He's a big softie, this one, but you don't have to tell anybody that. He looks pretty formidable when you first come across him."

Hashim waited by the cage and checked his watch.

A few moments later they heard the jingling of the front door.

"Hello," a young woman's voice called out. "Anybody home?"

The man turned to Hashim. "Would you excuse me for a minute? Feel free to look around."

"Of course," Hashim said.

When the man disappeared through the doorway, Hashim stepped closer to the cage. The dog made a low, rumbling growl. Hashim slid the latch up with his left hand and opened the door a few inches, preparing to extend his right hand into the cage—but then he reconsidered and switched to his left hand. He took a long, deep breath and slowly reached inside.

To his disappointment, the dog continued to growl but made no motion toward his hand. He withdrew his hand and thought for a moment—then he jabbed his arm back into the cage and slapped the dog across the snout.

This time the dog did respond.

In a blur of brown fur and a flash of white and yellow, the dog whirled and sank its teeth into Hashim's hand. Hashim felt its canines punch through his skin like paper and sink deep into the flesh. Now the dog began to twist and tear, and Hashim was astonished at its power; he thought the dog might pull his shoulder from its socket. He felt the muscle tear and heard the crunch of bone and tendon, and it was not a pretense when he screamed in agony.

The man rushed back into the room and saw the dog clamped onto Hashim's hand, jerking his arm left and right like the sleeve of an empty shirt. He shouted at the dog, but it showed no sign of relenting. He grabbed the hose from the floor, twisted the spigot, and shoved the nozzle into the dog's face until it reluctantly released its grip and backed away. He slammed the cage door and secured the latch, then turned and looked at Hashim.

Hashim was standing silently in the center of the room, holding his left wrist in his right hand. His left hand was a mass of shredded tissue and exposed bone. Blood dripped freely onto the concrete floor and followed the rivulets of water down the drain.

"What happened?" the man asked in astonishment.

"I only wished to pet the dog," Hashim said.

"I never thought that—I can't believe the dog would—Here, let me get you something to bandage that."

Hashim waited patiently while the man pulled a first-aid kit from the wall, took out a roll of gauze, and began to wrap it over and over around Hashim's wounded hand. As each layer of sterile bandage pressed against the one before it, it turned a crimson red.

"Look, you've got to get to an emergency room," the man said. "All I can do is slow down the bleeding. You're going to need stitches—a lot of them."

"Will the dog be destroyed?" Hashim asked.

"What? Oh—yes, definitely."

"How unfortunate. Perhaps the fault was partly mine. Perhaps I initiated too quickly with the animal."

The man walked Hashim to the front door, cradling his left arm like a dead trout. Jada saw them as they approached; she stared down at Hashim's bloody hand but said nothing.

"I can't tell you how sorry I am," the man said to Hashim. "Don't worry about a thing—we'll pay for all your medical expenses, and we'll definitely take care of that dog. We can't have a vicious dog running loose in Charlotte."

"No," Hashim said. "We can't have that."

Hashim exited and the man watched until he disappeared from view; then he turned and looked at Jada.

"Can I help you?" he asked.

"No thanks," Jada said, starting for the door. "I think I'll buy a goldfish."

CHAPTER 12

Cale studied the series of 8x10 photographs. The first displayed the back of a man's left hand with the flesh torn open in several places. Near the center, a surgical forceps held a flap of skin back from the wound, revealing two streaks of whitish-gray—the "Exposed 3rd and 4th Metacarpal Bones," according to a label in the lower left corner.

Cale looked up. "This looks awful."

"I have to agree."

The next photo showed an anterior view of the same hand. Here the damage was mostly to soft tissue, especially the plump, meaty area at the base of the thumb.

"And he's claiming that *my* dog did this?"

"That's what his attorney's letter says."

Cale sat in the office of a legal firm just down the street from McAfee & Nunn. The agency had three attorneys of its own, but their specialty was advertising law and FTC compliance regulations, not Mecklenburg County dog bite law—and that's what Cale needed right now. Besides, he was still a little new at McAfee & Nunn, and he didn't want his personal problems traveling around the office.

"I've reviewed everything you sent over," the attorney said. "The photos, the medical report, the legal documents. The claim is pretty straightforward. The injured party asserts that while walking through your neighborhood one evening, he was attacked and seriously injured by your dog."

"How does he know it was my dog?"

"Do you own a golden retriever that wears a braided leather collar with brass and silver tags—one shaped like a bone?"

"There could be hundreds of dogs in Charlotte that look like that."

"True—but he claims he followed the dog back to your house. He says the attack took place about 7:00 p.m. Is that feasible?"

"Yes, but—"

"Do you accompany your dog when it's out of the house? Do you always keep it on a leash?"

"There are no leash laws in my area," Cale said. "That's one of the reasons we built there."

"You're in Mecklenburg County, aren't you? The leash law is a county-wide ordinance. If a real estate agent told you there was no leash law, he was either misinformed or he was lying to you. What he should have said was, 'In this area, people don't bother with the leash law.'"

"But Molly is such a gentle dog. Why would she attack this man?"

"That's what he'd like to know."

"He must have done something to provoke her."

"That'll go over big. I wouldn't try that one if I were you."

Cale slumped back in his chair. "Is he filing a lawsuit?"

"Not necessarily."

"What does that mean?"

"It means he clearly has grounds for one, but his attorney makes no mention of money—not yet, anyway. At this point, the victim just wants to establish a basis in fact—that he was, in fact, attacked and seriously injured by your dog. Sometimes these things can be worked out with just a phone call. All some people want is a sincere apology and a promise to pick up their medical expenses—so I contacted his attorney for you."

"And?"

"And you're in luck. The guy doesn't want your money—he just wants the dog destroyed."

Cale jerked upright. "He what?"

"Hey, you can always get another dog."

"No, I can't. This dog is irreplaceable—she's like a member of the family."

"They all are."

"You don't understand—this is different."

"Look, everybody loves their dog, and I know the wife and kids might take it hard, but as an attorney, I advise you to look at this thing rationally. You let your dog out without a leash, and the dog attacked and severely injured a man. That's what the law calls *negligence per se*—it means you're liable if the victim decides to get nasty and file a claim for damages. He's entitled to recover the cost of his expenses for basic things like medical treatment, but he can also sue for future medical treatment, for cosmetic surgery to cover up the scars, for psychological counseling to deal with the trauma of the attack, and a whole lot more.

"Your homeowner's insurance will take the first hit. You probably carry $300,000 in liability coverage, maybe another thousand for med pay. Of course, some people keep an umbrella policy for an extra million or two in liability coverage. Do you?"

Cale shook his head.

"Take a look at those pictures again. Would a jury consider that a severe injury? There's muscular damage, possibly a broken bone or two—maybe even nerve damage. Suppose the hand becomes stiff all the time so he can't do what he used to do. What does this guy do for a living—do you know? Suppose he's a surgeon; suppose he plays the piano. Now he sues for loss of earnings from future employment—there's a nice little number for you. And don't forget the intangibles like physical pain, psychological suffering, and emotional distress—that's when it really starts to add up.

"So insurance picks up the first three hundred thou, but guess who's liable for the rest? How deep are your pockets, Mr. Caldwell? I promise you, that's what the victim's attorney is looking into right now. Maybe you've got a big house, maybe a nice boat out on Lake Norman. The attorney always wanted a boat—and don't forget, he's suing for a third of the damages—maybe half."

"You don't understand," Cale said. "Giving up the dog is just not an option."

"It's your best option. Maybe you can't see it right now while you're angry and your feelings are hurt—but cool off a little and think about it again. The bottom line is, a dog is a possession, and every possession has a price tag. What's this dog really worth to you—a million? Two? 'Cause that's what it could cost you."

"I can't do this to my daughter," Cale said. "She'd never forgive me. I can't explain it, but the dog plays too important a role in our family right now. I just can't give her up."

The attorney removed a document from a manila envelope and held it up. "See this? It's called a 'Probable Cause Notice,' issued by the bureau manager of the Charlotte Animal Control Department. This is informing you that in the next ten days he'll be deciding whether or not your dog is vicious and needs to be destroyed."

"Molly is not a vicious dog."

"'Vicious' is a legal term, Mr. Caldwell, not a matter of opinion. I did a little research on this; some states make the definition very clear. Here's the California code, section 31603: 'A *vicious dog* is any dog which, when unprovoked, in an aggressive manner, inflicts severe injury on or kills a human being.'"

"C'mon—Molly didn't kill anyone."

"That brings us to section 31604: '*Severe injury* means any physical injury to a human being that results in muscle tears or disfiguring lacerations or requires multiple sutures or corrective or cosmetic surgery.'" He pointed to the photographs in Cale's lap. "Think that qualifies?"

"I have to fight this," Cale said. "I can't just let them take my dog."

"You can fight it," the attorney said, "but you have to let them take the dog."

"What?"

"That's another part of the 'Probable Cause Notice.' It states that you must immediately turn the animal over to the authorities, where it will be quarantined to see if it develops rabies."

"And if I refuse?"

"Don't be stupid, Mr. Caldwell; this is the government. They have the legal authority to come on your property and take the dog if they want to."

Cale sat silently for a few moments, considering his options. "What happens next?" he asked.

"You can take the dog to the authorities, or the authorities will take the dog—either way, they get the dog."

"Okay, then what?"

"You have ten days to request a hearing, where you can present your own case that the dog is not, in fact, dangerous. If you take my advice, you won't request a hearing."

"Why not?"

"Think about it, Mr. Caldwell. Right now you have a man who only hates your dog. He doesn't hate you, and he doesn't want your money—unless you cross him, and then there's no telling what he'll want. This guy probably thinks he's doing the right thing, the generous thing. Hey, he's a public servant—all he's asking is for you to eliminate a threat to the public's safety. And you're going to show up at a hearing and say you won't even do that? Then what does he do, just forget the whole thing? I tell you what he'll do, Mr. Caldwell—he'll come after you in any way possible. He'll reach just as far down into those pockets of yours as he can."

"I don't have a choice," Cale said.

"You do have a choice," the attorney countered. "Even if you request a hearing, that doesn't mean you'll win—you could piss this guy off *and* lose the dog. Remember, he's got physical evidence that your dog is vicious—gory photos and all. You can't just give some big sob story about how much the dog means to your little girl—that won't cut it with Animal Control."

"No," Cale said, "but it might cut it with my little girl. She has to know I tried."

The attorney shrugged. "It's your choice—but you do have a choice."

"What can you tell me about this man—about the victim?"

"Only what he's told us in the documents. Why?"

"I want to know how old he is. I want to know if he's from the South, or if he moved down here from somewhere else. I want to know if he has children of his own; if he's married, if he's widowed, if he's ever lost anyone close to him. I want to know if he's a pet owner, and if he's a veteran."

"Why do you want to know all this?"

"I need to know how to talk to him. If I explain the situation, maybe I can make him understand."

"I strongly advise you not to."

"Why?"

"Like I said—right now, he only hates your dog. There are too many emotions involved on both sides. Right now you're just a name and a mailing address to him; but if you talk to this guy in person, if he doesn't like the way you look or you say the wrong thing, then you're the enemy too. Trust me, you need a buffer here; let the attorneys handle it. Let me work on this for a couple of days—I'll try to talk to his attorney again. I'll see if he'll allow me to talk to his client directly. But I should warn you: if I were his attorney, I wouldn't allow it. I always wanted a boat myself."

Cale gathered up the photographs and handed them back to the attorney. "I appreciate your advice," he said, "but I have to fight this. I really don't have a choice. If you were in my shoes, you'd feel the same way I do."

"No, I wouldn't," the attorney said with a grin. "I'm an attorney—I get paid not to feel."

Cale shook his hand and stepped to the door.

"Mr. Caldwell," the attorney said.

Cale turned.

"Juries are not very sympathetic to people who keep dangerous animals. Two million dollars buys a lot of puppies. Think it over."

CHAPTER 13

I t's just you and your dad here?" Jada asked, staring up at the elaborate brass-and-glass chandelier dangling like a giant earring over the center of the foyer. In front of her, a winding staircase curved up and to the left, joining into a semicircular balcony overlooking the floor below.

"There were three of us at first," Grace said, "but that was—before."

The foyer was cylindrical in shape, rising like the Cape Hatteras lighthouse to a ring of windows that flooded the room with afternoon sunlight.

"I feel like Dr. Frankenstein," Jada said, throwing her head back and shouting to the balcony. "It's alive! It's alive!"

"C'mon," Grace said, "let's get something to eat."

They passed through the great room on the way to the kitchen, and Jada let out a gasp. She found the sheer size of the room overwhelming; there were entire houses in Brooklyn that would fit inside.

"Look at this place! It's bigger than the Staten Island Ferry!" She made a quick pass around the room, running one hand over every desirable object. "I'll take one of these, and one of these, and—" She stopped in front of the fifty-inch high-definition plasma-screen TV.

"—and *two* of these." She picked up the remote and flopped down on the leather sofa. "You get cable?"

"Sure," Grace said, taking her usual spot in the overstuffed chair.

"What channel is MTV?"

"We don't get MTV."

"How come?"

"It's blocked."

Jada frowned. "Your dad tells you what you can watch? Hypocrite. What do you think he watches when you're in bed at night?"

"Sports, mostly."

"Yeah, I'll bet," Jada said, tossing the remote aside and jumping to her feet. "Hey, you mentioned food. C'mon—I'm starving."

Jada reached the refrigerator first, a double-wide unit with stainless-steel French doors. She swung open the right door and ducked her head inside, emerging a few moments later with lunchmeat, cheese, bread, and a plastic bottle of Dijon mustard. "Take these," she said, unloading it all into Grace's arms. "I'll get the rest."

They stood side by side at a granite-topped counter and assembled their sandwiches.

"What time does your dad get home?"

"About six, six thirty."

"You get this whole place to yourself 'til then? Not bad. Ever bring any guys here after school?"

Grace hesitated. "Not really."

"Too bad—perfect setup. What's he do?"

"Who?"

"Your dad—what's he do for a living? He must be a doctor or something."

"He works in advertising."

"You can make this kind of money in advertising?"

"I guess so."

"Man! Does he travel a lot?"

"Sometimes. Not as much as he used to."

"When he goes away, does he let you stay by yourself?"

"No—there's a lady from church who cooks and spends the night."

"A *church lady*?" Jada clutched her throat and made a gagging sound.

Grace grinned. "Where do you live?"

"Me? Just up the street. Hard to say how far—I'm used to the city, you know? In the city you say, 'It's three blocks away,' or 'Go uptown six blocks and make a right.' My place is maybe half a mile, but it's on the other side of the tracks, if you get my drift."

"What do you mean?"

"Not everybody lives in a place like this, Grace. I live in a big building, a little apartment, and an itty-bitty room."

"Half a mile," Grace said. "That's an easy walk. Maybe I can come over to your place sometime."

Jada looked at her. "Maybe. I'll ask my dad."

Grace picked up her sandwich and turned away. "C'mon—I'll show you my room."

They passed back through the great room and started down a long hallway. They stopped in front of the first open doorway and looked inside.

"This is my dad's room," Grace said.

Jada stepped in and looked around. To the left was a flagstone hearth and fireplace that extended up to a double-trey ceiling ten feet above. Across from the fireplace stood a king-size four-poster bed with an arching canopy top draped in silken sheers.

Jada walked across the room and flopped down on the bed. She lay on her back with her eyes closed and her arms and legs stretched wide, wallowing in the softness of the overfilled jacquard comforter.

"—and *definitely* one of these," she said.

Grace watched her for a minute, then slowly began to frown. "We shouldn't be in here," she said.

"Why not?"

"We just shouldn't. C'mon, my room is down here."

Jada shrugged, hopped to her feet, and followed Grace out the door.

"That used to be my room," Grace said. She pointed to the room directly across the hall but didn't enter.

Jada peered inside. The room was decorated in soft pinks and purples, and the walls were crowded with posters of sanitized music groups and snapshots of family and friends. The twin-size bed was a four-poster, too, but without the canopy. The rippling dust ruffle and thick, mounded comforter made the bed look to Jada like a giant pink cupcake. The dresser, chest, and nightstand were covered with trinkets and mementos. There was even a mirrored vanity with a delicate, lacy skirt; the top was scattered with bright-colored rings and bracelets that looked like little pieces of sugar candy.

"Where's your room now?" Jada asked.

Grace led her to a doorway at the opposite end of the hall. "I moved down here."

"How come?"

"'Cause it's farther away."

Jada stepped inside. The room was almost empty. There were a few scattered pieces of furniture, but none that matched. The bed was covered with only a blanket and sheets, and a green metal frame and rollers were visible underneath. The room looked familiar to Jada; it was just like the room she kept in Bushwick, a room you slept in and worked in but never put your heart in. It was like an empty appliance box the street people slept in; something to cut the wind, something to keep the weather out, but nothing more. Jada looked around at the walls—they were completely bare, and she understood why. To hang anything personal was to place a part of yourself in the room, and that was something you never wanted to do. It's nothing personal—it's just business. This was a place you had to be, not a place to belong. It was just a stop along the way—at least, that's what you told yourself every day.

Jada shook her head and tried to remember how old she was when she first moved into a room like this. She couldn't recall; she didn't want to.

The two girls sat down on opposite ends of the bed and picked at their sandwiches like a pair of disinterested hens.

"How did your mom die?" Jada asked.

"Car crash."

"Gross. Were you there?"

"No. She went to the store for milk, that's all. It was some drunk guy."

"Did they put him in jail?"

"Not yet, but they will."

"No, they won't," Jada said. "You think the cops are on your side, but they're not. Nobody's on your side except you."

"What happened to your mom?"

"Cancer. After she died, I got stuck with my stepdad. What a loser—I don't know why she ever married him. I didn't pick him, that's for sure."

"Can't you go back to your real dad?"

"He doesn't want me. I'm one of the reasons he left."

"I bet that's not true."

"Well, that's what he said—he told me right to my face. Then my stepdad called my real dad and they had a big fight on the phone about who had to take me. My real dad said, 'I don't have to take her 'cause I signed over all my rights. You married the woman, so you're stuck with the kid 'cause that's the law.' So my stepdad said, 'You can at least send money—you owe that much.' You wouldn't believe all the shouting and screaming. I heard the whole thing. I was standing right there."

"That's awful," Grace said.

"They're all the same," Jada said with a shrug. "Stepdads, real dads—they don't appreciate you. People don't know a good thing 'til it's gone."

Jada leaned forward and lowered her voice. "Does he hit you?"

"Who?"

"Who do you think? Your dad—does he hit you?"

"No."

"He will."

Grace blinked. "I don't think my dad would ever hit me."

"Stick around," Jada said. "Does he boss you around? Does he tell you what to do?"

"Sometimes."

"Well, that's how it starts. First he gets mad because he's stuck with you. He's got no wife, now he has to do everything, now he has to pay for everything. And he can't go out anymore; he can't go have fun with his friends 'cause he has to stay home and take care of you—so he starts to blame you. Does he ever yell at you?"

"Well—"

Jada nodded. "At first he yells and you jump; but after a while you get used to it, so when he yells you don't jump anymore—so then he raises his hand like this, like he's going to belt you one, and you duck; but after a while you don't even duck anymore, and that's when he starts swinging."

Grace didn't answer.

"And it's all because they don't appreciate you," Jada said. "Nobody knows a good thing—'til it's gone." She paused and looked at Grace. "Know what I did once?"

"What?"

"I went away for a weekend—just disappeared without telling him where I was going or when I was coming back. And when I did come back, let me tell you, he was whistling a different tune then."

"What do you mean?"

"He was worried sick—thought I died or something. Who knows, maybe he thought the cops would pin it on him. Whatever it was, he learned his lesson—he was a lot nicer to me after that. I think that's what you have to do from time to time: teach 'em a lesson. Remind 'em to appreciate you."

Grace seemed lost in thought.

Jada looked at her watch. "I'd better go," she said. "My dad gets home earlier than yours does."

"I thought we were going to work on math."

"Not today. I don't feel like it. I'll get the old man to help me—he oughta be good for something."

Grace walked her to the front door. "If you wait for my dad, he can give you a ride home."

"No thanks. Like you said, it's an easy walk." In the doorway, Jada turned and looked at her. "Do me a favor, okay? Don't tell your dad I was here."

"How come?"

"'Cause I'm not supposed to be here. I'm sort of—grounded. If you tell your dad, and he tells someone else—word gets around, you know? I'm supposed to come straight home after school. If my dad finds out, I'm in deep dirt. Okay?"

"Okay," Grace said. "You were never here."

Jada pulled a cell phone from her pocket and held it up in front of Grace's face. "Everybody say, *Chicago!*"

Grace grinned and Jada clicked her picture. She checked the image, then held it up for Grace to see.

"Something to remember you by," Jada said. "See you tomorrow, Grace."

When she reached the end of the sidewalk, she turned around and looked again. Grace was still watching her from the open doorway. Jada smiled and waved, and Grace waved back.

It's nothing personal, Jada thought. *It's just business.*

CHAPTER 14

What is this garbage?" Jada sneered, picking at a pile of pallid vegetables with a smear of thick white sauce across the top.

"*Badhinjan bil laban,*" Hashim said without looking up from his own plate. "Boiled eggplant with yogurt. It is a favorite dish in my country."

"Oh yeah? Well, you're in America now. How about something I can eat?"

"You are welcome to cook," Hashim said, nodding over his shoulder at the kitchen.

"Kids don't *cook,*" Jada said. "You're supposed to be the dad, remember? So how about it, Dad—where's dinner?"

"Perhaps you would prefer American fast food," Hashim said, "the unclean remains of some pathetic, slaughtered beast."

"Can I supersize it?"

"I agreed to provide shelter and clothing. I will provide food as well—but I will make no effort to cater to your American tastes. This is the dinner I have prepared. Eat it, or do not—it makes no difference to me, as long as you maintain enough energy and alertness to perform your duties."

"Hey," Jada said. "You do sound like a dad."

Hashim pushed his plate aside, wiped the corners of his mouth, and looked at her for the first time. "Tell me again about your encounter with the girl."

"I already told you," Jada said, shoving her own plate away in disgust. "Give it a rest, will you?"

"You described only her behavior—I wish to know more. I wish to know about her demeanor, about her emotional state."

"How should I know? You want to know how she feels, ask her yourself."

"You are a female, are you not? Have you no insight into the emotions of your own gender?"

"Look, you're paying me to do what you want and say what you want—beyond that, you're on your own."

"Did you take the photographs as I instructed?"

"Yeah, I took a photograph."

"Show me."

Jada pulled out her cell phone, pulled up the image of Grace, and handed the phone to Hashim.

He looked at the image and nodded. "And the others?"

"What others?"

"This is only a frontal view. What about the profile and the back?"

"Big deal. The front is all you need."

"I specifically instructed you to photograph all sides."

"What was I supposed to do, take mug shots? 'Smile for the camera, sweetheart! Now turn around and let me get the back of your head.'"

"The back is most important."

"I don't think so."

"I did not hire you for your capacity to think."

She narrowed her eyes at him. "What are you up to, anyway? What do you want from these people? What did they ever do to you?"

"That is not your concern."

"I don't like this," Jada said.

Hashim glared at her. "Please stop this annoying pretense. Why do you pretend to care about this girl?"

"I'm not pretending; I just—"

"Why do you suppose I hired you? Many women could perform these simple tasks with greater skill—an actress, or a counselor perhaps. I did not hire you because of any quality you possess. I hired you because of a specific quality you lack: You do not *care*. You people are well known for this."

"What 'people'?"

"Harlots, of course."

"I don't need this," Jada growled.

"What you need is forty-five thousand dollars—unless your situation has unexpectedly changed."

"Let's get something clear—"

"Yes," he cut in, "let us be very clear. I hired you to follow my instructions, and nothing more. If there is any confusion about those instructions, you are to call me—that is why you have been given a cellular phone. Do not think; do not improvise; and above all, do not *care*—that is not what I am paying you for. Do I make myself clear?"

Before Jada could reply, they were interrupted by a knock at the door. Hashim held up one hand and listened; a moment later there was a second knock. He crossed to the front door, peered into the peephole, and thought for a moment.

"Say nothing," Hashim whispered, then opened the door.

In the hallway stood an Arab man of similar age. He was shorter than Hashim, dressed in casual business attire with khaki slacks and a white, open-collared shirt. He was smiling broadly and holding a small plate draped with a colorful napkin.

"Good evening!" he said, beaming.

"Good evening," Hashim repeated flatly.

"*Katayif*," he said, extending the plate. "For your sweet tooth. My wife makes them—they are truly a delight." He glanced past Hashim as if he hoped to be invited in, but Hashim remained squarely in the doorway.

"Please thank your wife for me," Hashim said, taking the plate.

"I noticed you by the mailboxes," the man said. "There are not many of us here. Have you been in Charlotte long?"

"Not long."

"I noted the address on your mailbox. I was delighted to find that you had taken the apartment just across the hall. That is our apartment there—number 73. See?"

"Yes, I see."

"Please forgive my boldness, but as I said, there are not many of us here. My wife and I are hoping that you will join us for dinner one evening. My wife is very skilled at preparing traditional dishes. Perhaps you would enjoy a break from American cuisine."

"Perhaps."

"I am employed in pharmaceutical sales. My wife is an accountant. She is usually home by six o'clock. We could dine by seven."

"Yes. Thank you. I will call. Now, if you don't mind—"

But before Hashim could end the conversation, Jada squeezed into the doorway beside him.

"You have a daughter! How delightful! She, too, is invited for dinner."

"No eggplant," Jada said. "The stuff makes me gag." She turned to Hashim. "Dad, I'm going out. I took the car keys."

"Do you remember your instructions?"

"Don't I always?"

"You will come straight home."

"I'm stopping off at the Golden Arches first. I need something big and bloody—one of those McSlaughtered Beasts. I could use some money."

Hashim glared at her. "Your allowance is sufficient."

"Don't forget, you promised to help with my math. Maybe you could get started on that while I'm gone."

Hashim nodded. Jada slipped past the neighbor and started down the hall; both men watched her until she disappeared around a corner.

"My stepdaughter," Hashim grumbled.

"A delightful girl," the man said. "Very well mannered. Please be sure to bring her along."

Jada sat in a salon chair and stared at herself in the mirror. Her light brown hair dripped water from its curling tips, and little rivulets of hair snaked across her forehead. The smock that was pinned tight around her neck flowed down and out like a snow-covered slope, showcasing her face like one of the heads on Mount Rushmore. *It's true,* she thought, *my face looks so young.* She had always looked younger than her years. Sometime in her early teens her image had frozen in time, and the woman inside her moved on while her face remained behind. Now, ten years later, everything had reversed. Now the woman inside her had ceased to age while her body grew older fast.

But her face remained the same. It was a gift some women would pay a fortune for—but not Jada. To her, her youthfulness had an ugly side. Her face was the reason men desired her—not the woman inside; just the face. Her face was the reason Hashim hired her; not her abilities, just the face—and the fact that she didn't care.

And she didn't care. Why should she? But his words still stung like a razor strop: "*You people are well known for this.*" "*You people*"—the phrase made her blood run cold.

"So what are we doing today?" the stylist asked.

Jada glanced up. "If I had my way, I'd leave it like it is."

"I know the feeling—but I bet you didn't come all this way just for a shampoo and a rinse."

Jada took out her cell phone and held it up. "I want it to look like this," she said.

The stylist studied the tiny screen. "The color too?"

"Length, color, style—everything. Exactly like this."

"I can do that. No problem."

"Swell." Jada turned back to the mirror again and slumped a little lower in her chair.

"You don't sound too thrilled about this."

"It's not what I want—it's for my old man."

"Sorry," the stylist said. "Men can be so unreasonable."

Jada rolled her eyes. "Tell me about it."

CHAPTER 15

I'm sorry, can you speak up? I'm having trouble hearing."

Cale pressed the cell phone tighter against his ear. On College Street, noontime drivers roared past on their way to the exclusive shops and pricey restaurants of Charlotte's historic South End. Behind him, the smooth-faced glass-and-steel facade of the Westin Charlotte looked like a razor blade balanced on edge in the center of the city's financial district. A trolley clanged to a stop in front of him, and people began to noisily debark and scatter. Cale turned away and cupped his left hand over his ear.

"New York Public Health Department," the voice repeated.

"Thanks, that's better. I have a question about HIV testing and reporting."

"Hold, please."

"I'm in kind of a hurry here. Can you—"

But the operator had already cut him off. Cale checked his watch; he had already spent an hour on the phone this morning with Charlotte Animal Control, trying to understand the bizarre complexities of arranging a hearing for Molly, and he had been running behind ever since. He raised his eyes and peered through the smoky glass into the lobby of the Westin. Inside, the founder and principal partner of McAfee & Nunn was already seated in the gourmet Ember Grille restaurant—and Jack McAfee was not a man to keep waiting.

"C'mon, c'mon," Cale grumbled over the dead line.

A woman's voice broke the silence at last: "Public Health."

"Yes—my name is Cale Caldwell. I'm calling from the city of Charlotte this afternoon."

"Charlotte? In North Carolina?"

"That's where we keep it, yes, ma'am. I have a question about HIV testing and reporting in New York City."

"How can I help you?"

"I have a friend who was recently tested for HIV, and—"

"Excuse me. Before you go any farther, Mr. Caldwell, I need to tell you that in New York all HIV test results are confidential. I cannot release any information to you about your friend, even with his permission—not over the phone."

"It has to be done in person?"

"It's the only way to guarantee confidentiality."

"I see. Well—are these tests *completely* confidential? I mean, are the results reported to anyone else? Does anybody else know?"

"That depends," the woman said. "In an *anonymous* test you never give your name, so the results of the test can never be connected to you. In a *confidential* test your identity is known, but the results are strictly confidential—except, of course, in certain cases."

"What cases are those?"

"When AIDS is indicated."

"And how do you tell that?"

"When the HIV infection reduces the number of CD4 cells to around 200 per microliter of blood, that indicates the onset of AIDS. I'm sorry, I know this is a lot of information—am I going too fast for you?"

"That's okay," Cale said, "I'm in kind of a hurry anyway." He checked his watch and glanced at the hotel lobby again. "Can't you tell if you have AIDS without a test? I mean, aren't there obvious symptoms?"

"Not necessarily. HIV can be asymptomatic for years—even a decade or more. There aren't always symptoms at the onset of AIDS, either—not at the beginning."

"Tell me something: Is it standard procedure to have your test results *mailed* to you?"

"In anonymous tests, never. In confidential tests, sometimes. It depends on what you agree to at the time of the test."

"Is there ever a situation when someone comes to visit you in person?"

"Only when AIDS is diagnosed."

"What happens then?"

"The law requires all cases of AIDS to be reported to the Public Health Department for mandatory partner notification and contact tracing. In those cases, we sometimes send a Public Health officer to the individual's home."

"To get the names of people he might have come in contact with."

"Exactly."

"So in theory, I could go in for a confidential HIV test and suddenly find a Public Health officer knocking at my door."

"Well, we try to make contact by telephone first. But if that's not possible, then yes—you might find someone knocking at your door."

Cale looked at his watch again and groaned; the phone call was taking much longer than he'd planned. He turned and started into the lobby as he spoke.

"One more thing," he said. "Is there any way I can find out whether one of your Public Health officers ever paid my friend a visit?"

"Given what I just told you, that would be quite a breach of confidentiality, wouldn't it?"

"Well—if I described a man to you, could you tell me if the description fits one of your officers?"

"Not unless you're in law enforcement—and not unless you have a very good reason to ask."

"Okay, I get the point. Look, I've got to go—you've been really helpful, and I appreciate it."

"Mr. Caldwell?"

"Yeah."

"Tell your 'friend' to get that test—an anonymous test if he's worried about someone showing up at his door. Tell him to do it right away, okay?"

"Right. Thanks."

Cale had closed the phone and dropped it into his pocket before he understood her meaning.

He rounded the corner into the Ember Grille and spotted a stone-faced Jack McAfee at a table on the patio terrace.

"Jack," he said apologetically as he took a seat across from him.

"Thought you got lost," McAfee said with a minimum of pleasantry.

"Clients," Cale said. "Does it ever stop?"

"Not if you're doing it right."

Cale swept up a menu and opened it. A waiter slid a bourbon sour in front of McAfee and took away an empty glass. McAfee was on his second drink— maybe his third. The legendary three-martini lunch was a thing of the past for ad execs—at least for ad execs who needed more than a handful of neurons firing later in the day. But McAfee was from an older generation of ad men, a hard-drinking, hardworking Southern gentleman who almost single-handedly built one of the most respected agencies in the Southeast. Now McAfee was semiretired, but he still kept a hawk's eye and a lion's grip on the business. He did the hiring, and he wrote the bonus checks, and he occasionally invited one of his senior executives to dine with him. An invitation from McAfee was always polite to the point of being obsequious—but around the office it was known as "the summons." The term didn't give Cale any added confidence; this was his first toe-to-toe with the agency's founder, and he knew that his performance over the last six months had been less than stellar.

"Something from the bar, sir?" the waiter asked.

"Nothing for me. I'm working." Cale regretted the words the instant he spoke them.

McAfee ordered only a salad, and Cale followed his lead. The two men set their menus aside and made solid eye contact for the first time.

"Cale, I want to thank you for taking time out from your busy schedule to have lunch with me today. We've waited too long to do this—much too long."

"I agree, Jack. I've been looking forward to this."

"Me too. I want you to know, you were quite a catch for McAfee & Nunn. The pick of the litter, so to speak."

"Well, thanks, Jack. It's a privilege to work here."

"Up there in Chicago you were quite the boy wonder. You brought home— what—two Clios while you were there?"

"Three."

"Forgive me, *three*. That's most impressive—and that's just the kind of performance we're hoping for here at McAfee & Nunn."

"I'll give it my best."

"I'm glad to hear that, son, because your best is what it takes." He paused and took a drink. "Yes, sir, we were lucky to get you. A trophy wife, if you understand what I mean."

Cale winced at the analogy. McAfee knew about Hannah; the remark was deliberately crass. McAfee had been a copywriter in his early days; he knew the power of a carefully chosen phrase, and this one was no accident. He was trying to make a point here, and he didn't want it to be missed.

McAfee smiled reassuringly. "I mean that in the best sense of the term. I know about these things. See, I'm on my third wife, and each of them has been greedier and more empty-headed than the last. But each of them has been more beautiful than the last, too, and that's important to me—but not for the reason you might think. You see, my life is not about love; my life is about work. A beautiful woman attracts people to her, have you noticed that? That's not a criticism, you understand; it's just a reality of life. That's why I marry beautiful women: they draw people to me. And that's why I hire the pick of the litter: they attract clients. Are you following me here?"

Cale nodded.

"Nobody wants to do business with an old coon dog like me—they think I'm out of ideas; they think my brain is all dried up by now. But you—you're young, you're fresh. You're the reason Philip Morris turns to Leo Burnett instead of to McAfee & Nunn, even though they're just up the road from us in Richmond. You're a trophy wife, you see. You draw people to you."

"I like to think I'm more than a trophy wife," Cale said.

"Well, that's my point exactly. You see, my wife is beautiful, and she draws people to her—but when people do get up close, they discover that there is nothing whatsoever inside that pretty little head, and that's when they leave. You see what I mean? Beauty draws people in, but what keeps them around is performance."

The salads arrived then, and Cale was grateful for the interruption. It gave him an excuse to break eye contact, and he considered extending the reprieve by excusing himself to use the men's room—but he had already kept the old man waiting once. They took a few moments to settle down to the business of eating, and Cale hoped that might be enough to shift the conversation to a different topic. It wasn't.

"This business is the same way," McAfee said without missing a beat. "A man like you, a man with your reputation, you draw people in. Maybe a little of that Coca-Cola money over in Atlanta, or maybe a piece of that Disney account down in Orlando—now wouldn't that be nice? And make no mistake, those people are looking at McAfee & Nunn—but they won't be looking long.

"You're correct when you say that you're more than a trophy wife. I need you to be that; I need you to draw people in—but I need more than that from you. See, a trophy wife is expensive—I've learned this from experience. She spends a lot of money—she consumes, you might say, but she doesn't produce. I've had three trophy wives; I can't afford another."

McAfee stopped and looked across at Cale's plate with a look of genuine concern. "Is that salad all right for you? I believe mine is a little dry. Can I get you a little more dressing? Or would you like something else altogether?"

"This is fine," Cale said.

"You're sure? Because I want you to have what you want."

McAfee sounded deeply compassionate, almost grieved.

"I want you to know I've heard about your family situation," he continued in the same soothing tone. "I'm referring to the loss of your beloved wife. I want you to know how deeply sorry I am. As I said, my life is about work and not love—and I suppose I'm a much poorer man because of it. Nevertheless,

I've discovered a certain benefit in immersing oneself in work—a healing quality, you might almost say. Perhaps you'll have the opportunity to discover this for yourself. I make a poor physician, I know. Just think of it as a suggestion from a friend.

"Let me just say that I know you'll come back from this terrible tragedy. I'm counting on you to—everyone at McAfee & Nunn is counting on you. You're in our thoughts every day, and we hope that you'll be able to put this terrible thing behind you and move on—just as soon as possible."

Cale nodded but could not bring himself to say, "Thanks." Part of him wanted to quit—to walk out right now and look for a fresh start. He could land a job with another agency within a week, but not in Charlotte—not at this salary. That would mean moving, that would mean a new city and another new school for Grace, and the last thing Grace needed right now was another major upheaval. No, he needed to make this work, at least until the smoke had cleared in some other areas of his life.

The conversation went on for another thirty minutes, but Cale would never remember what was said. He kept thinking about Grace, and Molly, and the job he might not have much longer.

He wondered how much it took to make a man jump off a bridge.

CHAPTER 16

Grace looked so tiny at the opposite end of the double-leaf dining room table; she must have been ten feet away. This was not what Cale had in mind when he asked her to set the table for three. He imagined them eating at the much smaller pedestal table in the breakfast nook—but Grace chose the dining room instead, and Cale knew why. It was selfish, and rude, and obvious, and Cale wanted to tell her so—but those were not things you said in front of a guest.

Halfway down the table to his left sat a smiling young woman with blinding blonde hair. Her name was Melissa, known to everyone at the agency as Missy. Missy was an account rep at McAfee & Nunn, and according to the office rap sheet, she was approximately thirty-five, childless, and divorced. She dropped by Cale's office one day to express her condolences and to ask about Grace, and her brief visit turned into a half-hour conversation.

Missy seemed like a caring person. She was the oldest of four sisters, she said, and so possessed a mother's protective nature as well as a sister's loving heart. They talked about Grace, and the feelings she must struggle with, and how difficult it must be for her to find someone to share those feelings with. The things Missy said were fairly obvious, but coming from a woman, they somehow seemed more profound. She said that Grace was not a boy, but a girl. She said that Grace would soon be a young woman, and there were things about being a woman that no man could teach her. She said that every girl had only one mother, and a mother could never be replaced. She said what Grace needed now was a big sister—and she volunteered for the job.

So Cale invited her to join them for dinner. It sounded like a good idea at the time, but right now Cale felt a little sorry for Missy. She sat alone at the center of the long table, trapped in the no-man's-land between Grace and Cale, glancing back and forth between them like a referee at a tennis match.

That thought sparked an idea; Cale looked at Missy and smiled. "They tell me at the office that you play tennis."

She grinned from ear to ear. "Ah *love* tennis!"

Cale cringed a little. Missy was a true Southerner, and her accent reflected it. As a native of the South himself, he was aware of the giant sucking sound a Southern accent makes to those from north of the Mason-Dixon, and he wished that Missy would tone it down a little for Grace's sake.

"Did you hear that, Grace? Missy plays tennis too."

Missy turned to her. "Do you play tennis, Grace? Ah would *love* to play sometime."

Grace didn't reply.

"Grace—Missy's talking to you."

"I'm pretty busy," she replied without looking up.

"Grace used to play tennis," Cale said. "In Chicago we belonged to a tennis and swim club. She played a lot there; she was pretty good too. But she's gotten away from it lately."

"Well, we can't let that happen," Missy said. "What are the things you're busy with, Grace? Are you involved in other sports?"

"No."

"Are you in any clubs?"

"No."

"I'll bet you have a lot of friends, then."

"My friends are in Chicago."

"Well, that's just too far away. You need friends right here."

Grace looked across the table at her father as though Missy didn't exist. "May I be excused now?"

Cale turned to Missy to apologize, but Missy just nodded reassuringly. They waited in silence until they heard the sound of Grace's door clicking shut.

"Missy, I'm so sorry about—"

"Don't you dare apologize," she scolded.

"There's no excuse for her to act like that."

"She has every reason. That's why I'm here, remember? I didn't expect her to welcome me with open arms—not on the first visit."

"I'll talk to her."

"You'll do no such thing. She's just a hurt little puppy right now, and sometimes dogs get protective, know what I mean? I'm a stranger, and you're her father. She's just looking out for you, that's all. I need to find a time when I can talk to her alone."

"Thanks," he said. "I guess it's worth a try."

He looked down at Molly snoozing blissfully on the rug beside his chair. *It's true,* he thought. *Sometimes dogs get protective—but that's no excuse to bite.*

Grace carried the dishes to the counter while Cale scraped them off into the sink. Ever since she was little, Grace had been expected to do chores around the house: making her bed, doing her own laundry, helping with the dishes at night. After Hannah's death Cale was tempted to relieve Grace of her household responsibilities—until he saw how Grace was beginning to avoid him, and then he reconsidered. Sometimes, chores were the only thing that forced Grace to be in the same room with him.

This evening they worked in silence, immersed in their own thoughts. Cale thought about his lunch with McAfee—he'd thought about little else all afternoon. He had a bad feeling going into that meeting, though he wasn't sure what he had expected from his first "summons" from McAfee. Maybe he was hoping for a slap on the back, maybe just a "welcome to the family" speech. That's it—just a covered side dish, a hug from all the cousins, and a teary-eyed message from the preacher.

I should have known better, Cale thought, forgetting a lesson he knew full well about the South: that manners here were often just a form of anesthetic applied before the scalpel—or the ax. McAfee was a real charmer, just dripping with concern—like a water moccasin that flashes the white of its mouth just before it strikes.

Cale knew he had been hired because of his reputation, because of his ability to attract new business. "*But I need more than that from you,*" the old man said, and his meaning was clear: Put out or pack up. Beauty draws people in, but what keeps them around is performance.

The old snake.

For the first time Cale began reconsidering his situation at McAfee & Nunn. He was a bright and shining star at Leo Burnett—the pick of the litter, the old man said. He thought he might somehow be able to rest on his laurels at McAfee & Nunn—that his move to Charlotte would mean a slower lifestyle and fewer demands. He had already paid the price at Burnett—the endless hours and the constant travel—but that was when Hannah was alive. Hannah was the one who made it possible; now Hannah was gone, and Grace had no one else. Now every hour away from home was an hour away from Grace.

And then there was Molly; that little item had dominated more than a few hours of his thoughts—hours that he couldn't afford to lose. The attorney was having no luck arranging a tête-à-tête with the victim to explain Cale's difficult circumstances and to plead for the dog's life. The man's own attorney was shielding him like a Doberman, and Cale suspected why: there might be money in this, and the attorney was not about to let a tearful appeal for mercy cloud his client's better judgment. Cale thought about offering to sell the dog, but he doubted that would satisfy the victim: What's the good in selling a vicious dog so it can bite someone else? Besides, it wouldn't solve his problem; either way Molly would be gone. Cale would lose one more point of connection with his daughter, and Grace would lose one more thing to love.

He even thought about sending Molly away, maybe to Miss D.'s house in High Point—not to solve the legal problem, but to get Grace used to the idea of Molly being gone. But he knew that was a waste of time; there's just no way to warm someone up to the loss of something they love. Besides, he would have to explain to Grace why he sent the dog away, and he didn't want Grace to know—until she had to. If Animal Control decided that Molly had to be put down, Cale wanted his daughter to have every minute with her that she had left. He asked permission to keep the dog until the time of the hearing, and the authorities consented—with the stipulation that the dog be kept confined to the house.

Cale felt like a runner who had just crossed the finish line utterly spent, only to discover that he still had a few laps to go—and all by himself.

He felt an unfamiliar knot in his gut.

Grace interrupted his thoughts when she reached across to drop a handful of silverware into the sink.

Cale nudged her with his elbow. "You know, you weren't very friendly to Missy tonight."

Grace shrugged. "She's not my friend."

"You could use a few friends if you ask me."

"Not like her."

"She was trying, Grace—at least give her credit for that. She was just trying to talk to you, that's all."

"I didn't ask her to. I guess you did."

Cale stopped and looked at her. "Okay, let me put it a different way: You were *rude* to Missy tonight. I know you're angry, Grace, and that's okay. But *angry* is what you feel inside, and *rude* is what you do to someone else—and that's not okay. You understand me?"

Grace barely nodded.

What's the use? Cale thought. He could force Grace to change her behavior, but he had no idea how to change her heart. He wanted to shout at her,

"It wasn't my fault!" but he had no way to make her believe it—that was something she had to decide for herself. And while she was deciding, all he could do was stand there like a whipping boy and bear the brunt of all her bitterness and rage.

He looked at her again. "Is your homework finished?"

"Yes."

"Then I think you should go to bed."

She turned toward the hallway. "Ah would *love* to."

Cale shook his head. He knew he had to give her time, he knew he had to let her work through all this—that's what all the counselors said—but he was losing patience fast. What about his own anger? What about the things he felt?

Never mind Grace, he thought. *Maybe Missy should be my friend*—but the thought made him feel a little ashamed.

CHAPTER 17

It rained all day Saturday in Charlotte. By Sunday morning the clouds had lifted, but patches of fog still hovered in low-lying areas like long strips of cotton batting. On the bushes and trees the bright growth of spring had given way to a more enduring green as the land prepared itself for the serious business of summer. The sky, however, was still a crystalline Carolina blue—a last remnant of spring—and it would stay that way until the white summer haze bleached most of the color away.

Cale walked from his car to the asphalt footpath that meandered like a creek bed through Evergreen Memorial Park, and began the long, winding climb to Hannah's hilltop grave site. He came to a tall hedge of red tips; its spring coat of purplish-red leaves now lay mostly in scattered trimmings on the cemetery lawn. Rounding the end of the hedge, Cale found Walter raking the leaves into neat little piles.

"Morning, Walter."

"Mr. Caldwell! Pleasure to see you again."

"Just stopped by to have a word with my wife."

"Couldn't have a nicer day for it. If you don't mind, I'll walk with you a spell—something I want to show you."

Walter tugged off his leather gardening gloves, stuffed one in each of his back pockets, and joined Cale on the footpath.

Cale shortened his stride to match the old man's halting gait. "Guess it sounds a little crazy, doesn't it?"

"What's that?"

"Stopping by to have a word with my wife."

"Don't sound crazy to me."

"I suppose I could talk to her anywhere."

"Here you don't have to shout. Saves on the voice."

Cale smiled. "You married, Walter?"

"I was. Lost her to the influenza forty-three years ago. Buried her myself. Dug her grave with my own two hands."

"You're kidding."

"Martha—that was her name. See that blue spruce across the way, the one with all the branches on the one side? That's where she is, right at the base of it. I planted the tree too. It's a bit taller now."

"I'm sorry. Any kids?"

"Never had the chance."

Cale started to say, "Sorry," a second time but caught himself. The word seemed useless and superficial the first time; the second time it might sound insulting.

"Martha," Cale said. "I like that name."

"Never did stop talkin' to Martha; I talk to her all the time."

"Even after forty-three years?"

"That don't make no difference."

"I thought maybe you'd get over it after forty-three years."

"How does a man 'get over' a wife?"

"I was hoping you could tell me."

The two men made their way up the winding path side by side. Cale stopped to read a headstone from time to time to give Walter a chance to catch his breath. Even though the day was warm, the old man still kept his collar and cuffs buttoned tight.

"Were you ever in the Army, Walter?"

"Why do you ask?"

"You always look sharp—like an officer."

"No, sir, I never was. What about you?"

"I was in the Persian Gulf—in Desert Storm."

"You don't strike me as a military man."

"Trust me, I'm not. I was in the Reserves and I got called up."

"Foot soldier?"

"No, I worked in Psychological Operations. My job was to convince the enemy to surrender so we didn't have to kill him."

"Surrender—you mean just give up?"

"Yeah—just give up."

"Any luck with that?"

"Plenty."

Walter shook his head. "Why would a man give up just because you tell him to?"

"It's not quite that simple," Cale said. "You try to find a man who's tired, or hungry, or afraid. You find a man who doesn't have a whole lot to look forward to—a man with doubts. Most of all, you look for a man who's *isolated*—then all you have to do is whisper in his ear. If there's nobody to tell him otherwise, he'll believe anything you say."

"Sounds a bit like you."

"What?"

"Never mind me, Mr. Caldwell—just thinkin' out loud."

They arrived at Hannah's grave site now. Cale saw the familiar stone bench, the black granite headstone with the golden letters—and in front of it, a dozen and a half white roses in the bronze flower vase.

"That's what I wanted to show you," Walter said. "Don't they look nice?"

Cale approached the flowers and took a closer look. The stems were still stiff and erect; the flowers didn't droop or sag at all, and the velvety white buds had barely begun to open.

"These can't be the same roses," Cale said. "I haven't been here in two weeks."

"Just came this morning," Walter said. "Last week there were others. I figured you remembered the roses and liked the idea—I figured you sent these yourself."

Cale searched through the flowers for the small white florist's card. He fished his cell phone out of his pocket and dialed the number at the bottom of the card.

"Roseland Floral Company," a man's voice said.

"Hi, my name is Cale Caldwell. My wife is buried here at Evergreen Memorial Park. Hannah Grace Caldwell—does that name sound familiar? Somebody's been sending her flowers from your shop."

"Yes, sir, I remember the name. White roses, if I remember correctly."

"Well, who's sending them? There's no name on the cards."

Cale heard the faint tapping of computer keys.

"Here it is: Our Monticello Rose Bouquet. Eighteen white roses with pink waxflower and heather. To be delivered each Sunday morning to Evergreen Memorial Park. Section 273, Lot 1, Grave 1—Hannah Grace Caldwell."

"What's the name on the account?"

"There isn't one. The account was set up with a credit card."

"Isn't that unusual?"

"Not at all. It's what we call a 'standing order.' Some of our clients wish to have flowers delivered on a regular basis, but they don't want the bother of having to place an order every time—so they set up a standing order and we bill them automatically. No name is required as long as we have a valid credit card on the account."

Cale thought for a moment. "What about the white roses? Isn't that kind of unusual?"

"Very."

"Why?"

"It's a little expensive—on a weekly basis, I mean."

"How expensive?"

Another pause. "$95.99, plus tax and delivery."

"Do you get a lot of orders like this for fresh flowers? I mean, for graveyards?"

"Around Easter and Mother's Day we get a few. But on a weekly basis? No."

Cale thought for a moment. "Why white roses?"

"I'm sorry?"

"It seems to be white roses every time—nothing else."

"With roses, different colors have different meanings. Red roses signify love. Yellow roses mean joy, or gladness, or friendship. Pink roses symbolize grace or gentility."

"What about white?"

"White roses symbolize innocence or purity. Sometimes humility."

"Anything else?"

"Yes—secrecy."

Cale didn't reply.

"Is there a problem, sir? Is there something wrong with the arrangements?"

"I just wish I knew who was sending them, that's all."

"I'm sure your wife was greatly loved and admired, sir. You probably just have a friend or loved one who wants to honor her memory anonymously. It's a wonderful gesture. You should feel honored."

And for a hundred bucks a week, you should feel rich, Cale thought. "Thanks," he said and hung up.

On a hillside across the street from Evergreen Memorial Park, a car sat parked in the shadow of a hackberry tree. The lone figure behind the steering wheel trained a pair of Steiner binoculars on the two men slowly walking up the asphalt footpath. He wore a pair of headphones cupped over his ears like two black hands, and he aimed a sensitive parabolic microphone in the direction of the men.

He saw the two men stop by the grave site. He saw Caldwell take out his cell phone and make a call. He listened, and he heard every word that was said.

The man pulled off his headphones, started the car, and drove away.

CHAPTER 18

Jada rang the doorbell a second time and waited. Through the patterned glass of the door, she could see Grace jogging toward her across the foyer; her stocking feet made no sound at all on the hard ceramic tile. Jada used the last few seconds to recheck her appearance and to get back into character, turning up the brightness and volume several notches.

It's showtime, she thought.

The door swung open. Jada grinned from ear to ear and shouted, "Ta da!"

Grace just stared.

Jada's hair was different. The color, the length, the cut—everything about it had changed, and Jada could see that Grace found the new look eerily familiar. Jada had colored and styled her hair to look exactly like Grace's.

Jada bounded into the foyer and took Grace by the shoulders. "Well— what do you think? You're surprised, I can tell."

"I—I don't know what to say."

"You pretty much have to love it," Jada said. "If it stinks on me, it stinks on you too."

"Why did you do it?"

"I want to look like you—why do you think?"

Jada trotted past her into the great room and flopped down on her back on the soft, plush carpet. Grace turned and followed, sinking down cross-legged at her feet.

"But why?"

Jada propped herself up on her elbows. "I want to *be* like you, Grace. You're my best friend now—the only one who understands me. Before I met you, I had no one to talk to—not about things that really matter. But now I do, because you're like me and I'm like you—and I want to be even more like you. So now I am." She lay back on the floor again, folded her hands across her stomach, and smiled.

Grace just stared.

Jada sat up again. "What's wrong? Don't you like it?"

"No, I do. I'm just surprised, that's all—it's like looking in the mirror."

"That's the point," Jada said. "And now, I've got something for you."

Jada wore a black T-shirt that said "Cheetah" across the front in a glittered silver script. She pulled the shirt up and off over her head, revealing a second, identical T-shirt underneath.

"This one's for you," Jada said, handing Grace the shirt.

"What's 'Cheetah'?"

"Are you kidding? It's a club in New York on West Twenty-first Street. Very trashy, always jammed—it's where all the kids try to sneak in. Go ahead, put it on."

"Maybe later."

"No, *now.*" Jada took the shirt from Grace and started it over her head. Grace found the armholes and pulled the shirt down the rest of the way, smoothing out the front and straightening the hem.

"How does it look?"

"Let's find out."

Jada took her by the hand and led her into the bedroom, where they stood side by side in front of the closet mirror.

"It's like we're twins," Grace said.

"Exactly." Jada grinned. "Now I'm like you, and you're like me."

Grace looked doubtfully at her new twin. "I'm not sure I want to wear this to school."

"These aren't for school," Jada said. "These are just for us—when we're alone and we want to talk about important things. See, Grace, I was thinking: Your mom is dead and so is mine. That means we won't ever have sisters—not real ones anyway. I want you to be my sister, Grace—my twin sister. Someone who looks just like me and thinks just like me, so I can say things to you that no one else can understand."

Grace smiled. "Sisters. I like that."

The two girls embraced—but they were interrupted by the sound of the doorbell again.

"Probably just the mailman," Grace said.

The two girls hurried to the door and opened it. There stood Missy, looking back and forth between them.

"My goodness," Missy said. "You've multiplied!"

Jada looked at her friend for a cue, but Grace just stood there silent and without expression, staring up at the smiling blonde in the doorway.

"May I come in?"

Grace reluctantly stepped aside and let her pass.

"Who's your little friend?" Missy asked, turning the beam of her smile on Jada.

"I'm Jada," she said once it became apparent that Grace would not reply. "Who are you?"

"My name is Missy. I'm a friend of Grace."

"She's a friend of my dad," Grace corrected. "My dad's not here."

"I know that," Missy said with a wave of her hand. "He's still at work—I passed him in his office when I left."

"So he sent you here."

"He has no idea," Missy said with a wink, "and if you want, we'll keep it that way. It'll be our little secret. I just thought us girls should have a chance to talk alone."

Jada's eyes moved over Missy as she spoke, darting from point to point like a ravenous mosquito. She saw the dark roots exposed by the part in her hair; she saw the faint, hairline scars just below each of her eyebrows; she saw the empty ring finger of her left hand; and she slowly began to smile.

"Come on in, Missy," Jada said sweetly. "Let's all talk."

Grace turned and glared at her, but Jada just smiled and waved Missy into the great room. Grace and Jada sat next to each other on the sofa; Missy took a seat in the armchair and glanced back and forth from one of them to the other.

"You girls are two peas in a pod."

"That's right," Jada said, "alike in every way."

Missy flashed a quick smile at Jada, then focused her attention on Grace. "Grace, I've so looked forward to getting to know you better."

"What about me?" Jada said with a pout. "Don't you want to know me better?"

Missy blinked. "Of course I do," she fumbled. "Any friend of Grace is someone I want to know too."

"We want to know about you first," Jada said. "How old are you, Missy?"

Missy hesitated. "Well—girls don't usually talk about such—"

"I'm fifteen," Jada said. "I'm a year older than Grace because I was held back a year. Did I tell you that, Grace? Yeah—I flunked out last year, so I have to do it over again. Are you married, Missy?"

"No, I'm not."

"But you were, I bet."

"Why do you say that?"

"Because you're so pretty—someone as pretty as you just had to be married once."

"Why, thank you, sweetheart. Yes, I was married once."

"Did he die?"

Missy looked at her. "No, he didn't die."

"Oh, then you sort of flunked out too. I guess that means you have to do it over, and you know what that means: you'll be older than everyone else in your class. Do you have kids?"

"No, I don't."

"Well, you'd better hurry up—you should have a daughter Grace's age by now. We're just learning about these things in school. I don't think you can have kids forever—but what do I know? I flunked that class."

Missy tried to look at Grace. "Grace, I was wondering if you—"

"How long have you known Mr. Caldwell?" Jada asked.

"About a year," Missy replied. "Since he first came to Charlotte."

"He's delicious, isn't he?"

Grace punched Jada on the arm.

"Oh, c'mon," Jada said, "I saw his picture in your old bedroom. I think he's very attractive, that's all. Don't you think he's attractive?"

"He's my *dad*," Grace grumbled.

"So what? He's still attractive." She turned to Missy. "Don't *you* think he's attractive?"

Missy paused. "Yes. Of course. Grace's father is a very handsome man."

"You see, Grace? Missy thinks your dad is attractive—and she's known him for almost a year, even back when your mom was alive."

Missy glanced over at Grace; her face was darkening like a storm cloud.

"Don't you just love this house?" Jada said. "It makes me feel right at home. Don't you feel at home here, Missy?"

Missy didn't reply. She was fumbling for her purse.

"I think Missy has to leave," Jada said to Grace. "I'll walk her to the door; you just keep your seat."

As they walked across the great room and into the foyer, Jada spoke to Missy under her breath. "Thanks for dropping by, Missy. I feel like we all know each other a lot better now. But I don't think it went very well for you today, do you? I don't think Grace likes you, and that's not gonna win you any points with Mr. Caldwell. Maybe it's like you said; maybe your visit today should be our little secret."

Jada opened the door for her, and Missy walked out without responding and without looking back.

"Drop by again anytime," Jada called after her. "I'm here almost every day."

Jada closed the door. When she turned around, Grace was standing right behind her with a look of astonishment on her face. The two girls silently stared into each other's eyes—until they simultaneously erupted in laughter.

"You were so mean to her!" Grace said.

"She had it coming."

"But now I'm in trouble. She'll tell my dad what happened."

"Are you kidding? She wouldn't tell your dad in a million years."

"Why not?"

"'Cause she crashed and burned, that's why. If she told him, she'd never get another shot at him."

"You think she's after my dad?"

"You think she's after *you*? Wise up, Grace. She wasn't interested in you—she was only here to win brownie points with your dad. She knew it was true; that's why she didn't complain about the things I said—that's why she didn't disagree. The same thing happened to me, Grace. It's all about your dad now—nobody even knows if you're alive."

Grace frowned at the door. "If there's one thing I can't stand, it's a phony."

"Yeah," Jada said. "Me too."

CHAPTER 19

Cale sat at the pedestal table in the breakfast nook and sorted through the day's mail. There were the usual ads and circulars from landscaping and home repair companies, the little mom-and-pop businesses that attached themselves to large homes like ticks to a dog. Catalogs still arrived addressed to Hannah, from Pottery Barn and Talbots and Chadwick's of Boston. He removed Hannah's name from every mailing list he could remember, but the things had a way of returning from the dead. *If only Hannah could do the same,* he thought.

He resented the junk mail even more than usual this evening, because his hours at home were fewer and more precious than ever. He had put in a lot of overtime at the office the past week, attempting to display that stellar performance Jack McAfee was so eager to see. With the early morning departures and late arrivals home, it seemed as though he barely saw Grace anymore. That's what bothered him—the idea of Grace alone in the house so many afternoons and evenings, eating dinner by herself and thinking who-knows-what about her absentee dad. Who knows, maybe she liked it that way—that thought bothered him even more.

Cale was getting nowhere on Molly. The victim's attorney was adamant, and now it seemed certain that there would be no opportunity to appeal for mercy. Now he spent sleepless nights considering how to challenge the victim's complaint: how to deny that it was Molly at all, how to substantiate her gentleness, how to prove that the victim must have played some role in the attack. But he remembered his attorney's stern warning: a challenged victim is a vengeful victim, and Cale knew he had a lot more to lose than the dog. Cale felt blocked at every turn. He had only a few days until the hearing would take place; until then, all he could do was pray that the victim had a change of heart—or that his attorney didn't want a boat after all.

There had been no further word from Missy. He appreciated her offer to try to talk with Grace at another time, but now it looked as if that's all it really was—an offer. He couldn't blame her. She worked for McAfee, too, and she was subject to the same performance pressures and time demands that he was. Missy's "big sister" approach was worth a try, but now it looked as if it was all up to Dad.

Now if only Dad knew what to do.

Grace appeared unexpectedly from the hallway and crossed the kitchen without saying a word. She opened the refrigerator door and ducked her head inside. Cale searched for some clever or innocuous comment that wouldn't be instantly rebuffed—but before he could select the words, Grace had disappeared into her room again. Cale turned back to the mail more frustrated than ever.

At the bottom of the pile was a thick padded mailer hand-addressed to Cale. He hefted it; it wasn't especially weighty, but it was thick and packed to the very edges. He slid the other mail aside, opened the mailer, and shook its contents onto the table.

He found a bewildering assortment of items inside. There were clippings from newspapers, a small blue date book, matchbooks and menus from various restaurants, several photographs of various sizes, and two or three credit cards. Cale sorted through the pile without focusing on any specific item—until a face in one of the photographs caught his eye.

It was Hannah.

He picked up the photograph and studied it. It was a picture of Hannah
and another man seated at a restaurant table. Cale had never seen the man
before; he was tall and very good-looking. Hannah was dressed to the nines
and wore her hair up high, the way Cale liked it, and both of them were grinning for the camera. The man's right arm reached toward her across the
table, and Hannah's left hand rested on top of his. Cale looked closely at the
back of her hand; she was wearing a three-stone diamond setting in a plati-
num band. It was her wedding ring.

He felt a wave of nausea come over him.

He quickly spread the pile out in front of him; individual details now
began to assault his consciousness like a series of electric shocks. Hannah was
prominent in every photograph, sometimes alone and sometimes with the
same man. There was Hannah in an evening gown; Hannah in a tennis outfit; Hannah in a bathing suit. In some photos the man simply stood beside
her; in others, they held hands; in one, they embraced.

He sorted through the newspaper clippings. A few of them Cale had seen
before—items from the *Charlotte Observer* honoring Hannah's volunteer
work at the Children's Hospital at Carolinas Medical Center. Some of them
said nothing at all about Hannah, but mentioned instead a man named
Richard Maitlin. One of the articles included a photo of a man's face—the
man at the restaurant table with his wife.

He picked up the credit cards and looked at them again. Now he saw that
they weren't credit cards at all—they were hotel keys.

Now Cale sorted frantically through the rest of the items, searching for
something that might make sense of all this—and he found it. It was a handwritten letter on a single sheet of personal stationery. The letterhead presented *Mr. Richard Maitlin*—and the salutation was addressed to Cale. Cale
felt a rush of adrenaline, and his fingers began to tremble. He smoothed the
letter out on the table and began to read.

Dear Cale,

Though we never met, it seems appropriate to address you as if we were

acquainted, since we both shared something in common—we both loved the same
woman.

Cale squeezed his eyes tight. He had read only a single sentence, but already he felt utterly overwhelmed. He didn't want to read any more; that first sentence made no mention of Hannah's feelings, or anything Hannah might have done. If he never read more of the letter, his imagination would be left to supply the rest. The letter might be nothing more than fan mail, just a note from an ardent admirer. But his rational mind was still at work, too, and his rational mind reminded him that there were photographs, and embraces—and hotel keys.

He turned back to the letter again.

If it's any consolation, I knew Hannah before she was married. We were very much in love, but my own foolish fear of commitment kept us from marrying. That is the single greatest regret of my life. You, apparently, were not so foolish. I envy you that.

I moved to Charlotte from Chicago several years ago. When I discovered that Hannah had moved here as well, I asked her to meet me for lunch—just two old friends renewing an old acquaintance. To our surprise, we both discovered there was still something between us—more than either of us realized. More, I think, than Hannah wanted to admit—at first.

I have to tell you that the next few months were the happiest of my life. I say this simply as a tribute to Hannah and the remarkable woman she was. She had an incredible capacity to give pleasure, as I'm sure you know.

I make no attempt to justify what we did—just the opposite. I'm writing to ask your forgiveness. I now know that what we did was an act of betrayal, though I found it impossible to recognize at the time. I saw our many nights together only as an affirmation of our love, and not as a betrayal of yours. I now know better.

If it's any further consolation, I want to assure you that I have suffered greatly for my foolishness. I lived a dozen years without Hannah—that was the beginning of my penance. Then, when I learned of Hannah's death, I prayed that I would die as well. God has at least granted me that request.

I write you this letter because we will never meet in person. Not long after Hannah's death, I was diagnosed with lymphoma, and my condition has rapidly deteriorated. When I finish this letter, I will leave it with my attorney to be delivered upon the settlement of my estate. If you are reading this, I am now dead.

The few mementos I have enclosed represent my tangible memories of Hannah. I hope that you can overlook my presence in some of them and view them only as artifacts of Hannah's life. If you loved her half as much as I did, you will treasure them.

I'm sorry. I die without the consolation of your forgiveness, and I await further punishment for my sins.

> *Respectfully,*
> *Richard Maitlin*

Cale sat staring at the letter. Maitlin's words were like a storm surge pushed ahead of a massive hurricane, and now the storm itself rolled in with relentless force. He couldn't think; he couldn't bring his mind to focus on anything at all. He just sat there, still and lifeless, watching the debris of his life being carried out to sea.

He heard a sound and looked up. It was Grace, crossing the kitchen again with an empty cup and saucer.

Cale almost threw himself onto the table, frantically scraping the contents of the mailer onto his lap.

"What are you doing?" he shouted at Grace.

Grace looked at him in confusion. "What?"

"Why do you keep coming in here? Can't you see I'm doing something? Why do you keep interrupting?"

"I just—"

"Is your homework finished? That's why your grades are falling, you know; you don't spend enough time on homework. Get back to your room and put your nose in those books."

"I only wanted to—"

"Get out of here!" he shouted, half rising from his chair.

Grace spun around and ran from the kitchen in tears.

The first light of day pierced the windows like shafts of ice. Cale sat in his study, the door securely locked, staring blankly at his paper-strewn desk.

He had barely moved for almost eight hours now, and a part of him never wanted to move again. He felt like a man who had been walking blissfully across a meadow, only to find himself in the center of a minefield. One moment there was beauty, and pleasure, and peace; now everywhere he looked he found nothing but destruction and death.

He tried to remember back to the night before, back before the news, back when his life was still intact. He remembered shouting at Grace; he remembered her turning and running from the room in tears. He tried to feel bad about it, but he couldn't. Recalling the scene was like watching a movie; it was as if he were trying to feel bad for something someone else had done, someone long ago and far away, and he just couldn't dredge up the feeling. He couldn't feel anything at all.

When Grace ran from the kitchen, Cale gathered up all the items in the mailer and brought them into his study, spreading them out on his desk to examine each of them more carefully. In fact, he had barely looked at any of them—he simply sat there, staring at nothing at all, thinking of the infinite consequences of that one, simple letter. He was like a man in a house of horrors, opening door after door and finding each room darker and more terrible than the one before.

Richard Maitlin.

Cale kept repeating the name to himself.

Richard Maitlin.

He tried to remember if he had ever heard the name before—in some cryptic phone message, or in an unexplained Christmas or birthday card, or from an unguarded slip of Hannah's tongue—but there was nothing. He wondered if there was nothing to remember or if he simply hadn't been paying attention. He wondered if that was the cause of all this—a lack of attention.

They had talked about old girlfriends and boyfriends, of course, and Cale thought he knew everything about Hannah's past acquaintances. Now he wondered if she had held one back—the one who really mattered.

Cale found himself reviewing Maitlin's letter word by word and searching for hidden meanings. *"I lived a dozen years without Hannah,"* the letter said. Cale did the math: Maitlin said the affair began when they moved to Charlotte—but Grace was almost fourteen now. Was "a dozen years" just a rounded estimate, or was he revealing something deeper? Did the affair begin even in Chicago? He thought about all his nights of travel, all his weekends away from home . . .

He thought about Charlotte. It was Cale's idea to return to North Carolina, but Charlotte was Hannah's choice. *"I moved to Charlotte from Chicago,"* the letter reported. Hannah said she wanted a city, a place with malls and parks and decent schools. Maybe she wanted something else.

He found himself traveling back through time, reviewing the events of their marriage together, reconsidering each one from a different point of view. *Did she know then? Was she only pretending? When she said that, was she lying to my face? Was her passion for me, or was she thinking of someone else? She said she was too tired—was that really the reason? She was always late to pick me up at the airport—is this the reason why? If she lied about this, what else did she lie about? Did she ever really love me? Did I really know her at all?* Cale found himself trapped in a deepening spiral of accusation and doubt.

Worst of all, he found his mind turning to Grace, thinking about how much she looked like her mother. The thought had crossed his mind a hundred times before, and friends and strangers alike had made the comparison. But for the first time he thought of it in a different way: He thought about how little Grace looked like *him*. He thought about her stubbornness, her anger, and their difficulty getting along. He wondered now if the problem ran deeper—if it was really a problem of blood. But in his mental house of horrors, that room was the darkest of all, and to venture too far inside that room was to risk being lost forever. He quickly backed out again and locked that door behind him.

The words of the letter began to beat at him like bats pouring out of a cave. *"My own foolish fear of commitment kept us from marrying,"* the letter said. *"That is the single greatest regret of my life."* Was it Hannah's greatest regret as well? *"She had an incredible capacity to give pleasure."* Cale cringed at those words. *"I saw our many nights together only as an affirmation of our love."* Our *many* nights? How many nights, and when? *"I hope that you can overlook my presence in some of these mementos."* Was he joking? Did Maitlin think he was nothing more than some stranger who had wandered into the photograph, just a figure in front of the camera lens? He might as well have said, "I hope you can overlook the poison I put in your drink."

"If you loved her half as much as I did . . ." That was the blow that really landed; those were the words that hurt the most. Cale remembered stories he had heard about women with faithless husbands. "I don't care about my husband's affair," some were reported to say, "as long as he didn't love her." Cale always thought the idea was absurd, but now for the first time he almost understood. It wasn't Maitlin's claim of conquest that cut through his belly like a knife. It was his claim to have loved her—and to have loved her more than Cale did himself.

Cale tried to sort through this barrage of emotions, but it was impossible. He was like a broken dam, and there was no way to filter the debris-choked water that gushed out. He felt broken; he felt betrayed; he felt battered, and belittled, and deceived. But underneath it all he felt rage—rage that flamed up like a fire under a spit, blackening the impaled flesh above.

But there was nowhere to go with his anger—that was the worst part of all. He wanted to kill Maitlin—but Maitlin was already dead. He wanted to confront Hannah, to ask her a thousand questions, to beg her to explain it all away—but Hannah was already in the grave too. Cale felt like a child in a cruel game of tag, and suddenly he was "it"—but when he turned around, everyone else was gone. He felt like a man lying paralyzed in his sleep, surrounded by nightmares on every side, unable to do anything but scream.

Richard Maitlin.

He thought about the name again.

Richard Maitlin.

Every name has a place, a time, a history. Who was this Richard Maitlin? Was there anything he could learn about him? *If he's dead,* Cale thought, *he should be easy enough to find.*

He turned to his computer and typed in www.charlotte.com, the website of the *Charlotte Observer*. Then he clicked on "Obituaries" and began to search backward a day at a time—and there it was: *Richard Allen Maitlin,* buried less than a week ago. He called up the complete obituary and began to read the few brief lines of text: "Richard Allen Maitlin died Monday at Carolinas Medical Center in Charlotte. He is survived only by his brother, James, of Bedford, Oregon." Cale quickly scanned the rest—but it was the final line that caught his eye. "Funeral services will be at 2:00 p.m., Wednesday, at Northside Baptist Church. Interment will be at Evergreen Memorial Park."

Cale grabbed his car keys and ran for the door.

CHAPTER 20

Martha, I believe we need a new sprinkler head—this one's barely spittin' through its teeth." Walter knelt on a canvas gardener's cushion and poked at the fixture with a screwdriver. He heard a sound from the direction of the parking lot and looked up to see Cale Caldwell charging toward him across the cemetery lawn.

"Mr. Caldwell—surprised to see you back so soon."

Cale didn't return the pleasantry. "Richard Allen Maitlin," he called out. "Where is he buried?"

Walter watched Cale as he approached.

"*Richard Allen Maitlin,*" Cale repeated, almost shouting. "Do you know the name or not?"

"I know all the names," Walter said gently. "Got a memory like a mouse with half a tail."

"Where is he?"

Walter began to slowly pick himself up from the ground. "Well now, if you'll wait just a minute, I'll take you there myself."

"Just point," Cale said.

Walter paused. "Up the hill, past the tree, down the other side."

Cale turned and stormed off.

He followed the familiar footpath to Hannah's grave, but this time he didn't stop—he didn't even glance to the side. He continued twenty yards farther to the crest of the hill and the massive chinquapin oak that shaded it. He stopped at the trunk of the tree and searched the opposite slope; his stomach twisted in a knot when he spotted a single headstone less than twenty yards away.

The grave faced away from the hilltop. It was obviously fresh; in the casket area Cale could still detect the slight crown left under the sod to compensate for the settling soil. He circled the headstone and looked at the face. It bore the simple inscription:

RICHARD ALLEN MAITLIN
As Close to Heaven
as I Will Ever Get

At first Cale did nothing at all. He just turned and looked away—away from the grave site and the cemetery; away from Hannah and Charlotte and Jack McAfee; as far away as he could possibly look. Then a moment later his mind snapped back again like a rocket returning to earth, and he spun around and charged back up the hill.

He approached Hannah's grave in a fury and kicked again and again at the back of her headstone, but the massive stone didn't budge even a fraction of an inch.

"Mr. Caldwell! Mr. Caldwell!" Walter hurried up the footpath as fast as his arthritic knees would carry him, calling out as he approached. But the old man's voice didn't register with Cale—his thoughts were as cold and immovable as the stone he was trying to overturn.

Suddenly Cale vaulted over the headstone to the front of the grave and ripped the bouquet of eighteen white roses out of the bronze urn.

"Mr. Caldwell! What in heaven's name's gotten into you? You got no call to do that—that's your Hannah."

"Not *my* Hannah," Cale shouted back.

"What do you mean by that?"

Cale didn't answer. He just tore the flowers into shreds and threw the pieces as far as he could, scattering the lawn all around the grave with flecks of white and green. Then he twisted the bronze urn from its socket and threw that too; it landed with a clunk and rolled a quarter-circle before it came to rest.

Walter waited patiently until Cale finished venting his rage. Cale gave the headstone one final kick with the flat of his foot.

"Wouldn't do that if I were you," Walter said, taking a seat on the stone bench.

"Why not?"

"First off, you'll break your durn foot. The thing weighs half a ton, you know—they don't make 'em outta paper. And second, it just ain't right, that's all. Why you want to do that to your Hannah?"

Cale didn't know if he could speak the words. Thinking them was bad enough, but saying them out loud would lend them a certainty he wasn't sure he could bear to hear. After a long pause he said, "Because Hannah had an affair, that's why."

"What kind of nonsense is that?"

"I got a letter last night—from the man who's buried on the other side of this hill."

"Richard Allen Maitlin. Buried him myself Wednesday last."

"Maitlin sent me a letter—said he had an affair with my wife."

Walter screwed up his face. "And you believe such nonsense?"

"Walter, there were photographs, and a date book, and hotel keys. There was evidence—a lot of it."

"Evidence," Walter said as if deeply impressed. "Well now. And what about the woman herself—ain't she evidence too?"

"What?"

"Hannah—the woman you married."

"I know, Walter. What are you talking about?"

"I'm talking about Hannah, that's what. How long were the two of you married?"

"Fourteen years."

"Fourteen years—that's a pretty fair run. A man knows a woman pretty good after fourteen years."

"I thought I did," Cale grumbled.

"Think it over, Mr. Caldwell. You know Hannah; you know the kind of woman she was. Now somebody comes along and sends you a letter—somebody says different. Who are you gonna believe?"

"Walter, I can't ignore the evidence."

"You can't ignore Hannah, either. You see what I'm saying? You know the woman—you know what she was like. That's evidence, too, ain't it?"

"What can you tell me about this Richard Allen Maitlin?"

"Not much to tell. Buried him Wednesday—nobody came. No service, just a burial—no family hereabouts, I suppose. How do you know this man?"

"I never heard of him before last night."

"Maybe he made the whole thing up—ever think about that?"

"Of course I thought about it. But why would he do that? Why would a man I never met want to hurt me? And if he did, why would he wait until he was dead to send me the letter? It makes no sense."

Walter shook his head. "There's no telling what a man might do."

"No telling what a woman might do, either."

"You're talking about Hannah, Mr. Caldwell—you're saying, 'There's no telling what *Hannah* might do.' You really believe that?"

"I don't know what to believe anymore."

"I think you do. You don't know what to think, maybe, but you know what to believe. Sometimes a man just has to believe."

"Walter, can I ask a favor?"

"Sure thing, Mr. Caldwell—anything you want."

"Go away and leave me alone."

The old man sat quietly for a minute, nodding and blinking at Cale's feet.

Then he slowly rose from the bench and started back down the path. A few yards away, he turned back.

"You're letting the wrong voice inside your head, Mr. Caldwell. That's the devil himself talking to you, and you can't listen to him. You're tired and you're angry—I can see that. You're lonely, too, and that's not good for any man. When a man gets off by himself, that's when he hears the devil—that's when he starts to doubt. Don't you listen to that voice, Mr. Caldwell. *Don't listen.*"

Cale said nothing.

"Will I see you next Lord's day?" Walter asked.

"No," Cale said. "I won't be coming back."

Cale pulled out of the parking lot without looking back. He was driving fast, but he wasn't sure where he was going. Home, he supposed—but home to what? Home to a house he didn't want, to a daughter who didn't love him, to a job he couldn't stand. *Home*—he thought about the word, and for the first time in his life, he realized how empty the word could be.

Suddenly, in the corner of the rearview mirror, he saw a shape rising up in the backseat. He turned to look over his shoulder and the car began to veer—until an arm shot out and grabbed the steering wheel, steadying the vehicle.

"Easy, kid, you could get us both killed."

CHAPTER 21

Cale hit the brake and swerved toward the side of the road.

"Not here," Pug said. "Keep going. Find someplace out of the way where we can talk." He slid down a little lower in the seat again.

"What are you doing here, Pug? And what are you doing hiding in my car?"

"Told you I'd drop by sometime."

"That's not funny."

"It's not supposed to be. Look, you just find us a place to talk, and I'll explain everything. And try to breathe, will ya?"

Cale found an unmarked turnoff and plunged the car into a dense section of hawthorn and holly. As soon as the brush closed in behind the car he pulled over and stopped the engine. He turned and glared at Pug.

"You've got lousy timing," Cale said.

"You're right about that—but better late than never, I always say."

"C'mon, Pug, you're not just dropping in for a visit. What's going on?"

Pug stared at him blankly. "I'm trying to think where to start."

"Just jump in anywhere."

"Remember when you and me and Kirby worked together at 4POG? Not at Fort Bragg—in the Persian Gulf, I mean."

Cale frowned. It was an odd question, and it couldn't seem more out of context.

"Remember when we were in New York?" Pug went on. "You know—at Kirby's place, closing up shop?"

"Sure."

"Well, you asked me a question there, remember? You asked me if we were good—you, and me, and Kirby. You asked me if what we did in the Gulf made any difference."

"Yeah, I remember."

"Turns out it made a big difference," Pug said. "I need to tell you a story."

Kuwait, February 1991

Hashim scanned the western horizon with his binoculars. It was almost sunset, and the glowing red orb hanging low in the sky made the ruddy sands of the Kuwaiti desert look like the surface of Mars. The land around the Al Manaqish oil field was almost completely level as far as the eye could see. The only structures that interrupted the perfect flatness were the defensive barriers his own troops had constructed: the tank traps and trenches; the mounded sand berms; the sloping revetments designed to conceal their artillery and armor. The fortifications stretched for kilometers and had taken their engineers months to construct, but in the vastness of the desert, their defenses looked like so many anthills. And Hashim knew that's all they would be when the inevitable ground war began—nothing but anthills. Just a minor annoyance to the unstoppable American forces gathering like locusts somewhere beyond that horizon.

Hashim knew that in the flatness of southern Kuwait, the horizon line was less than five kilometers away. He did a quick calculation; at top speed, an American Abrams tank could cross that distance in four minutes—and troop carriers would not be far behind. Hashim's frontline position was well within enemy artillery range, and at any moment death might rain down from the sky just as it had done all over Iraq for the last thirty days.

Behind him, twenty-six black metal wellheads jutted up out of the sand like knots in a Persian rug. All but two, that is—two of the wells shot billowing pillars of flame high into the nighttime sky as a warning to the Coalition of how the earth would be scorched if they ever dared to attack. *Stupidity*, Hashim thought. The Americans cared nothing about a few million barrels of lost oil. They would quickly extinguish the blazing fires, and the oil would once again flow freely from Kuwaiti pipelines into the insatiable gasoline tanks of millions of American automobiles. The oil well fires were useless; they had only served to guide the American bombers and artillery spotters and to plague his own men. The deep, high-pressure wells of the Al Manaqish oil field belched out plumes of deadly hydrogen sulfide gas, and when the wind shifted in their direction, their lungs ached and their eyes and throats burned like fire.

Hashim stared harder through the binoculars, hoping that his own eyes might somehow add to the power of the lenses. The setting sun cast shadows toward them from even the smallest objects now, and it took little imagination to see a tank or a soldier where there was none. Night was even worse: a moonless night like this one would be as black as the petroleum beneath their feet. The nighttime desert was as still as death, and by midmorning the winter temperatures would drop below freezing—sometimes below zero. And all Hashim and his men could do was lie in their trenches and listen to the darkness around them, starting at every sound and imagining the horror that might be creeping toward them like a fog.

Only a few minutes of daylight remained, and Hashim decided to use the time for one last inspection of his men. He walked along the trenches, barking an occasional command to check a weapon or fortify a position, exchanging greetings and reminding his men of their inevitable victory—but it was all bravado. Hashim was dismayed at what he saw. Less than a month ago, Iraq's occupying forces in Kuwait numbered more than half a million men. Now, divisions that once mustered twenty thousand soldiers had been reduced by half. Instead of eight artillery tubes in a battery, there were now six; instead of seven tanks in an armored platoon, there were now four. And worst of all, the elite Republican Guard divisions that had spearheaded the attack had been slowly and quietly withdrawn, along with the best equipment and the best-trained officers and men. What Hashim now found in his trenches was an undertrained, underequipped, and underfed band of conscripts who were expected to provide the first line of defense against the best-equipped and best-trained army in the world. *This is not an army*, he thought. *This is just a handful of sand to be thrown in the face of a giant.*

Hashim paraded by with an exaggerated swagger as he had seen older and more experienced officers do, but he felt the doubtful eyes of his men as he passed. Hashim did not have the knowledge and experience to lead an army into battle; he knew it, and so did his men. At the tender age of nineteen, he had been promoted to the exalted rank of *Aqid*, a full colonel in the Iraqi army. The rank was ordinarily unthinkable for a man of his years and experience, but his promotion became necessary through the devastating attrition of war. Many of the true *Aqid*s were now enjoying the pleasures of Paradise, thanks to the nightly Coalition bombings. Now, through a series of battlefield commissions, Hashim found himself a pretend officer in command of a pretend army—just a paper head on a paper tiger. Hashim knew this was true— but he wished that he could find a way to convince his men otherwise.

He stopped and looked at the ragtag collection of conscripts in one trench, already huddled together in preparation for the bitter night ahead.

"You!" he called to one of them. "Come to attention!"

The man crawled out of the trench and stood shivering in the last rays of sunlight. Hashim looked him over; the parts of his uniform didn't match— if it could be called a uniform at all. None of their uniforms matched. It looked as if a village of common laborers had been handed weapons and ordered to report to the front lines—and Hashim knew that might not be far from the truth. There were whole villages here waiting to fight together; there were brothers and cousins; there were fathers and sons.

"Present arms!" Hashim commanded.

The man looked puzzled. Hashim reached out and pulled the rifle from his hands. It was an older-style Russian-made AK-47, a relic of the war with

Iran a decade ago. The stock was broken and it showed signs of rust. Hashim wondered if it fired at all—and if it did, he wondered if the man could hit a sand dune at twenty paces.

"Are you trained in the use of this weapon, soldier?"

The man hesitated. "Yes, sir."

"Are you ready for battle, then?"

"Yes, sir," the man replied with even less confidence.

"Return to your duties, then, and stay alert."

Hashim searched the faces of the rest of the men in the trench. Though none of their uniforms or weapons matched, every man wore an identical expression on his face—and that expression had changed dramatically in the last thirty days. At first, every man had worn a look of dogged determination, but the constant anticipation of battle and possible death quickly replaced that look with a look of fear. But fear requires energy, and these men had no energy left; now they wore only the vacuous look of exhaustion. Food and water had become scarce; the supply lines from Kuwait City had dried to a trickle, and their last decent meal had been more than a week ago. Now the men stood like scarecrows at their positions, their nerves etched raw by night after night of constant alertness, their senses straining in the darkness for the sound of approaching doom.

The Americans knew all of this, and they took full advantage. Night after night from just over the horizon came the low, rumbling sound of hundreds of tanks and mechanized vehicles. Iraqi Intelligence assured Hashim that this was only a deception, that the Americans were simply broadcasting the recorded sounds of vehicles over enormous loudspeakers—but deception or not, it produced the intended effect: Sleep was stolen from them. Every man spent the night staring wide-eyed into the darkness, anticipating the moment when each sound would be accompanied by a form.

But worst of all were the leaflets—the little slips of paper that rained down on them day after day, printed on one side to look like Iraqi currency or with a ridiculous drawing of smiling Iraqis and Americans shaking hands—as though the pain of all this destruction could be so easily forgotten. But the opposite side of that slip of paper—that was the scorpion's tail. Each leaflet bore a message written in grade school Arabic. Some simply listed the menu promised to prisoners of war; some reminded the soldiers of their lonely wives and children back home; some asked them to consider the harsh realities of living without arms or legs—or no longer being a man at all.

The Americans didn't drop the same leaflet on every position; each message seemed to prey upon the weaknesses of that specific unit. Some mentioned hunger; others shame; others fear of death or dismemberment. All were designed to create doubt—doubts about why they had been assigned to the frontline positions; doubts about the quality of their equipment and the ability of their officers; doubts about surrendering their lives for the personal glory of Saddam Hussein.

The leaflets worked with astonishing effect. Night after night, fearful and hopeless soldiers crawled out of their trenches and wandered under cover of darkness toward enemy lines. And morning after morning, *Aqid*s like Hashim counted their troops to find another handful missing. Some frontline units had been reduced by half; others were rumored to have surrendered to a man; all were destroyed without firing a single shot.

Hashim marveled at this.

To counteract the influence of the American propaganda, Hashim was instructed to warn his men that the leaflets had been treated with chemical weapons and that a single touch could cause death. When even that failed to curtail the number of nightly defectors, a more ruthless step was taken: assassination squads were formed to patrol the desert at night and shoot on sight any man attempting to escape. Even then, the numbers continued to decline.

It was completely dark now, and every man hunkered down in his foxhole and stared into the blackness toward the horizon five kilometers away. Once again from the darkness came the sound of thundering engines and clanking metal treads; once again they wondered when the real attack would come; once again there would be no sleep that night.

Hours passed.

Suddenly the recording stopped and a deathly silence fell across the desert. In alarm, a soldier at the opposite end of the line shouted out a warning, and panic began to sweep down the line like a wave. Hashim rose up from his position to command his men to be silent when he heard the dull pop of a magnesium flare. Moments later the sky exploded in a brilliant yellow-white, outlining the silhouettes of at least a hundred soldiers creeping toward them less than a hundred yards away.

There were panicked shouts and cries everywhere. Before Hashim could open his mouth to issue his first command, a single rifle shot echoed across the desert like the first drop of a torrential rain—and then the night erupted in fire. Gunfire blazed up and down the line as far as the eye could see; tracer bullets tore across the night sky, briefly illuminating the contours of figures as they fell to the ground. There were screams and shouts and cries of fear from every direction, and it was impossible to know if Hashim's men were repelling the Coalition attack or if death was finally upon them.

"Fire!" Hashim shouted uselessly, dropping back down in his foxhole. He had been told about the utter chaos of battle, and he knew there was nothing to do now but join in the desperate fight. He pointed the muzzle of his own weapon into the darkness and squeezed off bursts of bullets in the direction of the horizon.

It was half an hour before the battle subsided, and only then, Hashim knew, because his untrained and undisciplined men had completely exhausted their ammunition. The fools were like children with firecrackers; he doubted there was a bullet left among them. Hashim knew better. He reserved a few clips for the close-in fighting to come.

Now a great stillness fell across the desert again. There were no more flares; there were no more bullets; there were no shouts or commands that might divulge numbers or expose positions. There was nothing to do now but lie low and wait for daylight to assess the results of the battle.

Not a sound was heard for the rest of the night.

When the first rays of sunlight swept across the desert from the east, Hashim shouted to his men to stay down. He knew that the sun rising behind them would illuminate their positions before it revealed the enemy's. He waited until the sky was bright with the morning sun before he poked his head up from his foxhole and quickly scanned the area before him. The desert was littered with bodies for a hundred yards, and nothing was moving anywhere.

Hashim stood up for the first time in ten hours and slowly advanced toward the casualties with his weapon at the ready. Seeing their leader advance, Hashim's men began to cautiously emerge from their trenches and follow. Viewing the carnage before them, the men began to raise their rifles overhead and shout out cries of victory and praise to Allah.

But when they reached the first bodies, the shouting stopped.

The first dead soldier was not an American, or a Kuwaiti, or a Saudi—it was one of Hashim's own men lying facedown in the sand. Three bullet holes formed a triangle in the center of his back. Hashim hooked the toe of his boot under the torso and rolled the body over. He recognized the face—it was the man he had addressed just the night before.

Hashim heard a wailing cry fifty yards to his left. He turned to see one of his soldiers collapse beside one of the bodies. The soldier lifted the dead man's head and shoulders and sat cross-legged on the sand, weeping and cradling the lifeless form in his lap.

Hashim felt the hair stand up on his neck.

He hurried to a second body and looked; it, too, was one of his own men. Now his eyes jumped from body to body like a desert sand flea. They were all his men—every last one. There wasn't a Coalition soldier among them.

Mournful wails and cries of recognition began to rise all up and down the line as soldiers discovered friends, neighbors, brothers, and sons among the dead. Hashim took a quick body count; there was one dead man for every man still alive.

"This is your fault!" a soldier to his right screamed at him. "You gave the command to fire!"

"Soldier, control yourself!" Hashim shouted back—but there was no power or authority in his voice. The soldier was right—Hashim did give the order to fire, but only after firing had already commenced. He did not fire the first shot; he did not give the command to start the battle.

This is not my fault! Hashim wanted to shout those words more than anything in the world, but he knew they were useless. He was in authority, and in the eyes of his superiors, he was responsible for the actions of those under his command. Hashim was not at fault for this shameful humiliation—but he was still responsible. He knew that someone's head would roll for this, and he knew whose head it would be.

Hashim looked at the faces of his men. Each one glared back at him with a look of silent hatred, contempt, and accusation. They, too, knew that this was not Hashim's fault—but brothers had killed their own brothers, and fathers had killed their own sons. What man among them could bear to admit this to himself? No, someone else must be blamed, and Hashim knew that he would be the sacrificial lamb. Each of them would point the finger at him and say, "He was too young! He was inexperienced! He had no business being in command!"

Hashim wondered if they were right.

He looked down at the dead man at his feet, staring up into the searing desert sun without blinking. He saw a slip of white paper tucked under the man's belt; he pulled it out and looked at it. On the front was a drawing of a dead Iraqi soldier. His uniform was in tatters and stained with blood, and his left leg was twisted back at a grotesque angle. The simple caption, printed in Arabic, said, "Staying here means death."

Hashim looked at the bodies scattered across the desert, and he listened to the wails of his grieving men. *This is not my fault,* he told himself. *This is what killed them—this little slip of paper.*

Hashim tucked the leaflet under his belt. He would spend the day comforting his men. He would help them bury the dead. But that night, under cover of darkness, he would start off toward the western horizon himself.

But not to surrender.

CHAPTER 22

How do you know all this?" Cale demanded.

"Got it from the horse's mouth."

"You mean you've met this Hashim character?"

"Met him? He was one of my students."

"Are you serious?"

"I teach at Fayetteville State, remember? I'm in the master's program—I teach a PsyOps course that a lot of the 4POG officers attend. But the course is open to anybody who wants to take it, so last semester I got an Arab student who called himself Ahmad. He looked about thirty, thirty-five—pretty average for a master's student, fit right in. He was working on a degree in psychology, but he seemed to have a very keen interest in PsyOps—especially PsyOps during Desert Storm. Asked a ton of questions."

"And you answered them."

"Hey, that's what they pay me for. This 'Ahmad,' he always stuck around after class, chummed it up with the 4POG officers, followed them to the bars after class and asked even more questions. Claimed he was a Jordanian, said he hated the Iraqis too. But the questions he was asking started to strike me funny. Not just questions about strategies and techniques, but people and places—who did what to who and when, you know what I mean? So after a while I got suspicious and started checking him out. Guess what I found?"

"Hashim," Cale said.

"You got it. 'Ahmad' didn't exist. Apparently this 'Hashim' crossed the border into Jordan after the war—along with a few thousand other guys. He spent some time there, did an undergraduate degree in behavioral science at Yarmouk in Irbid."

"How did you find all this out?"

Pug gave him a look of disdain. "Hey, guess what I used to do for a living—Intel Officer, remember? Anyway, the main reason this Hashim guy was in Jordan was to launder his identity—so after a few years in Jordan, 'Hashim' faded away and 'Ahmad' took his place. Then Ahmad applied for a student visa to the U.S.—no problem there; the Jordanians are friendlies. Next thing you know he was sitting in my classroom at Fayetteville State."

"Why? What was he after?"

"I was hoping to ask him that," Pug said. "Never got the chance."

"Why not?"

"He disappeared. Dropped the class, dropped out of school, dropped off the planet. Somebody tipped him off. I think he got wind of the fact that I was checking him out. I tried everything I could think of to find him again—no luck. And if I can't find you, brother, you're gone."

"Where do you think he is now?"

"Where do you think?"

A look of realization came over Cale's face.

"Now you're getting it," Pug said.

"You think he's here? In Charlotte?"

"Yeah, I think he's here. I tracked this guy all the way back to his unit in the Iraqi army. I found a guy who served with him—he filled in some of the details. Their unit was on the front lines outside Kuwait. The leaflets that fell on their position—the ones that caused the massacre—they were your leaflets, kid. They were yours, and mine, and Kirby's—and Hashim knows it. So when you ask, 'What's he after?' it's not too hard to figure out."

Cale's mind was racing now. "Kirby," he said.

"That's right—Kirby."

"Then it wasn't a suicide after all."

"It was a suicide, all right. Hashim didn't want to kill Kirby—if that's all he wanted, he could have just walked up to him on the street with a gun. He wanted to do to Kirby exactly what Kirby did to him—he wanted to make him *surrender*. Understand what I'm saying? He wanted Kirby to surrender his life; he wanted him to kill himself."

"Dear God."

"Yeah," Pug said, "that was pretty much my reaction."

"But—how did he do it?"

"He forged a letter from the Army Medical Command telling Kirby he had to be tested for HIV. Remember his leg wound back in the Gulf? He needed a couple units of blood, remember? That was February of '91. Well, the Army didn't start screening its blood supply for HIV-2 until June of '92—that's what the letter told him. It also said that the original blood donor just died of AIDS.

"So Kirby hurried in for an HIV test, and a few days later a nice man from the New York Public Health Department came knocking at his door—only it wasn't a health official; it was Hashim. You get the picture? Hashim stepped in before the real test results came back."

"The guy in the business suit," Cale said.

"What?"

"At Kirby's apartment—I met a woman who lives across the hall. She told me that just before Kirby died, she saw a man in a business suit come to his door."

"Sounds like our boy," Pug said. "It isn't hard to figure out what happened next: He told Kirby he had AIDS; made his future sound like a nightmare; gave him all the gory details. Kirby looked at his future, and guess what? He didn't have one—so he decided to save himself a lot of pain and ugliness and do the job himself. He stepped off the Verrazano Bridge—and surrendered."

"Pug, how could you possibly know all this?"

"'Cause I found the phony letter from Army Medical Command. I got to the apartment before you did."

"What? Then why in the world didn't you tell me?"

"Just listen, okay? Once I figured out who this Hashim guy was, I knew what he wanted. When he disappeared, I was hoping he ran—back to Jordan or Iraq. But then I realized that he didn't run; he just went underground. I knew he was still coming after us—you, and me, and Kirby."

"How did you know that?"

"'Cause that's what I would do," Pug said. "So I asked myself who Hashim would come after first—and I knew it had to be Kirby."

"Why?"

"Wouldn't you? This guy is good, make no mistake about that. He understands PsyOps just like we do—only he's Intel, PsyOps, and graphic artist all rolled into one. So he asked himself, 'Who do I go after first?' Not me—too risky—I've been around too long. Not you—you're made of stronger stuff than Kirby was. Kirby, he was the weakest; he was the most vulnerable. You know it, I know it—so did Hashim. The minute that dawned on me, I picked up the phone and called Kirby to warn him—and you know what? I was one day late—one freakin' day late. Kirby did himself in just the day before.

"So I flew to New York and I searched his apartment and I found the letter from Army Medical Command. I checked it out; sure enough, it was a fake. That's when the whole thing came together for me. That's when I figured it out."

"What did the police say?"

"I didn't tell the police."

"Why not?"

"Think about it: This guy's got his antennae up. When I started checking on him the first time, he disappeared—not to get away, but to be able to come after us undetected. If I told the cops, they'd be searching for this guy in all the usual ways—they'd tip him off in no time. I don't want the guy going any deeper underground. I want to draw him out."

"You think *you're* going to catch him?"

"Of course not. I think *we're* gonna catch him."

"How?"

"By letting him think he killed Kirby and got away with it. I want him to let his guard down; I want him to get cocky; I want him to think the second time will be a breeze."

"The second time—then you think he's coming after me next?"

Pug shrugged. "Why do you think I'm here?"

"What do you think he's planning?"

"Not what he planned for Kirby, I know that much. It'll be something different, something tailor-made just for you—but it'll have the same goals: to cause discouragement; to create doubt; to knock all the props out from under you until you got nothing left to fight with. This is PsyOps we're talking about—you know how it works: first you pick a target; then you learn everything you can about your target—every strength, every weakness, every vulnerability; then you use that information to design your psychological attack. I don't need to tell you—that was your job."

"Yeah—but I never thought someone would be doing it to me."

"That's the whole idea. If he does it right, you never know it's happening—until it's too late."

"Wait a minute," Cale said. "You knew all this when I saw you in New York. If you're telling me now, why didn't you tell me then? Don't you think I had a right to know?"

Pug leaned back and drew a deep breath. "That part takes a little explaining," he said, "and I don't think you're gonna like it."

Cale's jaw dropped open. "You're using me as bait!"

"I wouldn't put it like—"

"How *dare* you!" Cale shouted. "This isn't just about me, Pug—I've got a daughter, did you forget that? Grace is involved in this too!"

"I know," Pug said in his most conciliatory tone. "I've been trying to keep an eye on you two."

"Big comfort that is! You checked up on Kirby, too, but you did it one freakin' day late—remember? You put Grace's life in danger, Pug! You put my life in danger too! Who gave you that right?"

"I know you don't wanna hear this, but I did it for you."

"What are you talking about?"

"If I told you what was going on in New York, if I told you what was coming your way, Hashim would know. The first time that he tried something and you didn't respond exactly the way he expected, he'd know—and he'd be gone again. Is that what you want? This nutcase, underground, with no idea what he might try next—or where, or when? We got one chance to catch this guy, and it's here and now. I needed you to play along, and the only way you could do it convincingly was if you didn't know."

"You should have told me," Cale said again.

"If I did, would you have told Grace?"

"Of course. She has a right to know too."

"Then both of you would have had to put on a perfect act. Could you both do that? Could you guarantee it? I couldn't take the chance."

"*You* couldn't take the chance!"

"Look, we can argue about this all day, but it's all water under the Verrazano Bridge, if you know what I mean. What's done is done. What we need to do now is talk about what happens next."

"First we tell Grace," Cale said.

"No way. The less she knows the better."

"If it's so important to put on this 'perfect act,' then why are you telling me all this now? Why didn't you just keep it a secret?"

"'Cause I was worried that things had gone too far. I just couldn't watch you hurt like that."

Another wave of realization washed over Cale. "The letter."

"Yeah—the letter. I've been watching your house at night and following you when you leave in the morning. When you visit Hannah, I've been watching and listening in from a hill across the road. You can learn a lot listening to a man talk to his wife—that's how I've kept track of what's going on in your life. I know about all you're going through with Grace, and I know that's gotta be tough. But this morning, when I heard you tell the old man about the letter—I knew that had to be Hashim's work. When I saw you go after the roses like that—when I saw you kicking her gravestone—that's when I knew I had to step in. I was afraid you were too close to the edge."

Cale closed his eyes. He felt overwhelming relief at the revelation that Hannah had been falsely accused; he also felt uncontrollable rage that someone had falsely accused her. More than anything else, he felt humiliated and ashamed because he had been so quick to believe it. In retrospect it all seemed so obvious: the phony letters, the digitally altered photos, even the mysterious flowers from the anonymous admirer. Cale was astonished at how easily he had been deceived, but he understood the reason why. It was a fundamental principle of psychology that he himself had exploited many times at 4POG: the mind is quick to believe the things it fears most.

At least now he knew it wasn't true. He felt eternally grateful to Pug for ending his torment—but at the same time he felt furious at Pug for ever allowing that torment to begin.

"What do we do next?" Cale asked.

"First off, you have to get back into character."

"What does that mean?"

"It means I need an Oscar-winning performance outta you. I want you to think back about thirty minutes—back to when you still thought Hannah had cheated on you. Think about how you felt. Think about the way you must have looked—then try to look and feel that way again. You have to go home the same way you left, 'cause Hashim is bound to be watching somewhere; he has to believe that everything's going according to plan. Think you can do that?"

Cale nodded, but he wondered if it was possible. How convincing did he have to be? He could remember his feelings—he would never forget them—but whether he could reenact them was another matter. Now he understood what Pug was saying: *The only way you could do it convincingly was if you didn't know.*

"I need to disappear again," Pug said. "Hashim can't know I'm here in Charlotte; if he does, he'll know we're onto him. We can't be seen together—that's why I watch your house at night; that's why I follow you with binoculars; that's why I hid in the backseat of your car. We can stay in touch by phone, and I'll keep watching from a distance—but we'd better not meet again face-to-face."

Pug opened the back door and got out. "Just drop me here. I'll wait a few minutes, then walk back to my car. Better not take a chance on being seen."

"Pug, wait," Cale called out the door. "What am I supposed to do now—other than act like a betrayed husband?"

"We wait until Hashim shows himself. He showed up at Kirby's door, remember? He doesn't seem to mind getting involved; let's hope he does the same thing with you. Keep your eyes open. I'll be watching too. When he shows up, we grab him—it's just a matter of time."

Just a matter of time. Cale wondered how many more "letters" he would have to endure before Hashim decided to make a personal appearance. Maybe they wouldn't be letters at all; maybe it wouldn't be that easy.

Pug saw the expression on his face and leaned back into the car. "Relax, kid, don't worry about it—remember, this is only a psychological attack. Now that you know what's going on, you're safe."

Pug closed the door and waved, and Cale backed the car out onto the road and shifted into first. *Pug's right,* he told himself as he pulled away. *If Hashim wanted to kill me, he could do it anytime. This is only a head game. Now that I know what's happening, I can be ready.*

But somehow, he didn't feel safe.

CHAPTER 23

There was a quiet knock on the apartment door. Jada checked the peephole—it was Grace, all right, clad in her black Cheetah T-shirt and wiping tears from the corners of her eyes.

"Do you understand your instructions?" Hashim whispered behind her. "This is most important."

"Shut up and get out of here," Jada said, "unless you want to talk to her yourself."

Jada waited until Hashim retreated into one of the bedrooms and quietly shut the door behind him, then turned back to the door again and opened it wide—and there was Grace, stooped and sobbing and staring at the floor. Grace stood perfectly still for a moment, then leaned forward slightly like a tree beginning to fall—then she rushed through the doorway and into Jada's arms.

"Grace, what is it? What happened?"

Jada walked Grace to the sofa with her arms wrapped around her shoulders like a sweater. They sat down together, and Jada waited patiently for Grace to pull herself together.

"I'm so glad you called, Grace. I'm so glad you came over. You wanted to see my place anyway—I just wish it didn't have to be like this."

Gradually, Grace's heaving sobs slowed and stilled like a subsiding storm.

"My dad hates me," she said, choking out the words.

"Why do you say that?"

"He barely comes home anymore. He doesn't want to be around me."

"Did he say that?"

"He doesn't have to—I can tell."

"Did something happen?"

Grace nodded. "Last night, he was in the kitchen and I walked in. All I did was walk over to the sink—I didn't say a word or anything, and he just blew up."

"What did he say?"

"He told me to get out and go to my room. It's not like I was interrupting or something. He wasn't even doing anything—he was just sitting there, and I walked in, and he started yelling at me."

Jada shook her head. "I told you—this is how it starts."

"What do you mean?"

"He's mad because he's stuck with you. He put up with you at first because he had a wife to take care of you—but now he has to do it all himself. That's why he doesn't come home, Grace; he's out having fun."

"He says he has to work late."

"And you believe that? He doesn't have to work late; he's rich—just look at your house. I mean, how much money does he need? That's just an excuse, Grace. That's just a reason to stay away."

Grace looked more despondent than ever.

"What did you do when he yelled at you?"

"Nothing," Grace said. "I just left."

"You should have *really* left," Jada said. "Right out the front door—just like I did once, remember? When he yells, 'Get out,' that's exactly what you do—you get out for a while; you go someplace where he can't find you. That'll make him think things over."

Jada watched for Grace's response, but there was none.

"Did you say anything to him?"

"No."

"Nothing at all?"

"I couldn't think of anything—I was just so surprised."

"You should have yelled back—that's what I do. You can't just let him yell at you; he'll think he can push you around. Let me ask you something: Did he hurt your feelings?"

"Sure."

"Are you mad at him?"

"Yes, I am."

"Do you hate him right now? You said you did."

"I—I guess so."

"Well, you can't keep all that bottled up inside—you'll get sick or something. You need to let that out."

"I can't say those things to my dad," Grace said. "I can't tell him I hate him."

"You can't keep it bottled up, either. Hey, wait a minute—I got an idea."

Jada went to a hall closet and opened it; she removed a small video camera mounted on a tripod. She carried it to the center of the living room, spread the legs of the tripod, and set the camera securely on the floor.

"What's that for?" Grace asked.

"This is your dad," Jada said, "or the next best thing. See, this is what I do: When I need to get something off my chest, but I can't say it to my dad 'cause he might belt me one, I say it to the camera. I pretend I'm recording it for him, like I'm gonna play it for him later—and I feel a lot better. No kidding, it really works. Come over here."

Jada positioned Grace across the living room from the camera, standing just in front of the open window.

Grace looked a little sheepish. "What am I supposed to do?"

"Just let it all out. You talk to the camera like you were talking to your dad—like you *wish* you could talk to your dad."

"I feel stupid," Grace said.

"You need to try this. I'm telling you, it really helps. Here, I'll show you what you do." Jada pushed Grace aside and stepped in front of the camera herself. She put both hands on her hips, glared at the camera, and narrowed her eyes.

"I hate you," she growled at the camera. "I've hated you ever since my mom dragged you home. You don't care about me—you never cared about me. You just acted nice to me so my mom would think you'd make a good father. Boy, you suckered her good. You're a mean, stupid, selfish bully, and the minute I turn eighteen, I'm walking out of here and I'm never coming back—because I *hate you, hate you, hate you!*"

Her anger crescendoed with those final words—then she abruptly turned and grinned at Grace. "Get the idea? Now you try."

Grace stepped back in front of the camera again. "I can't do it like that."

Jada stood behind the camera and focused in on Grace. "Do it any way you want—just let it all out. You ready?"

"I guess so."

"Okay . . . and *action!*"

At first, Grace just stared at the camera; then she slowly began to speak. "Dad, I'm mad at you," she began. "You didn't have to yell at me like that—you really hurt my feelings."

"Cut!" Jada shouted.

"What's the matter?"

"You sound like you're writing a letter. Put your heart into it, Grace—you're not just telling your dad what you think; you're telling him what you *feel*. Remember, you got poison inside you and you need to get it out. Now try it again."

This time, Grace stared at the camera for a long time before she spoke—but when she did, her words were full of venom.

"I hate Charlotte," she said. "I hate everything about it: the school, the house, the people—everything. My life was perfect in Chicago. I had a good school and lots of friends—real friends, people who really knew me and not just people who talked about me behind my back. There was you, and me, and Mom, and Molly—what was wrong with that, Dad? Mom was happy in Chicago too—you're the only one who wanted to move, back to the South where *you* could be happy. But what about us—did you ever think about us?"

From behind the camera, Jada nodded and flashed her an "Okay."

"I tried to be nice about it. I tried not to complain because you wanted to go so much, but it was really hard. I believed what you told me—that it would only be hard at first, that I would make new friends and that Charlotte would be even better than Chicago in the end. Well, you were wrong, Dad. You ruined everything—you ruined my *whole life*.

"I hate our house—it's like living in a cave! It's so big and empty and I'm alone there all the time now that Mom is gone. And now you're gone too—you never come home anymore, and when you do, it's just to yell at me and tell me to get out. Why did we ever move here? Why didn't you and Mom just stay in Chicago and send me away to some boarding school if you didn't want me? That would have been easier than this—at least that way Mom would still be alive.

"You ruined everything for me. You're the reason Mom is dead. You're the reason I have no friends. I hope you're real happy in Charlotte, Dad, because I have nothing left! I hate you! *I hate you!*"

She was almost screaming now—then she abruptly stopped and stood trembling and glaring at the camera. Jada said nothing but circled around to the left, out of view of the camera, and held out her arms to Grace. Grace turned and ran to her friend, collapsing in her arms and sobbing again.

"That was good, Grace. That was real good."

"Really?" Grace said through her tears. "I don't feel any better."

"Well, you've got to give it time. Wait 'til you calm down a little. You'll start to feel better then. Hang on, let me turn off the video."

Jada released her friend and returned to the camera.

"Wait a minute," Grace said. "I want to say something else first."

"Okay," Jada said. "Go for it."

Grace took her position in front of the camera again. She stared at the floor for a few moments, collecting her thoughts, then looked up at the camera and took a deep breath.

"I'm sorry, Dad," she said. "I had to say those things—I had to say them to somebody before I just blew up. I didn't mean all that. I'm just so angry right now, but I don't have anybody to be angry *at*—does that make sense? It's not your fault that Mom died. I know that. Sometimes I wish it was. Then I could at least be mad at somebody. I know that sounds crazy, but—I don't know—maybe it's like that for you too.

"I don't really hate you. If Mom heard me say that, I'd be grounded for a week—and maybe Mom does hear me, so I'm sorry. Just please don't yell at me anymore—'cause I love you, okay?"

Grace said nothing more.

Jada just stood and watched, expressionless, taking in every word of Grace's sorrowful sequel. The camera, however, did not.

Jada had turned it off before Grace began.

Hashim peered around the edge of the bedroom door. "Did you get the recording?"

"Hold on," Jada said, checking the peephole again to make sure Grace was out of earshot. "Okay—it's clear."

"Did you get it?" Hashim demanded again, emerging into the living room. "The recording—did you do as I instructed?"

"Yeah, yeah."

"And the camera—you're certain it was working properly?"

"Check it yourself."

Hashim gently steadied the camera with his bandaged left hand; with his right hand he opened it and removed a small silver disk. He took the disk back to the bedroom, where an elaborate desktop computer system covered the top of a wooden office desk. He opened the DVD tray and inserted the three-inch disk, then sat down in front of the monitor and waited for an image to appear—and up popped Grace in perfect focus.

"Dad, I'm mad at you," her voice said meekly. "You didn't have to yell at me like that—"

"This is worthless," Hashim said. "This is not what I require at all. Did you not understand what I—"

"Shut up and listen," Jada said from the doorway. "You got what you wanted."

Hashim waited; after several seconds he saw Grace look up at the camera and begin again. This time he heard the growing anger in her voice; he saw her darkening countenance; he saw the straightening of her posture and the tightening in her neck and jaw—and he slowly began to nod. And when he saw Grace turn to her right and disappear from view, he simply said, "Yes."

Hashim copied the contents of the DVD to the computer's hard drive and opened a video editing program. He marked the start and finish of Grace's soliloquy, cutting off the segment at the instant she vanished from the screen. Then he turned and said to Jada, "Now your part."

Hashim handed her a .22-caliber revolver.

"Open it," Jada said.

"I told you it would not be loaded."

"And I told you to open it. I want to see for myself."

He opened the cylinder and showed her the ring of empty chambers.

Hashim positioned himself behind the camera and replaced the disk. He closed his left eye and peered through the viewfinder, being careful not to jostle the camera. Jada took up a position to the left, at the exact location where she welcomed Grace into her arms just a few minutes ago.

"That is the precise position?" Hashim asked.

"Close enough."

"No—it must be exact."

"It's the right position, okay? Just run the camera."

"Do you know what to do?"

"Are you kidding? An idiot could do this."

I am relying on that fact, Hashim thought.

On Hashim's cue, Jada stepped in front of the camera—but unlike Grace, her back was to the camera and she faced the open window on the opposite wall. She stood motionless for a split second—then she raised the pistol to her head, pulled the trigger, jerked her head to the right, and dropped to the floor.

Hashim looked up from the camera. "That was very poor. Have you never seen a man shot in the head?"

"Never had the pleasure. Care to demonstrate?"

"Your movements are far too subtle. The pistol you hold—it is the kind often used by assassins because the bullet will penetrate the skull but not exit again. The bullet ricochets inside the skull and tunnels through the brain. The effect is immediate, somewhat like beheading—that is what you should try to imagine. Again, please."

Jada returned to her original position and they repeated the scene again—and again, and again. After the fourth take, Hashim shouted, "Have you no theatrical ability at all? A child could do this."

"All I'm doing is falling down," Jada shouted back. "It doesn't take Julia Roberts to do this."

"Your movements must be completely convincing; they must not allow the slightest doubt. Assume your position—I will show you."

Jada rose from the floor and begrudgingly positioned herself in front of the camera again. Hashim stepped from behind the camera and stood directly in front of her, cradling his wounded hand against his abdomen.

"This is how it is done," he said. "You step in front of the camera; you raise the gun to your head; you pull the trigger; and—"

He brought his good hand up from his side and slapped her hard across the face.

Jada felt a click in her jaw and saw a quick flash of light. Her head snapped to the right, her knees buckled under her, and she crumpled to the floor like a broken doll.

"Like that," Hashim said. "The movement of the head must be quick and sharp. The fall must be without restraint."

Jada glared up at him from the floor. She pressed her left hand against her crimson cheek; she could still feel the hot imprint of his hand on her skin. She slowly picked herself up from the floor and stood in front of Hashim again. She raised the pistol to his chest and shoved the barrel into the soft flesh just below his sternum.

She pulled the trigger three times and produced three hollow clicks.

"Don't *ever* touch me again."

Hashim shrugged indifferently and turned away. "As you said, an idiot could do this. Now—once more, please. Quickly, before you forget."

Jada slowly took her position off camera and awaited her cue. She ran her tongue over the inside of her cheek and tasted blood. Her face still stung and her head throbbed from the force of the blow. Strangely, all she could think of was Julia Roberts. She remembered the stories she had read in *People* and *Premiere* about demanding directors who pushed actors to the edge in order to coax out prizewinning performances. She wondered if Julia Roberts had ever been slapped; she wondered if a million a week and a percentage of the gross somehow softened the blow; she wondered if Julia Roberts ever wanted to kill a director—the way she wanted to kill Hashim right now.

"And—begin."

In one fluid motion Jada stepped in front of the camera, raised the gun, and pulled the trigger. This time there was no pretending, no sequence of actions that ran through her mind. This time it was all muscle memory: the hangman's snap of the neck, the jolting recoil of the head, the mangled toss of the hair, the helpless surrender of the legs. This time she did it perfectly and with no effort at all.

"Adequate," Hashim said, removing the disk from the camera and returning to his computer.

Jada continued to lie on the floor and stare up at the ceiling. She felt oddly at peace; she wondered if real death produced a similar effect. She thought about how many times she had been slapped or kicked or beaten by a man. She wondered if the scene she had just filmed was a kind of prophecy—a preview of her own eventual death, like a movie trailer for an upcoming release. *Coming to a theater near you,* she thought, *the feel-good hit of the season:* One Man Too Many.

At last she picked herself up and followed Hashim to the bedroom. She leaned against the doorframe, watching his fingers as they skittered across the computer keyboard.

"What happens next?" she asked.

"That's none of your concern."

"It *is* my concern. This is a nice girl, and I don't want to see her get hurt."

Hashim did not reply.

"I want you to promise me something," Jada said. "I want you to promise that nothing will happen to the girl."

"I made you a promise," Hashim replied, "the only one I will make: I promise to pay you forty-five thousand dollars when you complete your services to my satisfaction. Beyond that I promise you nothing."

"I don't like this."

Hashim waved off her words like an annoying insect. "Your performance has ended; you may stop pretending now."

"I'm not pretending."

"Harlots," he said under his breath.

Jada took a step into the room. "You think you know all about 'harlots,' don't you? Well, let me tell you something about men: We don't lead men on; they come looking for us—and then when they find us, they whine about how they were trapped or deceived. They love us and then they hate us—that's the way it's been for thousands of years. And the pathetic thing is that they don't really hate us at all. They hate themselves—they hate their own weakness. Men are *cowards*. At least we don't blame our weakness on somebody else."

"In my country, women like you are put in prison."

"In your country, all women are in prison. No wonder they bombed that litter box you call home."

Suddenly, Jada saw his face change like a jackal turning on its prey. He bolted out of his chair and reached her in two quick strides. He raised his hand as if to strike her again, but stopped; instead, his right hand shot out and grabbed her left arm just below the shoulder. He jerked her closer and glared down at her with eyes like burning pools of oil.

"Never speak about that again," he said, his voice trembling with rage. *"Never!"*

Jada looked down at the hand that gripped her arm. She raised her eyes and looked defiantly back into his—then her own right hand shot out and grabbed the bandaged hand that hung by Hashim's side. He winced and tried to pull away, but she kept her grip—and then she began to slowly squeeze until Hashim released her arm. He muttered a curse and stumbled back, examining his throbbing wounds.

"That just cost you five thousand bucks," she said.

"What?"

"I told you not to touch me. Now you owe me fifty thousand—or else I walk right now."

"We had an agreement!"

"You changed the rules. And in case you're thinking you might not have to pay me that fifty thousand, you might want to remember something: All I have to do is make one anonymous phone call. Wouldn't the feds love to get their hands on you."

Hashim glared at her. "Very well—five thousand more."

"Then we're still partners," Jada said. "For now."

CHAPTER 24

Cale made two wrong turns on the way home. His mind, like his car, kept turning down side roads that led nowhere and forced him to back up and start again. He kept thinking about everything Pug had told him, and the implications of his words kept expanding in his mind like an unfolding road map.

He had been right about Kirby after all—but only to a point. Kirby did take his own life, but only because a carefully planned psychological attack had driven him to the point of despair. That wasn't suicide; that was murder—surely the law would see it that way. Cale felt vindicated that his instincts had been right, that Kirby never would have taken his own life under ordinary circumstances. But he also felt an ominous sense of apprehension, because Kirby never saw it coming. *"Kirby was the weakest,"* Pug said; *"he was the most vulnerable."* Cale thought about the way he had felt just a few hours ago, and he wasn't so sure.

He wondered if Pug was right—if Hashim was really here, in Charlotte, and devising some plan of attack for him right now. He tried to step outside his life and consider it as an outsider would—as an Intel Officer would. He tried to assess his own weaknesses and vulnerabilities, and he didn't like what he saw. He saw a man who was lonely and isolated, overtired and underfed. He saw a perfect target for a psychological attack.

"That's the devil himself talking to you," Walter had said. The old man was closer to the truth than he knew. Maybe he did know; maybe the old man was able to see things that Cale was too tired or too distracted to see.

Cale thought back to his days at 4POG, when he and Pug and Kirby used to sift through intelligence reports and reconnaissance photos to identify an enemy component with the same characteristics: a frontline unit, isolated from reinforcement and resupply, exhausted from endless nights of vigilance. He remembered what a simple thing it was to prey upon those vulnerabilities, and how PsyOps had succeeded beyond anyone's wildest expectations. The Army referred to Psychological Operations as a "force multiplier," but the men of 4POG considered it a force reducer. Eighty-seven thousand Iraqi soldiers survived Operation Desert Storm only because of the work of the Fourth Psychological Operations Group. Cale thought about what a formidable power PsyOps was—and what a terrifying thing it was to be, for the first time, on the receiving end.

He found himself leapfrogging back and forth through time, revisiting all the misfortunes of the past year, wondering which—if any—Hashim might have been behind. He thought about his job, and the pressure from Jack McAfee to perform. Why had McAfee suddenly become so demanding, and why now? He thought about Grace, about her failing grades and her growing depression. He thought back to his decision to return to North Carolina, a decision he had made completely of his own accord—or so he thought. Now he wondered.

He even thought about Hannah. Was it possible? Could Hashim have somehow played a role in Hannah's death? Cale's rational mind told him that was impossible, but he was finding bogeymen under every rock now. Cale knew what was happening to him; his fear and ignorance were causing Hashim to take on mythic proportions—to appear more powerful than he could possibly be. He remembered Vietnam, when our own PsyOps forces manufactured condoms twice their normal size and left them on the trails for the Vietcong to find. Cale felt like a magician watching another man's magic show, knowing exactly how the trick is done but still marveling at the effect.

And, of course, he thought about Molly and the ridiculous claim that the gentle animal had mauled a man's hand. But what about the photographs of the severed tendons and torn flesh—were they all phony? Was it an outright lie? Was it possible to begin a legal action without any physical evidence? Or were they really photos of Hashim's wounded hand—was this man really willing to go that far?

At least he now knew that the accusation was a lie. Now he could see that the story about Molly had the same contrived appearance as the letter from Richard Maitlin, and he felt a little sheepish that he had ever believed it in the first place. Now it all seemed obvious; now he saw the whole thing clearly— just as he pulled into his driveway and parked behind a police cruiser and a van from Charlotte Animal Control.

He saw two men standing on his front porch, one dressed in a policeman's uniform and one in civilian clothes. He saw the officer push the doorbell, then turn to look at him as his car rolled to a stop. Cale scrambled out of the car and hurried toward the two men.

"Hold on a minute," Cale called out. "There's been a mistake here."

"Are you Cale Caldwell?" the officer asked.

"Yes, I am, but—"

"I'm here to pick up your dog, sir."

"Look, this is all a mistake."

"Do you own a female golden retriever that was accused of biting a man?"

"Yes, but I have permission to keep the dog until the hearing."

"That was on the condition that you keep the dog restricted to your yard, sir."

"I have—she's never been out of the house."

"We got a call this morning," the Animal Control officer said. "One of your neighbors says he saw your dog roaming loose again."

"What neighbor? He didn't give a name, did he?"

"Look, sir, our job is to—"

"You don't understand. The whole story about my dog—somebody made it up to get at my family—probably the same guy who made that phone call."

Just then the door swung open, and Grace stood staring wide-eyed at the three men.

"Dad—what—"

"Grace, go back inside."

"What happened? What's wrong?"

"Nothing. It's all a mistake. Just go back inside and close the door, okay?"

"I have a court order to impound the dog, sir," the officer said again.

Grace looked suddenly terrified. "Is he talking about *Molly?*"

"Hold on," Cale said. "Everybody slow down for a minute. This is all just a misunderstanding—I'm sure we can work this out."

"I'm sure we can," the officer said, "just as long as you give us the dog."

"You can't take Molly!" Grace shouted.

"No one's taking Molly," Cale assured her.

"Excuse me, sir, but we *are* taking the dog."

The Animal Control officer held up a piece of paper. "Mr. Caldwell, this is a Probable Cause Notice, issued by our bureau manager. Your dog will be impounded for a few days to watch for signs of rabies. During that time, we'll be evaluating whether the animal has to be destroyed."

Grace's jaw dropped open. *"Destroyed?"*

"No one's going to hurt Molly," Cale said.

"But why would they want to destroy her?"

"There's a man who says Molly bit him."

"You *knew* about this?"

"Yes, but—"

"Well, he's lying! Molly would never bite anyone!"

"Of course he's lying," Cale said, turning to the two men. "That's what I'm trying to tell you: I have evidence that this entire story is a fabrication."

"You'll want to be sure to present that evidence at the hearing," the Animal Control officer said. "But in the meantime, we have to take the dog."

"Dad, you can't let them take Molly!"

"Be quiet, Grace! Look, you can't expect me to just surrender the dog when I know the whole thing is a lie."

"And you can't expect us to leave the animal just because you *say* it's a lie. Come on, Mr. Caldwell, the man has a legal claim here. He went through all the right channels, and we're just following orders. Now be a nice guy and give us the dog."

The Animal Control officer held out a pole with a loop of nylon rope dangling from the end.

"You can't let them kill Molly! You can't!" Grace pushed between the men and ran weeping across the lawn.

"Grace!" Cale shouted after her. "Come back here! They're not going to kill Molly—they're just holding her for a few days! We'll get Molly back, I promise! *Grace!*"

But Grace had reached the sidewalk and disappeared around the corner.

Cale turned and glared at the two men. "You know, you guys have got really bad timing."

The officer narrowed his eyes. "Excuse me, sir, but so do you. I've got a daughter of my own, and a dog too. All you had to do was keep the dog in the house, but instead you made me come out here and look like the bad guy in front of your little girl. I don't appreciate that, you know? I'm a police officer, not a dogcatcher. I've got better things to do than this."

"I'm sorry," Cale fumbled. "Please, you've got to give me a chance to explain."

"That's what hearings are for," the officer replied. "Now I'd appreciate it if you'd bring me the dog."

"You have to let me go after my daughter first."

"I don't *have* to let you do anything—except bring me a dog."

"You *cannot* take the dog!" Cale shouted.

The officer paused. "Sir—do you really want to go there?"

Cale paused to get his anger under control. "Please—just let me go after my daughter first. After that, you can have the dog."

"I'll tell you what," the officer said. "You let me do my job, and I'll let you do yours. Just as soon as you bring me the dog, I'll let you go after your daughter—but first the dog."

Cale pushed past the men and hurried into the house.

CHAPTER 25

He let them take Molly!" Grace sobbed, burying her face in Jada's arms. "My dad just stood there and let them take her away! He could have stopped them if he wanted to, but he didn't do anything! Now they're going to kill her!"

"It's like I told you," Jada said, gently stroking Grace's hair. "He doesn't want to be bothered. He doesn't want to take care of a dog anymore. He doesn't want to take care of anyone—he just wants to do what he wants."

"I thought he loved Molly."

"He doesn't love anybody—except himself."

"But Molly was my mom's dog."

"But now your mom is gone and he's stuck with the dog. What can the dog do for him? Dogs cost money. Dogs have to be taken care of—might as well get rid of it."

Grace sat up and wiped her eyes. "They say Molly bit someone."

"You believe that? Your dog is about the nicest dog I ever saw."

"Then why would they say that?"

Jada shrugged. "Your dad needs some excuse to get rid of her—he can't just shoot her. Maybe he made the whole thing up. Maybe he just called the dog pound and said, 'Come and get my dog—I don't want it anymore.' That's all you have to do, you know. That's where they kill the dogs nobody wants."

"I don't believe it. My dad wouldn't do that."

Jada got up from the sofa and took a chair across from Grace. "You're not really my friend, are you?"

"What do you mean?"

"Friends listen to each other. Friends believe each other. You never believe what I say."

"Do so."

"Do not. I told you your dad would start yelling at you, and you didn't believe me, did you? So what happened, Grace? He yelled at you, just like I said—he told you to get out. I told you it would happen, but you didn't believe me. So now what happens? You open the front door and you find your dad with a cop and a guy from the dog pound. What a coincidence—they all just happened to be there at the same time! So you come running over here, and you ask me why it happened, and I tell you—but you still won't believe me."

"It just doesn't sound like my dad."

"Your *old* dad, Grace—it just doesn't sound like your *old* dad. But your old dad is gone—that's what I've been trying to tell you. Your new dad doesn't have a wife, and he doesn't want a dog, and pretty soon he won't want you either—unless you teach him a lesson."

"What kind of lesson?"

Jada crossed the room and knelt on the carpet in front of Grace. "Listen to me," she said softly. "Your dad is all mixed up right now. He can't remember what's important anymore. He used to love your dog—you said so yourself. But the dog doesn't seem important anymore, so what does he do? He gets rid of it; he has it put to sleep. He used to love you, too, Grace—now you don't seem important anymore. So what does he do? He yells at you; he sends you away. First it's 'Get out of the room,' then it's 'Get out of the house,' and pretty soon it's 'Get out for good.' He's forgetting, Grace—he's forgetting how important you are, and you have to remind him."

"How?"

"By going away for the weekend—just you and me, without telling any-one where we're going or when we're coming back."

"Where would we go?"

"My dad has a place in Myrtle Beach, right on the water. He's out of town. He'll never know. It's only three hours away."

"But—how would we get there?"

"I'll drive us. My dad left the car and I've got a set of keys."

"But you don't have a license."

"I'm fifteen, remember? I've got my permit—it's the same thing. C'mon, Grace, this is just what you need. I did the same thing to my dad once, remem-ber? It worked like a charm. He went crazy with worry, and when I finally showed up again, let me tell you, he was whistling a whole different tune."

Grace said nothing.

Jada got up from the carpet and returned to her chair. She sank down low and folded her arms across her chest. "You still don't believe me, do you?"

"I don't know what to believe."

"Well, thanks for stopping by. Say hi to your dad for me."

Grace blinked hard. "I can't go back home—not right now."

"I don't blame you. So what are you gonna do?"

"You said your dad's out of town. Can't I stay here tonight?"

"Then what, Grace? You just go home in the morning? In the morning your dad will be mad because you didn't tell him where you were going. See, that's how it works: the first day you're gone he gets mad; the second day he gets worried; the third day he'll give anything just to get you back."

"I could stay here—the whole weekend, I mean."

"You could, but what's the point? There's nothing to do around here. We could be having a great time at Myrtle Beach. Ever been there?"

"Not yet."

"Well, it's the best thing in North Carolina, I can tell you that. My dad's place is right on the beach, and it's got a huge pool in front of it. We can lay out all day, and at night we can head into town and check out the clubs. C'mon, Grace—whaddya say?"

Grace hesitated.

"Just you and me—two sisters spending a weekend together at the beach."

"Well . . ."

Jada jumped out of her chair and swept a set of car keys from the kitchen counter. She walked to the front door, opened it, then turned and looked back at Grace. She held the car keys in the air and jingled them.

"I'm going," she said. "Are you coming with me, or are you staying here alone?"

CHAPTER 26

By now the sun had set and the treetops and rooflines of Cale's neighborhood stood out in stark relief against the glowing blue horizon. Cale reached down and turned on his headlights. After three hours of searching, there was still no sign of Grace anywhere.

Cale had started his search by circling the immediate area over and over again, hoping that Grace had remained close by. Maybe she had no destination in mind, he thought. Maybe she ran just to burn off anger. Maybe Cale would find her somewhere nearby, sitting on a neighbor's front porch or on a curb just down the street—but Grace was nowhere to be found.

He gradually widened his search until he had covered several square miles of Charlotte suburbs, but still without success. Now he narrowed his search again, slowly circling in on his house like a dog preparing for sleep, hoping against hope that Grace would be waiting for him there—but when he pulled into his driveway, he found the house completely dark.

He cursed the stupid cop who delayed him from going after Grace in the first place. He could have reached her before she was a block away and all this would have been unnecessary. *It's all that moron's fault,* he told himself, but the policeman's words kept coming back to him: *"You made me come out here*

and look like the bad guy in front of your little girl." Cale was sorry for that—
but he knew exactly how it felt.

What bothered him most was the growing realization that Pug was
wrong. *"Relax,"* Pug had told him. *"Now that you know what's going on, you're
safe."* But Cale knew that the story about Molly was a lie, and he still couldn't
prevent the authorities from taking her away. It was a brilliantly executed
maneuver: Hashim knew that one complaint from a "neighbor" was all it
would take to force the authorities to seize the dog, and it allowed him to
control the timing perfectly. Molly was taken away right under Grace's nose,
and that's exactly what Hashim wanted—that would have the maximum
effect. If Hashim had only wanted to kill the dog, he could have shot it or
poisoned it—but then the enemy would have been an outsider, and that
would have brought Cale and Grace closer together. Hashim wanted just the
opposite; he wanted to drive them apart. He wanted Cale to have to surrender the dog, and right in front of his daughter's eyes. Then Cale would
become the enemy, and that would drive his daughter even farther away.

Cale looked again at the empty house. *Divide and conquer,* he thought. It
was a classic propaganda technique—and it worked.

He turned off the engine and leaned back in his seat. It was less than
twenty-four hours ago that he first received the news of Hannah's "affair," and
he had spent the entire night in sleepless agony, his emotions flooding back
and forth between rage and grief and shame. Then came morning, and the
angry trip to Hannah's graveside; then Pug's surprise visit and all the revela-
tions that came with it; and now this—now Grace had run away. Under ordinary circumstances he might not be so worried—but these were not ordinary
circumstances. Grace had disappeared into the darkness, and Cale had no way
to know what might be waiting for her there.

He opened his cell phone; the battery was almost spent. He had called
every one of Grace's friends, hoping to find her—every friend he could
remember, that is, and he was ashamed to admit that he could only remember two or three. Once again, Hannah was sorely missed. Hannah knew all
of Grace's friends; she knew all of their mothers, too, and she kept all of their

numbers stored on her phone. Cale only recognized a couple of Grace's friends, and he could never remember their names; now he wished he had paid closer attention.

He closed his eyes for a moment; he was utterly exhausted. He tried to imagine what he would say or do when he first saw Grace again. He tried to summon some anger, but there was nothing there. He had no anger; he had no desire to yell at Grace or to punish her at all. All he wanted was the chance to throw his arms around her neck and shout, "Thank God you're back!"

In the back of his mind he wondered if he would ever get that chance.

He felt sleep drawing over him like a warm blanket. He shook his head, rubbed his eyes, and stepped out into the cool night air. At the front door he paused to peer in through the glass, hoping that Grace might be home but already in bed, or maybe sitting alone in the darkness. But the moment he opened the door, he knew the house was empty—emptier than it had ever been before. Without even the sound of Molly's gentle panting or her nails clicking on the hardwood floors, the house was as still as a tomb.

He checked Grace's bedroom first—both her current one and the one she had abandoned after Hannah's death. Nothing had been taken or moved; there was no indication that Grace had returned home since she left that afternoon.

Cale searched the countertops and tables in every room for notes; there were none. He lifted the phone and checked for messages; the queue was empty. Last of all, he went to his study and sat down in front of his computer. He jiggled the mouse; there was a click and a buzz and the monitor slowly glowed to life. He checked for instant messages; there were none. He opened his e-mail program, clicked the *Send/Receive* icon, and waited while the spam filter sorted through the dozens of ads for low-cost mortgages and Canadian pharmaceuticals. Only one e-mail made it through to his inbox. There's no sender listed; in the subject line Cale saw the single word GOODBYE.

He opened it.

The e-mail itself contained no message, but it did include an attachment. It was an mpeg file, indicating some sort of audio or video clip, and it was large. He double-clicked on the attachment and waited. The file took almost a minute to load, and it was the longest minute of Cale's life.

A small frame appeared in the upper left corner of his screen, and an instant later an image filled that frame—an image of his daughter, standing in a room he had never seen before and staring angrily back at him through the screen.

"I hate Charlotte," she began. "I hate everything about it: the school, the house, the people—everything."

Cale was stunned; he had never seen Grace so angry. He held down a keyboard button and turned the volume up as high as it would go.

"Mom was happy in Chicago," Grace said to him. "You're the only one who wanted to move, back to the South where *you* could be happy. But what about us—did you ever think about us?"

Cale felt sick to his stomach. His own sorrow and regret made her words almost unbearable. Her sentences began to blur together, but individual phrases assaulted him like the strikes of a viper. "You ruined my *whole life*," he heard her say, and, "Why didn't we stay in Chicago? *At least that way Mom would still be alive.*"

Cale listened to her words; he heard the pain, the grief, the rage. It was like standing in front of an open blast furnace—it was all Cale could do to keep from turning away. Every word she spoke hit and stung, but her last words cut him like the lash of a whip.

"You're the reason Mom is dead," she said. "You're the reason I have no friends. I hope you're real happy in Charlotte, Dad, because I have nothing left! I hate you! *I hate you!*"

Then she turned and disappeared from the screen, leaving those words to echo in her father's mind.

Cale was about to reach for the mouse to close the window when Grace suddenly reappeared—only this time she was facing away from him. She stood motionless for a second, and Cale expected her to turn and continue with her angry tirade—but to his horror, he saw her raise a gun to her head and pull the trigger.

There was a deafening crack—then her head snapped violently to the left and she dropped from view. A moment later, the frame went black.

Cale sat staring at the blank computer screen. His hands began to shake, and his breathing grew rapid and shallow. His thoughts were like a retreating army, a thousand terrified voices shouting contradictory commands. He couldn't seem to focus his mind; a single image drifted across his consciousness, an image he hadn't recalled in years: the image of a fifteen-thousand-pound BLU-82, a bomb so devastating that from six hundred yards away it could reduce a man's body to jelly. He felt as if that bomb had just gone off eighteen inches from his face.

Logic and rationality tried to force their way into his mind like sunlight streaming through a crack. *It's a hoax,* his mind told him. *It has to be.* The dog bite was a lie—the letter was a lie—the video must be too. He knew it logically—he believed it—but somehow it barely helped. The emotional power of the image was just too overwhelming.

He had just watched his daughter die with his own eyes. And it wasn't like Hannah's death—there were no sober-faced officers knocking at the door to gently break the news. He heard the blast of the gun; he saw the recoil of her head as the bullet entered her brain; he saw her lifeless body crumple and collapse. He saw it all, and seeing is believing—almost.

It's a hoax. It's not real. It's not true.

He kept repeating the words to himself like a mantra—they were his firewall against insanity. He felt like a man in a flimsy life raft, watching the wreck of a huge ocean liner sink beneath the waves, knowing he was safe but wondering if the suction might still be enough to drag him under. He was on that ship just yesterday—what if he had never gotten off? What if Pug had never told him about Hashim? What if he still thought the letter from Maitlin was real—that Hannah had been unfaithful—and then saw this on top of it all? What if there was no life raft—nothing to keep him above water in an ocean of utter despair?

He let his mind slip over the edge of the life raft; he tested the darkness of the waters. He would have had no wife; no child; no one to survive him.

When he died, he would leave no mark on this earth. There would be no evidence that he had ever existed at all. *I'd be a ghost,* he thought. *I could see things, but no one could see me. I'd be as good as dead. I'd have no reason left to be alive.* Cale felt the overpowering emptiness of those words, and he thought of the long, lonely, unbearable years of life he still would have had to endure. He imagined himself walking alone down a long, dark street.

No, not a street—a bridge.

He looked at the screen again. *It's a hoax,* he told himself. *It's a fake. But that really was Grace . . .*

He remembered Walter's words: *"When a man gets off by himself, that's when he hears the devil—that's when he starts to doubt."*

He fumbled for the phone and punched a speed-dial button.

"Yeah, kid, what is it?"

"Pug, where are you? How far away?"

"Hey—you don't sound so good."

"How long will it take you to get here?"

"A coupla minutes. What's up?"

"Just get over here."

"On my way. Turn off your deck light—I'll come in through the backyard."

"Thanks. Hey—"

"Yeah?"

"Hurry—*please.*"

CHAPTER 27

Pug clicked the *Play* button and viewed the video clip for the third time.

"Unbelievable," he muttered.

Cale watched from over Pug's shoulder until the moment Grace put the gun to her head, then he looked away. Hoax or not, the image was too much for him to look at.

"No doubt about it," Pug said. "This is Hashim's work, just like the letter."

"How do you know for sure?"

Pug turned and looked at him. "You do know this is a fake."

"Yeah—but tell me how you know. I need to hear the reasons."

"Well, first off, who sent the thing? If it's really a video of Gracie blowing her —if it's really the genuine article, then somebody else had to e-mail you the clip."

"And you think that was Hashim."

"Or somebody working with him. Who else would want to?"

"Maybe Grace would. That was really her in the video, Pug. This isn't like the letter from Maitlin—photos are easy to fake. Hannah was a model before we got married; there must be hundreds of file photos of her that Hashim could have manipulated. But you can't do that with video—you can't just use PhotoShop to cut and paste someone into the picture."

"No, you can't—but you can still edit." Pug slid the *Clip Position* button back to the left and found the very end of Grace's words. "Now watch. There's Gracie, looking right at us—but look, she steps out of the picture, and when she comes back again, she's facing the other way. That's pretty convenient, don't you think?"

"Freeze the frame," Cale said.

Pug clicked the mouse button. Cale reached over his shoulder and pointed to the figure frozen in place on the screen.

"Look at her hair, Pug—it's exactly like Grace's. She's wearing the same shirt too. She's the same height, she's got the same build—"

"But not the same face," Pug said. "That's why she's looking the other way. I bet that's not Gracie—that's somebody he hired who looks a lot like her."

"But that *is* Grace at the beginning of the video."

"Yeah, it looks that way."

"But why would she record that? Nobody made her do it—look at her face. She doesn't look like some captured pilot propped up in front of a camera and forced to read a phony confession—she really meant those things."

"Sounds like it to me."

"Suppose you're right—suppose the second girl isn't Grace and the ending is a fake. At least the first part is real; how could Hashim get ahold of a video of Grace?"

"Beats me."

"And why would she ever—"

"Hold on," Pug said. "This is PsyOps we're talking about here. You need to start thinking like the guy dropping the leaflets instead of the guy picking them up. There are three kinds of propaganda, remember?"

"Sure—black, white, and gray."

"Right—it's all about the *source*. In white propaganda you tell them who you are right up front. You say, 'We're the U.S. Army—surrender or die.' In gray propaganda you let them wonder who you are. You say, 'We must surrender, or we'll die.' But in black propaganda you lie about who you are. You say, 'Saddam Hussein here, ordering you to surrender or die.'"

"What's your point?"

"The point is, black propaganda is a crazy maker. When you know your enemy is talking to you, all you have to do is decide whether to believe him or not. But when you think your own people are talking to you, that can make you nuts. You get what I'm saying? This is the black stuff. You think this video is a message from your daughter, but it's not—it's a message from Hashim."

"But—how do you *know?*"

"You gotta look at the big picture—you gotta take this thing in context. The letter from that Maitlin guy—the one that accused your wife of cheating on you—you know that's a fake, right?"

Cale hesitated. He *thought* it was a fake—but suddenly he wasn't so sure. He knew what Pug was getting at: since the letter was a fake, the video almost certainly was too—the video should be considered in the context of a previous lie. But what if it was the other way around? What if the video was real? That would mean the letter—

"Look at me," Pug said. "You know what I did this afternoon? I called a guy in Gresham, Oregon: Richard Maitlin's brother—the only family he's got. I asked him how he happened to pick that cemetery—and that particular spot. Know what he told me? He said a guy called him up about a week ago, a guy he never heard of before. The guy claimed he was a big admirer of his brother—said Maitlin did him some big favor a couple of years ago and he wanted to pay him back. But Maitlin died before the guy could repay the favor, so he wanted to pay for his funeral instead—to the tune of twenty thousand bucks. Now Maitlin's brother, he's no dummy—so he tells the guy, 'Send me the money and I'll take care of it.' But no, the guy wanted to take care of it himself. Said it was a personal thing for him—said he had a nice spot all picked out and everything. So the brother, he figured, what have I got to lose? Twenty thousand bucks is twenty thousand bucks—so he gave the guy the go-ahead.

"You understand what I'm saying? The flowers, the casket, the gravestone with the nice inscription, and the perfect location—right across from your wife. Hashim arranged all of it, and he shelled out twenty thousand bucks to do it. That's how far this guy is willing to go—that's what makes him so convincing."

Cale was stunned. He remembered something Adolf Hitler once said— something every PsyOps officer can quote from memory: *"The great masses of the people will more easily fall victim to a big lie than to a small one."* Pug was right—the thing that made the letter so believable was the sheer enormity of the lie.

"Okay," Pug said. "Now let me ask you again: You know the letter is a fake—right?"

"Right," Cale said. "The letter is a fake."

"Good. We need to get our heads on straight or we'll never get anywhere. *This is not a message from Gracie.* Got that? All we're looking at is a bunch of pixels on a computer screen. Forget how he did it; forget how he got the video of your daughter. We've got to proceed on the assumption that the video is phony—at least the last half of it. All we know so far is that for some reason Gracie recorded a message, apparently intended for you."

"A suicide note," Cale added.

"No—an *angry* note. She didn't say a word about suicide—play it back if you don't believe me. You read that in, just like Hashim wanted you to."

"She said, 'I have nothing left.'"

"I've said that once or twice myself, and I'm still around. Look, the kid's a teenager; she's a drama queen. She was just hurt and angry, that's all. It was only the ending that turned it into a suicide note—and that was a different girl, remember?"

Cale nodded—not because he believed it, but because he wanted to. He still wasn't completely convinced. Maybe the video was a phony; maybe Hashim was only playing a head game. But if Hashim really wanted to end Cale's life, there was no better way than to arrange for Grace to end hers. It was possible. It wasn't beyond his abilities—after all, he did it to Kirby.

Pug slid the *Clip Position* to the left and played the video again. This time he muted the volume to help them focus on the image alone.

"Look where she's standing," Pug said. "Recognize the place? A friend's room, maybe?"

Cale leaned closer to the screen. "It doesn't look like a bedroom—more like a living room or something."

"Looks pretty shabby for anyplace around here."

Now the moment came when Grace stepped away from the screen and an instant later returned, facing in the opposite direction. This time, Cale forced himself to watch. That's when he saw it.

"Hey!"

"What?"

"Play that part again—just the shooting."

Pug backed the clip up and ran the segment again. Cale mimicked each of the girl's motions: She stepped to her right; he stepped left. She moved back again; so did he. She raised the gun to her head; he pointed his finger and did the same. And when the head recoiled and the figure dropped from view, Cale looked at his hand—his right hand.

"That's not Grace," he said. "That's a different girl."

"How do you know?"

"Because Grace is left-handed."

Neither man said anything for a moment, but there was a tangible sense of relief in the room, as if a lid had just been lifted from a boiling pot.

Pug looked up at Cale. "Told you so."

"Grace is in trouble," Cale said. "We need to find her—and fast."

"Why?"

"Because Hashim wants me to believe that Grace is dead. He didn't send the clip until Grace ran out of the house; that's when he saw his opportunity. I don't know how he's got this whole thing worked out, but one thing's for sure: If Grace is supposed to be dead, he can't let her come home again—not for a while, anyway."

"You think he's holding her?"

"That's how I would do it. It's the only way he could guarantee she'd be away long enough to convince me she's really dead."

"So what do we do? How do we find her?"

"We've got to call the police," Cale said.

"If we call the cops, we'll blow our chance to catch Hashim. He'll know we're onto him and he'll run for sure."

"It doesn't matter," Cale said. "This isn't about catching Hashim anymore. Grace is in danger."

"Hang on a minute. Let's think this thing through."

"It's not your decision, Pug. Grace is my daughter, and this is my call—and I say we call the cops."

CHAPTER 28

Watch again," Cale said, pointing to the computer screen. "She raises the gun with her right hand, and—*bang*." He stopped the clip and turned to the Charlotte police detective standing behind him. "See, my daughter is left-handed. There's no way she'd put a gun to her head with her right hand."

The detective didn't seem particularly impressed. "Let's back up for a minute," he said. "You say you received this video last night attached to an e-mail."

"That's right—about nine o'clock."

"And you think you know who sent it—this man you call Hashim."

"Right."

"And you say he sent it to trick you into believing that your daughter is dead."

"Yes."

"And why would he do that?"

"Because we did it to him first," Pug said.

The detective turned and looked over at Pug, who was stretched out on a leather sofa in the center of the room. Pug lay on his back with his eyes closed and his head propped up on a cushion. His hands were folded neatly across his chest, giving him the appearance of a fresh cadaver in an open casket.

"And who are you again?" the detective asked.

Cale let out an impatient groan.

"I think the detective got the story the first time," Pug said without opening his eyes. "I just don't think he buys it."

"Sorry if I seem a little slow," the detective said. "It is three o'clock in the morning."

"You want some coffee?" Cale asked.

"No thanks. What I really need is for you boys to make a little more sense."

"What does that mean?"

"It means he doesn't buy it," Pug said again. "Our story sounds too far-fetched. The detective is looking for a simpler explanation."

"What kind of an explanation?"

Pug swung his legs off the sofa and brought himself to a sitting position. "When did you last see Gracie?" he asked Cale.

"Yesterday afternoon."

"And how would you describe her emotional state when you saw her last?"

"She was angry."

"How angry?"

"What do you mean?"

"You said she ran off. You said you searched for her for over three hours but didn't find a trace. It's been—what—twelve hours now? And you still haven't heard from her. Sounds like she was more than a little miffed, wouldn't you say?"

Cale didn't reply.

"Would you say she was furious?"

"Yeah—I guess so."

"Furious enough to want to hurt you?"

"What's your point, Pug?"

"It's not my point; it's his," Pug said, nodding to the detective. "He thinks we've invented a big fat conspiracy theory to keep from facing the facts."

"I didn't say that," the detective said.

"You didn't have to."

Cale looked at the detective. "And what are the facts, Detective?"

"Look," he said, "crimes are usually committed by stupid people—people who lose their heads and do something dumb. Seven times out of ten I can walk into a crime scene and tell you who did it, just like that—it's that obvious. Sure, we have to collect physical evidence, and sometimes we have to run some tests. But that's usually just to prove things in court, not to figure out who did it—we already know that. In this job you sort of learn to take things at face value, 'cause that's how things usually turn out. If it looks like the butler did it, then guess what? The butler did it, seven times out of ten.

"Now you show me this video, Mr. Caldwell, and I see a thirteen-year-old girl put a gun to her head and pull the trigger, and you ask me what I think. Well, I'll tell you what I think: I think your daughter is upset with you and she decided to play a very mean prank."

"I don't believe that," Cale said.

"Do you own a video camera, Mr. Caldwell?"

"Yeah, somewhere."

"Does your daughter have access to a computer?"

"All kids do these days."

"And would you consider your daughter a bright girl?"

"Sure."

The detective shrugged. "Kids have a lot of computer savvy nowadays; me, I'm still trying to figure out iTunes. Your daughter could have easily produced that video—and she could have sent it herself."

"Then where is she now?"

"You said you didn't recognize the room. She probably shot the video at a friend's house. That's most likely where she is now, holing up for a while just to let you stew. Like I said, it's a very mean prank."

"I called you because I need help finding my daughter," Cale said. "But if you think this is just a prank, you're not exactly going to mount a manhunt, are you?"

"You asked me what I thought and I told you. There is, of course, the possibility that the video is genuine—that it's a suicide note."

"I don't believe that either," Cale said.

"Why—because she held the gun in the wrong hand? Have you ever seen your daughter fire a gun before? Which hand does she usually use? I had a boy a couple years ago, stuck a rifle in his mouth and pulled the trigger with his toe—I bet he never did that before. We're talking about suicide here, Mr. Caldwell. You're not exactly thinking straight when you do something like this."

"I don't believe my daughter was capable of suicide."

"Your daughter was angry, maybe even depressed; the fact is, teenagers are prone to suicide."

"Not Grace."

"Yeah, so you said."

"Look at the video again," Cale said. "She steps out of the picture, and when she comes back she's facing the other way. What about that?"

"What about it? People do funny things when they commit suicide. Some people think ahead; they think about how they'll look, they think about the people who have to find the body. Some people curl up in the bathtub to keep things neat. Some people put a blanket over their heads to cover up the mess. Maybe your daughter just didn't want you to see her face; maybe she didn't want to see yours."

"But if it really is a suicide, then somebody else had to run the camera. Somebody else had to send the clip."

"Again, probably a friend. Adolescents sometimes take a romantic view of suicide; they see it as a kind of ritual. Sometimes kids do it together, in pairs; sometimes they help each other out."

"If you did believe it was a suicide, you'd be in a lot bigger hurry to find her, wouldn't you?"

"Sure. Like you said, somebody else had to run the camera. I'd be looking for two people—if I believed it."

"But you don't."

The detective just shrugged.

"What about the other option?" Pug called from across the room.

"What option is that?"

"You know—the conspiracy theory."

"You mean when the mysterious Hashim switches in a perfect double and fakes your daughter's suicide to drive you insane?"

"You've got to at least consider the possibility that we're telling the truth."

"I don't think you're lying, sir. I think you're just looking for a complicated solution to a simple problem. Trust me: seven chances in ten it's a prank; three chances in ten it's the genuine article."

"And the conspiracy theory?"

"Do either of you have any physical evidence that this man Hashim is involved in this?"

"It's—a long story," Pug said.

"I bet."

"Look," Pug said. "If you won't even consider the possibility that we're telling you the truth, what's the point in asking you to—"

"Hold it, Pug," Cale broke in. "The detective doesn't need to believe us. He just needs to help us find Grace—and he's going to do that, aren't you, Detective?"

"I am?"

"Sure you are. The way I see it, you've got three options here. If the video's a prank, then Grace is in no danger—but she's still missing. In another twelve hours I'll be calling you about a missing person, so you might as well start looking now.

"On the other hand, if the video's real, then you've got a body to find—plus an accomplice. Even if you don't believe it, it's a possibility you can't overlook. Three chances in ten; I've won a lot of poker hands with worse odds than that."

"And the third option," the detective said. "I assume that's your conspiracy theory."

"I don't blame you for not believing it," Cale said. "I didn't believe it myself at first. But whether you believe it or not, Detective, it happens to be true. So please, help me find my daughter—*and hurry.*"

It was almost 4:00 a.m. when the detective finally left. He spent the final hour collecting every piece of information about Grace that Cale could provide: photographs, names and addresses of friends, class schedules, favorite stores and restaurants, anything that might generate a lead. When Cale finally closed the door behind him, he turned and looked at Pug. "Do you think they'll find her?"

"Not fast enough."

"I agree. The detective didn't seem to be in a very big hurry, did he? He's convinced it's a prank, so what's the rush? We've got to try to find Grace ourselves. Maybe we can't convince the police, but we know what's going on here; we know Hashim is involved. It's like you said: this is PsyOps we're talking about here. We may be the best-qualified people to find Hashim—and if we find him, I think we'll find Grace."

"Where do you want to start?"

"Let's take another look at that video."

The two men pulled up chairs in front of the computer again. Cale closed the Media Player window and opened his e-mail program.

"Here's the original message," Cale said. "There's no sender listed. Is there any way to trace it back and find out where it came from?"

"I doubt it. You can log on to the Internet anywhere—a public library, a coffee shop. It's pretty easy to send an untraceable e-mail. Spammers do it all the time."

"Okay, then let's go back to the video. Maybe there's something we missed."

He opened the attachment again and the clip began to play. Once again Cale listened to his daughter's stinging soliloquy, and once again he prepared to watch his only child die right before his eyes. This time he tried to focus on the surroundings instead of on Grace herself; he tried to look past all of her anger and pain—but it was like wading through a swarm of hornets.

Cale cast a quick glance at Pug. "You know something?"

"What's that?"

"I almost threw in the towel last night."

"Whoa."

"I mean it, Pug. I walked right up to the edge of the bridge and looked down."

The two men watched again as Grace raised the gun, squeezed the trigger, and sent a bullet through the center of her brain.

"I even knew it was a lie," Cale said. "I kept telling myself, 'It isn't true. It's all a fake. The letter was a lie, and so is this.' The funny thing was, it didn't seem to make much difference."

He slid the button halfway back and released it. They watched the gun slowly rise and the skull recoil again.

"*Look* at that," Cale said. "Even if it is a lie—even if it's all pretend—just the thought of losing Grace . . ." His voice trailed off, and the two men sat staring silently at the screen.

"I'll tell you something else," Cale said. "It's a good thing you weren't one freakin' day late."

The clip began to run again. This time, Pug placed his hand on the screen to cover Grace's image.

"Just look at the room," he said. "Does anything look familiar?"

"It's almost empty—there's no way to tell. The room could be anywhere."

"What time did you say Gracie ran off?"

"Late afternoon. Why?"

"There's a window behind her. If she recorded this after she ran off, it should look like afternoon or later outside. Does the light look right to you?"

Cale maximized the window so that it filled the screen and backed the clip up to the beginning. This time, he focused his attention only on the window.

"Hold it," Cale said. "What's that?"

"What?"

"In the corner of the window—see there? Something outside in the distance."

"Looks like a billboard—but it's too far away to read."

"It says 'Central Carolina Bank.'"

Pug squinted. "How can you read that?"

"I recognize the layout," Cale said. "I should—I designed it."

CHAPTER 29

Grace looked at herself in the changing room mirror. It was the smallest swimsuit she had ever tried on. She grabbed the top and wrestled it up a little, but that only made it ride up in the wrong places; she pulled it down again, but that didn't solve the problem either: there just wasn't enough of it to go around. It was like trying to stretch a twin-size sheet over a king-size bed.

She held her hand up to the mirror to block her view of her face and looked at herself from the neck down. She would have really liked the suit if it were on somebody else; the problem was that it was on her, and it felt just awful. For years she had begged her parents for permission to look a little more like her friends and a little less like Anne of Green Gables. Now, at Jada's urging, she finally had the chance, but the sudden freedom made her feel a little awkward and unsure. For years she had been pushing against a locked door, and now the door had suddenly given way. Now she found herself standing in a strange and unfamiliar room, and she wasn't so sure she wanted to be there after all.

She turned and looked at the changing room door—if you could call it a door. It was just a pair of shutters on hinges, and they only blocked the view from her neck to her knees. They weren't even solid shutters; they had little angled slats like the ones on her house back home. If anybody in the store looked at just the right angle, they could see right in. *I guess you're not supposed to care about undressing in front of strangers,* Grace thought.

But she did care. She wanted to call out to Jada, who was somewhere in the store picking out a new suit for herself. She wanted to ask her to come and stand in front of the shutters to help block the view, and if it was one of her other friends, she would have done it. But it wasn't one of her other friends; it was Jada, and she knew Jada would only laugh and make fun.

"Hey in there," Jada called from behind a rack of T-shirts. "You about done?"

"Almost," Grace said.

"What are you doing, trying on a suit or growing into it? C'mon, the night isn't getting any younger. We got places to go and boys to meet."

The idea gave Grace a sudden shiver. She picked up the blouse she had worn down to the beach and slipped it on over the suit, buttoning it almost to the neck. The bottom of her swimsuit wasn't any larger than the top; that's why, despite Jada's wheedling, Grace also picked out a new pair of shorts— very short shorts, maybe, but at least they let her feel a little less exposed.

She gathered her things and pushed open the shuttered doors. Jada was waiting for her; she took one look at Grace and laughed out loud.

"What's wrong?" Grace said. "Do I look stupid?"

"We didn't come here to buy underwear, Grace. You're sort of missing the point."

Jada stepped closer and looked her over. "First of all, lose *this*," she said, pointing to the buttoned-up blouse.

"It's too cold."

"It's not cold at all—you're just chicken."

"Maybe I am. So what?"

"At least let me see the suit. Do you even have it on?"

"Sure I do." She unbuttoned the top two buttons and leaned forward a little.

Jada shook her head. She reached out and unbuttoned the remaining buttons, then flung Grace's blouse open like a pair of curtains.

Grace glanced around the store for prying eyes.

Jada just stood there, nodding and staring.

"Well? Say something."

"I love it," Jada said. "So will the guys, if you ever let 'em see it."

"They don't need to see it."

"Then what are you buying it for?"

"For me. I always wanted a suit like this."

"Liar."

"Shut up."

Grace began to button her blouse again, and Jada slapped her hands away. "Leave it open—you can at least do that much. And stand up straight—don't round your shoulders."

"You sound like my—" Grace didn't finish the sentence.

The two girls took their purchases to the register. Jada saw Grace take a credit card out of her purse. "No, this is on me," she said.

"You don't have to do that. I've got money."

"I want to, really. It's my treat." She took a roll of bills from her own purse and began to count.

"You carry a lot of money," Grace whispered. "Is that safe?"

"It's credit cards that aren't safe around here. Lots of identity theft and stuff—better if we stick to cash."

They stepped out of the beachwear shop and onto the crowded sidewalk. The moonless night sky sat atop the shops and buildings like a heavy canopy, but on the sidewalk below it was as bright as day. The T-shirt shops, bars, and tattoo parlors that packed both sides of the street were lit up like Vegas casinos. The glaring artificial light penetrated every crease and crevice and outlined every object with a laser edge, giving the entire scene a flat and cinematic look.

There were people everywhere. The crowd was young—mostly college regulars from UNC–Wilmington or USC just a couple of hours away, or high school students trying as hard as they could to act a few years older than they really were. Ocean Boulevard was an older, more run-down section of Myrtle

Beach, but the students all preferred it to the more sanitized and parent-approved amusements farther inland. It was loud and gritty, and there were more bars per square foot than in any other section of the beach. Besides, it was only a block from the water, and that made it the natural first stop for everyone wandering off the beach in search of nighttime adventure.

Grace watched the older girls passing by; compared to some of them, she was overdressed. Somehow, it didn't make her feel any better; it made it look as if she was trying to imitate them, and that made her feel even younger than she was.

"C'mon," Jada said, "let's have some fun."

They started down the sidewalk together in no particular direction. There were groups of men and women everywhere, roaming in packs of six or eight, laughing and waving and carrying on. Grace was content to stare into the store windows as they passed, but Jada, much to Grace's embarrassment, seemed to make eye contact with every passing male. Some of them stopped to talk with her—sometimes an entire group. One of them even hooked his arm around Jada's waist as they talked, and she just stood there and grinned back. Grace found herself slowly hanging back more and more, distancing herself from her more confident companion.

Thirty feet ahead, Jada suddenly realized she was traveling alone. She turned and searched the crowd for Grace; she spotted her, shook her head, and started back.

"What are you doing?" Jada asked.

"Just looking," Grace said, pointing to a souvenir shop window and a cream-colored conch shell with a spiraling tip and pearlescent tongue.

"Those are real rare," Jada said. "They pick 'em up by the truckload about a block from here. What are you doing, Grace? We got a street full of guys and you're looking at seashells."

Grace just shrugged.

"C'mon," Jada said, "we got better things to look at."

They started down the sidewalk again arm in arm. Jada pointed to a man across the street. "See that one? Now he's hot: broad shoulders, narrow waist—

dresses like a dork, though, doesn't he? See, that's the problem: men are like shoes—there's always something that's not quite right."

"He's cute, though."

"Yeah, but he's mine—you have to pick your own."

"What?"

"Go ahead, pick one. Show me the kind you like."

Grace looked sheepishly around the street. On the opposite sidewalk she spotted a young man who was easily a decade older than she was. He was tall and lean with wavy brown hair and round, doelike eyes. He was standing with a group of other men, louder men, but he seemed content to just smile and listen. He had his hands in his pockets, and he looked down and kicked at the sidewalk when he spoke.

"That one," Grace said.

"Who?"

"The one with the brown hair and the gorgeous eyes."

Jada nodded. "Okay. Wait here."

"Jada, *don't you dare*—"

But before Grace could finish the sentence, Jada was halfway across the street. Grace watched in horror as Jada approached the man, talked to him for a moment, then turned and pointed to her. The man looked over at her and smiled, and Grace instinctively smiled back—but when he started across the street toward her, Grace turned and ran.

She ran four blocks before she stopped, panting, almost in tears from embarrassment and rage. It took five minutes for Jada to catch up with her.

"Hey! Where did you go?"

Grace turned on her. "Don't you *ever* do that again!"

"Do what? I was just trying to set you up."

"I don't want to be set up, okay?"

"I thought you liked him."

"I said I like guys *like* him—that's different. I mean, look at him—he's old enough to be my dad!" The instant she said the word, the thought occurred to her that the young man looked very much like her dad, with his wavy hair and beautiful eyes. He even carried himself the same way. Maybe that's what she liked about him; maybe that's why she picked him out from the others. The thought made Grace feel deeply sad and suddenly out of place.

"Okay," Jada said. "My bad. Let's forget the guys for a while—we'll just have fun by ourselves, okay?"

Grace nodded gratefully.

Jada looked around; they were standing in front of the window of a crowded bar. "That's what we need," she said.

"Jada, we can't go in there—they'll card us, and we don't have IDs."

"I do," Jada said. "All the kids in New York have fake IDs. That's how we get into the clubs."

"Let me see."

Jada opened her wallet. She took out a card and handed it to Grace.

"This is a New York driver's license," Grace said.

"Looks real, doesn't it?"

"According to this, you're twenty-two!"

Jada held out both arms. "Do I look it?"

Grace cocked her head. "You know, sometimes you do."

"Wait here—I'll get us something to drink." And with that she turned and vanished into the building, leaving Grace alone on the sidewalk.

Grace stared through the window after her, doing her best to track Jada's silhouette through the throng inside—but Jada's shadow quickly merged with the others and disappeared. Grace suddenly realized that a group of young men were smiling back at her from a table on the other side of the glass; she quickly turned away from the window and walked to the curb.

It seemed to be taking forever for Jada to return. She folded her arms across her chest and looked around the street. It slowly began to dawn on Grace that virtually everyone else on the street was in groups of three, or four, or more. She seemed to be the only one standing by herself, and it made her feel glaringly conspicuous. She had just begun to refasten the buttons of her blouse when she heard a man's voice behind her.

"Hey there."

Grace turned to find three men standing and grinning down at her. She recognized their faces—they were the ones who were behind the window a few moments ago.

"Hi," Grace said and turned away again.

One of the men circled around and stood in front of her. Grace tried not to look at him, but she could see his halting walk—he was obviously drunk.

"Saw you smiling at me," he said.

"I wasn't smiling at you. I was looking for a friend."

"Well, I'm looking for a friend too. How 'bout you? Will you be my friend?"

Grace didn't answer.

"C'mon, you were so friendly a minute ago. You look friendly. You dress friendly."

"Leave me alone," Grace said. She thought about running, but the men seemed to surround her. She could hear the two behind her; they were so close she could smell their breath.

"Why don't you come inside with us and have a drink?"

"Because I don't have an ID."

"They won't ask if you're with us," the man said, slipping his arm around her shoulders. "C'mon."

Grace planted her feet and resisted. "I really don't want to. Please."

The man began to pull. "C'mon. Be friendly."

They heard the sound of breaking glass behind them, and the entire group turned and looked. There stood Jada, holding one beer bottle in her left hand and the jagged neck of another in her right. On the sidewalk was a foaming puddle filled with broken shards of amber glass.

"She said she doesn't want to."

One of the men looked at the broken bottle in Jada's hand and let out a snort. "Whaddya gonna do with that?"

"That's up to you, pinhead."

"Just tryin' to be friendly," he said.

"You tried and it didn't work. Now get lost."

The second man wasn't as easily cowed. "I could take you easy," he said.

"Not as easy as you think. I swear I'll punch a hole in your gut first."

No one moved.

Jada took a step closer. "Tell you what, I'll make you guys a deal: I got two bottles here. You can take this one and go," she said, extending the bottle that was still intact, "or you can take *this* one—and you won't go anywhere for a long, long time. Now—who's thirsty?"

The three men slowly came to life. The closest to Jada snatched the full bottle from her hand, and they slowly moved off down the sidewalk, growling and grumbling as they went.

Grace ran to Jada and threw her arms around her neck.

"You okay?" Jada asked.

"I'm okay now," Grace said. "For a minute I thought—"

"Forget it," Jada said. "No need to go there."

Grace pulled away and looked at her. "You know, sometimes you do seem twenty-two."

"Sometimes I feel like I'm forty-two," Jada said. She brushed the hair back from Grace's forehead. "Never let a man take advantage, Grace. Never."

"Sometimes that's not so easy."

"No," she said. "Sometimes it's not."

CHAPTER 30

There it is," Cale said, pointing to a billboard half a mile ahead protruding up from an asphalt parking lot like a flag on a mailbox. 'Central Carolina Bank'—you see it?"

"Got it," Pug said. He steered the car off the highway and onto a smaller access road, turning into the parking lot of a Carolina Sofa Factory outlet. He pulled directly under the billboard and stopped the engine.

The two men got out and stared up at the fourteen-by-forty-eight-foot panel. A single galvanized pole the size of a tree trunk supported the structure from the left; the billboard itself projected precariously to the right, giving it the look of a meat cleaver ready to fall. A series of flood lamps extended out from the bottom of the panel like a row of fingers, curling up at the tips to cast their light on the billboard's face.

"Think this is the one?" Pug asked.

"I can't tell yet." Cale looked down at the grainy print again, a single-frame photo captured and printed from the video of Grace's "suicide." The print showed the window and the corner of the billboard in the distance, but no other visual clues were observable in the window—no buildings, trees, or anything else that might place the billboard in a specific location. Only the

212

upper right-hand corner of the billboard was visible, just enough to allow
Cale to recognize the client company. Other than that single corner, there
was nothing in the window but Carolina blue.

Cale stepped out from under the billboard and looked back across the highway. It was an older, commercial section of town that had been effectively vivi-
sected by the construction of the highway a few years back. Nothing remained
now but a handful of aging one- and two-story business buildings scattered
along the highway like shoe boxes on a closet floor. It was not a residential
neighborhood; the billboard location had been selected by McAfee & Nunn
purely on the basis of its Daily Effective Circulation, the estimated number of
potential bank patrons driving past every day.

"This can't be it," Cale said. "There are no tall buildings in the line of sight.
This can't be the billboard in the background."

It was Cale's idea to call McAfee & Nunn and request a Location List, a
geographical listing of every Central Carolina Bank billboard in the greater
Charlotte area. Since the upper corner of the billboard appeared in the lower
portion of the window, it seemed logical to the two men that the window
must be in an elevated location—perhaps an upper-floor apartment. That
was Pug's job: to produce a list of Charlotte apartment complexes. By cross-
checking the two lists, they had assembled an inventory of possible locations
where the video might have been recorded—and where some clue to Grace's
whereabouts might still be found.

The plan had a real chance of success, and both men felt hopeful when
they first began, but it was now almost noon and they had visited every billboard on their list without success. Now they were checking even the most
isolated billboards, hoping to stumble upon a tall building or a house on
some adjacent hill—but there were no likely structures in sight.

The two men climbed back into the car again. The front seat was littered
with paper: computer printouts, phone books, notepads, and road maps of
Charlotte covered the floor in half-folded heaps. Cale put his head back and
closed his eyes for a moment. He was completely exhausted, and his mind
buzzed like an overloaded electrical box. He had managed to grab two hours

of fitful sleep in the morning while waiting for the first of his colleagues to arrive at McAfee & Nunn, and he hadn't slept at all the night before. His mind was still alert, though, thanks to generous doses of caffeine. They had made so many stops at Starbucks and Dunkin' Donuts that his urine smelled like coffee.

He opened his eyes and looked over at Pug. "This should have worked. What are we missing?"

"We could be working from a false assumption."

"What's that?"

"That the room is here in Charlotte. There must be billboards like this one all over the state—the video could have been shot anywhere."

"I don't think so," Cale asked. "Grace doesn't drive yet, remember? That means somebody had to transport her, and I don't think the place they'd pick would be very far away. I mean, why bother? It's too much trouble."

Cale sat silently for a few moments, continuing that line of thought. Then he turned to Pug again and asked, "Where'd you get that list of apartments?"

"From the phone book, mostly. Why?"

"Grace doesn't drive yet."

"Yeah, you said that."

"We're looking in the wrong place, Pug. When Grace left yesterday she was on foot—she probably didn't go very far before she met up with somebody. Our house is in the newest section of Charlotte, and that phone book you used could already be a year old. There could be an apartment building right down the street and it wouldn't even be listed yet."

Cale handed Pug a road map and picked up the list of billboard locations again. "I'll read you some addresses—you find them on the map. Find me the one that's closest to my house. How about Cleveland Drive?"

Pug found the street in the index and located the appropriate map grid. "Opposite side of town," he said.

"Okay. How about Orange Knoll Avenue?"

They repeated the process several times without success. Then Cale said, "What about Branchwater Trail?"

Pug ran his finger across the map and said, "Bingo. It's just down the street from you—couldn't be more than half a mile away."

Pug started the car and they headed toward home.

Twenty minutes later they pulled over under yet another billboard for Central Carolina Bank, and before they even got out of the car, they spotted it. Just two blocks to the east was a three-story apartment complex with a banner stretched across the parking lot that read, "Now Renting."

Cale got out and looked. Sure enough, the building's west wall offered an uninterrupted view of the billboard. He turned and looked at the billboard; it was the tallest object anywhere in sight, and there was nothing behind it but empty sky.

"That's got to be the place," Cale said.

"Great," Pug said. "Take your pick."

Cale looked at the apartment building again. The wall that faced the billboard covered half a city block. There were at least forty second- and third-floor units with windows facing in their direction; the video could have been shot from any one of them.

"Any suggestions?" Pug asked.

"I suppose we could call the detective."

"We could. He'd probably get a tenant list and start going door-to-door—if he believed us at all. In the meantime, our boy would spot the police cruisers in the parking lot and head for the hills. He'd be long gone before they got halfway through the building."

"You got any better ideas?"

"As a matter of fact, I do."

Pug went to the trunk of his car and opened it. He returned a moment later with a simple deck of cards. He removed the cards from the box, fanned the deck, and said, "Pick a card—any card."

Cale pulled a card from the deck and looked at it.

"Ace of spades," Pug predicted.

"Astonishing. So?"

Pug turned the deck over; every card in the deck was an ace of spades. "Remember these, Lieutenant?"

"The Death Card," Cale said. "Where'd you get those?"

"Had 'em since Vietnam. They're collector's items now."

"They told us about these in my PsyOps course back at Fort Bragg. Our soldiers used to leave them on the bodies of dead Vietcong to let people know the Americans had been there."

"Used to drop them on the trails too. It was supposed to scare the crap out of the VC, but it didn't. Turns out the Vietnamese had no idea what the ace of spades was supposed to mean. Our guys loved the idea, though. Used to order them in bulk from the U.S. Playing Card Company—whole decks like this one, with nothing but the ace of spades."

"So what's the point?"

"The point is, you heard about the Death Card in a basic PsyOps course. You know what it means, and I know what it means—so does anybody who knows much about PsyOps. Hashim knows, too, because I'm the one who taught him—and it's a good bet he's the only guy in that apartment building who does."

CHAPTER 31

Cale pulled into the parking lot of Huntersville Apartments and slowly circled until he spotted Pug's car; it was parked inconspicuously a few rows back from the building. He parked his own car even farther away, and once he was satisfied that no one was looking, he quickly walked to Pug's car and slid in on the passenger side.

"What kept you?" Pug asked, slumping low behind the steering wheel.

"I wanted to check for messages," Cale said. "I was hoping for something from Grace: a voice mail, an e-mail—anything. No luck."

"Did you check in with the Charlotte PD?"

"Yeah. Nothing yet."

"There's a surprise."

Cale stared through the windshield at the back of the building. The second and third floors were finished in beveled siding painted a buttery yellow, and the windows overlooking the parking lot were parenthetically marked with black louvered shutters in an unsuccessful attempt to give the boxlike structure a homier appearance. The ground-floor wall was a seamless facade of cinder block, broken only by two rectangular cutouts where stairways ascended from the parking lot into the building above. Between the two stairways was a long row of brass-finished mailboxes; that's where the two men focused their attention.

"Did you do the cards?" Cale asked.

"Put one in every box. There is a ventilation slit in each one; I just slid 'em in."

"Are you sure about this?"

"You got any better ideas?"

"Can't say as I do."

"There's a PsyOps story about Vietnam," Pug said. "When we wanted to clear out an area of jungle, first we'd fly over and drop Death Cards everywhere—then we'd follow up with napalm. Death Cards, then napalm; Death Cards, then napalm; over and over again. The story goes that after a while all we had to do was drop the cards and all the VC would hightail it for home, just like Pavlov's dog."

"Is that true?"

"No—but it makes a good story."

"Great."

"The principle still applies. Wait and see."

"You know, this could backfire on us."

"Look," Pug said. "That video was shot in one of these apartments, and it's a good bet that apartment belongs to Hashim. But we don't know which apartment it is, so we can't just knock on the door. If we can't go in, then we've got to make him come out. We've got to flush the bird."

"The problem is, once you flush the bird, the bird knows you're hunting him."

"Like I said—you got any better ideas?"

Thirty minutes later a white, red, and blue U.S. Mail delivery truck turned into the driveway and stopped in front of the mailboxes. The mailman turned a key in a lock at the top and the entire front swung down as a single unit, exposing the individual boxes like the cells of a honeycomb. He swung the canvas sack off his shoulder and began to distribute the building's letters, magazines, and packages with impressive efficiency. Ten minutes later he was

finished, and the truck roared off with two quick blasts of its horn as a signal to the tenants above.

"Things should start moving now," Pug said.

Cale squinted at the mailboxes. "I don't even know what this guy looks
like."

"Dark skin, thirty-five, black hair, mustache."

"You just described half the population of the planet. Can't we park a little
closer?"

"We can't take the chance. Hashim knows me, and he'd recognize your
face too—he's done his homework. We need to see him before he sees us."

Cale watched as figures began to appear as if by magic from the darkness
of the stairways and file to their mailboxes. The first to arrive was an old man,
a Caucasian; he removed his mail in a stack and returned to the stairway
without looking through it. Next came a young black woman; she removed
her mail piece by piece, examining each item carefully before reaching for the
next. Cale watched her remove the playing card and look it over. She flipped
it over and looked at the other side too; then she shrugged, added the card to
the growing stack in her left hand, and continued.

Now people began to come more rapidly—people of all ages and sizes and
ethnic groups. There were many with darker skin—some looked Hispanic,
some Indian, and some Cale couldn't distinguish. Some might be Arab; there
was just no way to know for sure, especially at such a distance.

"I can barely see their faces," Cale said.

"Never mind what he looks like—watch what he does."

"What if he's not the one who comes to the mailbox? What if he sends
somebody else—somebody who works for him?"

"Once the card gets back to him, it'll have the same effect. Don't just
watch the mailboxes—keep an eye on the stairways too."

Each tenant removed the ace of spades along with the rest of his or her
mail. Some looked at it quizzically and then tossed it aside; some returned it
to their mailbox as though they thought the delivery might be an error; some
simply took the card in stride as just one of the many strange advertisements

that arrived each day. But no one seemed taken aback; no one did a double take; no one's response seemed out of the ordinary in any way, and Cale wondered again if Pug's idea would work. If one of these men understood the meaning of the Death Card, he sure wasn't letting on.

"Nobody's taking the bait," Cale said.

"Give 'em time."

"This is a pretty cool character we're talking about; maybe he's not the kind to run. What if he sees the Death Card but doesn't respond? Then we've tipped him off, but we still won't know where he is."

"You're just full of worries, aren't you?"

"This is my daughter, Pug."

"Right. Sorry."

From his apartment on the third floor, Hashim heard the blast of the mail truck's horn. A few minutes later he stepped into the hallway, carefully locking the door and dead bolt behind him. Directly across the hall the apartment door was wide open. A friendly face leaned into the doorway and looked at him.

"Good afternoon," the Arab man said with a broad smile. "I believe the mail has arrived."

"Yes," Hashim replied, avoiding eye contact and starting down the hall.

"This is my day off," the man said. "Yours too?"

Hashim nodded but said nothing.

"My wife and I are still hoping you will join us for dinner!" the man called out as Hashim rounded the corner and started down the stairs. "Please bring your lovely daughter with you!"

At the bottom of the stairway, Hashim stepped out into the parking lot and turned to his left. A dozen other tenants were milling around the mailboxes; he waded through them without a word and inserted a brass key into his own box. As he opened it, he heard a woman's voice to his right speak two words.

"How odd."

Hashim glanced over—and then froze. The woman was holding a single playing card, frowning at it as she turned it from side to side.

It was the ace of spades.

He turned back to his own mailbox and took a step closer, shielding his face from the other tenants. He peered into the rectangular darkness at the small stack of paper awaiting him; he reached in with his right hand and began to sort through the pieces without removing any. The top item was a business-size envelope bearing the return address of his attorney. He curled up the corner with his thumb; underneath was a coupon-filled flyer for Papa John's Pizza. He lifted that one too.

Underneath was an ace of spades.

The air around him suddenly became electrified, and the hairs on his neck and back began to stiffen and tingle like thousands of tiny sensors. He strained to detect the sound of approaching footsteps but heard none. He imagined dozens of eyes trained on his back, and the tenants casually mingling around him seemed suddenly menacing. He imagined the point of a dagger plunging into his spine, and he almost jumped in response—but he forced himself to remain motionless, inhaling deeply through his nose and exhaling through his mouth, focusing his mind and reining in his irrational fears. He trained his ears on the voices of the other tenants.

"It has no address on it," someone said.

"Just a promotion," replied another.

"Maybe an ad for the new lottery," said a third.

He reached in and removed his own mail now. As casually as possible he flipped through each piece, pausing to examine both sides of the playing card just as he had seen the others do. It was not a facsimile; it was a genuine playing card with the trademark "Bicycle" printed across the top. And it was not just any playing card: it was the ace of spades—it was the Death Card. Everyone in the apartment complex had apparently received one—and Hashim knew there could be only one reason why.

He shrugged indifferently and continued sorting through his mail. Then he closed his box and slowly turned and strolled toward the stairway again—but when he reached the darkness of the stairs, he broke into a run.

Back in his apartment, Hashim edged up to the window that overlooked the parking lot and carefully pulled the drapes aside. He looked down, half expecting to see someone staring back up at him—but all he saw was row after row of vacant automobiles. The vehicles were all parked parallel to the building with their right sides facing him. He lifted his binoculars and began to examine each of them, beginning with those closest, looking through the glare of the passenger-side windows at the seats inside. But every automobile appeared to be empty—until the third row. There, in the passenger seat of a pearlescent-white BMW, he saw a form.

He focused the binoculars and looked again. He could make out nothing but a shadow—but then the shadow leaned closer to the window for an instant and he recognized the face: it was the face of Cale Caldwell.

Hashim lowered the binoculars and released the drapes. For several minutes he stood motionless, staring straight ahead as though he could somehow see through the curtains and down to the parking lot below. His mind raced; he tried to imagine what he had looked like standing at the mailbox. He tried to remember how long his face had been visible; he wondered if Caldwell had recognized him. He wondered if his attempt to feign nonchalance had been successful or if his involuntary reaction to the sight of the Death Card had given him away.

He pulled the drapes aside and looked again. The BMW was still there, and the shadow was still inside. Caldwell had not exited the vehicle; he had made no attempt to follow. Hashim listened, but he heard no sirens. He looked out at the street, but he saw no sign of the authorities. He wondered what Caldwell was planning . . .

Then he thought again about the Death Card, and he understood.

He sat down at the kitchen table and quickly scribbled a note.

CHAPTER 32

Cale's eyelids began to droop, and his blinking grew slower and more deliberate. He had watched people come and go from the stairways to the mailboxes and back again for more than an hour now, and they began to look like ants scurrying back and forth with tiny bits of bread. And just like ants, they all looked the same—the same size, the same shape, the same predictable motions. No one stood out; no one looked different. Cale was quickly losing the ability to distinguish shapes at all as exhaustion overtook him. He felt as if the car was slowly filling with warm water, and he desperately wanted to settle back and sink below the surface.

Cale shook his head and sat up a little straighter. He looked over at Pug, who was fighting off the same soporific seduction. Again and again Pug's chin slowly sagged to his chest and then bounced up again, giving him the appearance of a two-hundred-pound bobble head.

"Hey," Cale said, nudging his shoulder. "You still with us?"

"No problem," Pug said, scrubbing his face with both hands. "Could use some coffee, though—haven't pulled surveillance duty in a long time."

From the corner of his eye, Cale saw a shadowy form emerge from one of the stairways and race into the parking lot.

"Pug! Hashim—there he goes!"

Pug looked up and blinked to clear his eyes. "Where?"

"Ten o'clock, about thirty yards away! See him? He's in a big hurry!"

"That must be our boy," Pug said. "Watch him—we can't afford to lose him now. This only works once."

"He's getting into a car. Looks like a dark blue Corolla."

"I'm on him." Pug reached down and started his engine. He threw the stick into reverse, hit the gas, looked back over his right shoulder—and then slammed on the brakes. The car lurched to a stop inches from the side of a silver sedan parked directly behind him.

Pug jammed on the horn, then realized that the car had no driver. He twisted to his left and saw two young men standing in the parking lot just ahead of the sedan enjoying a casual conversation.

Pug and Cale both threw open their doors and rolled out.

"Hey!" Pug shouted. "You two!"

The two men stopped and looked over.

"Is this your car?"

"Who wants to know?"

"I said, 'Is this your car?'"

One of the men shook his head and whispered something to his friend.

"You're blocking us in! Move it!"

"In a minute. Take a chill pill, old man."

Cale looked across the parking lot; the blue Corolla was almost to the exit.

Pug took a step forward. "You move this car or I'll move it for you!"

At this, the two men turned and started toward Pug.

"We don't have time for this," Cale said. "Let's just take my car."

"You'd better go ahead," Pug said. "I'll make sure you get away. I'll follow as soon as I can—keep your cell phone on."

Cale dived onto the trunk of the silver sedan, rolled across, and hit the ground running.

"Hey!" one of the men shouted. "Get off my car!"

"That's the least of your worries," Cale shouted back.

He was into his own car in seconds. He stomped on the gas and screeched out of his parking space, leaving a two-foot gash and ripping the side-view mirror off the car beside him. He reached the exit a few seconds later, just in time to catch a glimpse of the Corolla speeding down the street to his left. When he reached the street himself, he glanced back at Pug. One of the men already lay motionless on the ground; Pug had the other one by the hair, slamming him facedown on the hood of his car.

He turned his attention to the Corolla now. Hashim was already three blocks ahead. Cale tried to close the distance between them, but the Corolla was moving fast and it was hard to pick up speed in this residential neighborhood. He approached an intersection and sped toward it, ignoring the stop sign. He saw the deep rain gutters that cut across the streets on all sides, marking off the intersection like a square on a quilt. He hoped his speed would be enough to let him jump the gutter, but it wasn't. He felt a jarring jolt and heard the sound of metal on metal as the shocks bottomed out and his gas tank slammed the pavement with a rasping thump.

Now the residential neighborhood ended and the houses gradually gave way to gas stations, used car lots, and strip malls—but the streets were still narrow and interrupted by intersections every few hundred yards, and Cale knew it would be impossible to catch up to Hashim on roads like this. He was greatly relieved when he saw the Corolla take the entrance ramp onto I-85. There was little difference between automobiles or drivers on the broken neighborhood roads, but on the freeway it was all about speed. Cale was sure he could catch the older Corolla on an open road.

The Corolla was headed south. Cale merged with the traffic, pulled out into the passing lane, and shoved the pedal to the floor. The car smoothly accelerated, and he began to dart in and out of traffic, keeping one eye on the blue Corolla a quarter mile ahead. The gap between the two cars began to close, and a few minutes later he pulled in tight behind the Corolla's bumper, his eyes locked on the back of Hashim's head.

Cale glanced down at his speedometer—both cars were doing close to ninety, and the other cars flashed by as if they were standing still. Hashim was driving wildly; more than once he almost overran the car in front of him, jerking the wheel at the last possible moment and swerving wide to pass. He seemed panicked, almost out of control, and Cale hoped he was the one responsible. He edged his car a little closer. *I'm right behind you, Hashim—let's see how you like it.*

Cale took out his cell phone and punched three buttons.

"Nine-one-one operator," a voice responded.

"My name is Cale Caldwell," he said. "I'm on I-85 headed south. I'm in pursuit of a blue Toyota Corolla, tag number KRR-8791. Did you get that?"

"Slow down, Mr. Caldwell," the operator said. "Try to describe your situation for me. First of all, are you in any danger?"

"Look, can you patch me through to the Charlotte Police?"

"I can, but first—"

"Then do it!" Cale shouted. Ahead of him, Hashim suddenly swerved to the left, exposing a slow-moving pickup truck overloaded with bedroom furniture and a mattress sticking up from the center like the fin of a shark. Cale dropped the phone and jerked the wheel to the right, barely missing the truck's rear bumper and forcing the car behind him to swerve off onto the shoulder of the road.

Cale glanced down; he saw the cell phone in the passenger floor well. He shifted his left foot onto the gas pedal and reached across with his right, dragging the phone back toward him with his toe. He checked the traffic carefully, then ducked down quickly and made a grab for it.

"Hello," he said, squeezing the phone tightly between his shoulder and ear. "Are you still there?"

"Charlotte Police," a male voice said. "Who am I talking to?"

"My name is Cale Caldwell," he repeated. "I spoke to one of your detectives just last night."

"What's up, Mr. Caldwell?"

"I'm on 85 South headed toward the city. I'm chasing a guy that I think might have kidnapped my daughter."

"Where are you exactly?"

"I just crossed North Graham. I think he might be headed for the airport."

"Can you describe his car for me?"

"Blue Toyota Corolla—I don't know the year. North Carolina plates, KRR-8791."

"KRR-8791," the man read back.

"That's it. What do you want me to do?"

"I want you to pull over, Mr. Caldwell—as soon as you can."

"Pull over? Why?"

"Because a high-speed chase is a dangerous business. Somebody's likely to get hurt, and it's likely to be you. If you cause an accident, you'll only slow us down. I've already forwarded the tag number and your location to the dispatcher; we'll have a cruiser there any minute. Please, Mr. Caldwell, pull over and let us do our job."

"I'm not pulling over until I see your cruiser," Cale said.

"What are you driving?"

"A silver Acura. I'll be easy to spot—I'm the only other car going ninety in a fifty-five."

"Mr. Caldwell, I'm asking you—"

"Gotta go," Cale said. "Tell your guys to hurry."

Cale straightened his neck and let the phone drop onto the seat beside him. Hashim was still dead ahead of him, and he showed no sign of slowing down. They were just north of the city now, and the traffic was getting thicker; their two cars weaved in and out like a pair of moths around a flame.

Cale knew the policeman was right: this was a dangerous business. It was only a matter of time until one of them made a mistake, and at ninety miles an hour, it wouldn't be pretty. *"Somebody's likely to get hurt,"* the cop told him, *"and it's likely to be you."* But the thought didn't bother him. If something had happened to Grace, he might just as well die now as later; he just prayed that he wouldn't take anyone with him.

To Cale's surprise, Hashim's car suddenly swerved to the right and took the I-77 South exit toward the heart of the city. Cale didn't understand; the airport was straight ahead, just off I-85. Why was Hashim heading into the city?

Did he have some other means of escape in mind? The roads would only get smaller and the traffic more congested—but maybe that was the idea. Maybe Hashim knew that he would never escape on the open freeway. Maybe his best chance of losing his pursuers was on the crowded city streets.

Cale fumbled for the phone and hit Redial.

"Nine-one-one operator."

"This is Cale Caldwell again. Put me through to the Charlotte PD."

A moment later he heard a familiar voice.

"Is that you, Mr. Caldwell? Where are you now?"

"I'm on 77 South heading into the city. Where are you guys?"

"There should be a cruiser right behind you. They saw you take the turnoff. You should hear the sirens any minute now."

Cale pulled the phone away and listened. Sure enough, he heard the rising wail of a siren in the distance.

"Hang on," Cale said, "the Corolla's slowing down again. He's turning—I think he's taking East Morehead, toward the stadium. Tell your people to hurry it up or we'll lose this guy."

"Don't worry, Mr. Caldwell, half of our units patrol the downtown area; he's driving right toward us. Now do us all a favor and slow down, okay?"

"Right," Cale said and hung up—but he had no intention of slowing down until that cruiser passed him and took over the pursuit.

A minute later it did just that. The police cruiser pulled up alongside Cale's Acura, and the officer riding shotgun glared at him, jabbing his finger at the side of the road and mouthing the words, "Pull Over."

Cale slowed down, but he didn't pull over. He let the cruiser slide in ahead of him, but he continued to follow not far behind. He followed Hashim and the police cruiser onto East Morehead, and he could see the flashing red lights of half a dozen police cars barricading the road just past the stadium under the shadow of the 277 overpass. Hashim's car slowed down now, but the cruiser behind him pulled up close and blasted its siren to keep him moving forward into the net. Hashim's car finally rolled to a stop about twenty yards short of the police line, and Cale pulled over to watch.

An officer on a loudspeaker instructed Hashim to step out of the car and keep both hands in view. There seemed to be no response. Now officers on all sides drew their weapons and began to close in.

Suddenly the driver's door flew open and an Arab man jumped out, frantically waving a piece of paper over his head.

"It's my wife!" he shouted. "She's been in an accident! I must get to the hospital at once!"

Hashim waited quietly on a street corner just a few blocks away from Huntersville Apartments. A taxicab approached and slowly pulled over to the curb in front of him. He opened the rear door and got in.

"Myrtle Beach," he said.

CHAPTER 33

Cale and Pug leaned back against the side of Cale's Acura. Neither man spoke. They waited side by side in silence, watching the two police cars that still remained behind, their signal lights flashing brightly in the shadow of the overpass. The roadblock had broken up the instant the police were convinced that "Hashim" was not Hashim at all. He was just a frantic and desperate husband trying to reach his wife at Carolina Medical just a few blocks down the road.

The instant Cale saw the man wave the paper and shout the message about his injured wife, he knew what had happened. He knew he had been duped, and he felt his stomach drop out from under him like a plunging elevator. Pug was right: Hashim understood the meaning of the Death Card, but he apparently understood a lot more than that—he also knew the reason for its use. Hashim knew that he was expected to run, and he knew that the only way to elude his pursuers was to give them someone else to chase instead. And Cale went for it like a hound after a bone, and now he felt stupid and ashamed.

Pug had arrived a few minutes after Cale called and gave him his location. Pug said nothing when he first arrived; there was nothing to say. Both men understood the gravity of their error, and they had no one to blame but themselves. Any excuse would have sounded cheap and childish, and right now any words of hope or encouragement would be an obvious lie. *"We can't afford to lose him,"* Pug had said back at the apartment. *"This only works once."* They had flushed the bird, and the bird was surely long gone by now. His own words came back to him: *"Once you flush the bird, the bird knows you're hunting him."* They had no way to know where Hashim would go next—and infinitely worse, they had no way to know what might happen to Grace.

Cale felt a wave of wrenching fear in his gut. He kicked himself for his recklessness and gullibility, and the last thing he needed was a slap on the hand from the authorities—but he knew he was going to get one anyway, so he bit his lip and waited while the detective slowly approached.

"Long time no see," the detective said. "Haven't seen you boys since— when was it? Oh yeah—last night. I can see why you two wanted to go ahead and stir things up: twelve hours is an awful long time to wait for the cops to get their butts in gear."

"We had an idea," Cale mumbled. "We thought it would help."

"That was real cute," the detective replied. "You pull this 'Death Card' stunt to make the bad guy run, and when he does you personally chase him halfway across town—only guess what? It's not the bad guy after all. It's just some poor sucker who thought his wife was dying."

"At least now you know there *is* a bad guy," Pug said.

"Thanks a lot. Now all I need to know is little things like, Where is he now? How do we find him? Does he know the whereabouts of your daughter? I sure hope you boys can help me out with those things, 'cause I have to tell you, I don't have a clue."

Cale stared silently at the detective's shoes. He knew this was a lecture and not a dialogue, and the less he said the sooner it would end. He wished that Pug would hold his tongue—but that was something Pug had never been good at, and it was a good bet he wasn't about to start now.

"We decided to let the poor guy go," the detective continued. "No sense adding insult to injury. I mean, somebody hands you a note that says your wife is hanging on by a thread—what would you do? You can't really blame him. But since he's not from around here, we explained to him how these things are supposed to work. We told him that here in America we've got these people called the *police*. They're hired by the city; they're professionals. And they're trained to do dangerous things—like drive ninety miles an hour without killing anybody. We told him next time, all he has to do is call us and we'll have a cruiser at his door within five minutes."

"We get the point," Cale grumbled.

"Well, see, that's because you boys are from around here. People around here understand that you're not supposed to take the law into your own hands. They know you're not allowed to drive ninety miles an hour, even if you think you're chasing a bad guy. 'Cause you know what, fellas? It might not be a bad guy after all."

"Do we have to stay after school?" Pug asked. "'Cause we got baseball practice."

The detective failed to see the humor. "A high-speed chase is considered *reckless endangerment*—that's a Class A misdemeanor. And putting those cards in those mailboxes was a federal offense."

"Gimme a break," Pug said.

"And worst of all, you interfered with an official police investigation."

"What investigation? If you guys were doing your job, we wouldn't have had to get involved."

"Pug, shut up," Cale said.

"No, let him talk. Go ahead, ace—tell me what my job is. I always like to learn from an expert."

"We told you about Hashim," Pug said. "You wouldn't believe us. It sounded like a big conspiracy theory to you, so you treated Gracie like just another problem kid. But Hashim is real—I know this guy—and he's behind all this. Gracie's gone, and we need to find her fast. We can't afford to sit around on our hands while you people check off items on your to-do list. Sorry, Detective, you guys are too slow."

"No, you guys are too fast—*way* too fast. You may not like it, pal, but there's a reason for the way we do things—it's called *procedure*. That's how we make sure nothing gets overlooked—that's how we avoid ninety-mile-an-hour chases where people can get killed. Maybe you think that's how things work because that's how they do it on TV—but in the real world, when we end up chasing somebody across town, it means somebody screwed up big-time."

"I couldn't let him get away," Cale said.

"Good for you. So where is he now?"

Cale didn't reply.

"I treated your daughter like just another problem kid because that's *procedure*. Odds are I would have found her just by talking to a few of her friends—and if it turned out you were right about this Hashim character, I would have found that out too. But no, you two were in a hurry—you wanted to play cops yourselves, only you don't know what you're doing. So the guy is probably long gone by now, and you just made my job a whole lot harder—and you may have endangered the life of your daughter in the process. Nice work, fellas. Let me see if I can get you a couple of badges."

Pug opened his mouth to reply, but before he could get the words out, Cale grabbed him by the forearm and squeezed.

"Are you arresting us?" Cale asked.

"I could."

"I know. Are you?"

The detective looked at both of them. "I don't see the point. Like I said, no sense adding insult to injury. This is *your* daughter we're talking about. If you screwed this whole thing up, you'll be sorry soon enough."

"Thank you," Cale replied. "Before you go, do you mind if I ask a couple of questions?"

"That depends."

"I'm assuming you questioned the man in the blue Corolla before you let him go. He must have seen Hashim."

"That's right. He said Hashim came up to him in a panic and handed him that note. Said it was from the apartment manager—said the manager gave it to him by mistake because he's a white guy and he can't tell Arabs apart. Apparently you can't either."

"Did you get a description?"

"A description—now why didn't I think of that?"

"Sorry," Cale said, keeping a lid on his temper and a grip on Pug's forearm. "Did he tell you anything else about Hashim?"

The detective shook his head. "Not a chance."

"Like you said—it's my daughter we're talking about here."

"I'll keep that in mind. Leave your number. I'll stay in touch."

Cale paused to let the tension ease. "How do you plan to proceed?"

"I plan to follow procedure, Mr. Caldwell. Now that we know where this Hashim lives—or lived, thanks to you—we'll get a court order to search his apartment. He probably left in a hurry; he might have taken the time to clean the place out, but maybe not. We'll see what we can find. We'll look for any indication of where he might have taken your daughter."

Cale stiffened. "Do you have some reason to think Grace is with him?"

"The guy in the Corolla says Hashim lived in the apartment right across the hall—with a teenage daughter. I asked for a description of the girl; the description matches your daughter, Mr. Caldwell. And that's your last question, right? 'Cause that's the last one I plan to answer. Go home, boys—I'll do my best to carry on without you. Next time you get a brilliant idea, run it by me first, okay?"

"Would you have tried the last one?" Pug asked.

The detective looked at him. "Why? Did it work for you?"

The detective turned and headed for his car, but not before giving Pug one last look of contempt. Halfway there, he turned back and looked at them again.

"So you boys are off the case, right?"

"We're off the case," Cale said.

"Good. Then we understand each other."

They waited until he was safely out of earshot.

"I don't like that guy," Pug said. "He's definitely off my Christmas list."

Cale turned and glared at him. "Can I tell you something?"

"I have a feeling you're going to anyway."

"I'm the Propaganda Officer—you're Intel. Persuasive appeals are my area of expertise—yours is supposed to be intelligence. So the next time we talk to anybody who has the power to throw us in jail, do us both a favor and *shut up*."

Pug looked annoyed but said nothing.

"Hashim was living with a teenage daughter," Cale said, "and it sounds like *my* daughter. But that makes no sense. Why would Grace hook up with Hashim? Why would she pretend to be his daughter?"

Pug looked at him. "Can I talk now?"

"Can I stop you?"

"Either that teenage daughter is Gracie or somebody who looks a lot like her. That Arab guy has never seen Gracie before—he wouldn't know the difference. Who knows, maybe all Caucasians look the same to him."

"We need to show the video to that Arab—we need to show him Grace's face and ask him if that's the girl he saw with Hashim."

"That's one of those brilliant ideas the detective was asking for," Pug said. "Why don't you run over and tell him about it? I'll bet he just bubbles over with enthusiasm."

Cale shook his head. "We'd never get within a mile of that Arab guy without the police knowing about it. Then they'd arrest us for sure."

They watched as the detective's car slowly rolled by and took the entrance ramp onto 77 North.

"What do you want to do now?" Pug asked.

"We've got to help find Hashim. We can't just sit here while the police run through all their 'procedures.'"

"You told the detective we were off the case."

"We're off *his* case, and I'm hoping he's off ours. Grace is with Hashim; that's all the more reason to help find him. If we've got anything to contribute, we need to do it—and fast."

"Any ideas?"

"The police are covering Hashim's apartment. Is there anything else we can check out? Is there anyplace we can look that the police won't think of?"

"Too bad Hashim didn't leave a forwarding number," Pug said.

Cale turned and looked at him. He took out his cell phone and dialed his attorney.

"Hi, this is Cale Caldwell. Got a minute?"

"I got your message about Animal Control picking up your dog," the attorney said. "Here's what we can do—"

"Never mind that," Cale said. "Have you made any headway with the guy's attorney? Any possibility of talking to his client directly?"

"Not a chance. Sorry."

"What's the victim's name? It must be listed on the formal complaint."

Cale could hear the shuffling of paper. "Here it is: *Robert Leonard.*"

"I thought so. It's an alias."

"What?"

"Did he give an address?"

"Just a P.O. box. Why?"

"No phone number?"

"Mr. Caldwell, I still advise you not to—"

"I want you to do something for me. I want you to call this guy's attorney and tell him I'll give him ten thousand dollars for his client's cell phone number."

There was a long pause on the other end of the line. "Mr. Caldwell, what are you doing?"

"I don't have time to explain. Tell him ten thousand dollars—and tell him I need the number *now.*"

"He'll never go for it."

"Why not? At this point, all he's getting is legal fees; if I make his client mad enough, he'll file a lawsuit, and then he'll get a percentage. What's he got to lose? This way he picks up a quick ten thousand bucks, and maybe more later."

"I still don't think he'll do it."

"It's not illegal, is it? All I'm doing is asking for a phone number. I could probably track it down myself if I had the time—but I don't."

"And it's worth ten thousand bucks to you?"

"Tell the attorney my offer is good for the next ten minutes—after that, I'll dig it up myself."

"Okay, if it means that much to you."

"I'll be waiting for your call." He closed the phone.

"You think it'll work?" Pug asked.

"If Hashim is on the run, the only way to reach him now is by cell phone— if he has one—and the only guy I can think of who might have his cell phone number is his attorney. It's worth a try."

"What if the attorney doesn't go for it?"

"I'll raise the price."

"Let's hope this guy's not a bloodsucker. What are you gonna do if you get the number?"

"I'm going to call Hashim."

"Just like that?"

"We're out of time, Pug, and I'm out of ideas."

"I know what the detective would say. He'd want to be the one who makes the call."

"He can't."

"Why not?"

"Because Hashim saw the Death Card, and now he knows somebody's after him—somebody with a PsyOps background. That's me, Pug. This is my town—he doesn't even know you're involved, remember? He doesn't know the cops are involved, either, but he will if the detective calls him. Right now it's just between me and him, and that's the way I want to leave it. No worries; no pressure; just a couple of guys working things out one-on-one."

The cell phone rang. Both men jumped, and Cale almost dropped it.

"This is Cale. Go ahead . . . Uh-huh . . . Yeah, I thought he would."

He jotted the number on the back of his left hand, quickly thanked the attorney, and hung up. He held out his left hand to Pug, and the two men stood staring at the number.

He opened his cell phone again and began to dial.

CHAPTER 34

ow much farther?" Hashim asked the driver.

"'Bout an hour to Myrtle Beach. Depends on traffic once we get there. Like I said, this is gonna run you a few bucks. Thought I'd better warn you."

"I understand."

"You might want to rent a car next time. Save you money in the long run—not that I don't appreciate the fare. Most of the calls I get are just airport runs, or little old ladies who need a ride to the Food Lion and back. Kinda nice to get out on the freeway once in a while—open 'er up, burn off the carbon, you know?"

The man's mindless chatter became an incomprehensible murmur in Hashim's mind, like the sound of a television from a distant room. Hashim was unable to focus on the man's words; his mind was occupied with more urgent matters.

"Where you from?" the driver asked. "We got folks from all over down here. Lots of retirees—people love to retire to North Carolina. We get lots of folks from Florida. Funny, you know? People from up north retire to Florida, but all the folks from Florida end up—"

"Please," Hashim interrupted. "I wish to think."

The driver shrugged and turned to the window. "It's your fare."

Hashim reached into his jacket pocket and removed the ace of spades. He studied it front and back, considering the full implications of its presence. He was astonished to find it in his mailbox, but even more astonished to find Cale Caldwell watching from a car in the apartment parking lot. The Death Card—only someone with a PsyOps background would recognize it, and he would only choose to use it on someone with similar knowledge. That meant Caldwell had discovered his identity—and he knew how.

Caldwell had traced him as far as the apartment building, but he apparently knew no more—thus the Death Card; thus the need for its use. It was an attempt to draw Hashim out of the building, to make him flee so that he could be followed and apprehended—and it almost worked. But he had sent another man in his place, giving him time to escape the apartment unnoticed. By now they had certainly cornered the man and had discovered the deception. By now the authorities were probably involved. By now they knew his identity and his address and were probably searching his apartment.

But Hashim was already halfway to Myrtle Beach, and it would take time for them to determine where he had gone. He had abandoned his car in the parking lot and had taken a taxi instead; he had arranged to be picked up four blocks from the apartment to conceal his point of origin. But they would soon find his car, and they would deduce that he was either on foot or had taken another means of transportation. They would eventually check with the taxi-cab dispatchers; they would eventually question the driver of this vehicle, who would recognize his description.

Hashim closed his eyes for a moment and allowed his thoughts to drift back in time. He thought again about the massacre that night at the Al Manaqish oil fields. He remembered the shock, the humiliation, the shame he felt upon discovering the bodies of his own men the following morning. He remembered how his shame gave way to anger in the months that followed—anger at how easily his men had been induced to lay down their arms and surrender.

But in Jordan, when Hashim undertook his study of behavioral psychology, he began to understand the frailty of the human psyche. Some speak of the will as a thing made of iron, but Hashim soon learned that the will is more like a spider's web—a delicate lacework of silken strands that allows the spider to remain precariously balanced in midair. The human will is inherently weak—just a tiny insect held aloft by a series of fragile support structures: a sense of dignity and value; a sense of place and purpose in the universe; hope for the future; someone to love and to be loved by in return. When a single strand of the spider's web is broken, the others might still support its weight. But if all break at once, the spider is lost.

The Americans understood this only too well. With their leaflets they told Hashim's men that their cause was hopeless; they said that their loved ones would not wait for them at home; they told them that they would not be honored as warriors, but pitied as cripples; they said that they would die meaningless deaths and lie buried in unmarked and forgotten graves. One by one they cut the silken strands until Hashim's men lost all will to resist and simply drifted away in the desert winds.

How quickly his men were willing to betray everything once dear to them: their wives, their families, their honor, even their country. They were uneducated and untrained, yes, but that was no excuse for their weakness of mind and will. At first Hashim felt nothing but contempt for them; truly they received only what they deserved.

He remembered the sting of the world's laughter and derision: eighty-seven thousand men lost without firing a single bullet! The shame was like a poison in his soul, and in the dark places of his heart, he wondered if the Iraqi people were somehow weaker, more cowardly than the rest of the world.

But now he understood that they were not different at all. Now he knew that any man can lose the will to fight, if only the right support structures are identified and taken away. A man on crutches can stand erect until his crutches are pulled from under him—then he falls to the earth, unable to rise again. But each man's crutches are different; what topples one man may not affect another at all. That is the art of psychological warfare—not to understand the mind, but to understand the mind of each individual enemy.

And Hashim understood the mind of Cale Caldwell.

After months of exhaustive research, he had pieced together a chronology of every significant event in Caldwell's life, dating back to his early childhood. By carefully sifting through these events, he had identified the common threads—the drives, the hungers, the motivational patterns that defined him as a human being. He knew every one of Caldwell's strengths, and he understood the corresponding weakness and vulnerability that accompanied each. A man of honor can be vain; a disciplined man can be unforgiving; a passionate man can be a fool. Caldwell was no different: He was faithful, and a faithful man can be crushed by betrayal. He was independent, and an independent man does not wait for others to act. He was responsible, and a responsible man blames no one but himself for failure.

Prior to marriage, Caldwell had no serious or long-term relationships and was never known to be promiscuous. From this Hashim understood that he was a romantic, reserving his heart for an idealized mate, and that he would feel the loss of that mate acutely. Since the death of his wife, Caldwell had not engaged in a single casual dalliance, indicating that his bond with his wife remained a powerful emotional force in his life. How fortuitous it was that Caldwell's wife had perished in an automobile accident; how much easier it made Hashim's task. How difficult it would have been to alienate such a fiercely loyal man from his wife; how much easier it was to simply poison her memory—and it would have precisely the same effect.

Caldwell was like an oak tree, possessing tremendous strength and resilience, but supported by only a handful of roots penetrating deep into the earth. With those roots intact the tree could withstand almost any external force; but cut those roots, and the tree's own weight could bring it crashing down. Hashim knew this from his own experience; when he was forced to flee in humiliation from Al Manaqish, he felt the roots of his own tree severed. He left behind friends, family, career—and a young woman he had hoped to one day marry. He had lost everything in a single night, and there was more than one occasion when he considered ending his life. But there was one root left that kept his tree still standing: he had an enemy, and revenge is a reason to live.

Hashim knew that after the death of Caldwell's wife, Caldwell's fierce loyalty would shift to his daughter. He would willingly dedicate the remainder of his life to her welfare. He would see it as a duty, as a debt he owed not only to his daughter but to the memory of his wife—which made failure unforgivable, because there would be no one to offer forgiveness. Hashim knew that all parents struggle with doubt and regret in raising their young, but parents have each other to pardon and encourage and console. Caldwell had no one. The responsibility was his alone, magnified by the idealized memory of his wife. To fail with his daughter was to fail at his one true mission. To fail with his daughter was to betray his wife.

But if Hashim could poison the memory of Caldwell's wife, he would remove her idealized memory. He would cut the invisible strand; then Caldwell's duty would be a duty to no one, like a man fighting for a country that no longer exists. He would still carry out his duty because duty does not easily release its debtors—but he would find no fulfillment in that duty. He would imagine no gratitude or pleasure from the spirit of his dear departed wife. And if he failed at even this hollow and meaningless duty, it would be the most bitter defeat of all—it would be to fail at life itself.

Hashim straightened the bandages on his still-throbbing hand. The pain was worth it; the removal of the dog was a brilliant bit of strategy, and he took particular satisfaction in it. He knew that the dog was a kind of nexus, a connection to the past and a common bond between father and daughter, and as such it had to be removed. But to cause Caldwell to surrender the animal in his daughter's presence—that was the stroke of genius.

Manipulating the daughter was the easy part, though he found the task distasteful. Hashim understood the tempestuous nature of the adolescent psyche, especially of the psyches of pampered and undisciplined Americans. He knew that adolescents are easily susceptible to depression and suicide. He knew that with the daughter's anger and grief, she would be fairly easy to maneuver, but only through the influence of an intermediary—only through someone her own age. Hashim knew that the daughter would resist the influence of all adults, because adults had failed her; her mother had failed her by dying. In the girl's irrational adolescent mind, she saw her mother's death as an act of betrayal, and now she would trust no one except a friend—and not just any friend: a wounded friend; a needy friend; someone as needy as herself.

That was the part he found most distasteful—involving the young prostitute from New York. Procuring her services was a necessity, no different from hiring a mercenary to serve the purposes of a military command. But sharing an apartment with her as though they were actually connected by blood— Hashim found the idea insulting and degrading. He found her very existence objectionable, a symptom of everything wrong with the West: the simmering lust, the limitless greed, the fatuous drive for instant self-gratification. Hashim felt tainted by her presence, like a worker in a chemical factory slowly being contaminated by his environment.

But it would all have been worth it when the plan succeeded—all the research, all the planning, even the polluting presence of the disgusting whore. By now Caldwell should have despised the memory of his wife; by now his dog had been seized and would soon be destroyed; by now the daughter had fled from the house and vanished without a trace. By now Caldwell had received his daughter's suicide video, and after a weekend of fruitless searching, he would conclude that his daughter was indeed dead—then all the final pieces would quickly fall in place.

But something had gone wrong.

He felt saddened that his original plan would now have to be altered. Caldwell now understood the nature of the psychological attack, so the deception was ruined. His wife's infidelity, his dog's false attack, his daughter's suicide—by now he knew it was all a ruse, and no further deception would be possible. What a shame—the plan had such a beautiful symmetry. It would have been truly satisfying to watch it play out like the workings of an intricate clock. But no matter; all that was required was a simple adjustment.

He took out his cell phone and a slip of paper with a number on it—Cale Caldwell's number.

But before he could dial it, his cell phone rang.

He checked the screen; he recognized the incoming number. He pushed

Send/Receive and pressed the phone against his ear. He said nothing at first; he simply listened, hoping for some ambient noise or background conversation that might provide a clue to the caller's whereabouts—but there was none.

Then he heard a voice say, "I want my daughter back."

"What a coincidence—I was just about to call you."

"I want my daughter back," Cale said again. "Tell me where she is."

The driver glanced over his shoulder. "I need to stop for gas," he called to the backseat. "It'll just take a few minutes. You can use the john if you want."

Hashim clapped his hand over the phone. "I wish to make an arrangement with you," he said to the driver. "At the end of our journey, I will pay you a gratuity of fifty dollars—if you will agree not to speak another word."

The driver shrugged and pulled off at the next exit.

Hashim uncovered the phone again. "Call me again in three minutes," he said and hung up.

At the truck stop Hashim exited the taxi and moved twenty yards away from both the gas pumps and the coffee shop, well out of earshot of any possible listeners. A few moments later his cell phone rang again.

"All right," Hashim said. "We can speak privately now."

"I want my daughter back."

"Your daughter is dead. Did you not receive her message?"

"The video was phony," Cale said. "My daughter is alive."

"Are you certain of that?"

"I want her back. Tell me where she is."

There was no reply.

"Look, just tell me what you want."

Again, no reply.

"I know this is about Desert Storm," Cale said. "I know what happened at Al Manaqish. I'm sorry."

"Half the men in my unit were destroyed in a single night. I was forced to leave my country—my family—my people. You're *sorry?*"

"It wasn't my fault."

"It was specifically your fault—just as your current misfortunes are mine. Tell me about the Death Card."

"What?"

"Only a man with your background would have thought of it."

"Please," Cale said, "just tell me if my daughter's all right."

"I have no wish to harm your daughter. I am not a murderer as you are."

"That was war."

"That word seems to justify everything to you Americans. Very well: My *war* is not yet concluded. We are still at war, you and I."

"Look—eighty-seven thousand men are still alive because of what I did."

"Alive without honor, without dignity—I consider that very much like death. And what about the men in my unit? Many are dead because of what you did."

"Just tell me what you want."

Hashim paused. "An exchange."

"Go on."

"Your daughter's life for my freedom. I will return your daughter to you; in exchange you will allow me to go free."

"Agreed. How do we make the exchange?"

"Your authorities will agree to this?"

"I can't guarantee what the police will do."

"Then you are not working in conjunction with the authorities. I thought not; you are too much of an individualist."

"I'm alone—this is just between you and me. The police don't even have this number."

"They will. The authorities will not be far behind you, and they will most certainly not agree to an exchange. We must hurry; if I am not allowed to go free, I will not allow your daughter to live."

"All I care about is my daughter's safety. Just tell me what you want me to do."

"Are you familiar with a city known as Myrtle Beach?"

"Myrtle Beach? Is that where Grace is?"

"That is where the exchange will take place. Do you know the area?"

"Yes."

"Then this is how we will proceed: you have exactly three hours to meet me in Myrtle Beach—exactly three hours."

"What if I can't make it in three hours?"

"Then your daughter will die."

"You said you're not a murderer!"

"I have no wish to be a murderer. And I will not become a murderer unless you make me one—as you made me one before."

"But what if my car breaks down? What if I get pulled over for speeding?"

"Then your daughter will die."

"Why the deadline? What's the rush?"

"I am not a fool. I am familiar with the manner in which these things are handled, and I do not wish to give your authorities time to become involved. This, as you said, is between you and me."

"I'm getting in my car now," Cale said. "I'll call you as soon as I get there."

"No—I will no longer respond to this cell phone. In exactly three hours I will call you and give you further instructions. If there is any delay, or if there is any sign of the authorities, your daughter will most certainly die."

"I'm starting now."

"There is one more thing: You possess a handgun—a service sidearm you retained from the War for Kuwaiti Liberation. Bring it with you, and be sure it is loaded."

"What handgun?"

"A Beretta 9mm. Would you like the serial number?"

"But I'd have to go all the way back to my house and—"

"Three hours—not a minute more. I wouldn't waste time arguing if I were you."

CHAPTER 35

Jada and Grace lay next to each other on plastic-webbed lounge chairs, staring up into the cloudless sky through sleek black Burberry shades. Beside them, a twenty-five-meter lap pool glistened like a blue sapphire in the afternoon sun. The water looked pristine and inviting, but the weather was still too cold for swimming and so the pool stood empty, just a preview of coming attractions in the summer months ahead.

The late spring sun, however, was perfect for sunbathing, and the sprawling pool deck was jammed with lounge chairs and beach towels stretched out on the concrete like candy-colored bedrolls. The deck was a quilt of human bodies covering every square foot of available space. Some lay faceup, some facedown; some read books and some sipped from foam-covered cans; some chatted with lounge mates while others snoozed and snored under the sleep-inducing sun.

Behind them, the Sunset Apartments towered twelve floors above the pool. The building was a simple rectangular prism, like a box stood on end. The wall that faced the pool was lined with row upon row of sliding glass doors, each exiting onto a six-by-eight-foot concrete slab surrounded by a black wrought-iron fence, making the building look like a zoo full of animal cages stacked in a twelve-story pile. But in this zoo the animals were doing the viewing; half of the patios held at least one figure staring down at the flesh-covered deck below. Some looked with only mild curiosity, but others made more intense scrutiny, searching through high-powered binoculars for the finest specimens of the human species. More than a few pairs were trained on Jada, who wore a revealing black two-piece. The bottom of her suit curved between her pelvic bones like a grin, exposing the top half of a blue-and-red rose tattoo on her right hip. The top of her suit was equally minimal, just an obligatory nod to the requirements of the law.

Opposite the building and across the deck was a series of green-and-white canvas cabanas lined up like a row of bedouin tents, giving the pool area the look of a Middle Eastern shopping bazaar. Behind the cabanas was a thin buffer of natural beach landscape, followed by the beach itself and the ocean beyond. The beach was sparsely populated; most of the regular sand-and-surf worshipers had retreated to the deck area, where the pool and concrete reflected the rays of the sun while the building and cabanas blocked the chilly spring breeze.

Jada grinned. "Is this the life or what?"

"Yeah, this is great." Grace rolled her head to the right and looked at Jada's hip. "I didn't know you had a tattoo."

"Got a couple. I'd show you the other one, but they'd arrest me."

"You never told me."

"There's a lot you don't know about me."

"Like what?"

"Lots of things."

"Tell me something—something I don't know about you yet."

"I don't know. I can't think of anything right now."

"Do you have a real sister?"

Jada turned away. "Where'd you get that suit, anyway?"

Grace looked down at herself; she wore a solid-color one-piece racing suit. "Why? What's wrong with it?"

"Nothing. It's fine."

"Well, I used to be on a swim team."

"I used to be a cheerleader, but I don't walk around in a pleated skirt any-more. You got the right stuff, Grace—you just need to show it off once in a while."

Grace hooked one finger under the right leg cut and tugged it down a little lower over her thigh. "I kind of like this suit."

"Your dad picked it out, didn't he?"

"No. My mom did."

Jada didn't respond.

Instead, she said, "Watch this." She folded her arms behind her head and smiled up at the side of the building. Instantly, a dozen pairs of binoculars turned her way.

"That's what I'm talking about," she said. "I can make a man look at me anytime I want. Look at 'em all up there—the morons."

"I don't want that kind of attention," Grace said.

"I like attention. I like to set 'em on fire and watch 'em burn."

"I don't want them looking at me like that. That's how they were looking at me last night."

"That's different," Jada said. "They decide when to look, but you decide when they touch. You got to learn to take care of yourself, Grace. You can't let men push you around."

"Did you ever have a boyfriend?" Grace asked.

"Sure, lots of 'em."

"I mean a serious boyfriend."

Jada cupped her right hand and made a little wave at the balconies. "Hi, morons—look at me."

Grace grabbed her arm and pulled it down. "Cut it out. They're looking at me too."

"They should. I'm trying to help you out here."

"I don't need any help."

"Sure you do. You think anybody's gonna look at you in a suit like that? That suit says, 'C'mon, I'll race you.' *This* suit says, 'C'mon.'"

"I want a suit that says, 'Go away and leave me alone.'"

"Congratulations—you found it."

The two girls laughed.

Jada wiggled her eyebrows at Grace. "C'mon, do it—give 'em a wave."

"No way."

"Just try it and see how it feels. Raise your little hand and make a little wave."

"Forget it. I'm not doing that."

"If you don't, I'll stand up and point at you. I'll yell and I'll point until everybody in the whole building looks at you. I swear I will."

"Jada, cut it out."

"Just try it. One little wave. C'mon, you can do it."

Grace finally rolled her eyes, raised her hand just to her shoulder, and made a quick wave. Half the binoculars swung her way.

Jada's smile disappeared.

Just then a cell phone rang, and people all around began to search through their pockets and handbags and shoes. But the ring was coming from Jada's purse; she opened it, took out the cell phone, and pushed a button.

"Yeah?"

"Where are you now?" Hashim asked.

Jada covered the phone and looked at Grace. "It's my dad. I'd better take this in private. If he hears all these people, he might know where we are."

Jada got up from the lounge chair and worked her way through the sea of people to the opposite edge of the deck. "Go ahead. I can talk now."

"Are you at the apartment building?"

"That's what you asked for."

"Are you in the apartment now?"

"We're down at the pool. How picky can you get?"

"I have further instructions for you."

Jada groaned. "I'm waiting."

"I want you to take the girl up to the apartment. I want you to hold her there until I arrive. Do you understand?"

Jada hesitated. "Wait a minute—you didn't say anything about you joining us here. You said I was supposed to keep her here until you called, then bring her home again."

"The situation has changed."

"Changed how?"

"That's none of your concern."

"Well, I'm making it my concern. It's a small apartment, and I don't like the idea of Daddy dropping by for an overnight stay. Do *you* understand?"

Hashim's frustration was obvious on the other end of the line. "You are to obey my instructions!"

"Then you'd better explain your instructions, 'cause I don't like the sound of them."

There was a long pause. "I am less than an hour from Myrtle Beach. I am bringing with me fifty thousand dollars in American currency—the balance of your payment. When I arrive, if you have followed my instructions—if you deliver the girl to me—I will pay you the money and your services will be completed. You will be free to go. But if you refuse to follow my instructions, I will tell the driver right now to take me to the nearest airport. I will leave you with the girl, and I will allow you to explain things to the authorities. I do not believe that would go well for someone with your background. I am familiar with your criminal record, as I'm quite certain the authorities are."

Jada bit her lip.

"Remember," Hashim added, "the girl has never seen me before, but she can describe you in great detail."

"I should leave right now," Jada grumbled.

"Without your fifty thousand dollars—money you have worked so hard to earn. This is not a gratuity; this is a debt you are owed. But, of course, if you no longer need the money . . ."

"I can go after you get here? I'm finished? That's it?"

"Within the hour you can be on your way, and you will never see or hear from me again."

"That suits me just fine," Jada said. "What happens to the girl?"

"That's none of your business."

"I want to know what happens to the girl."

"The less you know the better. Should the authorities ever question you, you will have no knowledge of the girl's fate. You will not be culpable."

"I want a guarantee of her safety."

Hashim's voice trembled with rage. "You parasite—how many lives have you ruined already, and for far less money? Why does one more life matter to you? Do as I say and leave with fifty thousand dollars, or defy me and go to prison. You decide!"

There was a long silence between them.

"And just how am I supposed to 'hold' her?" Jada asked.

"That's none of *my* concern. Must I decide everything for you? I don't care how you do it! Restrain her if you must—just be sure she is there when I arrive."

Jada heard a click on the other end of the line.

She looked across the deck at Grace. In Jada's absence she had covered herself with a beach towel, causing the binoculars to slowly drift away from her like flies from an empty table. Grace suddenly looked so young—more like a little girl than a young woman, and suddenly the ogling eyes that lined the balconies made Jada angry.

She began to work her way back toward Grace, thinking about her new instructions. Hashim would be there in less than an hour, and when he arrived Jada was supposed to just take her money and leave—leave her alone with Hashim, and who knew what might happen to her then.

"How many lives have you ruined already?" Hashim asked. But Jada wasn't the one trying to ruin a life here. She never wanted to hurt Grace; she told him so from the beginning. He was the one who was trying to drive some kind of wedge between Grace and her dad, and Jada only went along with it because she needed the money and because that's the kind of world we live in—a place where people get hurt, and you'd just better learn to deal with it. If Grace got her feelings hurt so Jada could make a quick fifty thou, so what? It happened to everybody sooner or later. She'd get over it; everybody does.

But now it was something more than hurt feelings. Now Hashim was going to put his hands on her, and the thought caused a strange queasiness in Jada's stomach—something she hadn't felt in years. She remembered what she said to Grace: *"They decide when to look, but you decide when they touch."* What a lie! How many men had touched her when she didn't want them to? *"You can't let men push you around,"* she told Grace, but men had abused her all her life. *That was my own fault,* she told herself. *I let them do it, and it's no good whining about it now.*

But she didn't have to let it happen to Grace.

In an hour she could leave with fifty thousand dollars, enough money to keep her off the streets for a year—maybe get her out of the business altogether. That was the original idea—that was what she signed up for. If she did leave, something might happen to Grace or it might not. Hashim didn't say he would hurt the girl; he just said he wouldn't make a promise. It wasn't her business, he said, and he was right—it wasn't. It never was.

And if she didn't deliver the girl, Hashim said he would leave her holding the bag, and she had no doubt he would do it. He was that kind of weasel; he didn't have a feeling bone in his body. Then the cops would blame everything on her, and even if she could convince them it was all Hashim's idea, what good would that do her? She was still a part of it and she would end up back in prison—for a long, long time.

Jada sank back down on her lounge chair, lost in thought.

"What did your dad want?" Grace asked.

"What? Oh, nothing. He just calls to check up on me."

"Was that your stepdad or your real dad?"

"I never talk to my real dad."

"Why not?"

"We didn't exactly get along. He used to beat me up. He used to—hurt me."

"I'm sorry," Grace said. "That's terrible."

Jada shrugged. "You get over it."

"I never would."

Jada turned and looked at her.

"Grace," she said, "would you come upstairs with me for a minute? I've got something I want you to help me with."

CHAPTER 36

Cale glanced at his watch and felt a knot twisting tighter in his stomach. Three hours to get to Myrtle Beach—was it even possible? The traditional route was to take I-77 straight south to Columbia, then make a ninety-degree turn onto I-20 and head due east to the coast. It was a huge dogleg, and people were willing to endure the extra miles because of the well-maintained interstates—but Cale didn't have time for sightseeing today. To make Myrtle Beach in three hours, he'd have to take the diagonal, making his way over narrow two-lane back roads through tiny coastal Piedmont towns with names like Polkton and Bennetsville and Dillon.

Besides, the big roads were more likely to be patrolled. He made it back to his house in record time, praying all the way that no cop would spot him streaking by on I-85 and pull him over for speeding. He had driven ninety miles an hour once today, and the cops didn't like it even when he was chasing a suspected kidnapper; how was he supposed to explain it when he was chasing no one at all? They'd arrest him for sure, and that was something Grace couldn't afford.

He looked down at the 9mm Beretta on the seat beside him—an even bigger reason not to get stopped. How would he explain that to the police? *I'm just taking it out for a drive, Officer. No, sir, I'm not sure what I'm going to do with it—I was just told to bring it along.* That would go over big.

How did Hashim know about the handgun? And why did he want him to bring it with him? Maybe he wanted a weapon to take with him when he fled. Maybe he wanted Cale to know for certain that he was armed so he wouldn't be tempted to follow. That's what Cale wanted to believe—but he didn't.

The gun gave Cale a very bad feeling, but it was only one of a dozen reasons to be worried right now. Hashim was still in complete control—that's what bothered him most. When Hashim saw the Death Card, he must have known his scheme was ruined. But even then he didn't panic; he kept his head and thought of a way to escape. Now he was making the calls again, and all Cale could do was follow his instructions and see what happened next.

And when Cale called him on his cell phone, why did Hashim say, "I was just about to call you"? Was that just a bluff? Was it just a way of concealing his surprise? He wanted to think so, but he wasn't so sure. Cale shook his head. Hashim was supposed to be escaping, and Cale was supposed to be in pursuit—but he couldn't help feeling like a greyhound chasing a phony rabbit around a track.

One thing was certain: when Cale made contact again, he gave Hashim a second chance. Hashim offered him an exchange: his freedom for Grace's life. But Hashim already had his freedom. He had already successfully escaped, and no one knew where he was going. Why would he make that offer? Cale knew the answer: it wasn't freedom Hashim was seeking; it was another shot at Cale. Cale knew it, and he was willing to give Hashim that shot—as long as it gave him a chance to get Grace back.

Cale had no way to anticipate what Hashim would do next; he could only consider what he *might* do by constructing a mental profile of the man. "*I was forced to leave my country—my family—my people,*" he said. That meant he was acting independently, without accountability and without restraint—exactly the kind of terrorist the authorities feared most. But he was not a religious fanatic, so he would not be so willing to take his own life. He spoke of escape. His driving motivation was the desire for revenge, and Cale knew that could be an advantage. Revenge involves payback, and payback requires a certain equivalence—doing to others exactly what they've done to you. That was the logic behind Hashim's entire plan: to do to Cale what Cale had done to him. He was probably telling the truth about Grace; he probably didn't want to hurt her, except as a way of hurting Cale—and that could provide an opportunity.

Cale could see one other advantage: Hashim was one man against many. Cale had the authorities on his side; Cale had the real power, and the only way Hashim could compensate for that was to keep Cale constantly off balance. That's why Hashim would no longer answer his cell phone; that's why he insisted on calling Cale instead: to keep Cale waiting, to keep him responding instead of taking the initiative. It was an old psychological principle: the man giving orders is the man in charge, regardless of his size or strength. Cale had to look for some way to give a few orders of his own.

He swerved to the left and passed the car in front of him as if it were parked. He didn't bother to check his speedometer; his speed didn't matter as long as he wasn't stopped. He drove as fast as the road would allow, peering as far ahead as he could for slow-moving traffic or lumbering farm vehicles. At intersections he braked only slightly, keeping his right hand ready on the horn, and the moment he was clear he pushed the pedal to the floor again. The road was narrow, but at least it was a flat, straight shot toward the coast. There was almost no shoulder on the road, and just a few yards away were perfectly vertical walls of dense lodgepole pines poking up through white sugar sand. It was like driving down the center of a hairbrush, Cale thought.

He glanced in the rearview mirror. Pug's white BMW was right behind him, just a few car lengths off his bumper. They agreed that Pug would come along, but it was too risky to take a chance on being seen together in the same vehicle. They had no way to know where Hashim might be waiting and watching. *"If there is any sign of the authorities, your daughter will die,"* Hashim told him. Pug wasn't the authorities, but Cale still couldn't take the chance. They agreed that Pug would follow close behind. As they approached Myrtle Beach, Pug would increase the distance between their cars and follow Cale to whatever final destination Hashim decided.

After that, they had no plan—they couldn't. All they could do was wait for Hashim's next instructions and improvise from there. But regardless of the situation, two of them were better than one—especially when one of them was invisible. Hashim still didn't know that Pug was involved, and that was a definite advantage.

Cale checked his cell phone; the battery indicator showed half-empty. What if his phone went dead? What if he was too far from a cell tower and couldn't get a signal? Did his company even get service in Myrtle Beach? There were so many things that could go wrong, and any one of them could mean the end of Grace's life. He felt a sudden rush of panic; there was just too much room for error, and there was way too much at stake.

Cale's mind was accelerating as fast as his car: What if Hashim lost his number? What if he changed his mind? What if he decided to simply kill Grace and leave with a head start? He never said he wanted to kill Grace; he talked as if it was something he wanted to avoid. Cale was the one he was after, not his daughter. But it was naive to think that a man like him would leave without wrapping up every possible loose end—and Grace was a big loose end.

He thought again about calling the police. It wasn't too late; maybe he should still make the call. They had warned him once about taking the law into his own hands; if something went wrong this time, they would blame it all on him. But Cale didn't care; if something did go wrong, what difference did it make? Whether the cops liked it or not, this was his best chance of getting Grace back alive. Hashim knew how the authorities worked: he knew they would try to buy time to formulate a strategy and get their people into position. Hashim wasn't playing that game—that was the reason for the three-hour deadline. Cale didn't have a single extra minute to plan or plot or arrange, and that's exactly the way Hashim wanted it.

Besides, if he did call the police, all they would do is ask for Hashim's number and then tell him to pull over again—and that was something he just couldn't do. If something did go wrong, he didn't want to have to blame the police; he wanted it to be his own responsibility. He thought about that for a moment, and he wondered if that was exactly what Hashim expected him to do.

The cell phone rang and he jumped, swerving onto the narrow shoulder. He looked down at his watch. He still had an hour to go—it was way too soon for Hashim's call. He opened the phone and looked at the incoming number: it was Pug.

"Make it quick," Cale shouted into the phone. "My battery's dying."

"Great," Pug said. "We're gonna need that thing."

"What do you want?"

"If a cop car comes after us, don't slow down. I'll take care of him; I'll make him follow me. You just keep going—get onto another road, but just keep going. Understand?"

"Let's hope that doesn't happen."

"Yeah, let's hope. When Hashim calls, you call me. Let me know where he tells you to stop, and I'll be right behind you. If you can, keep me updated. Otherwise, I'll just follow on foot and watch."

"Got it. Hey, Pug."

"Yeah?"

"In case I don't get another chance—thanks."

"Stay focused, kid. Try to think like he does. Better yet: try to think like you did back at 4POG. Remember, this guy doesn't want Gracie—he wants you."

CHAPTER 37

Hashim paused at the apartment door and listened. He heard no sounds coming from inside, but he was still confident of what he would find when he entered. He would find the prostitute and the girl together, just as he had instructed.

After their last conversation, he had sensed that greed alone was no longer enough to motivate the prostitute to follow his instructions. There was a slight possibility that the creature had actually developed some sentiment for the girl and would forgo the remainder of her salary and flee. Most likely not—but it was possible, and that's why he thought it wise to add the extra incentive of self-preservation. Faced with the possibility of imprisonment, the woman would have no choice but to do as she was told; he knew she would gladly sacrifice the girl to save her own worthless skin.

He glanced both ways before turning the key in the lock. He opened the door just wide enough to slip inside, then closed it behind him and locked it again. There, in the center of the room, sat Grace—just as he predicted.

The harlot had done as instructed: she had restrained the girl to make sure she remained in the room. Grace sat in a wooden kitchen chair, bound hand and foot with nylon cords cut from the draperies. Her shoulders were arched, pulled back by her wrists bound together behind the chair. Each of her ankles was tied separately to one of the rungs. A gag was stuffed into her mouth, and she was blindfolded with a colorful silk scarf that draped down like a pennant across her face. At the sound of the door, Grace lifted her head in anticipation—but when there was no further sound except the closing of the door and the ominous clicking of the dead bolt, her head dropped forward again.

Hashim shook his head. *"Restrain her if you must,"* he'd told the woman, and that's exactly what she'd done—no more, no less. He marveled at her lack of ingenuity—but that, too, was to be expected. She was a simpleminded creature, after all, but at least she was capable of carrying out basic instructions.

"Where are you?" he called to the back rooms. "Get your payment and go."

There was no reply.

Hashim took a step forward and heard a crumpling sound. He looked down; under his left foot was a sheet of notebook paper bearing a hand-scrawled note. He picked it up and read:

Hashim,

   I'm out of here. I thought about what you said on the phone, that you might ditch me with the girl and call the cops just to cover your own tracks—and you're just the kind of jerk who would do it. I'm leaving the girl like you said, so I kept my end of the bargain and I'm catching the first bus back to New York. Keep the rest of the money—but you'd better forget you ever heard of me, 'cause if the cops do come after me, I'll tell them everything I know about you. I meant what I said about the girl. If you so much as touch her, I'll come looking for you. I know people, and I can find you wherever you try to hide. So don't think that you can—

Hashim crumpled the note and threw it away. He gave a satisfied nod; his simple threat had a much greater impact than he anticipated. The woman had overcome her greed after all but had still acted out of her instinct for self-preservation—or perhaps simple fear. It didn't matter; either way it was all the better for him. He had saved fifty thousand dollars and was finally free of her annoying presence. He gladly would have paid the money just to make her go away, but their final encounter surely would have been an unpleasant one. This way he didn't have to listen to her hypocritical rantings; this way her silly and idle threats could simply be wadded up and tossed aside.

He walked to the balcony, pulled back the curtain, and opened the sliding glass door. The sound of the wind and the ocean and the crowded poolside below rolled into the room like the surf. He stepped out onto the balcony and looked down. It was ironic: from eight floors up the sea of bodies sprawling this way and that reminded him of a battlefield. They were all sleeping, or reading, or sunbathing, but he could very easily imagine them all dead. Some lay facedown, and some lay on their backs with one arm awkwardly shielding their faces. Some were half-naked with articles of clothing and personal items strewn around them. Mouths gaped open; hands lay open-palmed; limbs draped limp and lifeless. All of them lay perfectly still, unburdened by the cares of this life. Yes, it took very little imagination, and for a moment Hashim indulged himself.

On the tiny balcony was a patio chair and a small round table topped with scalloped glass. He pulled the chair up close enough to the railing to provide a clear view of the deck below, but he kept back as close as possible to the concealing shadows of the apartment. He pulled the glass table up beside him; on it he set a pair of binoculars, a cell phone, and a .22-caliber pistol. It was the same pistol he had used to fake the girl's death—only this time the gun held real bullets, and the sound it made would not have to be dubbed in later.

He wondered if he would have to use the gun.

He looked at his watch; he would soon know.

CHAPTER 38

Cale was still a few miles out of town when his cell phone rang again.

"Caldwell. Go ahead."

"Are you in Myrtle Beach?" Hashim asked.

"I'm here," he lied. "Is my daughter all right?"

"Are you familiar with the Sunset Apartments?"

"No. You'll have to give me directions." In fact, he knew exactly where Sunset was located. It was one of the largest buildings on the strip, and its sprawling pool area was a favorite gathering point for high school students visiting the beach for the weekend. But feigning ignorance was to his advantage; it would take time for Hashim to give him directions, and more time for him to follow them—and more time is what Cale needed most.

"You said you are familiar with the area. Did you lie to me?"

"No, I didn't."

"Then you have ten minutes."

"Wait!" Cale shouted. "There's no way I can get there that fast! The traffic on the main drag is murder this time of day—you've got to flex with me a little."

"I don't have to 'flex' with you at all."

"Look, you didn't bring me all the way down here just to kill my daughter when I'm a few miles away. Let me talk to her."

"No."

"How do I know she isn't dead already?"

"We agreed to an exchange. If I failed to keep my end of the bargain, would you keep yours?"

"You didn't need an exchange," Cale said. "You already had your freedom. You need to get rid of the girl so you can make a run for it—but you could have left her anywhere."

Hashim didn't reply.

"We're both professionals," Cale said. "We both know what's going on here."

Again no reply—but Cale wasn't looking for one; he just wanted to buy time by keeping Hashim on the phone. Cale decided to take a risk: "You don't want to hurt my daughter; there's no honor in that."

There was a long pause; when Hashim spoke again, his voice was trembling with rage. "That was a stupid and clumsy thing to say."

The gamble paid off. There was a saying in PsyOps: *Your life is in the hands of any fool who can make you lose your temper.* To lose your temper is to lose control, and this was the first crack in Hashim's authority—the first step in Cale's seizing power. He quickly followed up: "You think you know more about honor than I do?"

But once again there was silence. Hashim was no fool and no beginner either; he must have quickly recognized what Cale was trying to do. Now there was a chance Cale's ploy could backfire, and he needed a distraction.

"Hashim," Cale said, dropping the man's first name like a bomb.

No reply.

"Hashim."

A pause. "Yes?"

"If anything happens to my daughter, I'll spend the rest of my life looking for you. You don't want that. I'm the one who wrote those leaflets; I'm the one who made your men surrender. If you want another shot at me, here I am—just give me a chance to get there."

"How long?"

"I can be there in thirty minutes," Cale said, allowing himself an extra ten.

"I will call you again in thirty minutes. No more delays; I will consider any further delay an attempt to involve the authorities—and *you* don't want *that*."

The phone clicked off.

Cale took a deep breath and slowly let it out.

He turned onto 17 South, the main road that ran along the ocean through the center of town. He looked in the rearview mirror and saw Pug; he also took the turnoff, then slowly began to decelerate until he was three cars back. On his right Cale passed a Calabash seafood restaurant the size of a warehouse, with its stadium-size parking lot packed with tour buses and cars. There was an entire shopping area sitting on gray wooden piers constructed over the natural marshes and wetlands; there was a souvenir and beachwear shop that in a few hours would be lit like Atlantic Beach.

The left side of the street was lined with hotels, condos, and apartments competing for a glimpse of the ocean just a hundred yards away. When Cale was a boy, the drive down 17 had presented an ocean vista, but now the buildings blocked the view entirely. All of the big developers had properties in Myrtle Beach; over the years the little seaside hamlet had evolved into a full-blown tourist destination, complete with traffic jams and oblivious pedestrians—which Cale was cursing now. But at least he was moving, and he had only a few blocks left to go.

Then he saw it: Sunset Apartments, standing like a pink headstone over the crowded street below. Cale pulled into the parking lot of an old strip mall on his right and parked in front of a sign that futilely warned, "Parking for Customers Only." He took the cell phone and the gun from the seat and tucked them into the pocket of his jacket; the gun felt incredibly heavy, and he wondered if it might fall out if he had to run.

He exited the car and started toward the street when he heard a voice behind him.

"Hey! You in the jacket!"

Cale turned to see a man standing beside his car. Behind him, the door of a small office supply store slowly swung shut.

"Can't you read, you idiot? Parking for Customers Only!"

Cale took a few quick steps back toward him. "I'm sorry," he said. "I have a very important appointment, and I'm late."

"That's a crying shame," the man said. "Move your car."

"I can't. I don't have time."

"You had time to park it here. You had time to take one of my spaces so my customers can't find a spot. You had time to take money out of my pocket."

I don't have time for this, Cale thought. It suddenly occurred to him that his right hand was in his jacket pocket, resting on the hilt of his gun. He thought about sliding it out just enough to allow the man to recognize it. That would end the conversation—but that would bring the police, too, and that was something he couldn't afford.

Cale turned toward the street again, his frustration mounting. "I don't have time to explain."

"You leave it here and I'll tow it," the man called after him.

"Then tow it."

"I'm not kidding!"

"Neither am I."

Cale made his way across the street, dodging and weaving through the shouted curses and blaring horns. Halfway across he heard his cell phone ring. He jerked it out of his pocket and heard a clatter of metal; he looked down and to his horror saw his Beretta lying in the middle of the street. He snatched it up and shoved it under his jacket again. He glanced back across the street and was relieved to find that the angry proprietor had already returned to his store.

He turned and scrambled the rest of the way across the street, pressing the cell phone to his ear as he squeezed between the cars jammed end to end along the opposite curb.

"Okay," Cale said breathlessly, "I'm here."

"Where are you now?" Hashim asked.

"I'm on the sidewalk out front. Where do I meet you?"

"I agreed to an exchange, not a meeting. Did you bring your weapon with you, as I instructed?"

"Yeah, I've got it right here."

"Is it loaded? I will not accept excuses."

"It's loaded. Now what?"

"Do you know where the swimming pool is located?"

"Yeah—around back."

"I want you to proceed around to the swimming pool. I'll stay on the line until you arrive; I'll direct you from there."

Cale looked back and saw Pug making his way across the street toward him, still keeping a safe distance between them.

"The alley's narrow," Cale said to Hashim. "We'll lose the signal when I pass between the buildings."

"Then I will call you again in two minutes."

Click.

Cale waved frantically for Pug to approach. Pug hurried over and the two men stepped into the shadows between the buildings.

"What's going on?" Pug asked.

"I've only got a minute," Cale said. "Hashim wants me to come around to the pool. That's all he told me; he says he'll tell me what to do next when I get there."

"Then he's probably watching the pool area. He might be in the crowd, or maybe up in one of the apartments."

"I'll go first," Cale said. "Once he sees me he won't look for anybody else. When he calls I'll try to stall him if I can. Work your way around to the opposite side of the pool. Stay clear of me so he doesn't spot you. Find a place where you can stay out of sight but still keep me in view. If he sends me someplace else, you'll just have to follow as best you can."

"Right." He lifted a pair of binoculars hanging around his neck. "I brought these; I thought they might help." He quickly looked Cale over. "Where's the gun?"

Cale patted his jacket pocket.

"Any idea why he wants you to bring it?"

"I can think of a couple reasons," he said, but it was a lie.

He could only think of one.

CHAPTER 39

Cale stopped at the end of the alley before emerging onto the edge of the deck. The pool area was just as he remembered it as a boy: the long rectangular pool, the row of cabanas lining the far side, and the pool deck crowded with glistening flesh. It could have been the same group of people; only the hairstyles and swimwear had changed much. It was like a flashback to twenty years ago.

He scanned the crowd for eyes looking in his direction, but no one among the sun worshipers seemed interested in the shaded alley between the buildings. He searched for Hashim's face among the sunbathers, using Pug's rough description: a dark-skinned man with black hair and a mustache—but no one seemed to match.

His cell phone rang, and he answered it.

"Okay, I'm at the pool. Now what?"

"I cannot see you."

"I can't see you either."

"That isn't necessary. Where are you standing?"

"On the edge of the deck, by the alley."

"Step farther away from the building."

He's on a balcony, Cale thought. *That's why he can't see me yet.* He took a single step forward and waited. Hashim said nothing, so apparently he still was not in view. He took a quick glance at the building; he could see only the first column of balconies. He took a second step forward—still nothing. He took a third step, then a fourth, hesitating slightly between each step to give Hashim a chance to identify him and respond. From the corner of his eye, he watched column after column of balconies come into view.

"I see you now," Hashim said at last.

Cale turned and looked. He could see all the balconies on the near half of the building, and that meant Hashim was probably on one of them.

"Don't look at me," Hashim said. "Look straight ahead."

Bingo.

"I want you to walk to the center of the deck area—just to the left of the pool there is an open space. Do you see it?"

"I see it."

Cale started through the crowd of sunbathers. He felt silly and out of place in his jacket and khakis, but no one so much as raised his head or tipped her sunglasses as he passed by. He stopped just a few feet away from the pool, turned to the building, and raised his eyes to the upper floors.

"Okay. What next?"

Pug stood at the edge of the alley and looked out over the crowded pool. He watched Cale working his way across the deck; he waited until there was a safe distance between them, then started forward—but he abruptly stopped.

A thought suddenly occurred to him: Hashim might not be looking for him—but he would definitely recognize him if he saw him.

He searched the lounge chairs closest to him until he found a young man in a floppy, Gilligan-style beach hat.

"Hey, kid. Ten bucks for the stupid hat."

"Get lost."

"Then twenty bucks for the lovely hat."

"Deal."

The young man tossed him the hat while Pug fished a twenty from his wallet.

"Ten more for the beach towel," Pug said.

"Twenty," the boy countered.

"What's it made of, silk?"

"Get your own beach towel."

"Okay, twenty."

They made the exchange, and Pug pulled the hat down low on his head.

"Looks good on you," the boy said.

"Funny—it looked stupid on you."

He removed the binoculars and wrapped them in the towel, then made his way quickly around the left edge of the pool toward the cabanas. He found an empty one and took a seat well back in the shadows. He looked across the deck at Cale, who was now standing motionless in the center, staring up at the side of the building.

He's telling me Hashim's in the building, Pug thought. He unrolled the beach towel and took out his binoculars.

"Good," Hashim said. "I can see you perfectly now."

"Then let my daughter go," Cale replied.

"I hope to—very soon."

"What do you want me to do now?"

"Nothing."

He blinked. "Nothing?"

"My business is not with you; my business is with your friend."

Cale stiffened. "What friend?"

"You never told me about the Death Card."

"What?"

"It wasn't your idea, was it?"

"Of course it—"

"The Death Card had its origin in your country's Vietnam conflict. Only an older man would be likely to remember it."

Cale didn't reply.

"You called me by my name—you referred to me as 'Hashim.' Even if you were able to locate my apartment, you had no way to know my identity or my background—unless someone else told you."

"I don't know what you're talking about," Cale fumbled.

"Where is Colonel Moseley now?"

"Who?"

"Colonel Moseley—the man known to his friends and students as 'Pug.' Your colleague in the Fourth Psychological Operations Group; the Intelligence Officer in your three-man propaganda team; the man who revealed to you my identity; the man who suggested the use of the Death Card. Must I continue? You are beginning to insult my intelligence. Where is he? Somewhere nearby, I imagine."

"What do you want with Pug?"

"What I have wanted from the beginning."

"I don't understand."

"I know. Call him, please."

"You said this was between you and me."

"And so it is. If you wish to get your daughter back, you will do as I say."

Cale hesitated. "I don't want to involve Pug."

"Your friend has been involved from the beginning. Now for the last time—*call him to the phone.*"

CHAPTER 40

Pug scanned the side of the apartment building with his binoculars. It was a sunny day, and at least three-quarters of the balconies were occupied. Hashim was probably on one of them, watching Cale as he stood in the center of the deck—but which balcony? There were hundreds of them, and he didn't have time to study them one by one.

He began to sweep his binoculars back and forth, systematically eliminating some balconies and making a mental note to return to others for a closer look. He began by searching for individual males—but the deck was covered with sunbathing women, and the balconies were lined with eager males straining for a better look. That approach was useless; he needed a better filter than that.

He had another idea: instead of males, he began to search for binoculars. It was a good bet that Hashim would want the best view possible, and he wasn't likely to trust his unaided eyes from even a few floors up. Pug looked: he counted twenty-six pairs of binoculars trained on the deck.

He pulled his own binoculars away and looked across the deck; Cale was still talking to Hashim on his cell phone. Pug went back to those twenty-six balconies again, this time searching for males with binoculars holding telephones or cell phones. He found only three.

He studied each of the three remaining balconies carefully.

On the first balcony, he saw the patio door slide open and a middle-aged woman stepped out. The couple began to argue, and the man reluctantly set down his binoculars and retreated into the apartment.

The second man had dark skin and hair, but his face was completely obscured by his binoculars and the hand that held them. Pug waited. Now the man closed his cell phone and lowered the binoculars, and Pug could see his face clearly. It was not Hashim—but just to make sure, he checked Cale again. Cale was still talking on the phone.

That left only one apartment. Pug refocused his binoculars and stared. There was a single individual seated in a chair, but he was difficult to see. He wasn't positioned out near the railing like the others; he kept back in the shadow of the doorway. His face, too, was covered by his binoculars, but the shape of his head looked strangely familiar. Unlike the other two, this man's binoculars didn't sweep from side to side, sampling the delicacies below; they seemed to be fixed on a single point. Pug followed the viewing angle down—and found Cale standing in the center of the deck.

Pug looked at the building and counted. "Eighth floor, third unit from the end," he said. "That's our boy—let's go."

He raised his binoculars to check on Cale once more—and to his astonishment, Cale was no longer staring up at the building; he was looking directly at Pug, waving for him to come over. Pug took the binoculars away and looked with his own eyes, as though the lenses might be playing tricks on him.

Cale waved again and gave a huge nod.

Pug slowly picked his way across the crowded deck. He didn't like the look on Cale's face. Something was wrong—or maybe Hashim was on the move again. Cale wouldn't have risked exposing him unless Hashim was no longer watching—but if that was the case, why was Cale still standing there? Why did he wave him over—was there something he was supposed to see? And if Hashim was on the move again, why weren't they following—and fast?

Pug had to step across a final lounge chair to reach the clearing where Cale was standing. A young man in a bright red Speedo looked up at him and said, "Nice outfit, dude."

"Ever hear of skin cancer, bozo? Here—cover up." He took off his twenty-dollar hat and dropped it on the boy's head.

Pug stepped into the small clearing and looked at Cale. Cale was still holding the open cell phone, so Pug thought it best not to speak—he just held up his open hands in a gesture that said, "What gives?"

"He wants to talk to you," Cale said.

"He spotted me?"

"He knows, Pug. He knows."

Pug didn't reply. Both men just stood there, blinking, staring into each other's eyes with a dozen unspoken questions flowing back and forth between them.

Pug slowly took the phone and raised it to his ear—then looked up at the building and waved. "Eighth floor, third unit from the end," he said. "Why don't you come on out and say hello? Sort of a class reunion."

"Hello, Colonel Moseley."

"Hey, call me Pug."

"I prefer to think of you as a military officer. It reminds me of your crimes against my people."

"Well, we've all done things we regret. 'Course, I never looted a whole country or set any oil wells on fire."

Pug felt a hand grab his arm. He glanced over at Cale and saw the look of urgency and fear. The kid was right—this was no time to be a wise guy. Hashim still had Gracie, and he needed to play it straight.

"Step away from Mr. Caldwell," Hashim said. "What I wish to say to you next is a private matter."

Pug glanced at Cale and took a few steps away.

"What are you doing?" Cale whispered.

Pug ignored him and pressed the phone tighter against his ear. "How did you know? About me being here, I mean?"

"You make it sound like a discovery. I planned for you to be here all along."

"That's hard to believe."

"For a man of your arrogance, I'm sure it is."

"You killed Kirby."

"You killed the men in my unit."

"We only wanted them to surrender."

"That's all I wanted from your friend, and he was kind enough to comply. I suspected that his creative temperament would incline him toward melancholy and despair. I was correct."

"I tried to warn him."

"I assumed you would. I wasn't certain how long it would take you to understand my mission, but once you did, I was certain you would attempt to warn your friends. Tell me, did you warn Mr. Caldwell at the same time?"

Pug paused.

"Why not, Colonel Moseley? I could just as easily have selected Mr. Caldwell as my first target. Why did you warn Mr. Kirby first?"

"'Cause I knew you'd go after him first."

"Why?"

"'Cause he was the weakest."

"No. You were quite mistaken."

"How's that?"

"I approached Mr. Kirby first only because you expected me to. He was not the weakest member, Colonel—nor is Mr. Caldwell. You are."

"How do you figure that?"

"I knew that you would assume yourself to be the strongest because of your knowledge and experience. I knew that you would assume a definite order of events: first Mr. Kirby, then Mr. Caldwell, and last of all yourself. I approached Mr. Kirby first only to reinforce your assumption. Your arrogance has blinded you, Colonel. You are my primary target; you always were."

"That makes no sense. You could have come after me anytime."

"Not directly. In that sense your knowledge and experience were strengths. You would have been quite on guard against any direct attack. The only way to attack you was indirectly—by making you think I was after someone else."

"You went after the kid to get at me?"

"I knew that you would come to Mr. Caldwell's assistance. I knew that you would attempt to conceal your presence and that I would have to draw you out."

"Well, it worked. If you want me, here I am—come on out and fight like a man."

"The way your forces fought mine? You knew our unit's location, Colonel—why didn't you come out and 'fight like a man'? Instead, you hid behind your leaflets; how courageous of you."

"So the Death Card—you were expecting that?"

"On the contrary. I knew that at some point you and Mr. Caldwell might attempt to locate me, but your timing and method took me completely by surprise. That was quite ingenious, Colonel. Of course, the card also served to confirm your presence—but you forced me to change my plans. This is not the timing or the location I had in mind. Nevertheless, here we are, and it will have to do."

"So now that I'm here, you can let the girl go."

"You're missing the point."

"Cut the crap, Hashim. What do you want from me?"

"Can you see me, Colonel? As you said: eighth floor, third unit from the end. Just a moment—let me step closer to the railing."

Eight floors up and three units from the end, a figure rose and approached the railing, staring back through binoculars at the two men below.

"Yeah, I see you."

"Can you see what I'm holding?"

Pug saw Hashim's arm slowly rise to a right angle. He was holding a gun.

"Yeah—I see that too."

"Your friend's daughter is seated in the apartment just behind me. She is blindfolded and gagged and bound securely to a chair. In a few moments I will put this gun to her forehead and pull the trigger—unless."

"Unless what?"

"Unless you take the weapon from your friend, put it to your own head, and pull the trigger first."

Pug stood paralyzed, staring back at the figure on the eighth-floor balcony. His mouth went dry; he opened his lips to speak, but nothing came out.

"I'm curious," Hashim said. "During your career as an Intelligence Officer, did you ever consider what it would be like to be on the receiving end of a psychological attack? This is an area where I have experience that you do not."

"I'm listening," Pug said, trying to clear his thoughts.

"The men of my unit were ignorant and undertrained. In that sense they were weak—but as individuals they were very strong and brave. They knew our defense was merely a gesture; they knew we were vastly outnumbered and outgunned. They knew they would most likely perish—we all did. But we were willing to make that sacrifice because of our belief in things like honor, and brotherhood, and country.

"But after months on the front lines at Al Manaqish, my men were hungry and exhausted and afraid. You knew this; as an Intelligence Officer it was your job to know. You saw our weakness—you saw a vulnerability that you could exploit. My men had a choice: death with honor or surrender with disgrace. But you dropped your leaflets and you twisted the truth. You took that choice away from us and put another in its place: surrender with honor or death with disgrace.

"It is a terrible thing to be forced to choose between two options, knowing that both are evil—knowing that either choice will be a source of anguish and regret. But that was the choice you gave us, Colonel Moseley—and that is the choice I give you now.

"If you take your own life—right here, right now, as I watch—then you have my word that I will let the girl go. I have no wish to harm her; I have nothing to gain by her death. But if you refuse, I will kill the girl, and her blood will be on your hands.

"I instructed you to step away from Mr. Caldwell so that he would be unable to hear this request. He has no idea this offer has been made. If you refuse me, in a few moments you will hear a gunshot, and you will know for certain that the girl is dead. Mr. Caldwell will have no idea what went wrong; he will assume that I panicked or that I changed my mind. He will attribute the fault to me—but you will know better. You will know that *you* killed the girl, and you will have to live with that knowledge for the rest of your life.

"You and Mr. Caldwell might still remain friends—you might even draw closer because of this experience. He will express his gratitude to you for your assistance, for risking your life in an attempt to save his daughter. But each time he thanks you, you will hate yourself more.

"So there is your choice, Colonel. I believe you to be a man of honor and courage—just as my men once were. What will you do? Will you do the courageous thing and die with honor? Or will you become a coward right before my eyes?

"You have sixty seconds."

CHAPTER 41

Cale watched as Pug listened to Hashim's words. He couldn't hear a thing in the noisy pool area; he tried to read Pug's face like a barometer, but Pug had a face like a granite block, and Cale could pick up nothing from his stoic expression except one quick flash of something he had never seen on Pug's face before. The sight shook Cale to the bone, like a child first discovering that his father isn't invulnerable after all.

Hashim knew that Pug would be here—he seemed to know that Pug had been involved all along. He seemed to expect it; no, he seemed to have *planned* it—that's what worried Cale most. Pug was supposed to be the invisible man, the hidden hand in this ad hoc confrontation—but what if Pug wasn't hidden at all? What if he'd been hiding in plain sight all along? They thought they had been so clever: Pug hiding in the backseat, waiting until nightfall to sneak into the house through the backyard. Cale looked up at the balcony again; he suddenly felt like a chess piece on an invisible playing board.

Pug turned to Cale and pressed the cell phone against his chest to muffle the sound. He slowly extended his hand to Cale and said, "I'm gonna need that gun."

"The gun? Why?"

"I don't have a lot of time to explain."

Cale looked at Pug's face; it was even harder and more impassive than before. He was trying hard to conceal something, and Cale wasn't sure what it was—but he wasn't handing over the gun until he found out.

"Why?" Cale asked again.

"I think I can hit him," Pug said. "He's out in the open now—see him? I think I've got a clear shot."

It was a ridiculous lie. Pug was an Intelligence Officer, not a sniper, and he hadn't fired a gun in years. It would take an expert to hit a man standing eight floors up with a handgun, and before Pug even leveled the gun, Hashim would spot him and step away. It wasn't like Pug to suggest something like this; it would be insanity to even try it. It was a desperate lie, and it made Cale want to know the real reason even more.

"Tell me the truth," Cale said. "I'm not giving you the gun until you do."

"I can't," Pug said. "I'm asking you to trust me."

"That's not good enough."

"Look, I need that gun in the next thirty seconds. Don't make me take it from you."

"You won't get it from me in thirty seconds. Save us both the time and tell me now."

Pug took a step closer. "I'm begging you—give me that gun."

"Pug—what did Hashim tell you? What do you need the gun for? What does he want you to—"

Cale stopped. He saw the reason in Pug's eyes.

"Never," Cale said. "There's got to be some other way."

"There is no other way. He's holding all the cards."

"I will not trade your life for my daughter's."

"That's not your choice to make."

"It is as long as I'm holding the gun."

"Let me do this," Pug pleaded. "It's okay—really. Don't let her die while we're standing here arguing about it."

"I can't," Cale said. "I won't."

Pug turned away from Cale and pressed the phone to his ear again. "I need more time," he whispered.

"I'm afraid you're out of time," Hashim replied.

"Wait," Pug said. "I'm willing to do what you want, but my friend is not exactly cooperating here. I may have to take the gun away from him. I'm gonna need two hands for this, so I'm gonna have to hang up the phone—okay?"

"I can see your every move," Hashim said. "If you move from that spot— If you attempt to call anyone else—"

"I know, I know—I just need a minute. I'm gonna try to talk him out of it, and if I can't, I'll have to take it. Either way, you'll get what you want."

The line went dead.

Pug dropped the phone into his pocket. He spun around, glared at Cale, and charged forward. Cale shoved his hand into his right jacket pocket and held on to the gun. Pug reached him in two long strides and grabbed him by both lapels, jerking him closer until they were standing nose to nose.

He looked into Cale's eyes and asked, "How long does it take to run up eight flights of stairs?"

CHAPTER 42

Cale blinked. "What did you say?"

"I said, 'How long does it take to run up eight flights of stairs?'"

"How should I know? Four minutes, maybe five."

"That's about what I figure," Pug said, giving Cale's lapels another angry yank. "Two minutes to get to the building, four or five minutes up. How long you figure we been standing here?"

"What's going on?"

"Try to look pissed off, will ya? He's still watching."

Cale let go of the gun, hoping this wasn't a trick. He grabbed Pug by both shoulders and shoved back, but it was like trying to tip a cow.

"Is that all you got?" Pug said.

"What do you want me to do?"

"Smack me one."

"What?"

"Backhand me with your right. Do it now."

Cale did as he was told. He reached across with his right arm and came back hard across Pug's jaw. The blow stung the back of his hand but had almost no effect on Pug. Pug took a step back as if stunned, but a moment later he charged forward again and the two men locked arms like wrestlers tying up.

"My old lady used to wipe my face off harder than that," Pug said. "Is anybody watching us yet?"

Cale glanced to the side. Heads were beginning to turn in their direction. All around them people were beginning to set down their magazines and straighten in their chairs.

"Yeah," Cale said. "Would you mind telling me what we're doing?"

"Buying time," Pug said. "But we can't just keep doing the two-step here; he's too smart for that, so here's what we need to do: I only got time to go over this once, so listen up."

At the end of a long hallway on the eighth floor, a stairwell door flew open and a man burst out. He stopped for a moment, hanging his head and resting his hands on his knees, breathing hard. A few seconds later he started forward again, racing down the hallway toward the opposite end.

At the opposite wall he stopped and began to backpedal, counting the apartments as he went. At the third unit from the end, he put his ear against the door and listened, waiting for his breathing to quiet—but he heard no sound from inside. He dropped down to the carpet and tried to look under the door, but a band of rubber weather stripping blocked his view. He jumped up from the carpet and stood silently looking at the door, considering. He slowly raised his finger to the doorbell—then decided against it. Instead, he turned to the apartment on his right.

He moved to that door and listened again, but again he heard nothing. He knocked quietly and waited, counting the seconds; there was no response. *I don't have time to try them all,* he thought. He hurried to the next door and listened again: once again there was no sound from inside, so he moved on. He tried a third door, then a fourth. *Everybody must be at the pool.* He considered the idea of breaking down the door, but that would be too noisy—Hashim might hear it. Besides, things like that only worked on TV.

At the fifth door he finally heard a sound. He detected two voices inside, those of a woman and a small child. He knocked quietly on the door and waited. He placed his left hand over the peephole and planted his right hand securely near the doorjamb; then he widened his stance, braced himself, and held his breath. A few seconds later the dead bolt disengaged with a click and the doorknob slowly turned. He tensed. The instant he saw daylight between the door and the jamb, he shoved hard, forcing his way into the apartment.

Once inside he lunged for the astonished woman standing behind the door, cupping his right hand over her mouth. He reached back with his left foot and kicked the door shut behind him.

"This isn't what you think," he said quickly, hoping to ward off a scream. "I don't want to hurt you—I'm with the police. I don't have time to explain, so you just have to trust me. I'm going to take my hand away—please, I'm begging you not to scream. Okay?"

The woman nodded, though her eyes were filled with terror.

He slowly took his hand away, and she made no sound.

"Thank you," he said. "I'm sorry to have to barge in like this. I'm looking for the man who lives five doors down. The third unit from the end—do you know him? He's an Iraqi—black hair, mustache."

She shook her head. "These are vacation apartments. Nobody knows anybody here. What did he do?"

"He's holding a girl hostage."

"Right now?"

"Yeah. Is that your balcony?"

She nodded and pointed to the floor-length curtain on the opposite wall. He reached around behind his back and pulled out a gun. The woman drew a sharp breath, and her eyes widened even more.

"It's okay," he said. "Believe me, you're in no danger."

Just then a four-year-old girl wandered into the room; when she saw him, she stopped. She looked back and forth between the man and her mother and sensed that something was wrong. Her face began to twist and contort as if she were about to cry, so he quickly knelt down in front of her. He saw the woman take an anxious step forward; he looked up at her and nodded reassuringly.

"Hi there," he said to the little girl. "Know why I'm here?"

The little girl shook her head.

"I'm here to rescue somebody—a little girl like you, only a little older. I'm one of the good guys—want to see?" He unbuttoned the top three buttons of his shirt and pulled it open.

The little girl's face lit up. "Look, Mommy—it's Superman!"

Kirby got up and turned to the woman. "Call the police," he said. "Will you do that for me?"

"I thought you were the police."

"I lied—I'm sorry—I didn't want you to scream. But I wouldn't ask you to call the police if I wasn't one of the good guys, right? Just tell them there's a man in your apartment with a gun—that should get them here fast."

"What are you going to do?"

"Please don't say anything else—I'm going to open the balcony door and I don't want him to hear you. Just keep your little girl away from the balcony and you'll both be safe."

He stepped up to the patio door, then paused. He held up the gun and pulled back the slide halfway; a bullet was ready in the chamber. He took a moment to drop the clip and check it. Eight more rounds were ready and waiting; he hoped he wouldn't need them. He shoved the clip back in place and clicked off the safety. Then he quietly slid open the glass door and carefully peeked around the edge.

There was Hashim, standing on his balcony five apartments away.

The distance was much greater than he had imagined. In his mind he had pictured Hashim on the balcony next door, just a few feet away—but at this distance he could easily miss. Kirby had fired a handgun before, and he knew it wasn't like in the movies, where cops pick off bad guys at a hundred yards without even bothering to aim. In the real world, handguns are notoriously inaccurate. That's why so many innocent bystanders get shot: the slightest flinch or sideways tug on a trigger can send a bullet flying wide.

Kirby mentally reviewed the scenario again: *I take a single step onto the balcony, pivot left, level the gun, and fire.* It looked so simple in his head, and he knew he could manage the first part: Hashim was staring through binoculars; he had no peripheral vision at all. Kirby knew he could step out and take aim without being seen—but what if he missed?

Now he imagined a different scenario: *I step out, pivot left, level the gun, and fire—but there's too much adrenaline flowing; I rush the shot and it goes wild. I steady the gun for a second try, but before I can get the shot off, Hashim turns and ducks back inside. I start scrambling toward him, climbing from balcony to balcony, but before I get halfway there, I hear another gunshot—and it comes from his apartment.*

Kirby felt sick to his stomach.

He looked around the doorway again. Somehow, Hashim looked even farther away than before.

CHAPTER 43

Hashim steadied his binoculars and watched. He saw the two men standing face-to-face, quarrelling, but from eight floors up he could hear no sound. Their mouths were moving, apparently arguing, but he could hear no words. He watched Colonel Moseley seize Caldwell by the lapels and shake; he saw Caldwell grab Moseley by the shoulders and attempt to resist. Now Caldwell slapped him hard across the face; the colonel recoiled a step but immediately returned to the struggle.

Suddenly the colonel reached out toward Caldwell's pocket, but Caldwell grabbed his wrist and prevented him. But the colonel pushed forward, reaching over with his right hand to pull Caldwell's hand away. Caldwell added his left hand to the contest, and the two men wrestled back and forth—until suddenly all four of their arms swung up and around until they were pointed directly at the sky.

Caldwell was holding the gun because he was taller; but the colonel was gripping Caldwell's arms, and he was stronger. The two men stood motionless for a moment, eye to eye, struggling—and then a gunshot broke the stillness of the afternoon.

Hashim pulled the binoculars away and looked. The pool deck seemed to erupt in a panic of twisting bodies. There were screams of terror every-where; there were frantic shouts from parents to their wandering children. Some rolled off lounge chairs and crashed into their neighbors, collapsing in tangled heaps before scrambling to their feet again. People stumbled over upended chairs; shirts and towels whipped back and forth like flags in a hurricane. The gunshot, echoing off the building, seemed to come from everywhere, and people ran in all directions: some left, some right, some for the protection of the building, and some to the isolation of the beach. Some, trying to escape the gunfire, ran directly toward it.

Then there was a second gunshot, and the panic increased even more. Hashim looked through the binoculars and searched for the two men again. He managed to find them—but he could only catch glimpses of their actions through the sea of flailing limbs and crashing bodies. The gun still pointed to the sky—but now the arms swung down, and the gun disappeared from view.

An instant later there was a third gunshot. Hashim looked; as the panic subsided and the deck finally emptied, the two men were left standing alone in the center. For a moment neither man moved—then Hashim saw Pug slowly slump to his knees and fall face forward to the ground.

Cale dropped the gun and covered his face with both hands.

Hashim picked up his cell phone and hit *Redial*.

"Now what do we do?" Cale whispered through his hands.

"Shut up," said Pug's muffled voice. "I'm supposed to be dead."

"I can't just stand here all day."

"Give the doughhead a chance, will ya?"

"What did you say?"

Both men heard the muted ringing of a cell phone. Neither of them moved.

"Better answer it," Pug said. "That's your phone—it has to be Hashim."

Cale lowered his hands a little and looked up. Hashim raised his cell phone overhead, then put it back to his ear again.

"Which pocket?" Cale asked, bending over Pug's body.

"The right."

Cale checked the left pocket first just to maintain the deception; then he fished out the cell phone and opened it.

"Are you satisfied?" Cale said. "You got what you wanted—now let my daughter go."

"Why do you insult me? Do you think me a fool?"

"What are you talking about?"

"Do I have your assurance that Colonel Moseley is dead?"

"You can see for yourself."

"Then pick up the gun and fire a shot into the back of his head."

Cale froze.

"What's wrong? You cannot kill a man who is already dead."

He didn't reply.

"Your time is up, Mr. Caldwell. Tell your daughter good-bye."

CHAPTER 44

Jada kept thinking about New York; it seemed a million miles away. She had been in such a hurry to get out of the city, and now all she wanted was to get back. She thought about the restaurants, the music, and the Manhattan skyline at night. But that wasn't New York—not for her anyway. That was just a postcard of New York, a place for the snobs who live in high-rises on Central Park West. For her, New York was the streets, the drugs, and the life she knew she would never escape. It wasn't really New York she wanted to go back to; she just wanted, more than anything, to get out of *here*.

She kept trying to think about the city, but her mind kept going back to Grace.

Now she understood what Hashim was planning for the girl: he planned to kill her. All that crap about "making no promises"—he knew what he planned to do with her all along. *"I have nothing to gain by her death,"* he said, but he had a lot less to gain by letting her live. He probably meant what he said: *"I have no wish to kill the girl."* He didn't hate her; he didn't want to see her dead—he didn't care about her at all. Grace was just a detail to be wrapped up, just a thing to be used in the pursuit of his own desires.

And what about me? she thought. *I was a detail too—what was he planning for me?* There was no fifty thousand dollars—she felt sure of it now. She should have known better; she should have demanded more up front. Why should he pay her now? He had everything he wanted. He could have thrown her out without a dime, knowing she could never go to the police. And if she had demanded payment, would he have killed her on the spot? Or would he have tied her up next to Grace and settled both "details" at a more convenient time?

Jada knew he would have killed her for sure. He gladly would have put a bullet in her head—but he would have been careful not to touch her while he did it, because to him she was unclean—a creature—a parasite. The thought made her want to vomit. How many men had used her, only to be disgusted by her later? They were the real parasites—the ones who sucked the life out of others just to feed themselves.

Maybe he's right, she thought. *Maybe I am just a parasite.* After all, Jada was a part of all this too. She helped put Grace's life in danger, and not to settle some old score—she did it just for money. She did it to help Hashim settle *his* old score; if that's not a parasite, what is? Maybe Hashim really was better than she was. At least he had a reason for what he did.

I would have sold my soul for fifty thousand bucks, she told herself. And why not? She'd been selling off pieces of her soul for years, and fifty thousand was just today's bargain price. She never thought about Grace's soul; it never crossed her mind. It was just part of the bargain: Today only, sale ends at midnight, two victims for the price of one.

Jada punished herself with these words. She listened to her inner voice and tried her best to dredge up some feeling of guilt or shame—but it was like waiting for a glacier to thaw. Maybe there wasn't enough left of her soul to feel guilt. Maybe she was like that guy in the Bible, the one the nuns used to tell her about: *"He was rejected, for he found no place for repentance, though he sought for it with tears."* Maybe she was like that; maybe it was just too late.

Why am I doing this? Jada wondered; she wasn't sure of the answer. *Maybe it isn't too late,* she thought. She couldn't bear the thought of leaving Grace alone with Hashim. She wanted to prove to herself that in some way, she was better than he was. She wanted the girl to get away, and she wanted to keep Hashim from going after her. *I could still turn back,* she told herself. But she knew it was a lie—there was nothing left to do now but keep on going. She wondered in her heart if she had made this decision days ago.

Jada reached up and pulled off the blindfold that covered most of her face. She took the gag out of her mouth but left the drapery cords as they were, loosely wrapped around each of her wrists and ankles. *Maybe it's too late for me,* she thought, *but it isn't too late for Grace.* That's why she pretended to be tied up; that's why she took Grace's place. That's why, halfway up in the elevator, she sent Grace to a Kroger six blocks away to bring back pizza and chips.

Every girl deserves to be rescued, she thought. *Somebody should have rescued me a long time ago.*

She clenched her fists and started toward Hashim.

When Kirby heard the first gunshot, he had no idea where it came from. He peeked around the doorway at Hashim again and found him still staring down at the deck. The gunshot must have come from below, but it sure wasn't part of the plan he agreed on with Pug—what went wrong? Was Cale or Pug shooting up at Hashim? They couldn't be—Hashim hadn't ducked or taken a single step back from the railing. Then who in the world were they firing at?

When Kirby heard the second gunshot, he knew he had to find out what was going on—he had to step out onto the balcony and look down. But the balconies to his left were all empty. If Kirby stepped out into the open, Hashim would spot him for sure, and he would remember his face—they had met once before.

When Kirby heard the third gunshot, he knew something was definitely wrong—and he knew he was out of time. He had to step out on that balcony and take the shot whether he missed or not—he just had to take the chance. He ran his left hand across his chest and checked for his T-shirt one last time.

He held his breath and took one large step onto the balcony. He pivoted to his left and lowered the gun, placing the bead on the center of Hashim's head—but he quickly lost confidence and lowered his aim to the widest part of his torso instead. Hashim never moved; he seemed completely unaware of Kirby's presence; he remained focused on the deck below, and Kirby took advantage of his preoccupation to take a quick glance down himself. When he did, he saw Pug lying facedown on the deck, and Cale standing with his arms hanging limply at his sides.

Kirby's sideways glance was intended to take only an instant, but the shock of seeing his old friend dead added seconds to his gaze. When he finally turned back to Hashim again, Hashim was facing him and looking directly into his eyes—and he was holding a gun at his side.

A look of astonished recognition came over both men's faces at once. They looked equally electrified, as though they had both grabbed hold of the same high-voltage cable. An instant later Hashim jerked his gun to waist-level and fired off a wild shot that ricocheted off the wall by Kirby's shoulder.

Kirby slowly squeezed the trigger. His first shot had to count—he might not get another.

But before he could get the shot off, a figure darted out of the apartment behind Hashim and gave him a terrific shove, sending him halfway over the railing. It was Grace!

"Grace, get down!" Kirby steadied his gun and tried to take aim, but Grace was all over the man—pushing, pounding, shoving him backward, and Hashim was struggling to keep his grip on the railing with a gun in one hand and a thick white bandage on the other. There was no way Kirby could get off a shot—not without taking a chance of hitting Grace.

But when Kirby saw Hashim raise his gun to bring the butt down on Grace's head, he knew he had no choice. He aimed at Hashim's shoulder and fired twice; the first shot sailed wide to the right, but the second shot made a thick, smacking sound as it caught him in the flat of the neck. Hashim stopped; the gun dropped out of his hand and a jet of blood began to spurt from his carotid artery. When Grace pulled back to see what had happened, Hashim looked into her face; a look of utter astonishment came over him.

He began to totter; both of his hands shot out to steady himself; he grabbed Grace by the shoulders, locking on in a death grip.

Hashim tipped backward, over the railing and out into space, taking Grace along with him.

CHAPTER 45

Cale heard the gunshots from the balcony above. His arms went limp at his sides; the cell phone dropped from his hand and clattered on the concrete deck.

"Grace! *No!*"

Eight floors above he saw Hashim arch back over the railing and start to fall. He felt a split-second rush of hope—but as Hashim tumbled backward, Cale saw that he wasn't alone. There were two figures twisting together in midair, plummeting head over heels toward the deck below.

One of them was his daughter.

"*Grace!*"

The two bodies hit the ground as one. They seemed to fold into the concrete like accordions, like the crash dummies in his own car commercials—only there was no recoil, no rebounding off the dashboard and back into the seat. The bodies lay perfectly still. There was no further movement—no last gasps for breath, no convulsive reflexes—nothing. They were crushed by the impact, dead the instant they hit the ground.

He heard an agonizing scream, like the howl of an enraged animal; it was his own. He felt his body begin to shudder, and trickles of fire burned their way down both cheeks. He took one faltering step forward, but his legs buckled under him and he collapsed to his knees. He tried to struggle to his feet again but could not; he was paralyzed, incapable of movement. All he could do was stare straight ahead at Grace's broken body.

The image was more than he could stand. He squeezed his eyes tight, but it didn't help; it was as if his eyelids were transparent and the image still remained, seared onto his retinas forever. He was locked in a dark room with a demon from the pit of hell, and there was no escape. He knew he would be tortured forever.

He saw the whole scene again in his mind; he saw every detail of the two bodies as they plummeted down: One with black hair, the other auburn— beautiful auburn hair that fluttered out around her like a little cape. She wore a black shirt with something written in glitter across the front.

They made no sound as they fell. They didn't struggle; they didn't twist or stretch like cats trying to land on all fours. They didn't claw the air, desperately grasping for something to slow their descent, and in the final instant they didn't reach out and brace themselves for impact. They just held on to one another, each gripping the other's shoulders like two dancers on a ballroom floor.

Cale felt himself slipping into shock, and he welcomed it. His mind began to shut down, systematically locking out all sensory input. He heard nothing; he felt nothing; it was as though he had been instantly catapulted into the empty vacuum of space, staring down at a distant, cloud-covered world below.

Grace is dead.

The words drifted slowly across his mind like an advertising banner towed above a beach. He stared up at the banner as it floated by and saw the words in large block letters, but he couldn't quite make out the meaning.

Grace is dead.

Time went into slow motion. To his right he saw Pug scrambling to his feet, but he made no sound. His lips seemed to be moving—shouting—but Cale could hear no words. He saw Pug raise his right arm and point up toward the building. Cale's head slowly turned like the turret of a tank. He saw the building, but he didn't understand.

From the corner of his eye, he saw Pug rush to the two twisted bodies and kneel over them. Pug raised his head and looked back at Cale. His lips were moving again; he seemed to be calling to Cale, waving, gesturing for him to come over. Cale was astonished to find that he was on his feet again. His legs seemed to be moving of their own volition, but he couldn't feel them. He drifted forward like a ghost.

He stood over the two bodies and looked down; both bodies lay on their backs, eyes staring up at nothing through half-open slits. Cale stood by Hashim's side and looked at the man's face for the first time. The back of his skull was crushed flat, and a puddle of blood pooled beneath it. His face was completely vacant; he didn't appear cruel, or menacing, or vengeful. He looked peaceful and harmless—like a crayon melting on a hot plate. Whatever evil that had been in him had passed right through the concrete and into the belly of the earth, leaving nothing behind but an empty shell.

Cale slowly raised his eyes and looked at Grace.

She was positioned upside-down to him, and for that he felt a sliver of gratitude; it gave him a few seconds' slower introduction to the horror of her death. He saw her beautiful hair, so much like her mother's, spreading out around her head like a bridal gown. He saw her slender limbs, her skin so fair and smooth that it looked more like a child's than a woman's. He saw her black T-shirt twisted up under her rib cage by the fall. And on her right hip, just above the top of her swimsuit bottom, he saw a blue-and-red rose tattoo.

He blinked.

Cale slowly drifted around Hashim's feet to take a closer look; his eyes were fixed on the girl's face. From an upside-down perspective her features had seemed completely familiar—but as the face turned right-side up in his vision, the features seemed to morph into something else; into someone else—someone completely unknown.

Cale shook his head and stared. A thought kept trying to work its way into his conscious mind, like a bubble floating up to the surface of a pond, but he couldn't quite see it yet. He looked over at Pug; the man was smiling, grinning, and Cale couldn't understand.

Now Cale felt an urgent tugging on his left arm. He ignored it at first, but the tugging grew stronger and more persistent. He slowly turned to face the source and found himself staring into the face of a weeping girl; on the deck beside her were two crumpled grocery bags. He looked at her face again; she looked strangely familiar. She was shouting something over and over, but Cale couldn't make out the word. He looked back at the face of the figure on the ground; this time, it looked utterly foreign.

He felt like a man waking up from a horrible nightmare. He turned and looked at the girl again, and now he recognized her.

He heard her shout, *"Daddy!"*

Cale threw his arms around Grace and pulled her close.

CHAPTER 46

The deck was now surrounded by a yellow plastic ribbon bearing the words "Police Line—Do Not Cross." Just beyond the ribbon a crowd of wide-eyed onlookers stared at the tangled wreckage of lounge chairs, beach towels, and clothing. Some of the spectators whispered to their neighbors and pointed out locations on the deck that they had occupied less than an hour ago. Some eagerly described the recent events to late arrivers, vividly recounting details they had never witnessed in their panic to escape. All eyes were focused on two black body bags lying near the building and a handful of figures gathered around them.

Cale sat beside Grace on a lounge chair with his left arm curled around her shoulders. He hadn't let go of her once, and his arm was beginning to go numb—but he had no intention of taking it away. Cale kept looking over at his daughter as if she might vanish at any moment—like a man holding a feather in his open palm on a windy day. He kept pulling her in tighter against him, and for her part, Grace did not resist.

Kirby and Pug stood directly in front of them in a thoughtful attempt to block Grace's view of the body bags twenty feet away. Grace kept leaning out and looking around them, but her father kept gently pulling her back.

"Why did she do it?" Grace asked.

"I don't know, sweetheart," Cale said. "It'll take time to sort all this out."

"She sent me to the grocery store while she stayed behind."

Thank God she did, Cale thought.

"Why did she stay? We could've both run away."

"Maybe she knew he'd come after you. Maybe she didn't see any other way."

"But she was working for him—and then she did this. I don't get it; did she love me or did she hate me?"

"I don't know. Maybe both."

"How can you do both at the same time?"

"Trust me, you can. I hate her guts—but right now I wish I could give her a big hug."

"She didn't have to kill herself."

"Maybe she didn't mean to. Kirby says she tried to push him over the railing, but he grabbed ahold of her and took her over with him."

"But she must have known that could happen—she must have known something might go wrong."

"Yeah, I think she did."

Grace paused. "Then she loved me."

Cale pulled her a little closer.

He looked up at Kirby. "Thank you—you jerk."

"Talk about a mixed message," Kirby said. "What did I do?"

"You let me think you were dead, that's what."

"That was Pug's idea."

Cale turned to Pug. "Why doesn't that surprise me?"

"It was the only way," Pug said. "I told you the truth: when I figured out what Hashim was up to, I called Kirby to warn him—but I was one freakin' day late. Hashim had already made contact, and Kirby was feeling pretty low."

"But he wasn't dead."

"The reports were exaggerated," Kirby said. "I got a letter from the Army telling me I might have HIV. It looked just like the real thing."

"Smart," Cale said. "He knew it was the kind of thing you'd keep to yourself."

"So I went in for a test like the letter said, and then a week later Hashim showed up at my door. He said he was from the Public Health Department. He told me I not only had HIV; I had full-blown AIDS and I was going downhill fast. Pug didn't call me until the next morning. Man—that was the longest night of my life."

"So the letter I found at your mom's place," Cale said, "the one from the testing lab in New York—"

"Those were my real results," Kirby said. "Hashim stepped in before they arrived."

"What about your mom?" Cale said. "You let your own mother think you were dead!"

"Nah, she knew. You don't think I'd do that to my own mom, do you?"

"You could tell your mom, but you couldn't tell me?"

"Stop whining. I lost an apartment in Manhattan for this, you know."

"When I called Kirby, he told me what happened," Pug said. "Then I explained what was going on. We decided to set a trap for Hashim, so I grabbed the next flight to JFK and spent the next week hiding out in his apartment. We were hoping Hashim would show up again so we could grab him—but he never did. He must have figured the first time would do the trick."

"That's when we knew we had to play along," Kirby said. "We had to let him think it worked—let him think I was dead. That way he'd move on to you and we could get another shot at him—and since I was supposed to be dead, I could stay in the shadows and be ready to help."

"Kirby had to go dark," Pug said. "Like I told you, this guy was good. There was no way to tell what he knew and what he didn't; it turns out he knew about me all along. It's a good thing the doughhead came along."

"The comic book thing should have tipped me off," Cale said. "Who in their right mind takes the time to illustrate a suicide note? I should have known—that was way over the top."

"We didn't want people searching for a body," Pug said. "That's why we came up with the bridge thing. I told this moron to just leave a note, but no—he had to get dramatic."

"That was a very nice piece," Kirby said. "I'm thinking of developing it into a feature-length story."

"So you were here at the pool the whole time?" Cale asked.

"Pug called me," Kirby said. "He told me to follow you guys to Myrtle Beach. I was just a few steps behind you; I thought you might spot me a couple of times."

"Guess I wasn't looking for you."

"I was in the cabana with Pug. Once we figured out which balcony Hashim was on, we both decided to run upstairs and bust in on him—then you called Pug to the phone and I had to go by myself."

Cale looked at Pug. "What did Hashim say to you?"

"It's complicated."

"Pug—what did he say?"

He paused. "The same thing I thought he'd say to you."

Cale wondered what would have happened if he had handed the gun to Pug. He knew the answer—but he wondered if Pug's "surrender" would have been enough; after Pug was dead, he wondered if Hashim would have made the same demand of him.

"Thanks," Cale said. "That thing you came up with to buy Kirby more time—that was genius, Pug. You da man."

Pug just shrugged and looked away. "Who are we kidding? He had me cold—I never saw it coming. I thought he was after you, kid, but he was after me the whole time. I thought I was one step ahead of him, but he caught me flat-footed."

"So who's in the body bag, and who's standing here?"

Pug perked up a little. "That's true."

"Kirby was your idea, remember? And Kirby turned out to be the trump card."

"Some trump card," Kirby said. "I'm still not sure what happened up there. He fired at me, but he missed; he would have fired again if she hadn't gotten in the way. I got off two shots and hit him once—but that's not what killed him. She did that—she pushed him over the edge. I was supposed to save her life; I think maybe she saved mine."

Cale shook his head. "Like I said, it'll take time to sort all this out."

They looked again at the body bags.

"So she was the one," Kirby said. "The double—the girl in the video."

"What video?" Grace asked.

All three men turned and looked at her.

"Never mind," Cale said, "I'll explain it all later. And by the way, young lady: you've got some explaining to do too."

CHAPTER 47

Sunday was a flawless North Carolina day. Grace and Cale sat together on the small stone bench, basking in the afternoon sun. Grace closed her eyes and lifted her face to the sky.

"The sun feels so good," she said.

"I thought you'd had enough sunbathing for a while."

"I was just getting started. Some old guy with a gun came along and scared us all away."

Cale picked up a half-shredded tennis ball and threw it again. It disappeared over the hilltop and down the other side, and Molly happily bounded after it for the umpteenth time. She never tired of the game, and on a day like this, Cale didn't either. A few moments later Molly reappeared with her dripping treasure wedged between her jaws, bouncing over Hannah's grave and trampling down some of the flowers as she came. The bronze flower urn was no longer in use; it had been recovered and inverted and permanently retired to its underground hideaway. In its place, Cale and Grace had removed a small section of sod from in front of the headstone and planted a bed of geraniums, which would keep their color and hold their own throughout the hot summer ahead.

Cale got up and tended to the flowers, but he didn't say a word of rebuke to the dog. Why should he? Hannah wouldn't have minded—she would have laughed, because she was like that. It reminded him of Saturdays in Chicago, when Hannah would sleep in and Cale would wake her by throwing the tennis ball across the bed, sending Molly scrambling over her on all fours. And Hannah always scolded him but secretly enjoyed it; he liked to think she still enjoyed it now.

He sat down again on the bench and looked at Grace.

"What?" she said.

"Nothing. Can't I just look at you?"

"Dad, you've been looking at me every five minutes. I feel like I've got a big zit or something."

"You do. I've been trying to find a way to tell you."

"You keep putting your arm around me too. Kids are gonna think we're weird."

"Tell them I'm your boyfriend," Cale said. "I'll make a deal with you: I'll let you go out on a date when you're twenty-seven—until then, you're with me."

Grace grinned, and Cale smiled back. It had been a long time.

"I want you to do me a favor, Grace," he said. "I want you to promise me something."

"What's that?"

"Don't ever run away again."

"I didn't exactly 'run away.'"

"Whatever you want to call it—don't do that, okay? There will always be something trying to drive a wedge between us, Grace. We can't let that happen. That would break your mom's heart."

Grace looked over at the headstone. "Do you think she knows what happened?"

"I think she knows and I think she cares. That's why we have to stick together."

Molly nudged Grace with her nose until Grace wrestled the ball out of her jaws and threw it again.

"Molly didn't really bite anyone, did she?"

"No," Cale said. "You're in no danger from Molly—unless you're a tennis ball, and then you'll just get slobbered on."

Grace paused. "Why did he do it, Dad? Why did he try to kill you?"

"He didn't. He tried to take *you* away—and that's almost the same thing." He wrapped his arm around her shoulders again. "We're still a family, okay? All we've got is each other—don't forget that."

"For a while I thought I didn't have anything."

"Yeah, me too. But that was wrong, Grace—that's what he wanted us to think."

"But why did he hate you so much?"

"Hard to say. I guess I took something away from him, so he wanted to take something away from me."

"What did you do to him?"

"It was a long time ago—back when I was in the Army, back when I was in PsyOps. He was a commander in the Iraqi army. I wrote a leaflet that told his men to surrender, and half of them decided to do it. They tried to sneak off during the night; there was some confusion, and they thought they were under attack—and they ended up shooting their own men."

"Wow."

"Yeah—wow."

"But that wasn't your fault."

"He didn't see it that way."

"They didn't have to surrender."

"No, they didn't have to—but they were ready to. They were tired and lonely and afraid. When you get like that, sometimes all it takes is one voice to push you over the edge—or one voice to pull you back."

Grace nodded.

Cale heard a sound and looked across the cemetery lawn. He spotted Walter wheeling his rolling trash can onto the foot path at the bottom of the hill. Cale raised his arm and waved it in a huge arc; Walter saw it and waved back.

"Who's that?" Grace asked.

"An old friend of mine. His name is Walter."

"Were you in PsyOps together?"

Cale grinned. "You might say that. Walter's a real expert."

Thirty yards away a rabbit hopped out from under the foot of a juniper bush, and Molly dropped her tennis ball and began to bark. Grace went over to quiet her down; Cale watched her as she moved. Her walk had the same lilt, the same rhythm; she had the same way of carrying her delicate arms—it was just like looking at Hannah.

Cale turned to the headstone and said, "You would have been so proud of her."

He imagined Hannah's reply: "I *am* so proud of her."

"She reminds me so much of you."

"There's a lot of you in her too."

"I have a hard time seeing that sometimes."

"I never did."

"I'm so sorry, Hannah," Cale said. "I should have believed in you—I should have trusted you."

"You had to decide what to believe."

"I should have known."

"People forget. They have to remind each other."

He paused. "I'd give anything in the world to really hear your voice again."

"Talk to Grace. She sounds just like me."

"I love you," he said. "I'll be back next Sunday; we can talk again then. Tell God I'd still like to hear that voice from above, okay?"

Cale looked at Walter again, and he thought he heard Hannah say, "Maybe you already did."

Grace returned and sat down on the bench beside her father; Cale looked at her and stroked her beautiful auburn hair. "*Boy,* you look like your mom."

She smiled up at him. "Is that okay?"

"Yeah," Cale said. "That's *definitely* okay."

ACKNOWLEDGMENTS

I would like to thank the following individuals for their assistance in my research for this book: Major Ed Rouse (U.S. Army retired), twenty-year veteran of PsyOps and 4POG; Kent Middleton, Executive Vice President/ Executive Creative Director of Leo Burnett, U.S.A.; Colonel Mark Bontrager, U.S. Air Force; Lieutenant Colonel Andy Anderson, Assistant Professor of Military Science, University of North Carolina at Chapel Hill; Tina Beller, U.S. Army Civil Affairs and Psychological Operations Command; Lorraine Ramsey, City of Charlotte Cemeteries; Charles Hunter, Roseland Floral Company; Bill Strandberg, J.D., Nationwide Insurance; Terry Neely, piano tuner/technician; and all the others who took the time to respond to my e-mails, letters, and calls.

And thanks to all the others who helped make the publication of this novel possible: my literary agent, Lee Hough of Alive Communications; editor Ed Stackler for his story acumen and generous spirit; copy editor Deborah Wiseman for her usual eagle eye; my publisher, Allen Arnold, and my editor, Amanda Bostic, of Thomas Nelson Fiction for their helpful contributions to the story; and the rest of the staff of Thomas Nelson Fiction for their kindness, vision, and hard work.

The Facts Behind the Story
of *Head Game*

One of the earliest applications of psychological warfare was by Alexander the Great. Pursued by an enemy far larger in numbers, Alexander instructed his armorers to construct oversized breastplates and helmets that would fit men 7 or 8 feet tall. He left these items for the pursuing army to discover; when they did, they assumed that Alexander's men were giants and they abandoned their pursuit.

During WWII our PsyOps forces sometimes stuffed the bodies of dead rats with explosives and left them for the enemy to find. Soldiers would throw them into the furnace to dispose of them, setting off an explosion. When word of this practice spread, soldiers would no longer burn the rats, allowing disease to spread.

The ace of spades "Death Card" was commonly used in Vietnam, and appeared on many unit crests, patches, and insignia. The symbol was intended to strike terror into the hearts of the enemy. However, the Vietnamese deck of playing cards does not include the ace of spades, and most Vietnamese had no idea what it was supposed to mean.

Many Vietnamese villagers believed that if a man dies away from his village, his soul is doomed to wander forever. Taking advantage of this, American PsyOps forces recorded the voice of a Vietnamese man pretending to be a "lost soul." PsyOps soldiers then roamed the forests wearing backpack loudspeakers, playing the recording with a haunting reverberation. Many North Vietnamese soldiers heard the voice and ran for home; unfortunately, so did many South Vietnamese—so the recordings were discontinued.

During the Persian Gulf War, the 8th and 9th Special Operations Squadron dropped nearly 29 million leaflets from their MC-and HC-130s. A typical leaflet drop utilized between 24 and 40 boxes, each containing as many as 50,000 leaflets per box. The largest drop ever made was on the very first night of the war, when 2 million leaflets were dropped on frontline Iraqi soldiers along the entire southern Kuwait battle front. 87,000 enemy soldiers surrendered during Operation Desert Storm; 75% of them were carrying one of our leaflets when they did.

During Operation Desert Storm, 58% of all enemy prisoners of war reported listening to coalition propaganda broadcasts. Officially the broadcasts were known as the "Voice of the Gulf." Informally, they were referred to as "1-800-SURRENDER."

There was an actual Baghdad Betty employed by the Iraqis to broadcast propaganda messages to coalition forces. Like her predecessors Tokyo Rose and Hanoi Hanna, she did more to entertain the enemy than demotivate them. She was so unsuccessful that she was allowed to broadcast for only three months.

Some of our leaflets actually confused the enemy. Drawings of enemy soldiers portraying weakness or fear tended to increase their resistance; Iraqi soldiers often failed to recognize Saddam Hussein on the leaflets that included his caricature.

You can view several of the actual PsyOps leaflets used
during the Persian Gulf War on Ed Rouse's excellent website:
http://www.psywarrior.com/links.html

AUTHOR'S NOTE

I grew up reading comic books. I cut my teeth on DC Comics when they only cost 12 cents each: Superman, Batman, and the entire Justice League of America. Then, when Stan Lee spoke and brought the Marvel Universe into existence, I switched to a diet of Spider-Man, Captain America, and the Avengers.

Like a lot of boys, I learned to draw by copying my favorite comic book characters muscle by glorious muscle. Comic books taught me to love art; they taught me to love character, plot, and dialogue too. It's not an exaggeration to say that comic books taught me to tell stories.

So it only makes sense that I didn't turn out to be a mathematician or an engineer. For that matter, I didn't turn out to be a writer, either—not at first. That came years later. First, I became a cartoonist.

In 1975 I created a daily comic strip that I called *Downstown*. I began the strip while I was still a college student, and for the next five years I wrote it for college newspapers. In 1980 *Downstown* was syndicated by Universal Press Syndicate; for the next six years it appeared in daily newspapers all over North America. During my tenure as a cartoonist, I drew more than three thousand comic strips.

That's why I had so much fun creating the character of Kirby the comic book artist for *Head Game*. In the first draft of the story, Kirby's hand-drawn suicide note was only described; it was my publisher who suggested that I actually draw the note myself. The result became the first six pages of the book—and the most cartooning I've done in twenty years!